JOHN GREGORY DUNNE

Dutch Shea, Jr.

PUBLISHED BY POCKET BOOKS NEW YORK

POCKET BOOKS, a division of Simon & Schuster, Inc.
1230 Avenue of the Americas, New York, N.Y. 10020

Copyright © 1983 by John Gregory Dunne

Published by arrangement with Linden Press/Simon & Schuster
Library of Congress Catalog Card Number: 81-19355

ISBN: 0-671-46170-2

First Pocket Books printing July, 1983

10 9 8 7 6 5 4 3 2 1

POCKET and colophon are registered trademarks
of Simon & Schuster, Inc.

Printed in the U.S.A.

Books by John Gregory Dunne

Dutch Shea, Jr.
True Confessions
Quintana & Friends

Published by POCKET BOOKS

This is entirely a work of fiction. The city where it takes place is in equal parts the city where I spent the first eighteen years of my life and the city where I have lived the last seventeen.

This book is for my grandfather
Dominick Francis Burns
and for my beloved brother
Stephen Burns Dunne

May they rest in peace.

O, the mind, mind has mountains,
Cliffs of fall, frightful, sheer,
No man fathomed. Hold them cheap
May who ne'er hung there . . .

I wake and feel the fell of dark, not day.

GERARD MANLEY HOPKINS

. . . for we possess nothing certainly except the past . . .

EVELYN WAUGH

BOOK ONE

I

Lee was in the ladies' room when the bomb went off. In the loo, she would have called it. Lee always believed in speaking the vernacular wherever she happened to be. He never told her that her perception of the vernacular was rarely accurate. It would not have mattered if he had; she would not have heard. One should speak in the vernacular, Lee would say, as one should always drink the *vin du pays;* it was something one did. Lee always said "one" when she was in England. "One would like to go to Buscot for the weekend," she would say, "but one has so little time." Dutch Shea, Jr., could not stand her when she spoke like that.

The bomb shattered the plate-glass window in the restaurant on Charlotte Street. "Excellent French cuisine in quasi-provincial surroundings," Fodor's had said. "Expensive." Dutch Shea, Jr., had picked the restaurant. He would always blame himself for that. Not for picking that particular restaurant, but for the reason he had picked it. The recommendation in Fodor's had nothing to do with it. He had picked the

3

restaurant because he had seen Peter Jennings eating there one night. The ABC correspondent. Tall and languid, all side vents and wine expertise. A *blanc de blanc* perfectly chilled, twirled under and sniffed by the long Jennings nose. He had that sense television newsmen seemed to have of knowing he was recognized but not paying any attention to it, an implicit sense that he was a someone, a someone to be reckoned with. His words in the restaurant on Charlotte Street were clearly enunciated, not loud, really, but so projected that they were easily picked up two tables away. Beirut. Arafat. Cairo. Sadat. *The ambassador is a fool.* Peter Jennings had punctuated the ambassador's foolishness by snapping his fingers and calling for another bottle of *blanc de blanc*. A perfunctory smile. This is Peter Jennings, ABC, London.

In short, Lee's idea of perfection. How well he understood Lee, Dutch Shea, Jr., thought. And how they had both paid for his petty and private malice. I've made you a reservation at that restaurant on Charlotte Street, he had told Lee. The one where all those television people seem to hang out. That fellow from ABC. I can't remember his name. It would give Lee and Cat something to talk about. They did not have much to say to each other. Beyond movies they had seen. And where Cat's friends were going to college. It was what passed in Cat's late adolescence as mother and daughter talk. The Protestant perfection of Peter Jennings would provide an opening.

Isn't that Peter Jennings?

Peter who?

Jennings. The anchorman. On television. CBS, I think. Or maybe the other one.

I don't watch television, Cat would have said. In the same tone of voice she used when she said she did not eat the flesh of dead animals.

Oh, Cat, Lee Shea would have said. And picked up

her Hermes bag and gone to the ladies' room. Where she was when the bomb went off.

Dutch Shea, Jr., went into the kitchen and took a Coors from the refrigerator. The can was warm and there was a puddle of water on the bottom shelf of the fridge. Shit. I must have hit the defrost. There were four beers left. Well, warm is better than nothing. In the apartment next door, he could hear voices arguing in Spanish. *Puta,* he heard a man's voice say. *Puta, puta.* If he was talking about Ynez Cano, he was on the money. With change. From his kitchen window, Dutch Shea could see the boy in the Arco station across the street closing up. Staying open past ten in this neighborhood was an invitation to 211, P.C., armed robbery in the state penal code. Down the street, the lights in the adult bookstore were still on. "CUM One, CUM All," the sign in the window said. "Books. Tapes. Movies. Sex Aids."

Dutch Shea, Jr., turned on the television set in the bedroom. The newscaster said that at the top of the hour the big story locally was still the rain. Four days. Three point nine inches. The thruway was closed, route 395 was open, one lane only, northbound. Maintenance crews would work through the night. No letup in sight, isn't that right, Rod? Rod, the weatherman, opened an umbrella and the anchorman laughed. The anchorman would never make it at the restaurant on Charlotte Street, Dutch Shea, Jr., thought.

There was a commercial and then a story about the continuing strike of the gravediggers in the city's Catholic cemeteries. A spokesman for the union said that the gravediggers were striking for dignity and dignity translated into higher wages and then a spokesman for the archdiocese, a smooth young monsignor named Hawkes, said that His Excellency, Archbishop Clayton

Broderick, was considering the use of seminarians to dig graves and thus bring the fourteen-day-old strike to an end. A reporter asked Monsignor Hawkes if that could not be considered strikebreaking and Monsignor Hawkes answered that it would only be giving the faithful departed the dignity that was their due.

I could do without all this dignity, Dutch Shea, Jr., thought. He was the attorney for the Association of County Funeral Directors—the ACFD—and he supposed he would have to call Ben Goldman in the morning. Ben Goldman was the director of the ACFD and for some reason he was called Boomer. He knew that Boomer Goldman did not think he took the problems of the county's funeral directors seriously enough.

True.

Too bad.

So what.

The litany of my life, he thought.

He watched the rain bombard his bedroom window. He had replaced a broken pane with a shirt board from the Chinese laundry two doors down from the adult bookstore and now the rain had split the water-sogged cardboard and was staining the rust-colored curtain. Dutch Shea wondered if he had another shirt board. No. He did not pick up his laundry until tomorrow. If he did not forget. As he had forgotten to get the window fixed.

Why had Cat insisted on seeing her mother? It had not exactly been a habit since the divorce.

"We don't have a relationship anymore," Lee had said.

"I hate that goddamn word."

"No more than I hate her goddamn backpack. Why couldn't she go to Smith like everyone else?"

"Because she didn't get into Smith."

"I bet you think that's smart. And another thing,

6

why does she always stay with you when she does come home?"

"I'm her father. That might have something to do with it."

"Sleeping on the floor . . ."

"She has a sleeping bag . . ."

". . . in that slum you call an apartment. With all those pimps you hang around with . . ."

"Pimp. Singular. He's a client."

"God, you've got a crummy practice."

"Last week it was sleazy. Is crummy a step up or a step down?"

It was the way so many of his calls to Lee ended. There was a time when he would slam the telephone down, but now he would just quietly replace the receiver and then he would wait for the phone to ring when she called back. Ten, fifteen, twenty, thirty rings. He would not answer nor would she hang up. A clash of wills. What's the record? Cat had once asked. Cat had a way of storing incidental information. Fifty-seven rings, Dutch Shea had answered. Like Western Union, Cat said. And you counted them? You just sat there and counted them?

That was the spring they all wound up in England.

"I think I'll go to London this summer," Lee had said.

"Oh," Dutch Shea, Jr., had said. "I'm going to be there."

"Why?" Her tone hardened. Lee still suspected he followed her the way he had immediately after the separation. He was very good at it. It always seemed accidental when he ran into her at the movies or at the market. Lee was not fooled. She told Byron Igoe she wanted it stopped, but there was nothing Byron could do. He was very careful never to watch Lee and Byron when they spent the night together. He had Marty

Cagney do that. The private investigator he had known since Marty Cagney was a detective in the DA's office. Now listed in the Yellow Pages as PEEKABOO CAGNEY— DISCREETLY DETERMINING WHAT WAS DONE—WHERE & WITH WHOM.

"I'm going to meet Barry Stukin in Italy." Dutch Shea and Barry Stukin had once been law partners.

"Oh." Lee detested Barry Stukin. When they were partners, she refused to have him in the house. Though never mentioned, it was a factor in the breakup of the partnership.

"He has a client . . ."

"A hoodlum . . ."

"A client . . ." Barry Stukin was once a radical lawyer, the man you called if your son tried to blow up Fort Dix or was caught with a truckload of grass. If a case had a number at the end of it, there was Barry Stukin. The Hartford 7. The Albany 6. You think the Indianapolis 500 is an illegal detention case, Dutch Shea had once told him. Now Barry Stukin defended the civil liberties of upper echelon mafiosi.

". . . a client who was deported," he said.

"Of course."

"He died. I have a client. It turns out he's next of kin."

"Another hoodlum."

"A snitch, you want the honest to God truth. I think Barry'd like to make sure he doesn't snitch on the wrong people. Which is why he'd like my client to get his fair share of the will. So we're going to Italy to audit the assets."

It was the truth, but he knew Lee was not convinced.

"You said you'd be in London."

"I thought I might come over."

"Why?"

"Cat said she might meet me."

"Oh."

8

And Cat had shown up in London. With her backpack. And a boy named Charlie whom she deposited at Laker Airways. Nothing important, Cat had said. He had a Saab. I scrounged a ride. She had a bad cold. And an eruption of cold sores around her mouth.

"If you don't mind my saying, you look like shit."

Cat had smiled. "Is Mother here?"

"Buying china. Two sets so far."

"Have you seen her?"

"No. I've talked to her."

"I'd like to see her."

"Do you need money?"

"No, Daddy, I just want to see her."

"You want to buy some Lowestoft?"

"Daddy, don't be a pain in the ass."

"She'll ask if you've shaved your legs."

"Then I'll do it."

"I better go along with you."

"No."

"Somebody needs to referee."

"I can handle it, Daddy."

"You don't have the right clothes, Cat. You know your mother. You show up in Bibb overalls and she'll go into a terminal coma."

But Cat had prevailed. As always. She dug a wraparound burgundy-colored Danskin skirt from the backpack and a pair of lace-up lavender espadrilles and a blue button-down Brooks Brothers shirt with a frayed collar. Even a disposable Bic razor to remove the stubble from her legs. He wondered if Peter Jennings would have noticed the frayed collar. No: the PLO was up to something and the TUC was threatening a nationwide work stoppage and the IRA was blowing up underground stations. The world of Peter Jennings was a world of initials, not a world where the frayed blue collar of a Brooks Brothers button-down shirt affected the affairs of men.

9

In any event, Peter Jennings was not in the restaurant on Charlotte Street the night the bomb went off.

And Lee was in the ladies' room.

Peter Jennings was in Nicosia. There was no one famous in the restaurant that night. No one for Lee and Cat to talk about. In what passed as mother and daughter talk.

The bomb had gone off at 8:57 P.M., Greenwich mean time.

While Cat was picking at an endive salad.

While her mother was in the ladies' room.

In the goddamn loo.

The IRA took responsibility for the bomb. Retaliation for a Provo who had died of a hunger strike in H-Block at the Maze. Dutch Shea, Jr., could no longer even remember the hunger striker's name. The IRA communiqué listed no special reason for picking the restaurant on Charlotte Street other than it was favored by cabinet ministers and senior civil servants. Lackeys of English tyranny.

There was no mention of Peter Jennings.

Dutch Shea had insisted on reading the police reports. A habit of mind for the criminal lawyer. Read the reports, look at the forensic photographs. Even when the victim was SHEA, Catherine Liggett, female, Caucasian, 18. Time of death: 2057 GMT. A section of the restaurant's plate-glass window blew in when the bomb went off and severed Cat's head from her shoulders directly above the frayed collar of her blue button-down Brooks Brothers shirt. Her head had landed in a cut-glass Waterford bowl full of lemon sorbet on the sweets trolley, her right arm on the hood of a limousine belonging to the Danish chargé d'affaires, who happened to be passing the restaurant on Charlotte Street the moment of the explosion.

Forensic photographs.

SHEA, Catherine Liggett.

"An Austin Princess, sir," the inspector from Scotland Yard's bomb squad had told Dutch Shea, Jr.

"Excuse me," Dutch Shea had said.

"The limousine, sir. It was an Austin Princess." The inspector's tone was reassuringly confidential, as if the car's pedigree might assuage Dutch Shea's grief, and then he had added quietly, a man of the world exchanging a social confidence with another man of the world, "We call the Princess a Jewish Bentley over here, sir."

"Thank you," Dutch Shea, Jr., had said.

SHEA, Catherine Liggett.

No one else was injured in the restaurant on Charlotte Street. The wine cellar was destroyed. Nicosia was quiet.

And Lee was in the ladies' room

2

Dutch Shea, Jr., cracked another can of Coors, in the process cutting his right index finger on the pop-top opener. He swore at the inventor of the pop-top and then poured some warm beer over the cut, cauterizing it, and sucked the wound dry. The beer made a round damp spot on the blue cover of the preliminary hearing transcript on the bed and leaked onto the sheet. He swore again. On the television screen, Tom Snyder zeroed in on two screenwriters from Malibu, Barney and Faye, partners in work, partners in marriage. Barney and Faye had just returned from Biafra, and it was a tragedy, Tom, what was happening there, Barney said. A tragedy of human dimensions, Faye said, almost a humanistic tragedy. It was the most tragic two days of our life, Barney said. Absolutely, Faye said, without doubt, you see a famine like that and it puts film, not just our film, but any film, Barbra's or Warren's, in the proper perspective. Tom Snyder nodded vigorously and the camera picked up the third guest, a comic and game show host named Jackie Gross. The people in Biafra are black, right? Jackie Gross said. Right, Barney and Faye said. I knew a schwartze in the army, Jackie Gross said, a black guy, I mean, no offense to those beautiful people in Biafra, a sergeant about nine feet tall, a real Watusi—any Watusi in Biafra? I don't think so, Jackie, Barney said. Not to my knowledge, Faye said. Anyway, Jackie Gross said, this schwartze, this beautiful black guy, he was a real army sergeant, tough on the outside, but on the inside, a heart of steel. Your button is unbuttoned, he says. Take a lap. Around the world. A beautiful guy. He hands me a bayonet one day. You ever been circumcised? I swear to God. They're beautiful, those schwartzes. Black guys. Biafrans. Something else.

Barney and Faye seem dazed.

Oh, Jackie, Dutch Shea, Jr., thought. He had once defended Jackie Gross when he was called Jackie Grossbart and was the master of ceremonies at a strip joint in the North End. A violation of the liquor laws. A technical violation so that the Alcoholic Beverages Commission could close the joint. Watering the booze, the ABC claimed. The real target was the show. Jackie Grossbart would open every show the same way. The only thing wrong with oral sex, he would say, is the view. And then he would bring on the strippers. Direct from Shanghai, Princess Ming. I wouldn't mind being a Chinaman, looking at her, Jackie Gross would say. Chu Manchu. Then he would repeat the name slowly. Chew, man, chew. The charges were dismissed for insufficient cause. And Jackie Grossbart had gone on to better things and a shorter name. His own game show. A house in Las Vegas. He sent Dutch Shea, Jr., a Christmas card every year.

Dutch Shea wondered what had happened to Princess Ming.

He picked up the beer-stained transcript. A 1538.5 suppression hearing.

Q. How would you describe your job, Sergeant Crean?

A. I'm a jack of all trades, Mr. Shea. I analyze narcotics. I analyze blood, breath and urine samples for alcohol. I analyze blood and urine samples for drugs. I analyze all types of physical evidence for blood, and I do sex fiend cases, assault cases, homicide cases, anything like that.

Q. I guess you are a jack-of-all-trades, Sergeant.

A. Thank you, Mr. Shea.

Q. Now tell me about the test you ran on this substance. You tried to run a test to prove that this substance was cocaine, is that correct?

A. Right. I ran what I call a water test on it.

Q. I see. And what did the water test consist of?

A. The cocaine . . .

Q. Substance, Sergeant. You were running the test to see if it was cocaine.

A. Correct. Excuse me.

Q. Certainly. Go on.

A. The substance looked something like salt or soap powder. So we ran water in the portable bar that was in the room, and I tried to see what would happen to the cocaine . . .

Q. Substance . . .

A. Excuse me, Mr. Shea. I tried to see what would happen to the substance as the water hit it.

Q. That's what you call the water test?

A. That's right.

Q. What was supposed to have happened? If it was cocaine, say?

A. If it was cocaine, it would have immediately dissolved.

Q. Really?

A. That's right, Mr. Shea.

Q. And what would have happened if the substance was, say, salt?

A. It would have dissolved . . .

Crean always was a dumb bastard, Dutch Shea, Jr., thought. A worthless witness when I was in the DA's office, and worthless now. Salt, Bones Bloom said when the case was dismissed. About 10 K worth of salt. Bones Bloom was built like a Coke machine. He was wearing blue suede loafers and a lavender jump suit. Complementary colors, Dutch Shea thought. Bones Bloom was a hijacker. A good one. Cocaine was only a sideline.

"Dutch, I'd like to give you a little present," Bones Bloom had said in the corridor outside Department 127, Superior Court. "I got a hundred dozen Barca-loungers I wouldn't mind unloading. Take one. Any color. Burgundy. Champagne. Amber. Take two, they'd make a hell of a living room suite."

"They call that receiving stolen property, Bones. The courts frown on that."

"I got a load of barstools and dinettes. For the wet bar and the breakfast room."

"I don't have a wet bar. Or a breakfast room."

"Too bad, Dutch. You need a pinkie ring? Half carat? Blue-white diamond?"

"I don't think I'm the type, Bones," Dutch Shea said. "I'll just send you a bill."

"Listen," Bones Bloom said, "how's the Mrs.?"

"We're divorced."

"No shit." Bones Bloom hitched his jump suit over his size 50 waist. "Then I can tell you something,

Dutch. I always wanted to bang your wife. No offense meant."

"No offense taken."

"I was in the joint, I used to dream about her coming to see me on a conjugal."

"That's a nice compliment, Bones. I'll mention it to her."

"You wouldn't have her number, would you, Dutch?"

Dutch Shea, Jr., looked at the telephone. He wondered if Lee were still up.

Lee Shea picked up the telephone on the second ring.

"You must be awake," Dutch Shea, Jr., said. "You were asleep, you'd've let it ring four, five, six times, and then when you picked it up, you'd've said hello like you had a mouthful of feathers."

"Oh, for God's sake, Jack," Lee Shea said. She always called him Jack. There were times when he suspected the only thing they ever had in common was their joint dislike of his nickname. "It's almost two. Are you drunk?"

She never disappoints, he thought. "Not quite. Five Coors."

He could hear her steady breathing on the other end of the telephone. "Listen," he said. "I've got this client. Bones Bloom. Nineteen months in the federal slammer in Atlanta and he never got buggered. I think because he looks like he swallowed a set of dishes. Anyway. He wants to take you out. So if you get a call from a guy with a voice that sounds like he's gargling, that's Bones."

He waited for Lee to respond. Five, ten, fifteen seconds.

"Hello, are you still there?"

"Why do you do this?" Lee Shea said.

"Do what?"

"Oh, come on, Jack. It's after two. If you're going to call, do it earlier."

"You want a Barcalounger?"

Lee sighed heavily into the telephone. "Jack, I've got to go to sleep."

"Sure," Dutch Shea, Jr., said. "Just one last thing . . ."

Lee tried to control her voice. "I know what you're going to ask . . ."

"What were you doing in the ladies' room that night?"

Lee did not answer.

"Why did you go to the can and she didn't?"

"Jack . . ."

"It bothers me, Lee. I thought women always went to the can together. Like nuns. They always go in pairs."

"Jack, I'm sorry I wasn't killed that night." Resignation ran through her voice. She had repeated the answer more times than she could remember, but the words still came with difficulty. "I really am. And I'm sorry you can't go to sleep and God knows I wish Cat had been with me in the ladies' room. But she wasn't and I wasn't killed and calling me every night at this time isn't going to make it any different."

"Objection. Nonresponsive. That's not an answer. Why did she want to see you anyway?"

Lee Shea screamed into his ear. "Why did you pick that restaurant? Ask yourself that for a change."

Dutch Shea, Jr., hung up.

3

He dreamed of Lee. She had been named grand marshal of the Rose Parade. She was taking waving lessons. From Margaret Cusick. Margaret Cusick could teach her how to wave all right. Margaret Cusick had sat in a folding chair at their wedding reception, right at the edge of the dance floor, constantly fanning herself, not missing a beat. She was waving a cream-colored paper fan and on the fan was printed, FOR FUNERALS, IT'S SCULLY'S—THE COUNTY'S LARGEST CEMETERYMORTUARY COMBINATION—FOR THOSE YOU LOVE.

Oh, God, that wedding. At the reception, the Catholics sat on one side of the tent, the Protestants on the other. Like the House of Commons and the House of Lords, D. F. Campion had said. D.F. had raised him after his father died. The best way to explain D.F. is that he gave us a bomb shelter as a wedding present, Dutch Shea once said. The other presents—the Lowestoft and the Belleek and the Haviland Limoges and the Royal Crown Derby china, the Baccarat and the Waterford crystal, the silver urns and dishes and candlesticks —took up most of the dining room at the new house on Asylum Avenue that Judge Liggett had bought for his daughter and her husband. The bomb shelter was in the backyard, too big to hide, not yet lowered into the ground. D.F. had insisted on that. He had told the contractor that on no account was the shelter to be installed in its pit prior to the wedding. The shelter was fully stocked with bottled water, canned food and toilet paper. Sixteen rolls of double-ply Dulcey. " 'There's a definite difference with Dulcey,' as they say," D.F. told guests as they stared at the shelter. And then he would hum the Dulcey jingle. Fairfax Liggett looked as if he had swallowed something bad every time he heard D.F. humming. "It's the perfect place to keep your securities, Judge," D.F. Campion said. "Your tax-free municipals. Your will. You have to use that thing, you'll want to know where your will is."

He was gone now, Judge Liggett. A stroke when he was sitting on the toilet. He was wearing a nightshirt. The nightshirt, the circumstances of the death were comforting to Dutch Shea, Jr., a final reckoning that chipped away at Fairfax Liggett's rigid dignity. Judge Liggett had rarely talked to Dutch Shea, Jr., about the law. He had a tax practice, specializing in decedent trusts and fiduciary management, and he did not concern himself with the baser sections of the penal code. Except when the principal or the beneficiary of an estate he was planning found himself deep in trouble, having acted contrary to the criminal statutes or consorting with parties who might. Then there was a peremptory summons to lunch at the Club.

"How's Lee?"

"Fine, Judge."

"And the little girl?"

"Cat." Judge Liggett never referred to his granddaughter by name. He had advised against Cat's adoption. The judge did not trust the uncertainties of unknown blood. He believed in a continuum of heirlooms and family silver. "Short for Catherine."

"Of course." A gelid smile. Judge Liggett did not like to be called that way. Too bad. Dutch Shea, Jr., had a good idea why the judge had summoned him to lunch.

"Do you know the Pyles?"

"I know the Pyles." Old money. Insurance money. A continuum of family silver.

"They're clients of mine."

"Really." He was not going to help Judge Liggett out.

Fairfax Liggett took a deep breath. "Young Harry Pyle . . ."

"Just a minute, Judge," Dutch Shea, Jr., said. "He's twenty-six. That's old enough to know better. Though from what I know of Harry, not even his old man is rich enough to give him what he needs."

"And that is?" An arched eyebrow. The manner never failed to irritate Dutch Shea, Jr. He smiled so as not to let the annoyance show.

"An IQ of a hundred," Dutch Shea said pleasantly. "He's playing with a light deck, Harry."

"That's neither here nor there," Judge Liggett said. That Harry Pyle's intelligence was limited he seemed to accept as a given. "You have heard something, then?"

"I heard that someone held a blow dryer against his neck for twenty mintues or so. My feeling is that would hurt. It raised a big goddamn blister, I hear."

"A terrible thing."

"A great cure for the common cold, Judge." I think I could enjoy this conversation, Dutch Shea, Jr., thought. The slippery terrain of criminal misconduct and violation of the person was one where Fairfax Liggett was less certain, more tentative, where his arrogance was no protection, a swamp inhabited by Catholics and Jews and drunks and women, attorneys who could calibrate the nuances of criminal impulse as precisely as he could the clauses and subsections of the Fiduciaries Investment Act. "I think I'll have another drink, if you don't mind. And if you want me to tell you what I think you want me to tell you, you'd better have one, too, Judge."

Judge Liggett snapped his fingers and a waitress appeared. She smiled quickly at Dutch Shea, but did not look at the judge when she took the order. Her name was Nelly Treacy, Dutch Shea remembered. An elderly Irish spinster who had once worked for D.F. He watched her trying to avoid the judge's gaze. Wasn't

19

there a story there? He sorted through his memory. Oh, yes. The judge had once made her repeat a dirty limerick at a luncheon of the Club board in the conference room.

There once was a hooker named Booker . . .

A harmless enough lyric, but poor Nelly thought she had committed a mortal sin. D.F. told him that. And of course it had not occurred to Fairfax Liggett that he had violated Nelly Treacy's pious and stupid person as effectively as if he had fallen upon her and forced her legs apart.

"Well," Judge Liggett said.

"Well, Judge, the story around is that Harry stuck his dick into someone he should not have stuck it into." A pained look crossed Fairfax Liggett's face. This was not the language of the Decedents Estates Law. Dutch Shea was sure the language was more appalling to the judge than the act it described. "Namely Sara Cantalupo. Sara is short for Serafina, Judge, if that will make you feel any better. Her old man's name is Carmine Cantalupo. Sometimes known as Carmine Cantaloupe. The Melon man. That ring a bell?"

He permitted himself a small smile. Judge Liggett took a deep breath. Dutch Shea knew he was not telling Fairfax Liggett anything he did not already know.

"Carmine Cantaloupe is connected. I think that's the discreet way of putting it. He runs a fruit business. Wholesale fruit. At least that's what it says on his rap sheet. He works hard, he sends his only daughter—his only child—to Mount Holyoke. Not some Catholic school, you notice. Not Manhattanville. Not Marymount. He's got plans for her. What he did not plan on was having Sara knocked up by Harry Pyle."

"That's not been proven."

"No. It has not been proven."

20

"The girl could have had a number of lovers."

"They don't have a football team at Mount Holyoke, Judge, if you're thinking of trying to prove she fucked the varsity."

The two men stared at each other across the table. Judge Liggett drummed his fingers on the tablecloth. Finally he reached into his briefcase and pulled out a large manila envelope. He handed the envelope to Dutch Shea. "What do you make of this? It was in the Pyles' mailbox this morning."

Dutch Shea, Jr., studied the envelope. There was no name on it, no address. He opened it then and removed what appeared to be a set of X-ray photographs. He held first one and then the other up to the light for a moment and then he began to laugh.

"May I ask what is so funny?"

Dutch Shea ignored the edge in Judge Liggett's voice. "Any note?"

"No."

He slipped the X-rays back into the envelope and handed it across the table to Judge Liggett. Then he took a sip of his Gibson. Just to make the judge wait a moment longer. "Well, Judge," he said finally. "What you've got there is a picture of a broken kneecap. Two broken kneecaps. A right one and a left one I would suspect. I got a feeling Carmine wants Harry to marry his baby."

"They could have been misdelivered."

"You go right on believing that, Judge. Just tell Harry to line up a good orthopedics man."

"We can do a blood test."

"Judge, you can do a lot of things, but if Harry likes to walk, he'd better marry that girl."

Judge Liggett stuffed the X rays back into his briefcase. His voice was cold, as if the matter were closed. "You're familiar with the criminal statues. I think there are several sections of the penal code that would cover

21

this. If Mr. Cantalupo insists on taking this matter any further."

Dutch Shea, Jr., shrugged.

"Section five-twenty," Judge Liggett said. "Extortion."

Dutch Shea fished the onion from his Gibson and held it for a moment between his thumb and forefinger. "You're bluffing, Judge," he said after a moment. "You're not going to lay a glove on Carmine Cantaloupe. There's too many people between him and this." He popped the onion into his mouth. "Serafina Pyle."

Judge Liggett regarded him with distaste. "I don't appreciate your sense of humor."

"I'm sorry about that, Judge."

Judge Liggett pushed his chair back, preparing to leave. "Nor do I like your clients."

"Judge, I don't represent anyone here," Dutch Shea, Jr., said quietly. He reached across the table and put his hand over Judge Liggett's, lightly but with enough pressure to detain him. "So I'll tell you what I don't like. I don't like you acting like I'm your hired snitch. Just so you can check out if this is as bad as you think it is. I don't like that. I also don't like you thinking you can use me to cut a deal with Carmine Cantalupo. You want someone to tell him Harry's not carrying a full seabag, then you tell him yourself." He removed his hand from the judge's. "I come more expensive than lunch, Judge. So let's call this a legal consultation. I'll send you a bill."

The bill was for two hundred dollars. Judge Liggett paid it immediately. The judge did not attend the wedding of Serafina Cantalupo and Harry Pyle at the Immaculate Conception Church. Nor did Lee Shea, who claimed menstrual cramps. Dutch Shea, Jr., went by himself. He noted but did not tell Lee that when the bride and groom took their vows a string ensemble of six violins, a cello and a harp played the theme song from *The Godfather*.

Dutch Shea, Jr., opened his eyes. An actor in a three-piece white suit and a black silk shirt open at the neck was offering 20 Movie Masterpieces in a two-record set for $6.95 or 8-track stereo cassette for $8.95. Order now, stocks are limited. "Lara's Theme," two John Williams classics, the theme from *Jaws* and the theme from *Star Wars* . . .

Dutch Shea, Jr., checked his watch. Three o'clock. It was still raining. He switched channels. In a moment, a voice said, Alan Ladd, Veronica Lake and William Bendix in *The Blue Dahlia,* right after these commercial interruptions. He watched the man from Carpeteria and then he watched the man from Zachary All offering Hickey-Freeman, After Six and other namebrand suits, factory clearance, reduced for savings. He had once seen Veronica Lake in a bar in the East Nineties. The Park East Lounge. She was with three drunks who called her Ronny. Her face was bloated and stained with tears. He had told Cat but Cat did not know who she was. Olden times, Daddy, Cat had said. Olden times to Cat was the moment before she was born.

He closed his eyes and thought of Cat. In his study at the house on Asylum Avenue, he kept a drawerful of mementos from her childhood. First teeth. Locks of hair. Scraps of paper on which he had written her encounters with the language as she learned to talk. "Where you was?" she would say, and "Where did the morning went?" He wrote them all down and crammed them into the tiny secret drawer in the maple desk Barry Stukin had given him and Lee as a wedding present. Lee hated the desk. Chippenbaum, she called it. He could chart the decline of their marriage in the movement of the desk from larger to smaller rooms in the house, until finally it was dragged up still another floor and put in the attic maid's room Lee called his study. He loved the room in the attic. He wondered if Lee knew it was a tactical mistake to give it to him. He moved a leather chair in first, and then after suitable intervals, a television set, bookcases, a hide-a-bed. Castro convertible, top of the line. The hide-a-bed was the ultimate victory. He came home one day to find that Lee had put blankets in the closet and sheets and two down pillows. It was never mentioned.

He had made love to her once on the hide-a-bed. She had come to the third floor to ask still another year why day help could not be considered an income tax deduction and he had pointed to the bed and she had nodded yes and then unfolded the couch and removed the old sheets and replaced them with clean ones after first smelling them to see if they were mildewed. Then she had gone downstairs to get a tube of K-Y jelly and the telephone had rung and he had picked up the extension and listened to her plan the Junior League house tour with Chrissie Porterfield. D. F. Campion used to wonder why his vast old post-Victorian house on Prospect Avenue was never on the tour. He suspected that D.F. knew that the huge oil painting of the pope in the front hall might have something to do with it. Pius XII. The last real pope in D.F.'s thinking. Pius XII wasn't much of an attraction for the Junior Leaguers.

He was surprised that Lee remembered to come back upstairs, surprised even further that she had not forgotten the tube of K-Y jelly. She undressed as she always undressed for sex, humming quietly, folding her clothes neatly on the chair, every crease in place, as if preparing for the headmistress's inspection, and then she curled up the tube of K-Y as if it were an old tube of toothpaste until there was enough lubricant to squeeze

24

on her finger. She stood perched like a flamingo, her knee on the arm of the Castro convertible, naked, finger extended and glistening with clear gel, ready to stroke it on him, her glasses, which she never removed except when she was sleeping, hanging over her breasts from the cashmere cord around her neck. She always wore half glasses, even before they were fashionable. They were a perfectly incongruous touch, with their cashmere cord, an absurd detail for the perfect foreplay.

It was the last time Lee came to the study on the third floor. She left the curled-up tube of K-Y on the bookcase, on top of the penal code. He suspected it was still there, like a spent shell left on some forgotten battlefield of the war between the sexes.

Only Cat breached the sanctity of the study on the third floor. Cat in her school tartan. Cat who could call her bath a "bathment" and the butterflies for a kindergarten experiment "flybutters." Cat who had made up her first poem at the age of seven:

> I'm going to marry
> A boy named Harry.
> He rides horses
> And handles divorces.

He would make a note of each saying and when she went back downstairs he would stuff the piece of paper in the secret drawer above the pigeonholes in Barry Stukin's maple desk.

The Broken Man was in that drawer. The Broken Man was what Cat called fear and death and the unknown. I had a bad dream about the Broken Man, she would say. Don't let the Broken Man catch me. If the Broken Man comes, I'll hang onto the fence and won't let him take me.

25

He wondered if Lee had cleaned out the maple desk in the third-floor study on Asylum Avenue.

He wondered if the Broken Man had time to frighten Cat before she died.

4

William Bendix said, "How many fish did you give that house peeper?" William Bendix was Buzz. Buzz had a steel plate in the back of his head. The steel plate caused him to have blackouts. Alan Ladd was Johnny. Johnny was Buzz's best friend. Johnny's wife was a tramp. Her name was Helen. Helen had killed their son in a drunken car accident. Helen was murdered. The police suspected Johnny. Johnny suspected Buzz. Buzz could not remember. Because of the steel plate in the back of his head.

William Bendix said, "Baloney! Think we're going to help you tie a murder to a guy who's flown us on a hundred and twelve missions?"

William Bendix said, "Yeah, take it easy! That's all you do—take it easy. Think things out! Go slow! What does it get you? What did it get Johnny? Maybe you could answer that question, funny face?"

William Bendix said, "Move, motherfucker, and I'll blow your motherfucking head off."

No.

William Bendix would not say that.

Buzz would not talk that way. Even with a steel plate in his head.

Johnny struck a match with his fingernail and held it to the cigarette in his mouth. He inhaled deeply and then held the cigarette at arm's length. "Okay, kid," Johnny said to Buzz, "put it out."

Buzz aimed the gun.

Dutch Shea, Jr., could feel the steel barrel against his ear.

William Bendix said, "You hear me, motherfucker."

No.

That wasn't Buzz.

Dutch Shea opened his eyes wide. A black man was kneeling beside his bed.

No.

Sweet Jesus.

On the television screen, Buzz sighted and squeezed the trigger and shot the lighted cigarette from Johnny's outstretched hand.

The intruder jabbed the pistol deeper into Dutch Shea's ear, twisting the gun until it broke the skin. "You hear me, motherfucker?"

Dutch Shea, Jr., nodded. He was still groggy with sleep, still not certain whether the black man kneeling beside him hissing into his ear belonged in the unkempt bedroom or on the television screen with William Bendix. He wanted to turn his head to see what time it was, but he was afraid the slightest movement might make the gun go off. He wondered what kind of piece it was. The barrel was small enough to fit in his ear. A .22, probably.

A sour smell hung over the room.

"You piss your pants or something?" the black man said.

Dutch Shea wondered if he dared look at the intruder. "I spilled a can of beer." The words seemed to catch in his throat. His khaki pants felt damp. It occurred to him that he might have urinated at the first touch of the gun in his ear.

"Shit." The word seemed to have five syllables. "Beer's for drinking, not spilling."

Dutch Shea moved his head slightly. Immediately the gun was removed from his ear and pushed roughly into

27

his mouth. The barrel scraped the roof of his mouth and jammed his tongue so far back that he choked and gagged.

"Don't you go looking at me, Whitey."

Slowly the gun was removed. The taste of blood filled Dutch Shea's mouth.

"No, sir."

He could hear the black man laugh uproariously and slap his thigh. From the wet sound of the slap, Dutch Shea was sure that the man was soaked to the skin. He could hear the rain still pelting against the window.

"Son of a bitch. That's the first honky ever called me 'sir.' What's your name?"

"John."

"John what?"

"John, sir."

Again the loud laugh and the wet slap on the thigh. On the television screen there were half a dozen people in the office of The Blue Dahlia, many of them policemen. Oh, Christ, he thought, why couldn't one of them be here.

"I mean your last name."

"Shea."

"John Shea." The intruder drew the name out for several beats. "That is a shit name. You got any nicknames? Like Ramblin' Man? Chocolate Lightning? Sable?"

"Dutch."

"Dutch?" The voice was incredulous. "You some kind of Dutchman or something?"

"No." He thought for a moment, wondering if it were dangerous to volunteer anything else. "Irish."

"Then what the fuck they call you Dutch for?"

"It's a long story." He wondered if his father's cellmates had called him Dutch in prison. It seemed a good name to have on the yard. A man named Dutch was a man not to mess with.

28

I wish I were a man not to mess with, he thought.

"'Irish' is what I'm going to call you. Okay?"

"Okay." For a moment he thought of adding "sir," but held his tongue. He did not want the intruder to think he was being smartass. He was probably a hype and very nervous. Only a hype would be out looking for something to steal in this kind of rain. Not to mention this kind of building. In this kind of neighborhood. That was the worry now. The absence of anything of value in the apartment. Secondhand furniture. Garage sale lamps. The TV set from the Goodwill. A black-and-white TV set. Jesus, why don't I have a 19-inch color Panasonic. With push-button controls and automatic fine tuning. This spade would like something like that. He wondered if he should tell him that Ynez Cano in 3-G had a Betamax X2. With a pause button and a memory counter. She used it to record *Days of Our Lives* when she was turning a trick. No. Better not tell him about Ynez. Ynez would not turn tricks with *negritos*. She would begin to scream. Ynez had a reputation as a screamer. Especially in the courtroom. So much so that Judge Notreangelo in arraignments said that any vice officer who brought her into his courtroom would be cited for contempt himself.

Oh, God, I don't want to die, he thought. Keep thinking of something else. Even Ynez. Maybe this is not happening. It's the sound track from another movie, not *The Blue Dahlia*. It's what happens when you have a lousy TV set.

The black stood up and began shaking the kinks out of his legs. He was a hype all right. Dutch Shea could make out the hatchwork of needle tracks on his arms. And the gun was a .22. He wondered if the intruder knew that the .22 was the favored weapon for contract hits. Almost no recoil and small enough to fit into the palm of the hand. No unsightly bulges in a jacket pocket. Muzzle velocity 1000 feet per second. With a larger gun, a .38, say, the bullet might go right through you. Not so with a .22. The bullet from a .22 would rattle around inside you like a marble in a pinball machine. Tilt. Bingo. Sayonara.

This man is going to kill me, Dutch Shea, Jr., thought. Why can't I keep my mind on what is happening?

"I want to tell you something, Irish." The black kicked a cordovan Florsheim shoe away and stared balefully at him. "I should've known when your kitchen door was unlocked you was some kind of asshole. In this neighborhood no one leaves no door unlocked. You get the chain. You get the police lock. You get the dead bolt lock. Not that they would've stopped me, but when you didn't have none of them, I should've known what I was going to find in here."

He appeared to be about thirty, approximately six feet tall and 150 pounds. His hair was conked and his skin was of medium tone with no identifying marks or scars beyond the needle tracks on his arms.

Oh, shit, Dutch Shea, Jr., thought. I'm taking him down like a description for the IdentiKit man. Sweet Jesus, if he knew I was working up his WANTED poster.

"Shit is what I find in here," the intruder said. He pointed contemptuously to the easy chair with the broken spring on which Dutch Shea had thrown the glen plaid suit he had worn that day. "Shit. I got better shit in my place than you got here, Irish. I got stainless-steel lamps. I don't see you with no stainless-steel lamps. I been in jails turn this shit down. Where you get it at?"

"The Goodwill. I got a lot of it at the Goodwill."

"What's that? Some kind of honky welfare?"

"Close."

"Shit." The intruder pulled the soggy shirt board away from the broken windowpane. "You don't even fix the window. Like it's some kind of nigger welfare hotel."

Keep talking. Agree. "I suppose it does have that look."

"You ever seen a nigger welfare hotel?"

"No, no. I was just taking your word for it." As a matter of fact, he had once been inside a black welfare hotel. Correction: a hotel maintained by the Department of Welfare that happened to be inhabited entirely by blacks. The luck of the draw. Better not mention that. No. It was when he defended Gentle Davidson for murdering Lawrence Rivers. Aka Florence Rivers. Florence and Gentle had been sweeties. He liked defending in murder trials. One less witness. And a crucial one at that. Martha Sweeney was the judge on that one. It was the first time he met her. "Structured Setting Martha." So called because when she sent people away she always said, "I think you'd be better off in a structured setting." Judge Sweeney had let him bus the jury to the Cuthbertson on Ann Street, the welfare hotel where the killing took place. One look at the Cuthbertson was all the jury needed. There was shit on the stairwell and there was a one-eyed prostitute sitting on top of the shit trying to wrap a rubber cord around her arm. The visit had the desired effect, unspoken but there nonetheless: who cared who killed what nigger in a fleabag like that? Which was the reason he had petitioned Judge Sweeney to have the jury brought to the Cuthbertson in the first place. Gentle was acquitted. Justifiable homicide.

Gentle. Jesus. He had a dong like a hockey stick. I'd like to run this dude's ass up against Gentle Davidson, Dutch Shea thought. Gentle Davidson would fuck mud if he got horny enough. His sheet said that he had once tried to fuck a tree at the county work farm. Suddenly Dutch Shea, Jr., was furious. It's not much this place, but it's better than that toilet, the Cuthbertson.

Steady, he thought. This is the wrong time to get house proud.

He watched the intruder clean the money and the American Express card from his wallet on the dresser.

"Eleven dollars. That all you got?"

"I was going to cash a check tomorrow." He wondered if he should add that his American Express bill was two months overdue: $278. I have to see about that. I'll put Alice on it tomorrow. Pay it out of the O'Meara account.

Oh, God, no. Annie O'Meara. Why do I have to think about her now? Still hanging in there at eighty-seven. Eighty-seven years of age, as she invariably put it. A fixture at the Arthur K. Degnan Senior Citizen Center. The probate court had appointed him conservator of her estate when she was committed. He suspected that Annie was lying about her age. She wanted to be the oldest patient at Arthur K. Degnan's. The oldest patient sat in the aisle seat of the front row when they showed the Saturday cartoons on the Advent screen in the community room. Oh, that Bugs Bunny, Mr. Shea, Annie had said on his last visit. I wet my pants when I see Bugs. I hear my IT&T went up a point. Annie and Bugs. Maybe it would be better if the intruder let go. With muzzle velocity of 1000 feet per second, it would be over in a flash. Annie would come out all right after the audit. He was bonded. I'll go see Annie. I promise. It was like a prayer for salvation. If I'm still alive, dear God, I promise you that. I'll work it out. I'll bring her some rocky road ice cream. She liked rocky road. And Snickers bars. Snickers is my favorite, Mr. Shea . . .

Pay attention. He's talking. Don't let your mind wander.

"I stick up school kids with more than that. School kids carry more than that so they can score. I really picked shit when I picked you, you know that?"

Dutch Shea nodded. On the television screen someone seemed to be confessing to Helen's murder. Oh, shit, he thought. I've seen this movie before. Someone is going to shoot someone in a minute. This crazy spade's going to hear a shot on the tube and start blasting.

"Excuse me," Dutch Shea, Jr., said. He hoped the panic in his voice did not show. This wasn't the way Clint Eastwood would have handled it. Dirty Harry would have this guy in the electric chair by now. "This fellow, Newell, the house peeper . . ."

"The what?"

"The house detective . . ."

"What fucking house detective?" the black screamed. He crouched at the end of the bed in a shooter's stance, holding the gun in both hands, and aimed it directly at Dutch Shea's face.

"In the movie," Dutch Shea said. He nearly strangled on the words. "On the TV. He's going to get shot. I don't want you to get nervous."

There was a shot. On the television screen, Newell staggered. "Just a minute, gentlemen," he said. "You've got me all wrong . . ." Dutch Shea, Jr., closed his eyes and waited for the second shot. The real one. He thought of Cat. And of his father. Hanging from a wet sheet in his cell. Having learned after only four months in a structured setting that a wet sheet does not tear. A moment of peace. No more Annie O'Meara. The court of probate would sort that out . . .

Then he heard the laughter.

Slowly he opened his eyes. The black was at the foot of the bed, bent double, laughing so hard spit was exploding from his mouth.

"Oh, shit, Irish. Oh, shit." Another convulsion of laughter. "I bet you crapped your pants."

"I did not." The injured dignity of the craven. I hate this man. I hate him because he knows how terrified I am. I hate him because he knows he has nothing to lose if he shoots me. And he knows I know it.

The rage welled up.

Nigger!

Coon!

Dinge!

Jungle bunny!

The words ricocheted around his mind and for an instant they made him feel better. But only for an instant. The courage of the supine, he thought. He felt humiliated.

The black was trying to turn off the television set.

"Ain't you got no remote?"

Dutch Shea shook his head.

"Shit. They even got remote at the welfare hotel." The intruder crouched in front of the set. "Oh, I do like that blond pussy." His hand began to massage his crotch. "Oh, I got about a foot of nigger for her. Oh. What's her name, Irish?"

"Ronny." No. That wasn't it. That was her nickname. What was her name? Good God. Imagine being shot for not knowing the name of an actress on the late show. Not Ronny. "Veronica Lake."

"Yeah. Oh, yeah." The intruder turned and smiled at Dutch Shea. "You ever been fucked up the chocolate highway, Irish?"

Dutch Shea stared, not daring to blink.

"Don't you fret, Irish. I only do that in the joint. In the joint I am an asshole bandit. The sheriff of the brown trail." He winked at Dutch Shea, turned off the television set and then slowly patted his crotch again.

Dutch Shea, Jr., held his breath. The room was silent. He closed his eyes. Suddenly in the distance he could hear the wail of a siren, and then a second. The intruder tensed and then crouched and pointed the .22 at him.

34

"The po-lice."

"Fire," Dutch Shea, Jr., said quickly. His throat was so dry his words seemed to catch on little tentacles of panic. "Those are fire sirens."

"You sure?"

"Yes."

"How you sure?"

Dutch Shea stared at the gun pointing at his face. "They're not getting any closer." It seemed like a symphony of sirens now. He prayed that the explanation would suffice. He wondered if he had ever prayed so much. And invoked the name of God more often. No. Not even when Cat died. The will to survive left an acrid taste in his mouth.

Outside the sound of the sirens receded. The intruder parted the curtains and peered out the window. When he turned back to Dutch Shea, he was smiling. He put the gun in his belt.

"Lucky for you, Irish."

The intruder was at the closet now. Shirts and suits were held up, examined and then thrown on the floor.

"Ain't you got no suede?"

"No." He had bought a suede jacket once. Cat said it made him look like a trendy alderman. He had given it to the Goodwill. Honky welfare.

"You think I'd've robbed this place I knew all you had was this shit? Them wing-tip shoes and the white shirts with the little buttons on the collar. This isn't even honky shit. This is shit shit."

Dutch Shea nodded. "I guess you're right."

"You straight, Irish, you gay?"

"The former."

"The what?"

"Straight. I mean straight."

"Yeah. Shit like you got in your closet, you got to be straight. I bet you wear a rubber when you fuck."

35

Dutch Shea, Jr., considered the answer. How did he know that? Martha insisted. She refused to let her gynocologist fit her for a diaphragm or give her a prescription for the pill. She was afraid her father would find them. Tommy Sweeney went to Mass and communion every day. You never know when a fireman's going to go, he would say. A roof gives way under me, I want to be in a state of grace. The fire that gets me is the last fire I want to see, if you get my meaning. Martha still lived with her father. She was thirty-six years old, a superior court judge and she still cooked dinner every night for da. A goddamn fireman who sneaked into her bathroom and checked out her medicine cabinet. He wondered how Tommy had fathered Martha. He had just enough brains to hold up a hose.

"No." Dutch Shea, Jr., shook his head vigorously. Better to deny. "It's like going swimming in a raincoat." He wondered if he had it right. "It's like using an umbrella in the shower."

A chuckle. "You a good dude, Irish." The intruder was standing in the doorway to the living room. "You ain't going to move, is you?"

"No."

"You going to yell?"

"No."

"You do, I'm going to shoot you."

Dutch Shea, Jr., took a deep breath. He could still hear the fire engines far off. Martha, Martha. In bed she would hear a fire siren and bless herself three times.

Dutch Shea, Jr., watched the intruder through the bedroom door. The living room was littered with papers and manila folders and transcripts and briefs and lawbooks. Here it is. This guy finds out I'm a lawyer, that's it. I wonder if I ever prosecuted him when I was in the DA's office? Just my luck. The face wasn't familiar. But the faces were all a blur from his days in the DA's office. They weren't people, they were just numbers to deal. A 211 robbery, kick it down to 459 burglary, time off for time served, next case. I can't let him get a good look at my face, just in case.

The rage rose once again. You black bastard. I keep people like you out of the slammer now. And what for? So you can do this.

The rage subsided. Oh, God, I hope Cat is not watching this performance.

"Jesus." The intruder was at the bedroom door, the .22 still tucked in his belt, and in his hand he was carrying a transcript, some glossy photographs and a number of photocopied advertisements from what Dutch Shea knew was a sexual freedom newspaper. "What's this mean? 'Attorney for the Com . . .'" The rest of the word seemed too much for him.

"Complainant," Dutch Shea offered.

"'John Shea.'" The intruder was reading from the cover of the transcript. "That you?"

"Yes."

"You a lawyer?"

"Yes."

"No shit." He opened the transcript to a page he had folded back. "This com . . ."

". . . plainant."

"He sounded like a pimp."

Dutch Shea chose his words with care. "He runs an outcall massage service."

"Then he's a pimp, right?"

"That is the allegation."

"Don't give me that fancy shit. Yes or no?"

Oh, Myron, I would not say it if the man did not have a .22 ready to shoot me. "Yes."

"Myron. That his name?"

"Myron Mandel, right."

The black waved one of the Xeroxed advertisements from the sexual freedom newspaper. The ad was for an outcall massage service. "This his outfit? Camel Outcall?" He read slowly from the ad copy. " 'We Give You a Humping Good Time.' "

"That's his outfit, all right."

"Out of sight. And this one here. 'Teenagers Who Are Terrific.' "

"That's his outfit, too."

"That spell 'twat,' right?"

"Right. That's what it's meant to spell. That's why he chose that name, Myron. 'Teenagers Who Are Terrific.' It's what you call an acronym."

I sound demented, Dutch Shea, Jr., thought. Is living worth this abasement?

"Jesus," the intruder said. He drew the word out, as if he could not believe his good fortune. A smile lit his features. "You some kind of pimp lawyer. That is good shit."

Dutch Shea, Jr., nodded and smiled bleakly. A pimp lawyer. Even Lee never came right out and said it.

"Then what you doing living like this?" His hand circled the apartment. "There's good bread being a pimp lawyer. You drive a Seville, you a pimp lawyer. With wire wheels. AM-FM stereo. Tape deck. Tinted windshield. One of them antennas goes up and down from a button on the dashboard. Man, that's a heavy job, a pimp lawyer. I get some ladies, I don't want no lawyer lives like this." He leaned toward Dutch Shea. "You dig?"

"I dig."

The black began looking through the glossy photographs of the outcall masseuses. For each photo he had a word or a moan of approval.

"Man. That Myron. He got some string. Oh. You know these ladies?"

"Some of them."

"You fuck any?"

"No." It seemed late in the game to invoke the lawyer-client relationship, but there it was.

"You know her?" The intruder was looking at a photograph of a girl with long straight blond hair. She was wearing a T-shirt on which was printed the words, FRENCH CONNECTION.

Of course, he would pick that one, Dutch Shea, Jr., thought. "Yes."

"What's her name?"

"Crystal."

"Oh, that's nice. I like that. Crystal." He sat on the arm of the chair next to the dresser and stared for a moment at the photograph. Then he took the .22 from his belt and put it on the dresser. "Don't you move, Irish." His voice came in short breaths. "I got my piece right here."

It has to be a dream, Dutch Shea, Jr., thought. But it wasn't. The intruder unzipped his fly and took his member from his pants. Jesus. Christ. It's bigger than Gentle Davidson's. Dutch Shea watched, mesmerized. The black was breathing heavily. He held the photograph of Crystal Faye in one hand, his cock in the other. He began to masturbate slowly, his eyes not leaving the photo. I wonder what it would do to his hard-on if I told him Crystal was a cop, Dutch Shea, Jr., thought. An undercover vice cop. Oh, Crystal, I can't wait to tell you this boogie splashed right in your face. There'll be a laugh or two over that in the locker room down at vice. I can get off on that myself. Oh, yes.

There was a groan from the chair as the intruder ejaculated into the picture of Crystal Faye. He pumped himself until he was dry and then lay back until his breathing returned to normal, his cock draped over his thigh. For a few moments he seemed almost unaware that Dutch Shea, Jr., was even in the room. Then his eyes began to focus. He stared at Dutch Shea, fury mottling his smooth cocoa complexion. He grabbed the gun from the dresser and leaped across the room, his cock still dangling from his open fly. He jammed the .22 into Dutch Shea's mouth and put his face right next to his. The intruder's breath smelled of stale wine.

"You motherfucker, what you looking at?"

The gun in his mouth made an answer impossible. Dutch Shea began to make a perfect act of contrition. Oh, my God, I am heartily sorry for having offended Thee . . .

He could not remember any more. It's the thought that counts, oh, Lord. He wondered if the Almighty would see it that way.

"Motherfucker. Pimp lawyer . . ."

Dutch Shea held his eyes tightly shut. He was no longer afraid. The unknown was suddenly reassuring. A source of peace. The idea of peace at last suffused him, elevated him. He did not feel the barrel of the .22 when it came crashing down behind his ear.

When he awoke, the intruder was gone. He felt the knob behind his ear. He was surprised that he was still alive. And not too happy about it. My dirty little secret, he thought. Slowly he swung his legs over the side of his bed. It was still raining and it was dark outside. He wondered how long he had been unconscious. Ten minutes maybe. Nothing seemed to be missing.

Oh, yes. Nothing seemed to be missing because he had shit.

Dutch Shea, Jr., looked at the television set. Suddenly he was blinded by rage. He assumed a karate stance. Take this, you black fuck. He slammed the side of his right hand down on top of the TV set and the pain shot from his fingers to his elbow and then up to his shoulder. The blow had turned the set on. There was an exercise program on the screen. The picture on the tube was clearer than it ever had been. From the funny angle of his pinkie, Dutch Shea, Jr., was sure that he had broken at least two fingers and probably his whole hand.

When he was released from the hospital, his hand in a cast from fingers to elbow, he decided to go to Mass. He did not particularly want to go to Mass. He just wanted to return to his apartment even less. It was not quite six A.M. and the Pancake House was not open, so Mass it was. His parish since the divorce was Immaculate Conception, but this morning, a bit giddy from the pain-killers administered by the touchy Indian intern in the emergency room at Mother Cabrini Hospital, he was not quite up to the Immaculate. There was something about Immaculate that made him feel unworthy. Even when he called it Immaculate, as most of the parishioners did, he felt as if he were indulging in high irony. Immaculate was what used to be called a working-class parish. Working class translated into Italian. Mrs. Nick Del'Osso ran the Altar Society and Mrs. Punchy Iacovetti the Confraternity of C.D. and Mrs. Gianni Lombardozzi the Nocturnal Adoration Society. Good women he was sure, although he did not know any of the three. Women who wore black. All the women at Immaculate wore black. Black dresses, black shawls, black shoes, ankle fat spilling over the shoes.

Women with facial moles. And little hairs growing out of the moles. The women of Immaculate doted on the pastor. Father Mancuso. Father Ruggiero Mancuso. In the chancery of the archdiocese, Father Ruggiero Mancuso was known as Mancuso the Good to distinguish him from his twin brother, Father Fabian Mancuso. The Pallotine priest. Known as Mancuso the Bad. Father Fabian had absconded with nearly seven million dollars in funds credited to the Pallotine Missionary Society. Bad perhaps, but no piker. Fabian Mancuso was uncovered in a condominium he had purchased in Palm Springs under the name of Rhett Pincus. Dutch Shea suspected the archdiocese was less upset about the seven million than it was about the alias Rhett Pincus. He would like to defend Mancuso the Bad. He had his defense all worked out. Begin with Fabian Mancuso's Humble Beginnings. Show that Fabian Mancuso was a Builder. A Visionary who had put the Pallotines into the Teamster Pension Fund. The pope must be kicking himself, he didn't think to put the Vatican into the Teamster Pension Fund. Point out this was a dog-eat-dog world. Slide over Rhett Pincus. Who among us can cast the first stone?

Who indeed?

Not me.

Father Ruggiero Mancuso would make him think of Father Fabian Mancuso. Aka Rhett Pincus. Aka Rhett Pincus made him think of his own situation. And he was too fragile to think of his own situation this morning, thank you.

He did not go to Immaculate. He went to St. Robert Bellarmine instead. His parish when he was married to Lee. He liked the idea of a saint with a last name. Robert Bellarmine. Bob Bellarmine. Bobby Bellarmine. He pictured Bobby Bellarmine as a man with a golf handicap, a man with a taste for martinis, a man who did not get too terribly worked up about birth

control. St. Robert Bellarmine was more to his mood
this morning. There was no deadening piety about St.
Robert Bellarmine. No facial moles. The church
looked like an airline terminal. If airline terminals were
built of redwood. School of Eero Saarinen. Wings that
shot off like flying saucers. George Patton was in one
stained-glass window. Star-studded silver helmet liner
and ivory-handled revolvers. St. George Patton. Behind the altar was a huge Day-Glo green cloth tapestry,
school of Corita Kent, on which was printed in Day-
Glo blue:

> Youth is a gift of nature,
> Age a work of art.

It seemed to set the tone of St. Robert Bellarmine. As
did the printed Sunday announcements. You had to
search for the wedding banns and the month's mind
Masses between the advertisements. Get Your "Bug"
at Bill Barry Volkswagen. The Very Best in Domestic
Zinfandels at John Goll2g 's Packaged Goods. For
Life Insurance, Think Morgan Clancy. Where There's
Life, There's Morg. No ads for the Nocturnal Adora-
tion Society. Faith seemed a theoretical concept at St.
Robert Bellarmine, God a possibility.

Mass was said by a black priest. Surprising. There are
not only no blacks at St. Robert's, Lee had once said,
there are no brunettes either. With that infuriating
Episcopalian irony. I don't exactly hear no darkies
singing "Ol' Man River" at St. Bartholomew's, he had
replied. Another stand-off. He searched the announcements. There it was. Maryknoll From Africa Visits
Parish. Father Lionel Nkrumah. Lecture and slide show
in parish hall. He wondered what Lionel Nkrumah
would talk about. Communism vs. Catholicism in the
Subcontinent? Negritude and Religion: Can They Co-
Exist? No. Something in the St. Robert Bellarmine

manner. "Hiking in East Africa." As Lionel Nkrumah raised the host at the consecration, Dutch Shea noticed he was wearing Adidas sneakers. Orange and gold. Perfect for long walks in the hikers' paradise. He wondered if he should receive. Why not? He had made a perfect act of contrition the night before. The perfect act of contrition canceled out the three years since his last confession. So something good came out of the robbery after all. Take the long view. Lionel Nkrumah would not understand the intricacies of the Annie O'Meara situation anyway. Go. Lionel Nkrumah placed the host on his tongue and he felt a surge. A faith attack. Let him be run over in the parking lot. He would be heaven bound, in a state of grace, Annie O'Meara forgiven, sins of the flesh absolved.

His euphoria lasted until the parking lot. Where he was not hit by a car but waylaid by Elaine Igoe. Widow of Byron.

"What happened?"

He told her.

"Was it a colored man?"

"Yes."

"I didn't like that priest this morning, did you?"

Someone drove past and tooted the horn. The word would soon be out. The cuckolded husband was talking with the abandoned wife after the six this morning. She had her hand on his arm. Do you think they'll get together? The thought appalled him. Those terrible children. The boy's neck contaminated with flaming pustules, the girl always with a Kleenex wadded into her hand to dab at a permanently drippy nose.

"How are the children?"

"They need a father, Jack."

"Yes." But not me. Elaine Igoe was trolling for a husband and he knew that he was the catch she had in mind. No way. Except. The bait was enticing enough. The $2.7 million settlement she had received when three drunk teenagers ran over Byron and killed him instantly. On his way home from a rendezvous with Lee. He had read the autopsy report. Byron's semen bank was depleted. And he knew where the deposit had been made.

"Especially By." Byron III. "He needs a man to talk to." She brightened, as if lit up by a new thought. "Maybe you can talk to him, Jack."

"Yes." The three teenagers who had killed Byron were under legal drinking age. Barry Stukin, acting for Elaine, had sued the bar that served them: $2.7 million. One third for Barry, two thirds for Elaine: $1.8 million. Tax free. Plus Byron's portfolio. Plus Byron's life insurance. Maybe three million. In round figures. That had a nice ring to it. He did not need that much. The bait was appetizing enough. Enough to consider biting.

"That's swell, Jack." Elaine Igoe rubbed his cast. The fallish nip in the air seemed to make her forward. "You always were such a good father."

"Of course, I don't know what to say to a boy." But keep your options open. A bleak thought: hunkering between Elaine's vast thighs twice a week. He could feel the communion grace departing. No wonder Byron lusted for the slender Episcopalian thighs of Lee Liggett Shea. Stomach muscles unstretched by childbirth. He saw Lionel Nkrumah cross from the church to the rectory. Would Father Nkrumah still think him elevated by grace?

"Orange shoes," Elaine Igoe said. "It's a wonder Ralphie Keogh permits it."

Ralphie Keogh was the pastor at St. Robert Bellarmine. Ralphie Keogh could hardly complain about Father Nkrumah's footwear. Not a man who said Mass as if he were wearing track shoes himself. His record was nine minutes when he had a plane to catch for a pro-am at the Doral Beach Country Club.

"I don't think it matters that much." He opened the

door of his Toyota. If he did not leave, Elaine Igoe would announce the banns. He wondered if she and Byron had ever performed in anything but the missionary position.

"What you say to a boy, Jack, is not all that different than what you say to a girl." Elaine had neatly reversed her field.

"I'd feel strange, Elaine."

"Think about it, Jack."

"Of course."

She kissed him the cheek. Trolling.

Oh, God, don't let me bite.

III

"At least the cast should get you sympathy," Alice March said when he walked into the office. She was rearranging the magazines on the reception table. Copies of *Time* and copies of *Newsweek,* none more recent than three weeks old. No one steals old magazines, she had explained to him once. The people we run through this office, they'd steal the paint off the walls, you give them half a chance, he had replied. Because it's Tuesday, because they haven't stolen anything that day.

"I'd like to think I don't need sympathy, Alice."

Alice March shrugged and tore the wrapping off *The Forum,* a trade magazine published by the state trial attorneys association. She put the magazine on the reception table with the advertisement on the back cover faceup: Emergency Seminars on Death Penalty Cases.

"And, Alice, that ad is not going to stop anyone from stealing *Time* and *Newsweek.*"

Alice March ignored the sharpness in his voice. "You watch *Firing Line* last night?" She always watched

Firing Line. Dutch Shea, Jr., suspected she had a secret lust for William F. Buckley, Jr. She invariably referred to him as "Bill." She talked about his blue eyes and his perfect teeth and his custom-made ties, but never about giving South Africa an even break.

"I was getting stuck up last night, remember?" He wondered if Alice March were alone when he had called from the emergency room. Or if the Demerol shot into his buttocks had made him imagine the postcoital languor in her voice.

"He had a new blue suit. Chalk stripes. I've never seen him in chalk stripes before. Pinstripes, but never chalk stripes."

"The calls, Alice," Dutch Shea, Jr., said. He walked into his office and peered out the window. It was still raining so hard that he could hardly make out the Roman revival superior court building a block up the street. For a moment he contemplated writing Martha's initials on the cast. Discreetly, up by the elbow. M.S. He wondered idly of the effect of plaster on the libido. Not to mention the exercise of same. He had called Martha from the hospital. She was sitting as master calendar judge this session. No, she could not remember any defendant aka Sable who had appeared before her. Tonight? she had asked. He wondered if she had picked up the reserve in his voice when he answered yes, of course. He tried not to think what he would have done if Martha had been with him last night. In his mind he saw aka Sable rising and falling on top of her.

Maybe he would have killed me first.

A liberating idea.

But what if he had not? What if he had held his hit man's .22 on me and then climbed on top of Martha? How would I have reacted?

Consider that.

A not so liberating idea.

He felt the bump on his head. The swelling had begun to diminish. The X ray had confirmed a bad bruise but no concussion. No wonder he felt terrible. The bleakness of the office did not help. Since Cat's death, he had taken a perverse pleasure in the grubby. In becoming like his clients. First his apartment, then this office. There was a partner's desk by the window overlooking Washington Street that he had bought at auction for forty dollars and had refinished for five hundred. Conceivably an antique. Everything else was secondhand. Six file cabinets, two of which matched. A library table with a replacement leg shorter than the others and that leg propped up by a peace officer's abridged edition of the penal code. On the table piles of transcripts and appellate opinions. Two imitation Danish tubular chairs. Against the wall a Naugahyde couch with foam rubber cushions. His only fee from a woman he had represented in an action against her ex-husband. The ex-husband had been spray-painting walls around town with the words, "Call Eileen Gould 853-2210 for good head."

He wondered if Eileen Gould's husband had been correct.

Call Martha Sweeney for good head.

Call Alice March for good head.

Call Elaine Igoe for good . . .

You must be kidding.

Dutch Shea, Jr., examined the cast on his right hand and tried to wriggle his fingers. The pain was like a toothache. The Indian intern in the emergency room at Mother Cabrini had given him Demerol before he wrapped on the cast and a prescription for Darvon afterward, but the ache was constant. The intern wore a dirty white turban flecked with what appeared to be dried blood. His plastic name tag identified him as

M. Amin, M.D. M. Amin, M.D., seemed to take offense at Dutch Shea, Jr., staring at his turban.

"I am being from Trinidad," he had said.

Dutch Shea nodded.

"'Shrimp boats is a-coming/There's dancin' tonight . . .'"

"What?"

"Or maybe you are liking 'Jambalaya.'"

Dutch Shea, Jr., wondered what he had done to offend M. Amin, M.D.

"Sahib," the intern said. "If I were being an African gentleman, I would be calling you 'Bwana.'"

"Oh, fuck off," Dutch Shea, Jr., said, and immediately cursed himself for the outburst. He tapped the pulpy lump on his head and tried to explain. "Look, it's been a bad night. I just don't need shit from another . . ." His voice faltered.

"Darky," M. Amin, M.D., said. He continued wrapping the cast around the fracture, a small smile on his face. How did I get into this? Dutch Shea, Jr., wondered. A night like this, why do I have to meet up with a sensitive Indian? The Demerol was taking hold. He avoided the glance of M. Amin, M.D., and glanced around the emergency room. It was packed with the detritus of a rainy night. Broken bones. Knife wounds. Bullet wounds. Cardiac arrest. Old people. Young people. Babies. Male, female, black, white, yellow, brown. Peaceful, contorted, resigned, smashed, battered and bruised.

"There's a guy out there, you wouldn't believe it, Dutch," Jerry Costello said. He was standing in the doorway of the examining room, his gold detective's badge clipped to the lapel of his jacket. "Fag. His boyfriend sticks a ball-point pen up his cock. I swear to God. I ask him if it would write underwater. Isn't that rich?"

"That's rich, Jerry," Dutch Shea, Jr., said.

"Maybe he can write a check with it," Jerry Costello said. "It takes all kinds, don't it?" He sat on the edge of the examining table, not paying any attention to M. Amin, M.D. "One thing you can say for them fags. They always come with a new wrinkle."

Jerry Costello put a finger beneath his nose to head off a sneeze. His jacket was flaked with dandruff and his large bulbous nose mapped with a network of veins. He took a piece of paper from the manila folder in his hand.

"What we got so far is this, Dutch. Male, Negro. In that neighborhood, what the hell you expect? You must have terrible alimony is all I got to say. He's been in the joint, he's an asshole bandit, he might be nicknamed Sable and he's a hype. Also been on welfare. Aside from the Sable, that spells about half the coons in town . . ."

M. Amin, M.D., stared at Jerry Costello.

"Oops. No offense, Doc." Jerry Costello took the photograph of Crystal Faye from the folder. It was all crumbled and crusted with semen. "About this picture . . ."

"I told you, Jerry, He jerked off in it."

"Sure, Dutch." A large smile split Jerry Costello's face. "Crystal will be glad to hear that. She might even believe it." He held the photograph at arm's length. "Christ, he must've let go a quart."

"You're smearing the fingerprints, Jerry. That's about the only thing he touched in the apartment."

"Listen, if I was Perry Mason, Dutch, I'd be making a hell of a lot more money than I am now. Tell me something. Just between you and me. She really fuck that guy, Crystal?"

His head throbbed. "What guy?"

"Myron. Your client."

"I thought we were discussing my case, Jerry."

"Shit, Dutch, we're never going to catch this guy, you know that. You were still in the DA's office, you'd drop the charges. He beat his meat is all he did." Jerry Costello tapped the photograph. "And we only got your word for that."

"I'll take the picture, Jerry," Dutch Shea said.

"Sorry, Dutch." Jerry Costello began to laugh. "Got to dust it for prints." He so appreciated the joke that the laughter turned to a cough. His face turned red and a piece of phlegm flew out of his mouth and landed on the white hospital shoe of M. Amin, M.D. "Listen. Sorry about that. Take my handkerchief." He dug into his pocket and handed a handkerchief to M. Amin, M.D. The intern looked at him for a moment and then shook his head.

"Okay, have it your way," Jerry Costello said. Then in a low voice to Dutch Shea, he added: "I hear they got a lot worse than snot on their shoes in India, is what I hear."

"Dr. Amin is from Trinidad, Jerry."

"No shit." Jerry Costello turned toward the intern. "You're from Trinidad, I hear. How'd you ever get to this part of the world?"

Dutch Shea, Jr., closed his eyes. The voices faded away. A moment, two. He awoke with a start. Jerry Costello was standing at the elbow of M. Amin, M.D.

"Look at this tie," Jerry Costello said. He was wearing a dark brown polyester tie with a pattern of beige diamonds. "Pull it."

M. Amin, M.D., looked from Dutch Shea, Jr., to Jerry Costello, his sad brown eyes reflecting the conviction that he was meant to be the butt of some obscure joke.

"Go ahead," Jerry Costello said. "Pull it."

The intern hesitated and then pulled the tie with both

hands and when he did the polyester expanded and each diamond formed the words, FUCK YOU.

M. Amin, M.D., dropped the tie as if it were a snake.

"I wish I'd've been in on the ground floor of this one," Jerry Costello said, shaking the end of his tie. "I'd've made a mint, I'll tell you. You get the rights, you can make a fortune back home in India, Doc."

"Trinidad," M. Amin, M.D., said.

"Whatever," Jerry Costello said. He nodded toward Dutch Shea, Jr. "I tell the counselor here, it's my courtroom tie. The judges we got these days, you got to make a protest somehow. What kind of judges you got back home in India, anyhow?"

The rain was coming down harder.

Dutch Shea fingered the bottle of Darvon on his desk. He noticed that the fingers extending from the cast had begun to turn black and blue.

Call Lee Shea for good head.

Debatable.

Scratch good.

Call Lee Shea.

Period.

"You hit him then?" Lee's telephone voice. Cool and impersonal. Grace Kelly in *The Swan*. All right, not good. Not bad either. Considering the breeding, not bad at all.

"No, not exactly, no."

"Then how did you break it?"

"I got mad and hit the television set." For a moment he considered whether he should add the circumstances. "After he left."

"Of course." He had often hit inanimate objects when they were married. Tables, bookcases, walls, doors. It never seemed to make any impression on her.

The only bone he ever broke was when he kicked the bathtub after her salpingogram. A fractured toe. A fractured little toe. Little toe, little marriage. He wondered if he should tell her about the Indian intern and Jerry Costello. No. It was just another pointless anecdote. Their marriage had been a mosaic of pointless anecdotes.

"I'm glad you weren't hurt. Seriously, I mean." Cool but at least not grudging.

"Thanks."

"And Jack . . ."

"Yes."

"My check."

Back to basics. "I'll put it in the mail."

"It's never on time."

"I'm sorry."

"It makes life easier if it arrives on time."

"I heard you, Lee. The first time." If she had married Byron Igoe, he thought, the alimony would have been one less worry.

Money.

Always money.

He suddenly remembered Annie O'Meara. And the promise he had made during the robbery to see her if he survived. *Mea culpa, mea culpa, mea maxima culpa.*

Speaking of money.

"And Jack . . ."

"Yes."

"Don't let anyone write on your cast. It's vulgar."

So much for calling Lee Shea. For good anything.

He swallowed a Darvon. Lee always had that effect. A cough.

Alice March was standing in the doorway of his office. He wondered if she had listened to his conversation with Lee. "You want your calls?"

He nodded.

"Mr. Campion said not to come by tonight if you weren't feeling up to it."

"Tell him I'll be there."

"The clerk of the probate court called. Judge Baum's still waiting for the inventory of the O'Meara estate."

An insignificant tightening of the trigger finger and aka Sable could have spared him that worry.

"Call him and say I'll get on to it." No. That would involve Alice. His hand began to sweat beneath the cast. "Don't bother. I'll call Judge Baum myself."

Buy time.

He considered Alice. Her face was impassive. He wondered who was with her when he called. Better to conjecture about that than to think about Annie O'Meara and her estate. Outside the office efficient Alice March was good old Alice. Dewar's, no ice, water back. A little flutter on the Jets if the spread was right. Season tickets for the Whalers and a corner seat at the bar of the Stadium Club. Dewar's, no ice, water back. Show me a man who drinks Chivas and I'll show you an asshole. Repartee at the Stadium Club bar. Watch it, buster, it's got teeth. Hit me again. Dewar's, no ice, water back. Dutch treat, Dutch. Stadium Club rules. A snap of the fingers. Dewar's, no ice, water back.

Good old Alice.

"Our municipal wart called," Alice March said.

Dutch Shea, Jr., took a deep breath. "Our municipal wart pays your salary. As well as much of the overhead of this office. So I would appreciate it if you called him Mr. Mandel. Or if you must be familiar, Myron."

"I don't like his hair," Alice March said. Myron Mandel wore his hair long on the sides and swirled it over the top of his scalp to cover a rapidly advancing bald spot.

"There's a lot to dislike about Myron, Alice. He's

devious, deceitful, dishonest and a liar. For a start. He's also a pimp. A first-rate pimp, mind you. Except he's so goddamn greedy. So if you don't like him, fine. But don't tell me it's because of his hair."

Alice March stood her ground. "I still don't like his hair."

Dutch Shea shrugged. It was an appealing if sometimes irritating characteristic of Alice that she never made value judgments on right or wrong, only on hairstyles or the relative merits of Dewar's versus Chivas. "What did he want?"

"He wondered why the hearing had been trailed until tomorrow. I told him about the robbery and he said he had better things to do than wait for you to get well and maybe he should get himself another lawyer."

Vintage Myron. "And you think his hair is the only reason to dislike him."

Alice March did not smile. "I told him you were under sedation and would see him at the hearing."

"Thank you, Alice."

Alice March flipped the pages of her steno pad. "Barry Stukin called to see how you were."

Dutch Shea scratched under his cast with a pencil and wondered which of his clients his former law partner would have tried to steal if he had been seriously injured in the robbery. Myron. Definitely Myron.

"And Thayer Pomfret."

Thayer. As straight as Barry Stukin was devious. He wondered why he preferred Barry. Perhaps because he had the courage of his deviousness. He kept you on your toes. And yet he supposed if he needed a lawyer it would be Thayer. "When" he needed a lawyer. Not "if." "When" was more like it.

"Who else?"

He listened as Alice March rattled off the names in her notebook, half-attentive, occasionally offering a cryptic instruction. Philly Little said he was going to buy the man's immunity package. Eddie Killian wondered if the police property office would release his burglary tools. Darrel Adkin's probation was revoked. Orville Moon's diversion hearing had been postponed. Terry Dailey's mother said she had talked her son into accepting an MDSO program rather than go on trial. Charlie Considine wanted to talk about his brother's appeal.

Charlie's brother Packy. The dumbest client he had ever represented. Which took in considerable territory. Currently in county jail awaiting sentence on an armed robbery conviction. Wheelman in an armored car stick-up. His first mistake. The second mistake was the take. One hundred seventy-six thousand dollars. Except it was in nonnegotiable bonds. Plus twenty-nine dollars cash. All of it in pennies. Mistake number three was the getaway car. Stolen by Packy. A Ford Galaxie. Innocuous enough. Except for a bumper sticker that said, I'VE GOT MY SHIT TOGETHER BUT NOW I CAN'T PICK IT UP. Three armored car guards and seventeen eyewitnesses remembered the bumper sticker. It made for a difficult defense.

He wondered how high Charlie Considine would go for an appeal.

It was hopeless, but Charlie didn't know that.

Charlie was an optimist.

"Is that all?"

"Except for the Harriet Dawson interview at two thirty," Alice March said. "You sure you don't want me to postpone that?"

For a moment he could not place Harriet Dawson. Then he had it. 187, P.C., murder. It often struck him now how faces only took on an identity with a section of the penal code attached. The amnesia of the criminal attorney. The district attorney's office seemed willing to kick Harriet Dawson's 187, P.C., down to a 192.1, P.C., voluntary manslaughter, as long as she agreed to do a year. Just a touch, Dutch, just a touch. Not a bad deal as deals go. She'd be out in eight months. Less time off for time served. A good deal, in fact. Which he was not inclined to take. "Harv Dawson's mother, right?"

Alice nodded.

"No, don't postpone that." His head hurt when he shook it. "I want to get rid of it. I'm going to try and get her sprung at the prelim next week."

Alice March closed her notebook.

"Thanks, Alice."

He watched the rain for a moment after Alice returned to her desk. Harriet Dawson. Packy Considine. Myron Mandel. And the others. All the others whose faces and names he could scarcely remember. Each defined by a set of fingerprints, a yellow sheet, a charge sheet, a discovery motion. Foot soldiers in the armies of the night.

I've been in the trenches too long.

Solly Baum.

Judge Baum.

The probate court.

He checked his watch. Solly went to the Marble Pillar for lunch precisely at noon every day. Clamato juice. Broiled whitefish. Lettuce salad with lemon. Tea. How many times had he eaten lunch with Solly Baum? His first employer when he got out of law school. D. F. Campion's lawyer for thirty years before he went to the bench. Much of what he knew of the law he had learned from Solly Baum at the Marble Pillar. Solly sat down and the waiter brought his Clamato juice. Never a menu to interrupt the flow of memory. No tale twice told, each example of the illicit and the illegal confirming Solly Baum's view of human nature.

Twelve thirty.

A perfect time to telephone.

He would get credit for returning the call and he would avoid having to talk to Solly.

He tried not to think of Annie O'Meara.

"Judge Baum's chambers . . . Oh, Mr. Shea, you're in luck. The judge is eating in today."

Luck. All bad.

"Jack, how are you?"

"Fine, thanks, Your Honor." "Your Honor" until he could calibrate Solly's intention. "I didn't expect to find you in." A bad thing to say. Why did he call, then? Jesus, I'm as jumpy as a con. Calm down.

"I looked at the rain outside and decided I could not face another glass of Clamato juice. Fish urine. I've eaten like a dying Jew for thirty years. Well, I don't have to get wet on top of it."

Dutch Shea chuckled.

An appreciative chuckle. He began to sweat.

Solly Baum asked about the robbery.

"I was held up once," Solly Baum said when Dutch Shea, Jr., finished. "With your father. We played poker once a week. Your father, D.F., me, several other fellows. Cut-throat poker. Deuces wild, one-eyed jacks. Your father was a loser this night. He was a terrible loser, your father. Hated it. Put him in a foul temper." It was a side of his father Dutch Shea did not remember. "He must have lost a hundred dollars this night and you would have thought he lost the family homestead. Well, we were walking up Park Street after the game, it was maybe twelve, one o'clock in the morning, and this fellow came out of an alley with a gun and asked for our wallets and your father just hauled off and clipped this fellow in the jaw. Broke it, it turned out."

Dutch Shea wondered if the story were true. From the day his father went to prison, he had not heard a story about him in which he had not performed more admirably than other men.

"Puts me to shame."

Solly Baum seemed embarrassed. "Different circumstances, Jack."

"Nevertheless."

Solly Baum was silent for a moment. "This O'Meara matter . . ."

"Which is that, Your Honor?"

"I appointed you conservator."

"O'Meara," Dutch Shea said doubtfully.

"Mrs. Walter O'Meara."

"O'Meara," Dutch Shea, Jr., repeated. "That must be Annie O'Meara. Is she the one?"

"I believe so, yes."

"How can I help you?"

"Our records show you're very tardy in submitting the accounting of her estate."

"I was not aware of that, Your Honor."

"Six months."

"Good God. I'm sorry."

"My clerk says he's sent you three notices."

"Well, in a one-man office, the paperwork is apt to get a little sloppy." He hoped his voice sounded natural. "You used to get on me for sloppy paperwork."

Solly Baum was not about to be deflected. "You're bonded, aren't you?" he said curtly.

"Of course."

"Fully?"

"Absolutely." Be helpful, he said to himself. Don't be evasive. Solly Baum always had a nose for the evasive. "For three hundred thousand. That's a little more than the estate is worth." He added quickly, "By my reckoning." If he had not done an accounting how would he know what the estate was worth? "She's well taken care of out there. . . ."

"Where is that?"

"The Arthur K. Degnan Senior Citizen Center. Out on Sisson Avenue."

"You see her, then?"

"Whenever I can, Solly." He thought it safe to switch to the familiar. "Poor soul. She doesn't really notice if I'm there or not. She watches Bugs Bunny on television. It's her favorite television show."

Solly Baum laughed. "In a way I envy her."

Dutch Shea took a deep breath. The moment of danger had passed. "I guess I do, too. Not a care in the world."

"Hmmmm." A pause. "Try and get that accounting in to me, Jack."

"As soon as I can, Solly." He looked at the cast on his hand. Maybe it was a godsend. Make use of it. "With this damn hand and all . . ."

"When you can, Jack, when you can." With a lack of urgency Solly Baum said, "There's another conservatorship here when you give me the O'Meara accounting."

Good God.

"Well, thank you, Your Honor." He thought of his father and wondered how often he had been tempted.

"How's D.F.?"

"Cantankerous as ever."

"They broke the mold with D.F. We'll have lunch, Jack."

"I look forward to it, Solly."

He wondered how much time he had bought. Enough to try and figure something out. I hope. Annie O'Meara. She always made him think about his father. He supposed that was not surprising. Solly Baum's story about his father depressed him. The father he remembered was not the legend created by his contemporaries to ease the son past the shame of a penitentiary sentence. It occurred to him that all his father's friends used the word penitentiary. As if the extra syllables made it a more equivocal word than prison. Anyway, he preferred the man in prison to the man who was alleged to have broken the jaw of a street hoodlum. The father of the ten-year-old boy was not a street vigilante. Or is that what I want to believe? He remembered a Sunday drive. Father and son. After Mass. Heading east on Farmington Avenue toward the railroad station. His father always bought *The Times* at the railroad station after Mass on Sunday. Never say train station, his father had said. Why? he had asked. Because it's not right, his father said. You say bus station, he had said. But you don't say train station, his father said. Railroad station. Again. Railroad station. It was a lesson he had tried to teach Cat. Because it was the only imparted wisdom from a grandfather who had died in prison. People fly today, Cat had said. The train station is closed. Olden times.

Sunday.

After Mass.

He remembered his father running a red light and nearly hitting a pedestrian. The street was empty and the pedestrian ran down the middle of Farmington Avenue, chasing the car, shouting after the car. His father pretended not to see the pedestrian and did not slow down. His father who did not take his eyes from the rearview mirror. He went home on Asylum Avenue. Not Farmington Avenue.

He wondered if he were ashamed of his father that day.

Or if it were just another pointless anecdote.

A story for Lee. He had told it to her one night at the Club. She was drinking a Scotch old-fashioned and sucking on the orange slice. I thought Asylum Avenue was one way those days, Lee had said.

That was later, he had said.

Oh.

He was eleven the day his father died. He remembered the Dodgers beat the Pirates four to two.

Vic Lombardi pitched for the Dodgers.

With relief help from Hugh Casey.

That was another pointless story he had told Lee.

IV

"Let's take it from the top, okay?"

"From the what?"

"Let's start at the beginning."

"You mean with the baby?"

"No, I definitely don't mean the baby. The baby is for later. All in due time."

"I thought it began with the baby. Baby Harriet. She was named after me."

"I know that."

"I'm her grandma."

"Forget baby Harriet."

"I'll be thinking of baby Harriet every day for the rest of my . . ."

"Fine, but not right now."

"I don't know why you want me to forget about baby Harriet."

"I don't want you to forget about baby Harriet. I want you to build up to baby Harriet."

"Like how?"

"Tell me about your husband."

"I don't want to talk about him."

"It'll be a help."

"He's a motherfucker."

"That's a start."

"What do you mean?"

"I mean I can understand that."

"Then why you ask me about him?"

"Because I want to have the whole story. Having the whole story will be a big help."

"For who?"

"For me. And for the judge. Especially for the judge. When we go into the preliminary . . ."

"What's this preliminary?"

"A preliminary hearing. To see if your case will be bound over to the superior court. For trial. I don't think this case should go to trial."

"What's Purvis got to do with this?"

"Who is Purvis?"

"That motherfucker."

"Your husband?"

"Yeah."

"What Purvis had to do with this is this: when we go into the preliminary I want to have all the facts. The facts will be a big help. The fact that your husband, that Purvis, is a motherfucker will be a big help."

"I don't want to talk about him."

"Okay."

"Baby Harriet is dead."

"I know that. That's why I'm here. Try not to cry."

"Easy for you to say."

"I suppose it is, yes."

He waited until Harriet Dawson finished sobbing. Behind her in the visiting room was a bank of ten closed-circuit television screens which showed the interior of the various blocks of the county jail. The camera for this visiting room was right above the bank of screens and he tried to look at both the camera and the screen at the same time, looking at himself looking at himself. On the other nine screens he could see prisoners in blue work denims with a thick white band around each pant leg mopping floors and watching game shows on television. A prisoner in the mess hall interrupted his mopping, picked his nose vigorously, examined the findings on his finger and then put it into his mouth and began to chew.

"I'm okay now."

"Fine. You're forty-one, Harriet."

"Thirty-nine."

"Fine. Who is Hector?"

"He my man."

"And he is also your husband's brother. Purvis' brother."

"My man."

"And Leo?"

"Hector's brother."

"And also Purvis' brother, right?"

"I don't want to talk about that motherfucker."

"Okay. Is Leo your man, too?"

"Sometimes."

"And Harv is your son?"

"Baby Harriet's papa."

"And Marvis is . . ."

"A whore."

"Also baby Harriet's mother. And Harv's wife."

"They never got married."

"I see."

"He went to jail, she just run out on him."

"And left you with baby Harriet."

"That's what whores do. I loved that little baby."

"Where is she now?"

"Whoring."

"And Harv is right here in the county jail."

"He wants to get in a drug program. He gets the right kind of supervision he won't do drugs no more."

"You know he's charged with over a hundred burglaries?"

"See what I mean?"

"Not really."

"To pay for his drugs. He in a drug program, he wouldn't do no hundred burglaries."

"I see."

"He shoots all day to relieve his disappointments."

"Of course."

"The judge give Harv a chance, he could function in society properly."

"Well said."

"His lawyer tell him to say that."

"I'm his lawyer."

"That was you tell him that shit?"

"Right."

"No shit. No wonder Hector got you."

"Actually it was Leo's idea."

"Because you told Harv that good shit."

"Harv's not going to get probation, Mrs. Dawson. Nor into a diversion program."

"Why not? He shoots all day to relieve his disappointments. The judge give Harv a chance, he could function in society properly."

"The judge is going to give Harv a chance to cop to possession of burglary tools. A year in the county lockup. Time off for time served. With good time, he'll be out in eight months."

"No state time?"

"Only county time."

"That sounds good."

"Thanks."

"What about me?"

"That's what I'm trying to find out."

"Leo is a good man."

"Leo is a canary."

"So what. Better than jail."

"Okay."

"He doesn't give them good shit, Leo."

"Oh?"

"He make it up."

"I hope no one finds that out."

"You going to tell them?"

"Calm down, Harriet. This is privileged. Lawyer-client."

"You sure?"

"I'd get disbarred."

"What that mean?"

"I'd be hip deep in shit."

"I like that."

"Thanks. Hector murdered your husband. Purvis."

"Manslaughter. Purvis hitting on me, Hector hit on him."

"With a knife."

"You think he didn't have no blade, Purvis? Purvis always carried his blade. Purvis called his blade his baby. Purvis naked without his blade."

"Purvis was hitting on you."

"Yes."

"And Hector hit on Purvis."

"Yes."

"With his blade."

"Yes."

"And Harv?"

"He gets all uptight."

"And starts doing drugs."

"Yes."

"And stealing to pay for his habit."

"You got it."

"And Marvis?"

"Whoring."

"Leaving you with baby Harriet."

"Right."

"Why was Purvis hitting on you?"

"He wants to get married."

"You were married."

"To another woman. That's what he sees me for. About getting divorced."

"You said no."

"Fucking A."

"The other woman . . ."

"Marvis?"

"The one Purvis wanted to marry . . ."

"Jenny Williams."

"Did you know Jenny Williams?"

"She used to be with Hector."

"I thought Leo."

"What you asking me, you know so much?"

"Just checking."

"Leo, too."

"Keeping it in the family."

"They's close, Purvis, Hector and Leo."

"You were once separated from Purvis."

"Shit. Not separated. Divorced."

"When?"

"I don't know. Harv was little."

"Why?"

"Why what?"

"Did you get divorced?"

"I got to tell you that?"

"Everything."

"I had Harv, he wants to intercourse with me."

"Purvis?"

"You got it."

"When?"

"Right away."

"Before you were healed."

"In the back."

"In the rectum?"

"That mean ass?"

"Yes."

"In the ass, that's it."

"I see."

"It tears me up."

"How exactly?"

"It rips the skin between my thing and my rectum."

"I see."

"I got to tell the judge this?"

"It would help."

"What's it got to do with baby Harriet?"

"Everything."

"I don't like to talk about it."

"You're sensitive about it."

"Shit, yes. He get drunk, Purvis, he tell people I got to shit through my pussy."

"I see."

"Harv was hard to birth."

"Go on."

"I had to have stitches to tie up the tear in my thing."

"Yes."

"Purvis said it didn't matter. We could do it in the other place."

"Your rectum."

"That's the place."

"What happened?"

"It tore the stitches."

"You go to the doctor?"

"Purvis wouldn't let me."

"Why?"

"He didn't want no doctor to know he took advantage of me."

"But he told Hector and Leo."

"Yeah. He tell them I shit through my pussy. He didn't tell them it's his fault."

"And you divorced him."

"Yes."

"And then remarried him."

"That's right."

"Why?"

"He wouldn't let me alone. I was a maid. Working

for white folks. And he wouldn't let them folks give me a ride home. In their car. He says, 'I catch you riding in any car with some small dick honky, I'm going to take my blade to him and you.'"

"It seemed simpler to remarry him."

"Yes." Harriet Dawson glanced at the bank of television screens. For the first time she was aware of the camera. She smiled and waved.

"And then he came and said he wanted to marry Jenny Williams."

"That's right."

"What then?"

"Hector and Leo tell me Purvis telling Jenny I shit through my pussy."

"And you said you wouldn't divorce him."

"Right."

"And he hit on you."

"Right."

"And Leo hit on him."

"Hector."

"Sorry." He stared at Harriet Dawson. She seemed transfixed by her face on the closed-circuit screen. She touched an ear, pulled at an eyelid and when the gesture appeared simultaneously on the screen she seemed genuinely astonished. "Why didn't you want to divorce Purvis? The second time? After what he said?"

"Because of baby Harriet. Harv was in jail. Trying to learn how to function in society properly. And Marvis took off."

"With who?"

"Leo had a crack at her, I think."

"And you thought baby Harriet needed a grandfather."

"Right. With Harv in jail and all. And Marvis whoring."

"And then Hector killed him. Purvis."

"They dropped the charges."

"Self-defense."

"That's what the man say. A nigger kills another nigger, no one seems to care much."

"And so you had custody of baby Harriet."

"I was her grandma. She named after me."

"You do drugs?"

"Never."

"Grass?"

"Little bit."

"Smack?"

"I'm clean."

"How long?"

"Long time."

"Since Purvis said you shit through your pussy?"

"That sound good."

"You were arrested once, it says here."

"Disturbing the peace. Charges dropped. That was when Purvis told Henrietta Frick what I did through my thing. I tried to run her down with baby Harriet's baby carriage."

"I see."

"Pretty carriage. Harv stole it."

"For baby Harriet."

"No. From baby Harriet. To pay for his habit. Harv didn't know how to function in society proper."

"I see. And you lived at your house . . ."

"Eleven Fourteen Bishop's Terrace."

"You own the house?"

"Since Purvis died. It's mine."

"And Hector and Leo live there with you."

"That's right."

"Anyone else?"

"Tenants sometimes."

"You take care of that house on Eleven Fourteen Bishop's Terrace?"

"Yes."

"Clean up?"

"Yes."

"Cook?"

"Yes."

"Mow the lawn?"

Harriet Dawson began to weep. She saw herself crying on the closed-circuit screen and the weeping turned into a wail. He waited until she quieted down.

"How much do you drink?"

"Nothing. It gets to me."

"Beer?"

"A little."

"When you're sad?"

"Yes."

"And you were sad that day."

"Yes."

"Because Harv was in jail."

"Trying to rehabilitate himself."

"And Marvis had gone away."

"Whoring."

"And Purvis was dead."

"Yes."

"And Purvis said you shit through your pussy."

"Yes."

"And your mind wasn't on what you were doing."

"I was sad."

"When you were mowing the lawn."

"Right."

"Watching out for baby Harriet."

"Amen."

"Who's named after you."

"Amen."

"And you didn't notice her."

"Right."

"Laying there on the lawn."

"Right."

"And you were sad."

"Amen."

74

"And you didn't see her."

"Right."

"And you ran the lawn mower right over her."

"That's how it happened. Her little fingers were flying all over the lawn. It was one of them big gas jobs, it could cut hay, let alone a little baby's fingers."

"No need to say that."

"Harv stole it for me."

"Don't volunteer."

"I'm sorry."

"You were sad . . ."

"Oh, yes."

"Because of your life."

"That's right."

"That little baby's death was just one more unhappy thing in a long unhappy life."

"That's right. You tell the judge that."

"No, you can tell the court that, Harriet."

"I will."

V

"You're going to shoot yourself with that."

Martha Sweeney held the .38 in her hand as if examining an exhibit she was about to admit into evidence. Coolly. Without prejudice. She was wearing a slip. A pale blue slip. A pale blue slip with lace across the hem and another fringe of lace at the bosom.

"That's what I told him," Dutch Shea, Jr., said. He loved to watch Martha undress. The last woman he could remember wearing a full slip was his mother. The same kind of slip. Except for the color. Pale blue was racy. Too racy for his mother. Dead at thirty-two of an aneurysm. A little blister on the brain and then the blister exploded. He was seven. He scarcely remembered his mother. Except for the slip. He wondered how pale blue could be considered racy. Pale blue with a lace fringe. "You know D.F."

"Stop looking at me that way," Martha Sweeney said.

"I was just thinking about your slip. It reminded me of my mother."

"Thanks."

"You know what I mean."

"I'm not sure that I do, but I'll take it under advisement that it's not Oedipal."

Martha Sweeney checked the .38 to see if the safety was on and then replaced it in its holster with the practiced air of one used to handling guns. She had a permit to carry a handgun and often did on the bench. She had never worn a gun in her courtroom until an incident six months earlier when she was held up in the parking lot of the superior court building by three young toughs—Martha's description—who forced her into her Trans-Am and drove her nearly to the state line with the intention of exploring her body and stealing her car. It was a situation that demanded a cool head and Martha had not panicked. She ascertained that the youths were attracted first by the white Trans-Am and secondly by her and had no idea that she was either a judge or a former assistant district attorney, thus eliminating revenge for either a prosecution or a sentence as a factor in her kidnapping. Taking a calculated risk, she then explained to the three that she was a judge, an officer of the court, and that if any harm were done to her, the authorities would track them down with unrelenting zeal and would prosecute them, when they were apprehended, to the limit allowed by the law. It would therefore behoove the youths, she said, to let her out of the car, here on this dark and lonely road where there was not a house in sight, thus giving themselves a head start of several hours before an alarm could be spread. For her part of the bargain, Martha promised that should they be apprehended—and with such a head start this was by no means certain, especially if they ditched the car— she would ensure that they would not be prosecuted for violation of Section 207, P.C., Kidnapping, or Section 220, P.C., assault with intent to commit rape, but only for violation of Section 499b, P.C., joyriding, which could be reduced, so long as they did not take the

Trans-Am across the state line and depending on their prior records, to a misdemeanor with the possibility of a suspended sentence. The cool reason of Judge Sweeney took the three toughs by such surprise that they agreed to her bargain almost without argument, their only violence being verbal—a few obligatory references to her cunt, twat and pussy. It was nearly three hours before Martha, cold but unharmed, was picked up by a passing truck. Her Trans-Am was discovered abandoned two days later, the three toughs arrested a week after that on another joyriding charge. Martha picked the three from a lineup, but she was good for her word. No 207, no 220, but because of the second joyriding charge, the three were sentenced to nine months in the county jail.

"Were you wearing a blue slip the night you were kidnapped?" Dutch Shea, Jr., said.

"No, I was wearing black that day." Trust Martha to remember that. She was nothing if not precise.

"You were a lot cooler than I was last night."

"Does that bother you?"

"Damn right."

"There was one thing I've never told anyone."

"What?"

"I was having my period."

"So."

"I thought if they tried to rape me and discovered I had the curse they might kill me."

"Why?"

"I prosecuted a rape case four years ago when that happened. A rape murder. Over on Collins Street. The victim was having her period and it so enraged the defendant that he strangled her."

Victim. Defendant. It amused him that Martha found it so difficult not to use the stilted language of the statute books. Even in private conversation with the man she would soon join in bed. Soon join for lewd and

78

lascivious conjoining when penetration is perpetrated by the party of the first part on the party of the second part, she would probably say.

"That's what I like about you, Martha. You always have a precedent handy."

"Precedents make you think straight." Martha handed him the holstered .38. "Put this away."

Dutch Shea, Jr., held the gun in his hand and watched Martha walk toward the bathroom. I wonder what she means by that? he thought. Maybe that I don't think straight. He suddenly wondered if she would ever refer to him as a defendant. The thought chilled him. He opened the drawer to the bedside table and laid the .38 inside.

D.F. Campion had given him the gun and holster earlier that evening at his house on Prospect Avenue.

"What the hell is that?" Dutch Shea, Jr., said when D.F. bounced into the living room, holding the gun in one hand and the holster in the other.

"It's what they call a Milwaukee Legster," D.F. said, holding up the small leather holster for a moment. He looked like a retired tap dancer, a small, perpetually exasperated man with a fringe of white hair surrounding a permanently reddened face, and he seemed to bounce rather than walk, every step a preamble into a never-executed buck-and-wing. He sat down in a cracked leather chair, pulled up his right pant leg and began fastening the holster to his upper calf. "You tie it to your leg, Jack, and then you put the gun in." He took a catalog from his jacket pocket and began to read: " '.38 Snub-Nosed Revolver. Popular with detectives, undercover agents and the CIA.' " D.F. holstered the .38 in the Milwaukee Legster. "You can't beat that for references. Those guys are champs."

"What do I want a gun for, D.F.?" Dutch Shea, Jr., said.

"You were held up last night, weren't you?"

"I don't know how to use it."

"It's simple. You point it. Then you pull the trigger. That puts a hole through the next coon that tries to stick you up."

"I was in bed when he came. It will be hard sleeping with that tied to my leg."

"Then put it under your pillow," D. F. Campion said. He unfastened the gun and the holster and handed them to Dutch Shea, Jr.

"I'll shoot myself."

"Not if you're pointing it in the coon's direction, you won't."

Dutch Shea, Jr., knew it was pointless to argue with D. F. Campion. Better to put the .38 and its Milwaukee Legster on the end table and conveniently forget them when he left. But when he stood up after he finished his drink, D.F. bounced to his side, retrieving the gun and holster from behind the vase of tulips where Dutch Shea had deposited them.

"Don't forget the gun, buster," D. F. Campion said. "Leaving it there on the end table like you thought I wouldn't notice."

"No fast ones on you, D.F.," Dutch Shea, Jr., said.

"You better believe it, buster."

Dutch Shea, Jr., held the gun and holster warily. "I'm going to take my Milwaukee Legster and become the local bounty hunter. A shooter of holes in obstreperous coons."

The irony escaped D. F. Campion. "That's the ticket. You come by for dinner tomorrow night, Jack. Clarice will be here."

Clarice Campion was D.F.'s second child and only daughter. Until recently Sister Domenica of the Salesian Sisters of St. John Bosco. Clarice was five years younger than Dutch Shea, Jr., and he knew that her departure from the convent was a sore point with her father. And the reason for the invitation to dinner. Clarice confused D.F., and after a lifetime of getting his own way he did not know how to deal with the confusion. He had made his money in real estate, a property here, a tenement there, a right-of-way across town, establishing a pyramid of companies that had made him a rich man at forty and a respected one at fifty, but now, well over seventy, he had a daughter with whom he did not like to be alone. Ever since her return from the convent, Clarice had tried to enlist D.F.'s financial support for a media service for former nuns and nuns still under orders. Dutch Shea, Jr., knew it was an idea that drove D. F. Campion nearly around the bend.

"I'd like that."

"You heard from Hugh?"

Dutch Shea detected the note of reticence in D.F.'s voice. He wondered if any man had ever been so out of sync with his children. Both of whom he had given to God. Clarice the nun and Hugh the priest.

"As a matter of fact, yes." There had been a message from Hugh Campion on his answering machine that very afternoon when he got home from his interview with Harriet Dawson. "Jack. Hugh. I'll be in town next week to settle some things. Have lots to talk about. How about lunch Thursday. The Club, twelve forty-five. I'll book." And then Hugh's singing voice. " 'Will you still need me,/Will you still feed me, When I'm sixty-four.' " Followed by Hugh's distinctive cackling laugh. Dutch Shea, Jr., was sure that Hugh had neglected to tell his father he was coming to town. "He said he might be here in a week or so."

It pained him to be equivocal with D.F. He knows I can be more precise than that, he thought.

"Oh."

"We should all get together."

"Swell, Jack."
"The whole family."

The whole family. He supposed that Hugh and Clarice and D.F. were his whole family. Certainly the only family he had after his father died. Even before that. After his father went to prison. He thought of Hugh. They were only a year apart and had shared a room when they were growing up. He was eleven when he moved in with Hugh and it never was a difficult situation. "Tell me about your dad," Hugh had said. "How is he?" It was always "your dad." There was never a hint that there was anything wrong with a dad being in prison. Dying in prison. Your dad is your dad.

Your dad is your dad.

There was not a song lyric Hugh Campion did not know. Or a recipe that Hugh could not whip up in the kitchen. The only surprise about Hugh was that he was able to capitalize on both his specialties in the priesthood. No bishop seemed to know what to do with him. He was the chaplain on a cruise ship and the technical adviser on a television series that had a priest character. The questions he was asked as technical adviser were nondoctrinal: We have this terrific scene at a wedding reception and the bride asks Father Phil to dance and is it okay for him to do that as long as she doesn't rub her tits up against him? Father Phil was canceled after thirteen weeks and the next season Hugh became a contestant on *Name That Tune*. Dutch Shea, Jr., remembered the look on D.F.'s face when he saw the advertisement in the newspaper: "See If the Absolutely Lovable Father Hugh Campion Will Win the $100,000 Golden Medley." There was a photograph of Hugh in the ad, smiling broadly and holding up both hands in a V for Victory salute. Winning the Golden Medley was a piece of cake for Hugh Campion. "That's when I found myself, Jack," he told Dutch Shea afterward. "I stood in that booth and they played that last song and it all clicked, music and lyrics by Alec Wilder and Lee Kuhn, Mabel Mercer had the single, the only one that was any good, and I said, 'In the Spring of the Year.' The place went wild and I knew there was nothing I couldn't accomplish in the priesthood."

Your dad is your dad.

Dutch Shea, Jr., knew how much Hugh's accomplishments in the priesthood perplexed D.F. "I've got a son who can tell you the Top Forty and can't remember the Ten Commandments," he complained to Dutch Shea one evening. They had eaten dinner and were watching Hugh on television in his latest celebrity priest incarnation. Host of *Father Hugh's Kitchen*. The highest rated cooking show on the air. Prime time on public television. Hugh was wearing a black-and-white striped apron over his clerical cassock and there seemed to be a spot of marinara sauce on his Roman collar. James Beard was the guest gourmet on that show and he and Hugh were cooking up bracciolette ripiene and discussing the role of veal in ecumenicism. "He'll be saying Mass on top of a stove next," D.F. said. "And start seasoning the Host." The cooking show had put Hugh on the cover of *Time* ("Kitchen Catholicism" was the slash line), and the cover of *Time* put him on the *QE II,* where three times a year he shepherded a pilgrimage on a gourmet tour of Catholic shrines.

Your dad is your dad.

I'll forgive Hugh any lunacy for that, Dutch Shea, Jr., thought.

The whole family.

Home.

Home was the house on Prospect Avenue where D.F. Campion still lived. Even though the neighborhood was deteriorating, he knew that D.F. would never leave. It was simply a matter of ego. The large post-

Victorian relic, all polished wood and unexplained corners and areaways and window seats where there were no windows. It expressed exactly the personality that D.F. Campion wanted to express, a folly that in better times better people did not think was a folly. Dominating the center hall was the large and ugly oil painting of Pope Pius XII that Dutch Shea suspected was the reason the house was eliminated from the Junior League house tour. Every evening at dusk the painting was lit, the tubular lighting catching the ascetic face, the long bumpy aristocratic nose, the white cassock, the ruby pontifical ring. Lee had once complained that the papal eye rested on her seat at the dining room table, followed her across the hall, tabulated the third vermouth on the rocks at the drinks table in the living room. Dutch Shea was certain that D.F. only kept the painting up because Hugh and Clarice so hated it. If anything, his own father had detested the painting even more than Hugh and Clarice did now, but by a window seat where there was no window his wake had been held under the forbidding Pacelli gaze.

The Twomeys and the Clarkins had come to his father's wake, the McNultys and the Maras, the Galvins and the Riordans and the Bolands and the Bogans, the McNamaras and the Igoes, even little Byron Igoe in glasses and braces, Byron who would cuckold him, be his wife's lover, an object of Marty Cagney's surveillance, PEEKABOO CAGNEY—DISCREETLY DETERMINING WHAT WAS DONE—WHERE & WITH WHOM. Yes, the Igoes were there, and the Pomfrets and Judge Fairfax Liggett and the Cahills and the Keleghans and Alderman Billy Cullerton leading the delegation from the City Council and District Attorney John Ginna who had prosecuted his father and Judge Walter Manning who had pronounced sentence, and wasn't that a nice thing for them to do, that was the measure of Dutch

Shea, Sr., that men like John Ginna and Walter Manning would show up at his wake, proving there was nothing personal, old Dutch was a champ, that's right, a champ to the end, pleading guilty so as to spare so many people so much embarrassment. It was an enormous wake, a wake that other wakes were compared to for years to come, the quantity of the liquor and the quality of the food setting a standard that even today many thought had never been matched, lobster Newburg and creamed chicken in patty shells, all white meat in the creamed chicken and a little sherry in the cream, and more goddamn shrimp than you can shake a stick at, it must have set D.F. back a mint, and isn't it swell him taking in little Dutch, Jr., a champ like his dad, little Dutch, big Dutch and D.F., they were like this, it's the least D.F. could do, a spread like this, considering . . .

Considering.

Voices and memories, Dutch Shea, Jr., thought. There were so many voices in the house on Prospect Avenue, so many memories. He remembered Byron Igoe, a particle of green vegetable caught in his braces. Byron at ten unable to look him in the eye as he would be unable to look him in the eye at forty, Byron who took his hand and mumbled the Irish benediction, I'm sorry for your trouble.

Byron, Byron, poor dead Byron, you can't begin to know the trouble.

And he remembered late in the evening when the mourners were gone and the drinks put away and when the only lights in the center hall were the candles flickering around his father's casket, and he had sneaked downstairs in his pajamas, leaving Hugh still asleep in their room, and he had stared at his father's face, trying to will him to breathe, trying to coax movement into fingers bound with rosary beads. He had listened for a heartbeat, as years later he would bend over Cat's crib and listen for her heartbeat, and he remembered wondering if he had told his father he loved him the last time he saw him in prison. The second visiting day.

Visiting day. The words sent a shiver through him.

He opened the drawer to the bedside table and looked at the .38 in its Milwaukee Legster. I've got to get rid of it, he thought. I can't have it lying around. The old equalizer. My conscience's equalizer. Maybe Marty Cagney might like it. No, not Marty. Marty still had the service revolver from his days in the Police Department. Marty Cagney had spent twenty-two years in the Police Department before becoming a private detective. Marty would not need a Milwaukee Legster for his matrimonial work. PEEKABOO CAGNEY— DISCREETLY DETERMINING WHAT WAS DONE—WHERE & WITH WHOM. It pained Dutch Shea, Jr. to remember Marty Cagney's reports on Lee and Byron Igoe: 10:47 P.M., Subject A wearing white halter dress checks into Chateau Blanche Motor Hotel, 1 Constitution Plaza, driving silver BMW 528i, license plate LEE S. Subject A proceeds to Room 701, West Wing, where she is admitted at 10:52 P.M. by male Caucasian previously identified as Subject B. 1:16 A.M. Subject A exits Chateau Blanche Motor Hotel, 1 Constitution Plaza. Subject A is barefoot and is carrying what appears to be one pr black satin sandals in hand. Subject A tips doorman Michael Haughey 45¢ and departs Chateau Blanche Motor Hotel in silver BMW 528i, license plate LEE S.

Forty-five cents. Perfect. Lee's signature. If there had been pennies in her purse, she would have thrown them in, too. The 45¢ was a touch that must have appealed to Marty Cagney. He tried to imagine Marty Cagney's conversation with the doorman. Michael Haughey. Marty Cagney was always specific.

LEE S.

A vanity license plate.

I need to know who I am, Lee had said.

LEE S.

Beside him, Martha Sweeney groaned slightly. The sheet had fallen away, exposing her breasts. He tried to imagine Martha with a vanity license plate. MARTHA S. No way. Martha was perfectly aware who she was. No JUDGE. He smiled. STRUCTURED SETTING MARTHA. Too many letters. But right to the point. He ran his finger lightly over her breasts, tracing the shape of one and then the other. Her nipples were perfectly centered. A fact he noted because Lee was so sensitive that hers were slightly off center. When she was naked, she kept her arms folded over her breasts. An imperfection. Lee would not countenance imperfection.

They work.

That's not the point.

They're pretty.

Ugly.

He wondered if she had folded her arms over her breasts when she was with Byron Igoe.

Martha snored. A low phlegmatic rattle in the back of her throat. Easy. Rhythmic. Exhale. Inhale. Lee had maintained that she did not snore. As if it were an imperfection. Un-Episcopalian. He would prod her in the night. Push her thigh. Put his hand between her legs. Rearrange her pillow. Cough loudly. And still she snored. And insisted she did not. Until finally he brought a tape recorder to bed one night when she was asleep and for thirty minutes he had taped her on the A side of a Sony C-60 magnetic tape. He had played it for her in the morning. She listened to all eighteen hundred seconds on the tape, each sibilant whistle, each guttural snort, her face tight. At first he thought she would cry, but she did not. Wordless embarrassment gave way to wordless anger. He supposed it was as mean-spirited a gesture as any he could remember in their marriage. Unnecessary. A violation of the compact between civilized people.

At least that was what Lee had called it.

It embarrassed him to remember the tape. He had not thrown it out. He had put it in the maple desk in his attic office on Asylum Avenue.

In the same drawer with Cat's mementos.

Martha rose on an elbow, plumped her pillow, brushed the hair from her face and then turned over, all without waking. Martha of the pale blue slip with the lace fringe. And the panty girdle. And the nylon stockings that were clipped to the garters and the panties with the lace fringe that she wore over the panty girdle. Not briefs. Panties that came almost to her navel. He had never slept with a woman who wore so many underclothes. Who truly could be said to wear foundation garments. All neatly hung over the back of a chair, nothing inside out. Neatness in the bedroom was perhaps the only trait Martha shared with Lee. Certainly Lee did not wear a scapular pinned to her slip. Only Martha would entrust her sexual guardianship to the Infant of Prague. Martha, at thirty-six, with only two sexual experiences before she met him. The first with a sophomore at Holy Cross who had ejaculated in her hand. The second, thirteen years later, at an airport hotel in Montreal when fog closed down airports up and down the East Coast, diverting all flights to Mirabel International Airport. And there in the airport hotel in Montreal, Martha met and willingly gave herself to an industrial engineer from Atlanta, Georgia, with a wife, three children and a Siamese cat named Dawson after the town of Dawson, Georgia, where the industrial engineer and his wife were born and raised.

It was time, Martha said.

Sweet Martha.

No names, Martha said. That was the arrangement.

Precedent. Codification. Ground rules. A laying out of the articles. That was Martha's way.

The industrial engineer's Diners Club card, however, had fallen from his wallet in the night. Or perhaps in his haste to leave the room in the airport hotel in Montreal the following morning. Edwin J. Higgins, DC3817 178107 0003. The card was under the bed when she awoke the next morning, certifiably not a virgin, a member of the bar who had fellated, an assistant district attorney who had been cunnilingued by DC 3817 178107 0003. Edward J. Higgins, DC 3817 178107 0003 had left a note. "That was swell, Must run. Got an early flight home. That was SWELL." The second "swell" was uppercased. SWELL. Martha was pleased to get the note. It seemed to codify the experience. She was an assistant district attorney. She knew the criminal definitions of sodomy and penetration and she knew that the insertion of the male part into the female parts, however slight, was an offense complete without proof of emission. She had prosecuted prostitutes and rapists, demanding the full penalties for illegal entry into illicit orifices, but SWELL was a new and totally gratifying subsection of the sexual statutes. She wished, however, that the male part was not encumbered with a name. Not to mention a number. DC 3817 178107 0003. The carelessness of the male part in leaving his Diners Club card seemed to Martha a breach of their articles of confederation. For nearly half an hour she sat in her bathroom in the airport hotel in Montreal and tried to tear DC 3817 178107 0003 into small enough parts to flush down the toilet. It was an effort that tended to cast a shadow on SWELL.

SWELL became a person.

Edward J. Higgins.

DC 3817 178107 0003.

Which was not so swell.

Lower case.

The digital clock on the bedside table said 12:27. He wondered if Lee were waiting for him to call, wondered if she suspected that on the nights he did not call someone was with him.

Someone. He was sure that Martha would not appreciate the anonymity of "someone."

12:28.

Why can't I sleep?

Lee.

Cat.

Annie O'Meara.

Three good reasons.

The women in my life.

Martha. I did not include Martha.

The woman in my life.

12:29.

He picked up the digital clock to see what time Martha had set the alarm for. 5:45. Of course. Plenty of time for her to shower and to shave her legs and under her arms and to dress for seven o'clock Mass. Martha would only spend the night with him when her father was working the lobster trick: 11 P.M. to 7 A.M. And even then only with a covering excuse. I'll be at the Canon of Ethics meeting tonight, Dad. It'll run late and so I think I'll stay with Joan Murtagh. I don't like to come in alone that time of night, you're not there.

It's the colored is the reason, Tommy Sweeney said. In Tommy Sweeney's opinion, the colored were the reason for every social aberration and dysfunction. Tommy Sweeney had scarcely been able to mask his disappointment that the three toughs who kidnapped Martha were not colored.

Why don't you meet me at Mass?

Swell, Dad, Judge Sweeney said.

And Martha would kneel next to her father the following morning at St. Justin's, Tommy in his blue fire captain's uniform, Martha with a tube of spermicidal foam and a vial of strawberry-scented vaginal spray at the bottom of her imitation Chanel black quilted bag.

I'm surprised he doesn't check out your bag, Dutch Shea, Jr., said to her once. You can tell him the foam's for putting out fires.

That's not funny.

Do you go to confession?

Of course.

How do you plead? Lascivious conduct?

That's not funny either.

12:37.

Sleep.

In the distance he thought he heard a fire siren. Martha stirred.

Sleep.

"What time is it?"

"Nearly two."

"Why are you up? You set the alarm for five forty-five."

"Listen."

He could hear the sirens melding one into another. Martha was dressing. She raised her arms and the pale blue slip fell into place. The scapular medal of the Infant of Prague rested on Martha's right breast. She tucked it back inside the slip.

"I called FIC," Martha Sweeney said. FIC was the Fire Department's Fire Information Center. "It's a bad one, Jack."

"Tommy?"

"He's all right. So far."

"Where?"

"The Cuthbertson. Downtown."

"Jesus. Any dead?"

"Fifteen anyway. Probably more."

"Any idea what happened?"

"Probably arson."

VI

Dutch Shea paused at the newsstand on the ground floor of the superior court building and read the headline: 18 DEAD IN HOTEL FIRE—ROOKIE FIRE FIGHTER KILLED IN BLAZE—ARSON SUSPECTED. The fireman's name was Cloonan. A particular favorite of her father's, Martha had said, the son of another fireman now retired to Pompano Beach. Tommy Sweeney had brought the boy home for dinner not two weeks before. A young man with a plague of pimples who had taken three helpings of apple brown Betty and who to his mortification had become flatulent over coffee in the parlor, which was what Tommy Sweeney insisted on calling his living room. The roof at the Cuthbertson had collapsed under the boy.

"You think this is some kind of library," the news vendor whined. His name was Angie and he was legally blind. He wore glasses with one opaque lens and when he was handed a bill he held it against his usable eye to see what it was before he made change.

"Sorry, Angie." It occurred to Dutch Shea that although Angie had been at this stand for as long as he could remember he had never bothered to learn his last name.

"You going to buy the paper or not?"

"Thanks, no."

"Cheap bastard. I hope your pimp goes to jail."

It was the sort of remark that had made Angie an institution in the superior court building but which for some reason always irritated Dutch Shea, Jr. He looked at the cast on his hand and hoped he was not becoming sensitive to being a pimp lawyer. The superior court building was home to him in a way that not even the house on Asylum Avenue ever was. He felt comfortable here, even safe. The building was huge and dirty, with chewing gum ground into the grouting of its polished aggregate floors, but its immensity gave it a kind of grimy dignity. Everywhere he looked there were knots of people, the guilty and the bureaucrats of guilt, the retinue of the law-abiding dependent on and supported by the guilty. Lawyers with briefcases and district attorneys and public defenders with manila folders filled with case material and policemen appearing as witnesses wearing their badges clipped to their off-duty windbreakers and lumber jackets. Even the innocent took on the tainted look of the guilty. No one seemed to talk out loud, certainly not the blank-faced relatives of the accused. It was a building of whispers, of furtive looks and missed eye contact, of snatches of overheard conversation. I got carried away . . . You hit her with a hammer you got so carried away . . . You got to hear my side of it . . . Yea, I got to hear your side of it. . . . Nothing in the building ever seemed to work. The toilets were stopped up, the toilet paper holders empty, there was no soap in the soap dispensers, the floors were littered with candy wrappers, there were used condoms in the stairwells. The building reminded him of the system of justice itself. Why do I love it? Why do I love the assumption of guilt?

The elevator was out of order so he had to walk. When he reached the second-floor landing, a black youth bounding down the stairs two steps at a time crashed into him and nearly knocked him down.

"You blind or something?" The youth was ripping open a bag stenciled SHERIFF'S PROPERTY OFFICE.

"Sorry." Dutch Shea looked at the bag. The youth must have just got out of custody. The bag contained the belongings he had surrendered when he was arrested. "You just get out?"

"What's it to you?"

He realized he was staring at the youth. For an instant he wondered if it were the same one who robbed him. He remembered the fear of two nights before and then the consuming rage.

"What the fuck you looking at?" The youth had a scar from his left ear to his chin.

"My mistake," Dutch Shea, Jr., said, and continued on up the stairs. Thayer Pomfret was waiting on the next landing. He was wearing a Cottage Club tie and carrying an old cracked leather briefcase embossed with gold initials. TWP II. Thayer Wilson Pomfret. The second.

"I thought that was going to get ugly."

"You were a big help." It annoyed Dutch Shea, Jr., that Thayer Pomfret had seen the incident. Thayer always made him feel as if he were being graded.

"A little touchy, aren't we?"

"I thought it was the guy who stuck me up," Dutch Shea said. "I suppose you were going to come to my defense if it did get ugly."

"With alacrity."

That damned smile, Dutch Shea thought. TWP II. The second. Senior partner of Howard, Carey & Pomfret. Founded by his father and once Judge Liggett's old firm. The judge was too fastidious to allow his name on the letterhead. He thought it inappropriate for a former member of the bench. That was a laugh. The judge had a flexible sense of the inappropriate. TWP II was the author of the school district's busing formula and was always being hailed for his public commitment. He had also handled Cat's adoption. And been her godfather. Lee's idea. Lee had also asked him to represent her in the divorce. Thayer had tactfully refused. Thayer was always tactful. Theirs was a tactful relationship.

"Lucinda said to thank you for your present." Lucinda was Thayer Pomfret's youngest child and Dutch Shea's goddaughter. A quid pro quo for Cat, he was sure. He had given Lucinda Pomfret a bottle of Perrier Jouet for her birthday. "Fifty-five dollars. An expensive bottle of wine for a fourteen-year old."

"You didn't price it."

"Of course I did. I told her she could drink it when she was eighteen. If she got into Smith."

Smith. Where Cat had not been accepted. He wondered if Thayer Pomfret knew the names of Cat's natural parents. It was a private adoption. He had never had the slightest interest in Cat's natural parents until her death. One day he wanted to tell them what sort of child she had been, what sort of daughter. But then Cat never had been their daughter. He wondered if Cat were even of interest to them. Cat. This angel boarder. *That* angel boarder.

They stopped at the door of the hearing room.

"Coffee?" Thayer Pomfret said.

"I'll meet you in the cafeteria." He could not decide why Thayer so irritated him this morning. Perhaps because he did not think a busing formula should be written by someone who wore a Cottage Club tie. Whose daughter would drink a bottle of champagne when she was accepted at Smith.

96

Where Cat had not been accepted.

The hearing room was empty. It was a small room, a room generally reserved for minor civil matters, for hearings on easements and variances. Dutch Shea, Jr., squared a legal pad at his place and checked the calendar entry:

BEFORE THE PUBLIC UTILITIES COMMISSION

HON. MILES O'T. LEFEBVRE, Examiner,
Presiding
Case No. 3049

MYRON MANDEL,
dba CONSOLIDATED SERVICES, INC.
  Complainant

—vs—

UNITED TELEPHONE COMPANY
  Defendant

Appearances:

JOHN SHEA, Attorney-at-Law, appearing for
    ᵗon Mandel, dba Consolidated Services,
    ., Complainant.

HOWARD, CAREY & POMFRET, by THAYER W.
    POMFRET, Attorney-at-Law, appearing for Unit-
    ed Telephone Company, Defendant.

JOHN J. TORIZZO, Deputy District Attorney, ap-
    pearing for the DISTRICT ATTORNEY and for
    CLINTON K. MURTAGH, Chief of Police, Interve-
    nors.

DALE W. SNYDER, Attorney-at-Law, appearing
    for the PUC staff.

He wondered how many pimps had made it before the PUC. As a constitutional issue. It did not make Myron Mandel any more likable to have to consider him a constitutional issue.

It occurred to him that he did not seem to find a whole lot of people likable this morning.

As usual before court opened, the cafeteria on the fourth floor was crowded. When he bought his coffee, Dutch Shea moved through the room, nodding, winking, giving the high sign, cocking his finger, pulling the trigger, exchanging the gossip of the courthouse. This guy, Dutch, he's a real hard ticket, he's in the interrogation room there and he's no dummy, he's been there before, he knows someone is trying to finger him through the two-way mirror, so what does he do, he picks up a chair and heaves it through the mirror. Scares the shit out of the witness, which is what he had in mind, I think.

Dutch Shea saw Thayer Pomfret talking to the banking commissioner and the new federal attorney designate and decided he was not up to that. From a table in the corner, Barry Stukin was waving at him. He was wearing a three-piece gabardine suit with a red silk polka-dot handkerchief in the breast pocket, a custom-made suit with buttonholes in the sleeves, one button undone on each cuff.

"I remember you when you used to dress like Buffalo Bill," Dutch Shea, Jr., said when he sat down. "Buckskin, sandals and work shirt. You never missed a sit-in in those days."

"My version of ambulance chasing." Barry Stukin smiled. "Stukin's my name, illegal detention's my game." His neat black beard was flecked with gray and a pair of pink-tinted glasses was perched on top of his head. "Listen, tell me something. If two black guys in a black Caddy is black power, and two white guys in a white Caddy is white power, what's two Puerto Ricans in a red Caddy?"

"Grand theft, auto."

"Oh, you heard that one." Barry Stukin tapped a

photograph of the burning Cuthbertson Hotel in his newspaper. "I hear they picked somebody up. A transient. Kid with a history as a firebug."

"The PD have him?"

Barry Stukin shook his head. "Conflicted out. I hear the kid's a snitch in another case of theirs. It'll be court-appointed."

"Your turn?"

"Unless I can find a calendar conflict."

"I wonder why that makes me think of Morrie Wishengrad." Morrie Wishengrad was a political activist Barry Stukin had defended when he and Dutch Shea were first partners, a college student who had poured lighter fluid on a Dow Chemical recruiter he had then set on fire.

"Morrie Wishengrad owns a car wash now. Two Budget Rent-a-Car franchises and a parking lot. He put me into gold futures six months ago. I lost twenty-two K." Barry Stukin cut his doughnut in two and handed half to Dutch Shea. "The times, they are a-changin', as the troubadour of my radical youth used to say." He dunked the doughnut in his coffee. "Didn't you have a homicide in the Cuthbertson once?"

"Gentle Davidson. He had a pecker like a telephone pole."

"You tend to remember things like that," Barry Stukin said. "How's Lee?"

"Fine." He remembered that Lee had once said if she were a writer she would introduce Barry Stukin this way: Hello, he lied. It was not often that Lee could make him laugh.

"Tell her I said hello."

Dutch Shea nodded. He wondered what Barry Stukin had on his mind. With Barry it was always best not to appear too interested.

"You know that the prostate is the last organ de-

99

stroyed by fire?" Barry Stukin asked. "A real tough bastard, the prostate."

"I didn't know that, no."

"And the uterus in a woman."

"I didn't know that either."

"I had a damage case once. Two, three years ago. A kid and his dog were killed in a fire. Nothing left of either one of them. The kid's parents, they got it into their heads the dog was buried in the kid's grave. So they came to me and I got a court order to exhume the body. The pathologist took a look at the prostate and lo, and behold, it was Spot. Parents sued the shit out of the hospital."

"How much?"

"Five seventy."

"One ninety for you."

"Not bad for a prostate."

"No."

"It's interesting, arson." Barry Stukin corrected himself. "Fire, I mean. You see a guy, he looks unidentifiable. But he's not. Take carbon granules. If he's got carbon granules in his bronchial passages, it means he was alive when the fire started. The top of his head is gone, the arms and the legs, the abdomen and most of the chest. The guys looks like the inside of a barbecue after a cookout. But those carbon granules are still floating around."

"Persistent little buggers." Dutch Shea sipped his coffee. He was almost sure now he knew where the conversation was heading.

"Like the fat globules." Barry Stukin said.

"Which fat globules?"

"In the lung tissue. Of our friend who was barbecued. If there are any fat globules in his lung tissue, it means he was attacked before the fire. You're hit in the head, it dislodges a certain amount of fat and this fat is carried through the bloodstream to the heart and from the heart to the lungs. But the blood vessels in the lungs are so small the fat globules are strained out. And stick in the lung tissue. You find any fat globules, it means our pal was clobbered before he was cremated."

Hello, he lied.

"Why do I get the feeling, Barry, you're trying to unload this baby on me? You recommended me, didn't you?"

Barry Stukin smiled. "You always could see through me, Jack."

"Fat globules." Dutch Shea shook his head. "Carbon granules. All you had to do was ask."

"I'm too devious for that."

Dutch Shea, Jr., laughed.

"Maybe we should go partners again." Barry Stukin raised his coffee cup until it covered the lower half of his face. "There's no impediment anymore."

Dutch Shea wondered how Lee would react to being described as an impediment. "That's not necessary."

"The stuff you do, you can't make that much."

"I get by."

"I'm serious, Jack."

"Even if I don't take over this kid?" He knew he was going to take on the case. Why not? The intractability of the prostate. The asbestos quality of the uterus. Fat globules. Carbon granules. They were a means for him to avoid the contemplation of his own life.

"Sure."

"Hello, he lied."

"What the hell is that supposed to mean?"

"It means I'm going to do it, Barry. You can take the carrot back."

Thayer Pomfret was making his way toward their table.

"You're not kidding?" Barry Stukin said.

"Not kidding," Dutch Shea said.

Thayer Pomfret set his tray down, took a paper napkin from the container and brushed off his chair and then the sugar from the table. He said, "If two Negroes in a black Cadillac are black power . . ."

"Grand theft, auto," Dutch Shea, Jr., said.

VII

Myron Mandel tapped a finger on Dutch Shea's cast. "How do you think this will affect my case?"

Dutch Shea, Jr., surveyed Myron Mandel's clothes and did not answer. "I thought I told you to wear a jacket and a tie."

Myron Mandel ran his hands down his purple body shirt. "So what's the matter with this?"

"You want sympathy, Myron, I don't think you're going to get it with a purple shirt opened to your belly button. Not to mention all those gold chains."

"It's a Star of David."

"Tastefully set in a chestful of hair."

"I don't need your cheap shit, Dutch."

"What you need is a suit, Myron. Button your shirt."

Myron Mandel reluctantly began buttoning his shirt. "You're nothing but a pimp lawyer, don't you forget that."

"Pimps get pimp lawyers, Myron. Don't you forget that."

A pimp lawyer. Today's received wisdom. A pimp lawyer with a pimp client the vice squad could never make a pandering case against. Forcing said vice squad to ask the telephone company to terminate telephone service to the pimp's outcall massage agencies on the grounds that said outcall agencies were contravening Sections 266h and 266i, P.C., pandering and procuring. With which request the telephone company complied. Forcing the pimp lawyer to ask the PUC for interim relief on the grounds that no criminal charges had been filed against the pimp and that the telephone effectuated the pimp's right of free speech as guaranteed under the First Amendment of the Constitution of the United States. Which made Myron Mandel a constitutional issue. A constitutional issue in a purple body shirt.

A pimp. With a pimp lawyer.

House counsel for Consolidated Services, Inc.

Not bad.

And for its subsidiaries Wet & Willing, Hot Stuff, Camel Outcall, Teenagers Who Are Terrific, The Farmer's Daughters, Think Pink, The Honey Pot and The Ball Game.

Not so good.

John Shea. Attorney-at-law.

He wondered what his father would think.

His father had been a tax lawyer.

And look where it got him, Dutch Shea, Jr., thought.

Miles Lefebvre cleared his throat and called the hearing to order.

"You're sure you wouldn't like a continuance, Mr. Shea?" Judge Lefebvre said.

"No, Your Honor."

"It would be entirely legitimate. I'm sure that Mr. Torizzo and Mr. Pomfret would concur."

At the defense table, Thayer Pomfret winked at Dutch Shea, Jr. Johnny Torizzo stared straight ahead, ignoring him. Dutch Shea checked Myron Mandel to see if his shirt was buttoned. "Thank you, Your Honor, but I'm ready to proceed."

"Then let the record reflect that Mr. Shea, attorney for the complainant, is present in the hearing room and prepared to proceed in spite of a grievous injury received in a dastardly attack on his person since this hearing last adjourned the day before yesterday. Mr. Shea's presence here today does honor to the bar."

Myron Mandel nudged Dutch Shea, Jr., sharply with his elbow and under his breath whispered, "You should get a cast on the other arm, too."

Dutch Shea, Jr., rose. "Thank you, Your Honor."

Miles Lefebvre cleared his throat again and surreptitiously examined his hand for sputum. Dutch Shea caught Thayer Pomfret's eye at the defense table and they exchanged quick smiles. Miles Lefebvre was a hypochondriac. Throughout the hearing he had interrupted testimony to spray his throat and swallow lozenges and drink Phenergan expectorant laced with codeine from a medicine bottle. The judge seemed especially wary of Myron Mandel's masseuses. Both Dutch Shea and Thayer Pomfret had noticed that whenever one of Myron's girls was called to the stand, the judge kept a handkerchief between himself and the witness, a filter, as if he were afraid the girl's breath might contaminate him. The things they take in their mouths, Miles Lefebvre had said during a recess two days before. It was not that the judge had any special moral reservations about fellatio. It was the health hazard that concerned him. Herpes. The high sodium content. Salt makes you puffy, Judge Lefebvre had said in chambers. A salt-free diet, that's the ticket. It was the only time Dutch Shea, Jr., had ever heard the high sodium content advanced as an argument against fellatio.

Myron Mandel had not been amused by Judge Lefebvre's musings on health.

"The guy's a nut case, Dutch. Pure and simple. Fruit salad. That's some diet, not copping joints. Nathan Pritikin must be wondering why he didn't think of that."

"Don't worry about it, Myron," Dutch Shea, Jr., had said.

"That's easy for you to say, don't worry."

"It's not relevant, Myron. What's relevant is whether they can take out your telephone lines. That's what this hearing is all about. Telephones. Not whether your girls give good French."

"My girls are masseuses. They hook on the side, I don't know about it."

"Swell, Myron."

Miles Lefebvre sprayed his throat with antibacterial mouthwash. "You may call your witness, Mr. Torizzo. I believe she is still under oath."

Candy Cane was wearing a black dress with long sleeves. As she passed by Dutch Shea on the way to the stand, she touched his cast and blew him a kiss.

Johnny Torizzo came to his feet. "Let the record reflect that the witness blew the attorney for the complainant a kiss."

"That's not all she blew," Myron Mandel whispered.

"Mr. Torizzo, that's not necessary," Miles Lefebvre said. He was wrapping a handkerchief around his hand to filter any germs that might emanate from Candy Cane's mouth.

"On the contrary. Your Honor, it shows that this is a hostile witness with perhaps a special relationship with the attorney for the complainant," Johnny Torizzo said.

"Objection," Dutch Shea, Jr., said. "No foundation. Argumentative. Innuendo. Slanderous. Unethical. Mr. Torizzo can't seem to see a belt without hitting below it."

"Gentlemen," Miles Lefebvre said. "I'm going to

106

sustain your objection, Mr. Shea. I will also caution you against any future outbursts such as your last remarks about Mr. Torizzo." He turned toward Johnny Torizzo. "As for the alleged kiss directed toward Mr. Shea by the witness . . ."

"Actual, Your Honor, not alleged," Johnny Torizzo said.

"Mr. Torizzo, I did not see it," Miles Lefebvre said. There was an edge to his voice. "It is not significant to the record as far as I am concerned. Let the record proceed from the point where Miss Cane was called to the stand."

Johnny Torizzo said, "Did you do nurse calls?"

"Occasionally," Candy Cane said. She looked at her hands and at the purse in her lap.

"Would you describe what a nurse call is?"

Candy Cane reached into a bag for a Kleenex and wiped her nose with it. "It's someone who wants to play doctor."

"I see. He's the doctor and you're the nurse."

"He's the doctor and I'm the patient."

"I see. A gynecologist, I presume."

"It's a little sicky, I'll admit that," Candy Cane said.

"I'm glad," Johnny Torizzo said. "Are there any other permutations of the nurse call?"

"Some guys want an enema."

"And who gives them an enema."

"I do."

Miles Lefebvre lowered his handkerchief filter and looked directly at the witness for the first time since she took the stand. "What sort of equipment do you use?"

Candy Cane seemed baffled by the question. "Your Honor?"

Jesus, he thinks it's a health matter, Dutch Shea, Jr., thought.

"How did you effect the enema?" the judge said deliberately. "Give it."

"The normal way, I guess."

"With a rectal syringe?"

Candy Cane looked for support from Dutch Shea, Jr. When none was forthcoming, she said, "Yes."

"Did you use castor oil or a warm water detergent mixture?"

"I didn't check," Candy Cane said.

"Fruit salad," Myron Mandel whispered into Dutch Shea's ear. "I lose this one, there's the grounds for your appeal right there."

Johnny Torizzo coughed. "Miss Cane, were there any calls you did not do?"

"I don't do Greeks."

Miles Lefebvre roused himself. "I will not tolerate ethnic slurs in this courtroom."

"Your Honor," Johnny Torizzo said carefully, "in the context of this hearing, 'Greek' is not a nationality." He paused for effect. "A 'Greek,' or 'doing a Greek,' means to perform anal intercourse."

"Oh." Miles Lefebvre's handkerchief-bound hand shot back to his face, blocking his view of Candy Cane.

Thayer Pomfret put his hands behind his head and stared up at the elaborately molded ceiling of the hearing room. Dutch Shea knew Thayer was trying not to laugh. He also knew there was no reason for Thayer to attend the hearing. The district attorney was the de facto leader of the defense and the interests of United Telephone could have been handled by a junior associate at Howard, Carey & Pomfret. He suspected that Thayer was bored with handling only United's rate increases before the PUC and wanted some entertainment for the long tedious hours he had spent interpreting PUC tariffs.

Johnny Torizzo handed Candy Cane an advertisement for an outcall massage service called The French Connection.

"You were employed by The French Connection, were you not?"

"Yes."

"Do you have any opinion as to what the words 'French Connection' mean?"

"Objection," Dutch Shea, Jr., said. "It's immaterial and irrelevant and beyond the scope of the witness's expertise. She had nothing to do with the ads. She didn't place them. She didn't compose them."

"Overruled." Without looking at Candy Cane, Miles Lefebvre said, "You are directed to answer the question."

"What question is that?"

She's going to get smartass, Dutch Shea, Jr., thought. A bad tactic with Johnny Torizzo.

"What is the meaning of 'French Connection'?" Johnny Torizzo said.

"Oh, it means the movie. It was a swell movie. You ever see it?"

"And that is all."

"As far as I know."

Johnny Torizzo took another advertisement. "This one says, 'Our outcall girls play ball.' What does that mean?"

"Objection," Dutch Shea said. "Calls for a conclusion."

"Overruled."

"I think it means the girls are athletic and like baseball and if you like baseball you should call this service for a massage."

"I see," Johnny Torizzo said. "And this one here. 'Quick draw sugar. I will be in and out of your pants in a splash.' What does that mean?"

"Objection. Calls for a conclusion."

"Overruled."

Candy Cane said, "Well, that one means if the girl is nude and you give her a pair of pants, she can put them on and then if you have a pool or a Jacuzzi she can take them off and splash around."

Myron Mandel put his arm around Dutch Shea's shoulder and whispered, "That's not bad for a whore."

Dutch Shea, Jr., did not answer and moved his body slightly until Myron Mandel removed his hand. He concentrated on Johnny Torizzo. He did not like Johnny Torizzo, but he was a good lawyer and Dutch Shea liked to watch a good lawyer lead a hostile witness. It was a way to keep awake. He had heard it all before in all the cases against Myron Mandel and there were no surprises. He played with his pencil and doodled on his legal pad, any break in the familiarity of the testimony a signal for an objection. He suspected that Johnny Torizzo was as sick of seeking a judgement against Myron Mandel as he was of defending him. No wonder Johnny Torizzo lost his temper and tried to put on the record a special relationship with Candy Cane. A special relationship indeed. He had defended Candy Cane as Candy Cane and he had defended her as Susie Sweet and he had defended her under her real name, Shirley Potts. In a way he regretted defending her as Shirley Potts. It was as Shirley Potts that she hit a john over the head with a credit card imprinter when he became abusive and she had fractured his skull. In the Chateau Blanche Motor Hotel. Where he had lost a wife and gained a client. The client being Myron Mandel who employed Shirley Potts aka Susie Sweet aka Candy Cane. The first masseuse of the first tycoon of outcall. A contributor to the United Way, a member of the Chamber of Commerce.

On the stand, Candy Cane fluttered her hands over her breasts as she talked. An instinctive gesture. He

110

had noticed that in moments of judicial stress the hands of a prostitute seemed to hover around her preliminary or secondary sexual organs. The organs in which she had whatever faith she possessed. Johnny Torizzo was leading her skillfully, letting her expound on the numerals and the fractions and the nationalistic nomenclatures of sex, on dates and tricks and johns, on the professional distinctions between heavy and light dominance.

"You did heavy dominance?" Johnny Torizzo said.

"No. A girl named Monica did. She carried a bag of chains and whips. She set that thing down and it would rattle."

"So heavy dominance was physical abuse?"

"I guess."

"And light dominance is verbal abuse?"

"That's it."

"Have you ever engaged in light dominance?"

Candy Cane pressed her hands against her bosom. "Let's say I know how it's done."

"Give an example."

"You kick the door open and say, 'Get in there, you son of a bitch, I'm here to punch your ticket.'"

In the chair next to Dutch Shea, Jr., Myron Mandel stirred. Dutch Shea knew what was coming. Myron's routine. The performance of shock and dismay he put on at least once in every court appearance. He shook his head as if he were hearing the litany from the witness box for the first time, as if Candy Cane were a valued associate who had betrayed his trust and was now testing the boundaries of his forgiveness. Dutch Shea graded the act badly. He suspected that Myron's heart was not in it. He stared Myron down until he sagged deep in his chair, a fold of fat bulging against his purple body shirt. It seemed to Dutch Shea that Myron might profitably use several of the massages he claimed his masseuses gave.

Johnny Torizzo took a tape recorder from the exhibit table.

"You carried a tape recorder on your dates, Miss Cane."

"Yes."

"On whose instructions?"

"Myron's."

"And did Mr. Mandel give you any further instructions?"

"About what?"

"The tape recorder."

"Well, I was supposed to tape myself asking the gentleman if he was a member of any federal, state or municipal law enforcement agency."

"These instructions came from Mr. Mandel."

"Yes."

"Why did Mr. Mandel so instruct you?"

"Objection. Calls for a conclusion."

The tape recorder was a weapon against entrapment by a vice officer posing as a john. An example of the ingenuity Myron Mandel lavished on outcall. The mogul of massage. A mogul with an eye for detail. Every girl also carried a credit card imprinter. Myron Mandel took Master Charge. And Visa. Carte Blanche. Diners. American Express. Each date was charged to Consolidated Services, Inc. A more ambiguous name than Wet & Willing. A name that would not make a wife suspicious when it turned up on a Visa printout. Myron was nothing if not thorough. Which was why he was so successful. And why vice had never been able to make a case against him stick.

Johnny Torizzo said, "Miss Cane, I direct your attention to exhibit number ten, previously admitted into evidence. What would you call this?"

Candy Cane took a list of names from Johnny Torizzo and looked at it for a moment. "A heat sheet."

"For the record, would you explain what a heat sheet is?"

"Asked and answered," Dutch Shea said.

"Not by this witness," Miles Lefebvre said. "Please answer, Miss Cane."

"Well, a heat sheet is a list of policemen."

"Any special kind of policemen?"

"Vice."

"Vice officers."

"Yes."

"And why are they on the list."

"Because they busted one of the girls."

"You were supposed to check this list if you got a call?"

"The dispatcher was."

"And if the date's name was on the list, you did not take the call?"

"Right."

"Did any other names go on this list?"

Candy Cane said the list also included every john a girl suspected of being a vice cop. Every john staying in a hotel who did not have a return airline ticket. Every john whose name did not match the name on his driver's license.

"Who compiled this list?"

"I guess Myron."

Dutch Shea, Jr., glanced down the names on the heat sheet. Boland, John J. Dioguardi, Renato. Dwyer, Arthur P. Faye, Crystal. Hughes. Ito. Moran. Tante. Touhy. Vice cops all. Every name written in a neat Palmer penmanship hand. Only parochial schools still taught the Palmer method. He wondered if the prostitute who had copied the list had been taught by the nuns. He remembered Sister Cletis who had told him that if he received his first communion not in a state of grace the Host would fly out of his mouth and hang in

113

the air above him. The Host hanging in the air would tell everyone at St. Justin's he had committed a mortal sin. Mortal sins unspecified. He wondered what Sister Cletis would think of the mortal sins committed by the prostitute with the neat Palmer penmanship hand.

"Why do you think Mr. Mandel compiled this list?"

"Objection. Speculative. Calls for a conclusion."

"Sustained."

The heat sheet was a business tool, Myron Mandel said. He often talked like a time and motion man. Check. Check the name. Check the address. Check the credit card number. Do not dispatch a girl until everything checked. Have the girl recheck when she met the date. Name. Address. Credit card. Driver's license. Telephone number. Leave if something did not check. Call the dispatcher when everything did check. Good rules make for efficiency, Myron Mandel said. The robber baron of the orgasm, Dutch Shea, Jr., thought. They should teach me at the Wharton School of Finance, Myron Mandel said.

"Miss Cane, did you ever have sexual relations with the complainant?"

"Objection. Irrelevant."

"Overruled."

"Oh, that's embarrassing."

"Please answer the question."

"Yes."

"And when was that?"

"When I went to work for him."

"Was there anything unusual about that occasion?"

"Objection. Calls for a conclusion."

"Sustained."

"Let me put it this way. When you had sexual relations with Mr. Mandel, did he put it on videotape?"

"Yes."

In case the trainee masseuse was an undercover vice officer. A house rule. I don't think they teach that rule

114

at the Wharton School of Finance, Dutch Shea, Jr., thought.

"I have nothing further," Johnny Torizzo said.

"Your witness, Mr. Shea," Miles Lefebvre said. "But let's take a ten-minute recess first."

2

He tried to place the voices. Norm Brewer probably and he did not recognize the other. It always surprised him the way lawyers talked in men's rooms. As it would surprise them that he listened. He often locked himself in a stall during a recess simply to listen, propping his shoes on the struts of the stall so that his feet could not be seen under the door. The secondhand life of the eavesdropper appealed to him.

"So what happened?" The unknown voice.

"He put his golf clubs in the trunk of the car that morning and when they found him that night, he was in the trunk along with the clubs, that's what happened."

"Any ideas?"

"Wasn't the ginneys."

"So how do you know that?"

"Whoever did it lifted his wallet. It's a point of honor with the ginneys, they never touch what's in the wallet, they hit somebody. The PRs are different. They figure what the guy's got on him is part of the deal. An extra, you know what I mean?"

"Included in the price of the hit."

"He was a client of Barry Stukin's, wasn't he?"

"He unloaded him, Barry."

"Maybe he knew he was going in the trunk is why, I bet."

"He's an expert when it comes to unloading, Barry. He dumped that arson kid on Dutch Shea."

"Can you blame him? Two fifty a day is all you get,

115

court-appointed. That's why all the schwartzes are after it."

"His shoes cost more than two fifty, Barry."

"Is that right?"

"That's what I hear."

"I got a couple I wouldn't mind unloading on him, Shea."

"Give it a try. He'll take anything, I hear."

"The city dump."

Dutch Shea, Jr., heard water splash and the automatic hand dryer blow and then the door open when the lawyers left. The city dump. He guessed a men's room was as good a place as any to find out what your reputation was. It occurred to him that he did not even know the name of the firebug he was supposed to defend. Oh, well, everything in due time. When he was sure no one was outside, he unlocked his stall door.

Marty Cagney was standing at a washbowl, examining a badly shaved spot on his chin in the mirror. Marty Cagney always had been quiet for such a big man. He had not made a sound when he came into the men's room and now he seemed embarrassed, as always, to see Dutch Shea, Jr. He touched the cast.

"You want me to check out that spade?"

"Jerry Costello said to forget it."

"If Jerry Costello had a brain, it would be tapioca pudding."

Dutch Shea smiled. "What brings you here today?"

Marty Cagney rubbed the rough spot on his chin before answering. "I'm a witness."

"In what?"

Studiously Marty Cagney avoided Dutch Shea's eyes. "Domestic relations."

Of course. A divorce. PEEKABOO CAGNEY—DISCREETLY DETERMINING WHAT WAS DONE—WHERE & WITH WHOM. Dutch Shea was touched by Marty Cagney's reluctance to answer. In all the years he had used him since the

116

divorce, Marty Cagney had never alluded to the reports on Lee and Byron Igoe.

A BMW 528i.

LEE S.

Room 701, West Wing, Chateau Blanche Motor Hotel.

A 45¢ tip.

"How's Mary?" Dutch Shea, Jr., said. Mary was Marty Cagney's daughter. It was safe to talk to Marty Cagney about his daughter and her nitwit ex-husband and his grandson. Neutral subjects. No discreet determination of what was done, where and with whom.

"She wants to open a bar."

Dutch Shea dried his hands under the automatic blower and tried not to sound doubtful. "Mary? That's nice."

"A gay bar." Marty Cagney headed out the men's room door. Dutch Shea followed. In the corridor, Marty Cagney said, "For her many friends in the gay community. That's what the prospectus says. It comes in the mail, asking me to invest. That's the first I hear about it, in the mail. Martin Peter Cagney, Esquire, it's addressed. Even the mailman doesn't like to touch it. Martin Peter Cagney, Esquire."

Marty Cagney sat on a window ledge oblivious to the people passing by.

"She's thirty-eight years old, Mary, she plays bridge on Wednesdays and tennis on Friday, she's a terror in racquetball is what they tell me, she's got a Chrysler LeBaron station wagon and a new Fleetwood, she's on top of her game since she dumps that rich nincompoop she was married to and now she wants to open a gay bar. For her many friends in the gay community. I never met those friends in the gay community, they were never around when I came by with my Christmas present. I go by once a month, have the roast lamb and those little potatoes, I don't see any friends from the gay community. The husband maybe, but he smokes a pipe, I'm around, and wears a plaid shirt like he's a lumberjack, Paul Bunyan, and he takes me into the wet bar and tells me dirty jokes. You hear about the girl with three tits, one in the back for dancing, and he slaps me on the back and says have one for the road. I don't even have my coat off and he's giving me one for the road."

Two black prostitutes sat down on a bench opposite Marty Cagney. One of them took off her gold wig and the other tried it on.

"A gay fucking bar," Marty Cagney said, shaking his head. "I got friends on the Liquor Commission, I'm going to make those friends very unhappy, they give her a license, Dutch. I got stories on two or three of those guys on the Liquor Commission, how much it costs to get a license, speed things up, things like that, the DA might be happy to hear what I had to say, they give her a license, Mary. He might even call it a shakedown, I go to see him, a dirty word like that. Graft is another word he might use, I ask him to check out how a couple of guys on the Liquor Commission got condominiums in Hilton Head, take tennis lessons from Evonne Goolagong there. It's better than the exercycle, the tennis, is what I hear. It keeps the pulse rate up, and you're on the Liquor Commission, you want the blood pumping all the time, steady like Hoover Dam, so you got the energy to keep stuffing it in the pockets with both hands, maybe get a little place on Kauai, too. They don't have condos in any slammer I know about, tennis lessons either, for that matter, and the slammer is where a couple of people are going to go, they give Mary a liquor license, and you can bet the house on that, Dutch, everything you can steal, get a bet down, take the points."

Dutch Shea nodded and watched the two prostitutes

across from him and Marty Cagney, who were now comparing frosted lipsticks.

"It's no day at the beach having kids, Dutch."

Except for Cat. It was always a day at the beach with Cat. No. I'm forgetting the days when she was a pain in the ass. P.I.T.A. That was what he called it when she got on his nerves. P.I.T.A. Pain in the ass. P.I.T.A., Cat would say. Pronounced like the bread.

"I hear you're getting this arson case."

"It seems that way." Barry Stukin wasn't wasting any time getting the word out.

"You want some help?"

"It's court-appointed, Marty. They don't allow a whole hell of a lot for investigation."

"Oh, for Christ's sake, Dutch . . ."

Dutch Shea, Jr., did not look at Marty Cagney. He knew that Marty Cagney gave him a cut rate and he knew the reason that Marty Cagney gave him a cut rate was because of his surveillance of Lee. It was not often that he continued doing business with cuckolds, business that had no connection with the tailing of a BMW 528i. Other business. Business concerning pimps and car thieves and dealers and murderers and burglars and drunk drivers. Business that took him to the Hall of Records and the registrar of voters and the Department of Motor Vehicles and the probate court and all the offices with the computers that printed out the statistical parameters of a life. Even after all this business, however, the adultery was there between them. The cut rate was like a neon advertisement. Dutch Shea, Jr., suspected that the adultery was the reason he continued to use Marty Cagney. It was a bond far stronger than friendship.

"Okay, Marty." Down the corridor he could see Thayer Pomfret at the door of the hearing room, pointing to his watch.

"You got the pimp's hearing?"

Dutch Shea nodded.

"He's a giant, Dutch, you got to admit that. The PUC. How many nigger pimps get hauled before the PUC? Those spade pimps, they think PUC is a new way to spell pussy."

Dutch Shea squeezed Marty Cagney's elbow. "I'll call you."

3

Candy Cane tried not to smile. The laugh lines around her mouth were like ski trails and they made her seem older than thirty-one. Thirty-one with a hysterectomy. Dutch Shea, Jr., wondered why whores told him things like that. Things they would not tell Myron Mandel.

"Miss Cane, how much did you charge for a massage?"

"Forty dollars."

"And of that forty dollars, how much went to Consolidated Services?" He could have phoned in the cross-examination. Even Johnny Torizzo was bored.

"Thirty-five dollars."

"For the massage?"

"Yes."

"Leaving you five dollars." Dutch Shea, Jr., remembered the night he met her, the night when she was still Shirley Potts and had hit the john with the credit card imprinter. She was wearing green underwear. He had never seen a woman in green underwear. What do you expect a whore to wear? Lee had said. Lee who had never met a whore. And he who was always being surprised by them.

"Correct."

"Did you receive tips?"

"Yes."

"What was the average size of your tips?"

"Fifty dollars minimum." She was so practiced he thought she would answer before the question was out of his mouth. "Usually seventy-five or a hundred."

"The massage was for forty dollars. But your tip was often a hundred?" He remembered he had Christmas lunch with Candy Cane the first holiday after he and Lee had separated. In the coffee shop of the Chateau Blanche Motor Hotel. He was having the Xmas Special —Roast Tom Turkey, Dressing, Giblet Gravy, Sweet Potatoes, Choice of Vegetables, Salad, Dessert, Coffee and Favor—$7.95. She had been turning a trick upstairs and when it was finished she had come into the coffee shop to buy a package of Larks. He had given her the favor as a Christmas present. A sample bottle of shaving lotion.

"Yes."

"Did you perform a service for your tip?"

"Yes."

"What kind of service?"

"Depends." Oh, Shirley, he thought, don't get coy now. Even Johnny Torizzo looked sharply at her.

"A sexual service?"

"Yes."

"So in other words, the tip was not a tip for the massage. The massage that Consolidated Services had arranged for you to give. The tip was actually a payment for the performance of a sexual act?"

"I guess."

"And not for the massage?"

"That's right."

"Would you give Mr. Mandel any part of that tip?"

"No."

"Not a dime?"

121

"Correct."

"Of any money you received for oral copulation or sexual intercourse or whatever?" Johnny Torizzo was smirking at the "or whatever." He thought suddenly of Cat. The "or whatever" would have broken her up.

"Right."

"Did you ever discuss with Mr. Mandel that your tips were based on the performance of a sexual act?"

"No."

"Did you ever tell him that you were engaging in sexual activities with customers who would call his service for a massage?"

"No."

"Did he ever tell you to engage in sex with any customers?"

"No."

"When you went to work for Mr. Mandel, did you sign a form under oath before a notary public that you would not engage in any sexual activity for hire?"

"I did."

Dutch Shea picked up a document from the exhibit table and handed it to Candy Cane.

"Is that your photograph clipped to this document?"

"Yes."

"And your signature that has been notarized?"

"Yes."

"Would you read the document?"

Candy Cane reached into her bag for a pair of reading glasses. Even with the glasses, she held the paper away from her eyes. "'I understand that if I solicit for or perform any act of prostitution while engaged by Consolidated Services, Inc., I will be immediately terminated. If any customer complains that I did perform any such act or solicitation, I will be immediately terminated.'"

"Who asked you to sign this document?"

"Myron."

"Mr. Mandel?"

"Yes."

"No further questions."

VIII

"I gather Poppa's bought you a gun," Clarice Campion said.

"Popular with the CIA, the FBI and undercover narcs," Dutch Shea, Jr., said.

"Narcs?"

He realized how long she had been away. Narcs were not an issue in the convent. "Narcotics agents."

Clarice nodded vigorously. "You always were a good shot, weren't you, Jack? I seem to remember you being a terrific shot. A sharpshooter, I think."

He wondered where Clarice had come up with that idea. She had written him regularly twice a year in the seventeen years she had been in the convent and every letter recalled events he was sure he had never shared. The picnic when Margie Dunn fell into Lake Elizabeth with all her clothes on and the party after Transubstantiation High ("Transy," Clarice called it) beat Kingswood for the first time in seven years on Phil Bogan's field goal and that Sunday Mass, the nine, when Father Quigley ran out of communion wafers just as he reached you, Jack, I don't think I've ever seen anyone so embarrassed.

124

"That must be someone else, Clarice," he said carefully. "The prevailing opinion is that I'll shoot myself. I hope it's not a self-fulfilling prophecy."

"I hope so, too, Jack." There was not a trace of irony in her voice. "You ever see Transy play anymore?"

"I'm afraid not, no."

"We used to have such fun at those games." She drew her voice out in the mournful moan of a school cheer. "'Go Transy, Kill Kingswood.' Remember that cheer?"

It seemed easier to say yes.

A momentary silence fell between them. Neither seemed to know what to say. Dutch Shea reflected that between him and Hugh silence was always a punctuation and never an embarrassment. He concentrated on an itch underneath his cast and listened to D.F. on the telephone in his study. Was there any reason for D.F. to remain on the telephone this long? He wondered if D.F. were trying to keep them alone together. Long ago, before Clarice had entered the convent, he had suspected that D.F. wanted them to get together.

Clarice drained her drink. "Could you make me another highball, Jack?"

Dutch Shea, Jr., took her glass. A highball. Were they still saying highball when Clarice went into the convent? He deliberately made the drink light and handed it back to her.

"Poppa hates to see me drink. He thinks I'm a sexual misfit." She said it with a brightness that weighed on him. "I think he wonders if I'm still a virgin."

Dutch Shea laughed to cover his discomfort. In a way Clarice touched him as few women ever had. She was well into her thirties but because she had entered the convent so young she still had the physical and social ungainliness of an adolescent. Her hair caught for so many years under a nun's cowl was still unfashionably short, her eye makeup too pronounced, her lipstick too bright for her pale, almost translucent coloring. Given time, she would be attractive, but sitting in that deep leather chair in her father's living room she did not seem to know what to do with her hands or whether she could cross her legs without her underclothes showing, and when she talked about her virginity it was with the adolescent daring of a field hockey player. She was an adult subject to the same mortifications as a child and he remembered that once when she was seventeen, the summer before she entered the convent, he had seen her naked. She was using his bathroom because of a leaking pipe in her own and he had walked in on her as she prepared to shower. She had blushed but for a moment she had not moved her hands from the shower curtain to cover herself and he had noticed how prominent her nipples were, so prominent that he wondered if she had been stimulating herself before he walked into the bathroom. Later that night he had awakened with an erection and had masturbated, thinking of Clarice, of the prominent nipples and the thick dark triangle disappearing between her legs. The summer before she became Sister Domenica of the Salesian Sisters of St. John Bosco. It was the only sexual spasm he had ever had for her and it embarrassed him that he remembered it now after so many years. He smiled at her and as if she knew what he had been thinking she lit a cigarette and began smoking it in short, jerky puffs. In effect Clarice was his sister and he hoped suddenly that she was not a virgin.

He changed the subject.

"How's the consultancy service, Clarice?"

"Oh, I'm having a ball, Jack."

He nodded and tried not to smile. Even her slang was dated. "I'm glad."

"Well, I'm not," D. F. Campion said, bouncing into the living room from his study. "A nutcake scheme if I ever heard one."

"Oh, Poppa," Clarice said. She seemed to shrink in her chair before her father's presence. With D.F., Clarice would always be the adolescent who became Sister Domenica. "There's a real need for it, Jack."

"There's a real need for cancer, too," D. F. Campion said. He stood at the ice bucket making himself a drink, throwing each cube into his glass in a fury.

Clarice tried to ignore him. "There's a communications revolution going on, Jack. Nuns have got to package themselves."

"I see." Dutch Shea, Jr., sneaked a quick look at D.F. He knew the old man was making an effort to hold his tongue. He knew D.F. better than either of his children, both of whom had left home so young, but as always when he was with one or both of them and they called D.F. "Poppa," he felt apart. He had never been able to bring himself to call D.F. "Poppa," nor had D.F. ever insisted. As a child he had waited until he caught D.F.'s eye before speaking to him. It was only as an adult, a member of the bar, an assistant district attorney that he had begun calling him "D.F." He knew that it pleased the old man and that it pleased him even more that he called him "Dominick" when they were alone together. Never "Dominick" in front of Hugh or Clarice. Dominick was his name and Poppa was theirs. It was what his father had called D.F.

"We want to help them get their media act together," Clarice said. "We can tell them what kind of cosmetics to use. How to travel. Acquaint them with feminist issues. Let it all hang out."

"Let all what hang out?" D.F. said. His face had turned a deeper shade of red than usual and for a moment Dutch Shea, Jr., was afraid he would have a seizure.

Clarice acted as if her father were not in the room. "Teach them how to combat church authority."

"Jesus, Mary and Joseph," D.F. said.

"Nuns have got a communications problem," Clarice said.

"Because they're nuns," D.F. said. "Seen and not heard. That's the way it should be."

"No, Poppa. We want them to get out. Into second careers. Start over. Lawyer nuns. Doctor nuns. Nun power. That's the answer, Poppa."

"What in the name of Jesus is nun power?" D.F. said.

"It's something like gay power, Poppa."

"Jesus, Mary and Joseph," D.F. repeated. He sank into a chair and stared into his drink.

"You're too simplistic, Poppa. You've got to go with the times."

"You mean you want the altar boys running around the convent, passing out the pot," D.F. said. "What about the prophylactics? You can get them out of a machine now, I hear. Three for a dollar, I hear."

"You've hit on an important subject, Poppa. I think you're finally getting with it."

"Good God," D.F. said.

"Nuns have sex drives, too. We want to open sex information clinics for emerging nuns."

"Not a nickel out of me," D.F. said. "Not a nickel for this fruitcake scheme."

"I have my dowry, Poppa. When I left the convent, the mother general returned the dowry I entered with and wished me luck."

D.F. was bouncing in his chair. "You mean you took the money I gave the Sisters when you went into the convent and you're using it to endow this loony set-up?"

"I think the mother general is behind us, Poppa."

"Then she ought to be the mother private," D.F. said. "She ought to be shot. I didn't even want you in the convent. That wasn't my idea. The convent's a

128

place for girls with mustaches. You could've married Georgie Duggan."

"Oh, Poppa," Clarice said. "Georgie Duggan was the biggest makeout artist at Transy."

D. F. Campion looked at Dutch Shea, Jr., as if seeking a translator.

"A real twerp," Clarice said.

Dutch Shea wondered if she knew she had D.F. on the run. The old man was a stranger in this country of adolescence. He did not know how to deal with this half-formed child-woman who one moment talked in an archaic tongue about highballs and makeout artists and the next about the sex drive of nuns. It was a country for which he had no visa.

"Let's eat," D. F. Campion said.

They had corned beef. The menus at D.F.'s table rarely changed. Meat one night was followed by a casserole of leftovers the next, except on Friday when the pattern was broken by fillet of sole. Even after the laws of fast and abstinence were loosened, D.F. still had sole on Friday. Not out of devotion to past strictures but because he believed in fish one night a week and Friday was as good a night as any. Once a week every week of his adult life Dutch Shea, Jr., had dined with D.F. Lee always came when they were first married, then less often, then seldom, then not at all. There was a Junior League meeting, a classmate from Smith was in town, PTA, a whole range of charities, headaches and strains of influenza. D.F. always accepted each excuse with equanimity. "A grand girl, always busy, not run down, is she, Jack? You got to watch that, being run down. Lil was like that, run down. Then bingo! Lights out, time's up." Lil was D.F.'s late wife, dead almost forty years and only vaguely remembered by Dutch Shea, Jr. The word pleasant came to mind.

129

And the image of a muffin. Warm and without taste. He wondered what it would be like to be remembered as a pleasant muffin. And to have his death chronicled as bingo! Light's out, time's up.

"How's Lee, Jack?" Clarice said brightly.

For an instant Dutch Shea, Jr., was not sure Clarice was aware of the divorce. No. Of course she was. Clarice had written him. Clarice had said he would be quite a catch for some gal. Was it really five years ago? Had it been that long?

"Fine, Clarice."

"Not run down, is she, Jack?" D.F. said.

"Not that I know of."

"I'll send her some flowers," D.F. said. He had always been fond of Lee. "Daffodils is nice this time of year. I'll call Jack Cully that's got the bad hemorrhoids in the morning, he's got a swell selection of daffodils, and have him send some out. Not himself. She might get upset, Lee, as run down as she is, if he shows up at the door with the daffodils and starts babbling away about the hemorrhoids and what a grand cure Preparation H is. They do that, florists. Smelling flowers all day makes you nutty, I hear."

A puzzled look crossed Clarice's face. Dutch Shea knew she was trying to track D.F.'s conversation from Lee to a strange florist's hemorrhoids. He was not surprised that neither one could understand the other. He buttered a piece of bread and contemplated D.F. The old man had been a widower for over thirty-five years and he wondered suddenly if D.F. had been sexually continent during those three and a half decades. Of course. No doubt. There was money to be made and the making of money was more than enough compensation for celibacy.

"Terrible about Artie Nangle that was in Water and Power," D. F. Campion said.

Dutch Shea, Jr., mumbled noncommittally. He had

no idea who Artie Nangle was, but he was also sure he was going to get a complete genealogical history. Not a morning went by that D.F. did not telephone Mother Cabrini Hospital and the various Catholic florists and funeral homes to see who had died during the night. If there was a familiar name, however tenuous the connection to himself, then D.F. had a subject with which to dominate his table that night. He had never understood what advantage D.F. got out of it, but then an advantage was an advantage.

"Thirty-eight years he was there and when he retired they gave him a watch that didn't work. A seventy-five-dollar watch, which averages out to less than two dollars a year. And the guarantee didn't cover it when it went on the fritz. So he sued Water and Power and they had to fight it."

Dutch Shea glanced across the table at Clarice. She seemed absorbed in the slicing of her corned beef. It occurred to him that over the years he and Clarice had received capsule biographies of most of the minor clerical help at the Bureau of Health and the Department of Sanitation. A strange way to torment your loved ones.

"Your pal, Jack, he was the attorney for Water and Power then . . . ?"

"Which one is that, D.F.?" The maid served him the cabbage and he shook his head. She was an Irish girl in a white uniform, scarcely into her teens, it seemed, with fair reddish hair, and when he smiled and said no to the cabbage, her cheeks turned almost scarlet.

Oh, no, not that again, he thought.

"The one with the fifty-seven teeth in his head, and when he was running for Congress later, he kept talking about his Jacuzzi to that gang up in the North End." D.F. waved the cabbage away impatiently. "That bunch, they hear the word Jacuzzi, they think you're talking about a congressman from New Jersey."

"Thayer Pomfret," Dutch Shea, Jr., said.

"That's the one," D. F. Campion said. "Settle, he tells Water and Power. You don't need the bad publicity. Which is the one smart thing Thayer Pomfret ever done in his life. Except for a little thing he done for me once."

Dutch Shea looked at Clarice and then at D.F. "What was that?"

"Imagine giving a nitwit like Artie Nangle a cheap watch," D. F. Campion continued without answering. "So he sits down with Artie, your pal, Mr. Thayer Wilson Pomfret, and he says, 'What do you want in place of that watch?' and Artie says, 'A trip to Providence.' Think of that. A trip to Providence. That's a man who knew what he wanted and what he wanted was a trip to Providence. Thirty-eight years in Water and Power, Artie. He must've spent his time watching the water go drip, drip, drip." D.F. leaned toward Clarice, and as if she were still a schoolgirl and not a grown woman and an ex-nun, he said, "There's two hundred and seven thousand people in Providence, many of them Italians."

From across the table Dutch Shea could see Clarice's jaw muscles bunch and harden. "Yes, Poppa."

"That's a good thing to remember, you ever want to go to Providence."

"Yes, Poppa." Clarice did not look up from her plate. Dutch Shea knew that in some obscure way D.F. was paying her back for trying to mobilize nun power.

"He was eighty-two, Artie. They were keeping him alive at Mother Cabrini with the tubes and the machines. They should've plugged him in over at Water and Power. He was wearing the watch when he died. Which still didn't work. He must've worn it to remind him of his trip to Providence."

But D.F.'s heart was clearly no longer in the passing of Artie Nangle, late of Water & Power, and he lapsed into silence as the maid cleared away the dishes, occasionally glancing at Clarice, who studiously avoided his gaze. Dutch Shea pretended not to notice the tension between father and daughter and concentrated on the maid. He was struck by how much she resembled Clarice. Clarice the virgin teenager. Clarice the postulant of the Salesian Sisters of St. John Bosco. He was not surprised by the resemblance. For as long as he could remember, it had been D.F.'s policy to bring over poor and humble nieces and grandnieces from Ireland as household help. The daughters and granddaughters of second and third cousins D.F. had never seen but who were the sometime recipients of his sporadic largesse. He paid for each girl's passage and in return got for two years what amounted to an indentured servant. Only at Christmas and Easter was the blood kinship ever acknowledged. On those holidays the girl of that particular year would eat at the table in her white maid's uniform and call D.F. "Uncle Dominick," but when the meal was over and the last wishbone snapped, she would retire to the kitchen and until the next holiday D.F. was once again "Sir" or "Mr. Campion."

Pure D.F. Always on the lookout for a bargain.

Kathleen.

He did not like to think of Kathleen as a bargain.

How many years had it been?

Kathleen.

The wild child.

No.

He watched Clarice. Clarice seemed to count every dish the maid cleared. He knew that the servant cousins were always a particular burden on her. She had always hated being called "Miss" or "Miss Clarice" by girls who were contemporaries and relatives, but the more democratic forms of address were never permitted except when D.F. was seized by the annual spirit of holiday goodwill. Even now, twenty years older than the child clearing the dishes, Clarice could not look her in the eye.

When the girl disappeared through the swinging door into the kitchen, Clarice hissed, "Really, Poppa, it's obscene."

"What?"

"That girl."

"Maeve, you mean. One of the Kellehers. From Galway. Poor. Not a pot to piss in, the Kellehers. I can say that now, you're out of the convent."

Clarice flushed. "It's slave labor, Poppa. It always has been. Isn't it, Jack?"

Dutch Shea smiled and raised his hands. "I suppose it depends on your point of view." A brave stand. Controversial. Clarice looked disgusted.

"I'm giving these girls a once-in-a-lifetime opportunity," D. F. Campion said.

"How can you say that, Poppa?"

"They come over here and they learn to cook and clean and shave under their arms," D.F. said.

"Oh, Poppa. This is the twentieth century."

"Not in Galway, it's not," D. F. Campion said. "You remember the one didn't shave under her arms. You stuck chewing gum under there. Wrigley's Juicy Fruit." D.F. looked at Dutch Shea, Jr., with satisfaction. "That was before she started talking about slave labor."

"Kathleen." The memory seemed to embarrass Clarice. "Kathleen Donnelly. I'm ashamed I did that, Poppa. No excuses. Just ashamed." She took a deep breath. "As you should be ashamed for still bringing those girls over from Ireland."

Kathleen.

I am the victim of memory.

Kathleen. She had never mentioned the chewing gum Clarice had deposited in her armpit. He saw D.F.

staring at him. He wondered how much D.F. knew. God knows there was little D.F. did not know about what went on under his roof.

Clarice put her napkin down and stood up. "Must run."

"Where are you going?" D.F. seemed petulant. His children did not leave the table until they were dismissed.

"The medium is the message, Poppa. We're trying to organize the Sisters of Mercy."

Clarice kissed Dutch Shea, Jr., on the cheek. "Good to see you, Jack." The spontaneity of the kiss made her blush. She touched his cast. "Remember. We used to sign them at Transy. Y.A.T.O.A.O. You are the one and only."

He smiled but did not remember. D.F. saw his daughter to the door. Dutch Shea, Jr., could hear them arguing on the front porch. He tried to pick up the gist. It was rude to leave. Jack was depressed. Couldn't she see that? Why didn't she live at home? The voices faded and suddenly he was aware of the maid hovering at his shoulder.

"More coffee, sir?"

Dutch Shea, Jr., shook his head. The girl flushed and started for the kitchen.

"Maeve."

"Sir."

"Maeve Kelleher, right?"

"Yes, sir."

"How long have you been here now, Maeve?"

"Six months, sir."

"Are you going back?"

"Where, sir?"

"Galway."

"Oh, I don't know, sir."

"How old are you?"

"Seventeen."

"You look younger." He smiled at her but he knew immediately that Maeve Kelleher did not appreciate being told she looked younger than seventeen. He stirred his cold coffee and on an impulse said, "Did you ever know Kathleen Donnelly?"

Maeve brightened. "Not know her, sir. Personally, I mean. Know about her."

"Ah." He picked up the inflection in her voice. So Kathleen was someone they knew about in Galway. And talked about. As an object lesson, no doubt.

"Her da and my da are second cousins, once removed. They're from Sligo, the Donnellys."

"I see." Her tone suggested that the Galway Kellehers thought themselves ever so slightly superior to the Sligo Donnellys.

"She didn't come back." He detected just the faintest brushing of belligerence.

"She didn't?" He was at his most noncommittal. The art of cross-examination. Let her go on.

"No, sir." The idea of Kathleen Donnelly seemed to appeal to Maeve Kelleher. "I think she went to the state of Nevada."

"Really." That would be like Kathleen. The state of Nevada. An unsanctified state I think Maeve might fancy herself, he thought.

"Yes, sir. She would write to Sligo."

"And the Sligo people would tell the Galway people."

"Yes, sir."

"I see."

"She had a flat there." Maeve Kelleher corrected herself as if he might not understand. "An apartment, I mean."

"I understand."

Again the whisper of belligerence. "Of her own, I mean."

Dutch Shea, Jr., nodded.

"She was a waitress in the state of Nevada."

Oh, Jesus.

A look of ferret fear passed over Maeve's face and she backed suddenly toward the kitchen door. Dutch Shea could hear D.F. bouncing toward the dining room.

"Look sharp now, Maeve," D. F. Campion said, clapping his hands. "The dishes should have been cleared away by now."

"It was my fault," Dutch Shea said. "We were just chatting about Galway."

"Rocks and cows, that's all Galway is," D.F. said. "And harps. As dumb as the cows and hard as the rocks." He clapped his hands once again and Maeve vanished into the kitchen, tripping over her own feet. From the other side of the door, they could hear the crash of the silver coffeepot onto the kitchen linoleum. "See what I mean?" D.F. said. "Galway."

They walked across the varnished wood floor of the center hall into the living room. Past the hideous portrait of Pope Pius XII. Dutch Shea poured himself a brandy. Lee was right. Pius XII was staring at him. He gave himself an extra dollop of brandy.

D. F. Campion was in a foul humor about Clarice.

"Why does she need her own apartment?" D.F. said. "She's got a swell room upstairs, with her own bathroom. I just put in new fixtures. A push-button toilet. I could understand it if she had to share a toilet."

D.F. seemed to expect an answer. "Well, you know, Dominick." Weak. Try again. Anything but the truth. He was not about to tell D.F. that Clarice would rather return to the convent than have her own new push-button bathroom upstairs. Even with gold fixtures. Better the mother general than a steady diet of Artie Nangle stories. "Clarice is a grown woman."

"So that's your idea of a grown woman."

D.F. had him there. He swirled the brandy, appraising the old man over the top of the snifter. Something off the wall to change the subject.

"Whatever happened to Kathleen Donnelly?"

"How'd you happen to think of her?"

"We were talking about her at dinner."

"We were?"

"Clarice stuck Juicy Fruit in her armpit."

"Oh, that one."

"That one."

"I don't know."

Why did he want to know about Kathleen anyway? There were already too many women in his life. In every pigeonhole a new one. And the only one who could help him out was Elaine Igoe. Sweet Jesus, don't let the thought take hold. "She's in Nevada, I hear."

"Las Vegas." So D.F. did know. Pius XII would not let him dissemble.

"Really."

"A bad apple, that one. I had her checked out."

"Oh."

"You got to watch out for that type."

"Why?"

"She's like someone you defend."

Like someone I defend. You had to hand it to D.F. He was very neat with the old one-two. A hard man to pin against the ropes. And he always had been. About so many things.

"Don't pull that silent act on me, buster. You know what I mean."

Yes, he knew what D.F. meant. The decline of John Shea, Jr., attorney-at-law, former husband and father. It was the subject that seemed to end all their conversations these days. "I know that when you call me 'buster,' I'm meant to stand at attention and salute." He smiled at D.F. A tolerant smile. That was a mistake. D.F. hated being tolerated. "I'm tired tonight. How would parade rest be instead?"

"Always the jokes," D.F. said. "You never used to be such a weisenheimer."

"I've always been a weisenheimer."

"And look where it got you."

I should have seen that one coming. Never give D.F. an opening. "Oh, come on, Dominick."

"You're about a foot and a half from the funny farm and you think I don't know it. I told your dad I'd look after you, Jack . . ."

Your dad. The words filled him with dread. His father was a subject he tried never to discuss with D.F. An instinctive decision. A discreet decision. He was sure the discretion served them both well. "You have, Dominick."

"You're depressed all the time. All the time. It's the way you live. You never lived that way until Catherine died." D.F. had never called Cat anything but Catherine. "You got a boogie practice now. You live like a boogie now. You think no one else ever had a few hard knocks. Those boogies you keep out of the cooler where they ought to be, even they had a few lousy breaks. Being black is enough to put you down for the count. But there's some of them came out okay. That King fellow and O. J. Simpson . . ."

Dutch Shea, Jr., smiled.

"Go ahead and laugh, wise guy," D. F. Campion said. "But you know I'm right. Ever since Catherine . . ."

Dutch Shea took a deep breath. "It happened, Dominick."

"And that's all you got to say?"

"It's like a highway accident. I'd go crazy if I thought about it any other way."

"You're going to go crazy keeping it bottled up," D.F. shouted. "Living like a goddamn boogie."

The sound of D. F. Campion's shouting brought Maeve Kelleher to the kitchen door. She peeked out, her face frightened, and for an instant Dutch Shea, Jr., was reminded of the look on Cat's face when he and Lee shouted at each other. In that brief moment it struck him that Maeve was approximately the same age. Would have been the same age. If. Then Maeve disappeared back into the kitchen.

D.F. settled back into his chair. "I loved that little girl, Jack," he said quietly. "More than you'll ever know. More than you'll ever know," he repeated. "But you've got to shake it off . . ."

Dutch Shea, Jr., nodded. He tried not to think of Cat in her lavender espadrilles and her blue button-down Brooks Brothers shirt, tried not to imagine her various appendages scattered all over Charlotte Street.

"You're all I've got, Jack."

"Don't say that, Dominick," Dutch Shea said sharply. He knew it was an irrevocable thought that once uttered could never be retracted. "You've got Hugh . . ."

"Wearing an apron and whipping up an omelette. I gave my son to God and He threw back a chef . . ."

". . . and Clarice."

"Packaging nuns like they're tollhouse cookies. The sex drive is that little chocolate bit." D.F. shook his head in bewilderment. "That's not what they used to talk about in the convent, Sister Annunciata and them. We were a lot better off when nuns talked about mite boxes for the Chink missionaries and how long a Communist spent in purgatory if he made a perfect act of contrition on his deathbed and what a swell cake sale for the Children of Mary that birdbrain Father Phil Gorman had in the parish hall last Sunday."

The grandfather clock in the center hall struck ten and Dutch Shea, Jr., counted every chime, thankful for the interruption. He considered the family. His family. They were like parts to four different automobiles. And D.F. For more than three quarters of his life, D. F.

Campion had been his only parent, a surrogate father who had never tried to sweep away the shards of memory about his real father. He wondered if gratitude was a bond stronger than love.

Suddenly D.F. was on his feet, bounding around the living room. "Don't be so down in the mouth, buster." Momentarily, Dutch Shea was startled, but then he relaxed. D.F. had always had the ability to transfer responsibility for his black moods onto whomever happened to be with him, blaming the pall he had created on anyone but himself. "I stay around you long enough, I'm going to start acting like I live in some coon neighborhood. He's a champ, Hugh, and Clarice, too, and don't you forget it. Great kiddos. The best." D.F. shook his finger in Dutch Shea's face. "And as for you, buster, I told your dad I'd take care of you and I don't think I've done a bad job."

"Not a bad job at all, Dominick."

D.F. put his hand on Dutch Shea's shoulder and squeezed it slightly. "I love you, Jack."

Dutch Shea, Jr., nodded gravely. Why did love remind him of the communion Host the priest placed on the tongue? With all the tastelessness of sanctifying grace. He noticed Pius XII staring at him from the hallway, warning him not to be equivocal.

"I know you do, Dominick."

BOOK TWO

BOOK TWO

I

Sunday, and the weekly dilemma. To Mass or not to Mass. That is the question. Whether 'tis nobler in the mind . . . In general, he felt about God as he felt about the Kennedy assassination conspiracy theories: he was willing to believe. Suspended belief. Or was it suspended disbelief? Whatever. He had his script worked out. Confession on his deathbed. Penance. Extreme unction. Two sacraments for the price of one. A perfect act of contrition. Not to mention a perfect way to hedge his bet in case he had backed the wrong horse. No harm done either way.

Reason(s) to attend Mass: (1) It took up an hour. Counting ten minutes to drive to church and ten minutes to drive home, an hour and twenty minutes. Throw in ten minutes in the parking lot, Hiya, Jack, Hello, Charlie. Plus breakfast at the Pancake House. Another thirty minutes. Two hours in all. Mass was like taking on another Legal Aid case. Religion as anesthesia. Ditto the law. Ways to anesthetize memory. (2) See 1.

Reason(s) not to attend Mass: (1) Sloth. (2) More sloth.

In the end he went to Mass, the urge to fill his time overcoming suspended belief. He wished he lived on the West Coast. On the West Coast the NFL double-header started at 10 A.M. with a game from the East, the pregame show at 9:30. Roll out of bed at nine and into a shower and from 9:30 until 4 total immersion in a world of stunts and blitzes and double coverages and zones and shotguns. A half-dozen beers, a pleasant buzz, a frozen Swanson's chicken pot pie and into bed, another day safely negotiated. Far better the Fellowship of Christian Athletes than Father Ruggiero Mancuso on purgatory. Mancuso the Good made it sound like a medium-security slammer. A place that his brother, Mancuso the Bad, aka Rhett Pincus, could hack if worse came to worse. He perused the printed announcements, wondering what the Confraternity of C.D. was up to. The power base of Mrs. Punchy Iacovetti. Imagine the impetus to call yourself "Punchy." No quotes. A legal name. Not Luigi (Punchy) Iacovetti. Punchy Iacovetti. Husband of Mrs. Punchy. "Punchy, is that you? We're having your favorite tonight. Osso bucco." At one point in his life, Hugh Campion was nicknamed "Squirrel." Yet Hugh never had the urge to change his name legally to Squirrel Campion. *Father Squirrel's Kitchen.* It would not play on public television. A difference in style between Immaculate and Bobby Bellarmine.

The congregation stood, knelt, sat. A cough worked its way like a wave from front aisle left to rear aisle right. Sniffle, snuffle, clearing of throats back of Immaculate to front. Offertory bells and the moment of truth—the collection. He checked his wallet. A five, a ten and a twenty. No singles. He did not like to give the collection more than he gave valet parking. Slowly he inched his way toward the door. Take in the sights of Park Street until the collection was safely passed. There a tire mart, there a body shop, here a Thom McAn. But it was raining outside now and he came back inside and busied himself with the holy water font. Good God! Carmine Cantalupo was taking the collection. He checked the various exits. At every one a soldier in Carmine's army. Melon men. Each in a hound'stooth jacket and a blue silk shirt buttoned to the neck, no tie. Carmine Cantalupo approached, collection basket outstretched. Dutch Shea took the five from his wallet. Carmine Cantalupo shook his head, put his hand on Dutch Shea's arm, said, "It's on me, Mr. Shea." Sweet Jesus. Charity from the Melon Man. A favor repaid after how many years? Serafina Pyle must have five children by now. No, six. The last two were twins. Guido, Rocco and Lou were the boys; Ames, Lindsay and Daisy the girls. It was said that Harry Pyle doted on the girls. He had difficulty with a son named Guido. No wonder Harry Pyle never spoke to him. It's on me, Mr. Shea. Your money's no good at Immaculate. Five dollars. Did that square things with Carmine Cantalupo? Do I come that cheap?

Dutch Shea escaped Immaculate before the consecration. Another mortal sin in the eyes of God, but what the hell? In the vestibule he considered putting the ten-dollar bill in the poor box, but he resisted the temptation. An empty gesture. No spectators. Look at it this way. The Melon Man had saved him a fiver. What to do? The apartment was uninviting. Bed unmade, sink full of dirty dishes, newspaper and dirty laundry all over the floor. Damn Martha. When Martha spent the night, she always made the bed before she left, first wiping the crusted semen off the sheet with a damp washcloth. The little things. Martha was not fastidious about sex. If anything she was realistic to a fault. "You watch it in the movies with the camera floating around and the music playing and Julie Christie's head thrown back and the camera making another circle and you think, hey, that's not bad. Except when I do it, my legs are locked around someone's neck and there's hair all over his back and there's this big ass pumping up and down and there's no background music and there's a big wet spot I get to lie in, I'm so lucky."

"That's swell, Martha. I'm glad you told me that, it really turns me on. And I don't have hair on my back."

"The one in Montreal did."

"I don't think I want to ask you about the big ass."

"Hyperbole. And, Jack, I didn't say I didn't like it."

True.

But Martha had spent last night with Tommy getting ready for the Cloonan boy's wake. Oh, yes, the Cloonan boy's wake. A must in his social calendar. Kevin Cloonan was the first fireman to die in the line of duty in three years and the Fire Department was not only paying for the funeral expenses but also pulling out all the stops. Uniformed firemen at either end of the casket at Goldman & Flowers, a color guard promised for the funeral, as well as the governor, who was up for reelection. Taps, a rifle salute and no need for equal time on the six o'clock news. And already a touch of drama. Kevin Cloonan's father in Pompano Beach had collapsed with a massive coronary when told his son had died. A definite no-show at the wake. The boy's mother was dead and so Tommy Sweeney had prevailed on Martha to take over as surrogate mother and mistress of ceremonies. Martha, sweet Martha, had extracted a promise that he would come to the wake.

"It's going to be difficult, Martha. I am representing the guy who's accused of killing him."

"Jack, it's going to be a circus. Judge Sweeney needs a friendly face."

"If it pleases the court . . ."

"It pleases the court."

All in all a social highlight he would just as soon avoid. Too many firemen talking about too many close calls. About too many roofs that gave away. About too many walls that caved in. Too many pints of Irish concealed in too many brown paper bags. Sooner or later someone was going to try to pick a fight with counsel for the accused. All because Judge Sweeney needed a friendly face.

So what.

Fuck them.

A fight might prove he was alive.

2

Back home he made a stab at cleaning his apartment. Pulled up the bed. Piled the newspapers. Sprinkled All on the dirty dishes and then filled the sink with soapy water. He took a dish towel from a kitchen drawer and made a pass at the dishes, but the egg clung tenaciously to the first plate and the idea of much more such exercise fatigued him. Still two hours to kickoff. He tried the TV. An evangelical preacher on the cable promised eternal damnation. Better Mancuso the Good's paean to purgatory. He wondered if he were up to dealing with BEAUBOIS, Robert No Middle Initial. The ultimate time killer. Not to mention the alleged killer of seventeen indigents and one probationary fireman.

FILE NO: 1077–187/447a–1334–136.

ARRESTEE'S NAME (Last, First, Middle Initial): BEAUBOIS, Robert NMI.

AGE: 19.

DATE & TIME ARRESTED: 10/14 0617.

TIME BKD. 1639.

CHARGE (Section, Code, Definition): 447a, P.C., Arson, 1

Ct., 187, P.C., Homicide, 18 Cts.

He took another document at random from the file and wondered how many police reports he had read. Five thousand. Ten. He never read them sequentially. An old habit. Sequential officialese seemed to plane the edges off perception. Subject. Perpetrator. Alleged. Deceased. Vehicle. Female person. Male person. Cau. Neg. Susp. The language invariably made him sleepy, but if the files were read in no particular order, things stuck in his mind—the inconsistency, the odd fact, the quirky memory. PHYSICAL EVIDENCE HELD. A good enough place to start.

Item #1—$3.38. Item #2—two (2) city bus tokens. Item #3—one (1) Greyhound bus schedule. Item #4—one (1) paperback book, "Star Trek Night."

A firebug Trekkie.

Dutch Shea checked his own pockets. Change. Wallet. Handkerchief. Kleenex. Menthol inhalator. Parking lot stub. Cigarettes. Zippo lighter.

BEAUBOIS, Robert NMI. No wallet. No ID. No cigarettes. No lighter, No matches. At least not in PHYSICAL EVIDENCE HELD.

What did he set the fire with?

A thin straw, but a straw nevertheless.

What else?

Seventeen prior arrests. Not bad for a kid of nineteen. Two prior jail sentences. Juvey detention for grand theft, auto, 487, P.C., and the State Industrial School for arson, 447a, P.C. Three other arson beefs: "rel., insuff. evidence."

This kid is a walking torch.

SUPPLEMENTARY REPORT:

Susp. admitted setting five (5) fires for which he was not caught and no charges were brought.

150

Why didn't the nitwit keep his mouth shut?
Dutch Shea went back to the arrest report.

> The Following Statement Was Read to the
> Arrestee: "You have the right to remain
> silent . . ." This Admonition Was Read to the
> Arrestee by (Name & Serial No.): Costello,
> Jerry, Det. Sgt., 6218.

He wondered if Jerry was wearing his FUCK YOU
courtroom tie.
SUPPLEMENTARY REPORT:

> When Det. J. Costello lit a cigarette, susp.
> jumped and stared at flame as if hypnotized.

Oh, for Christ's sake, Jerry.
The telephone rang. He let the answering machine
pick up the call. He was not up to speaking to anyone
this morning, thank you.
Where was this kid busted at 6:17 in the morning?

> Officers Kehoe & Fair proceeding westbound on
> Albany Avenue detected susp. sleeping on bus
> bench n.w. corner Bishop's Corner approx 0613.

The buses stopped running at 11.
The fire was reported at 12:21 A.M.
Bishop's Corner was the halfway mark in the city
marathon, which made it at least ten miles from the
Cuthbertson.

> Officers Kehoe & Fair thinking susp. might be
> runaway juvenile awoke susp. from sleeping posi-

151

tion. Manner of susp. appeared suspicious to Officers Kehoe Y Fair. Susp. calm and cool at first and then susp. became extremely agitated in an agitated manner.

Cop English.

Time to check the answering machine. Perhaps it would wake him up.

"Jack. Elaine. Igoe. Uh. I've got, uh. Someone, uh. Someone gave me, uh, an extra ticket to the auxiliary next week. Uh. The women's auxiliary dance, I mean. At Mother Cabrini. I mean, uh, for Mother Cabrini. It's a benefit. At the Club. Black tie. That's optional. I mean, uh, you can wear a blue suit. Hey, I haven't even asked you. I mean, would you like to come? Uh. I took care of the tickets . . ." There was a silence on the machine, as if Elaine Igoe knew she had made a tactical error about the tickets and was trying to think of a way to erase the tape. "Uh. Call me, would you? Elaine. Igoe."

So Elaine had taken care of the tickets.

And Carmine Cantalupo had taken care of the collection.

Everyone takes care of old Dutch.

The thing to do.

He thought of Elaine Igoe's three million. That would take care of a lot of things.

For sure.

No-win thinking. Back to the firebug.

PROBATION OFFICER'S REPORT. What for?

487, P.C., grand theft, auto. Referred for pre-plea. Defendant lived with paternal grandparents for reasons unknown since infancy. Father corporal U.S. Army now stationed in Canal Zone. Father had not seen defendant since defendant was 2 yrs. old. Mother a German national now living in Wertheim am Main, West Germany, since divorce from father. Defendant first arrested for setting alley fires. Remanded to State Industrial School when he was 14. Defendant left school in ninth grade. Defendant shows apitude for mathematics and shop.

For reasons unknown since infancy.

Elaine Igoe. Good God. Elaine. And Byron. And Lee. Oh, yes.

He remembered the day he realized Lee was having an affair. "There's a letter from Hugh," Lee had said. "I didn't open it." She said it in a way that suggested he frequently accused her of opening his mail. That suggested that Hugh Campion was his responsibility. That suggested . . .

Oh, Christ.

"He's going to be here next week," he said after finishing the letter.

"Lecturing on the nouvelle cuisine?"

He tried to keep his irritation in check. "He wants us to reserve him a small . . ." The letter had said "suite," but he hesitated to say the word to Lee.

"Monastic suite."

"Bingo."

"The Chateau Blanche."

"Fine."

"OLdfield 6-1010." Had Lee run a finger down his cheek? Or did he wish to remember it that way? "You know, I really like Hugh." She had smiled. "As ridiculous as he is."

"You say that because you can't make a perfect lemon soufflé."

The tired banter of the disintegrating marriage. He had called the Chateau Blanche and reserved Hugh Campion a small suite. Then he had gone shopping. He spent a lot of time shopping the year his marriage was breaking up. Checking the Gouda at the Cheese Corner. Sampling the blanched almonds at the Nut Tree. Feeling avocados and tomatoes and Crenshaws and casabas. He was weighing a honeydew when it hit him.

OLdfield 6-1010.

Lee had difficulty remembering his office number.

OLdfield 6-1010.

Just like that. Off the top of her head.

OLdfield 6-1010.

A hotel.

She was having an affair.

With someone at the Chateau Blanche.

The honeydew slipped out of his hands and split on the floor of the fruit department. Seeds and liquid squished over his tennis sneakers.

My God.

No.

Vaccinate yourself with the present.

ARSON REPORT:

Conclusion: It is the opinion of undersigned investigator that this fire was set in a mattress located in first-floor service area with an open flame held in human hands. L. L. Hackett, Arson Squad, 5959.

The Cuthbertson. He had driven past on his way home from Mass. Another way to kill time. It was a charred ruin now. Half the third floor sagged under the weight of the rain, the fourth floor was gone except for a bathtub that hung out over Ann Street, the roof had disappeared, the roof that had collapsed under Kevin Cloonan. It was raining and the rain washed down the swollen and blackened timbers and the smell was like a roomful of half-smoked cigars. The way the bathtub perched precariously on the remaining fragment of the fourth floor was etched against the sodden sky had reminded him of the kind of photograph that was usually titled *Metaphor for Western Civilization* in the photography magazines. He detested the cheap easiness of photographs like that—the shoe left on the street after an automobile accident, the pair of rosary beads wrapped around the stock of an infantryman's AR-16. The Cuthbertson to him was a place the world was better rid of . . .

. . . and that's the end of that tune. Try that on a jury and the state could start checking out the wiring in the electric chair.

OLdfield 6-1010.

Another inoculation. An eyeball witness who placed BEAUBOIS, Robert NMI, at the Cuthbertson the afternoon before the fire.

> He just shouted is the reason I remember him. Joe the Polish fellow at the desk said he didn't want no rough trade queers at the old Cuthbert. Young fellow, maybe 17, 18, long hair in a kind of ponytail and glasses. Skinny. No ass on him at all. Would have been like fucking [street jargon for fornication] a pencil.

NAME OF WITNESS: Mrs. Minerva Harper.
RESIDENCE: Cuthbertson Hotel.
Like fucking a pencil.
First things first with Minerva.
Fucking.
[Street jargon for fornication.]
Lee.
With whom was she [street jargon for fornication].

He had watched for the signatures. The look. The unexpected flush. The averted eye. The hand resting a fraction of a second too long on the arm. He had not expected to find the signature at a PTA meeting. The issue was sex education. Our bodies, ourselves. Menstruation and masturbation. The textbook had reduced Cat to uncontrollable giggles. Instructions to masturbate with a peeled cucumber. A cucumber! Oh, Daddy! The mind boggles! Byron Igoe protested. Stood, waving his hand, demanding to be recognized, a concerned father. Finally he was called and when he began to speak, Byron instinctively massaged the back of Lee's neck. Lee who was sitting immediately in front of him, Lee who flushed.

Byron Igoe.

Busted by a peeled cucumber.

Which led to PEEKABOO CAGNEY—DISCREETLY DETERMINING WHAT WAS DONE—WHERE & WITH WHOM.

No.

Do not think.

Concentrate on BEAUBOIS, Robert NMI.

Chemotherapy for a metastasizing memory.

II

Martha Sweeney was nowhere to be seen. So much for the friendly face, Dutch Shea, Jr., thought. From the hallway of the Goldman & Flowers funeral home he could see that the viewing room was almost empty. Only a few of the metal folding chairs set up along the walls and in orderly rows in the center of the room were occupied. Not even Ben Goldman was visible and the Boomer was always on tap for important wakes. Dutch Shea wondered if he could slip in without encountering Tommy Sweeney. Tommy invariably referred to Martha as "the judge" in front of Dutch Shea, Jr. Not out of any pride in her accomplishments, Dutch Shea was sure, but as a warning: hands off, shyster.

Tommy Sweeney detached himself from a knot of firemen in the lounge and approached, switching the rosary beads in his left hand to his right. An excuse not to shake hands, Dutch Shea suspected. As if Tommy could shake hands with a plaster cast anyway.

"I hope God knew what He was doing," Tommy Sweeney said.

Dutch Shea, Jr., nodded. It was as near as he had

ever heard Tommy come to equivocation. The absolute was more Tommy Sweeney's style. And Martha's, too, when it came right down to it. Structured Setting Martha. He supposed the appeal of the structured setting was genetic. "I hope so, too."

"What's that supposed to mean?" Tommy Sweeney said truculently.

"It means I agree with you," Dutch Shea said carefully. Poor Tommy. Always wondering if I'm getting into Martha's pants.

"Oh." Tommy Sweeney mashed the rosary beads in his meaty hands. "It's hard to tell with you sometimes."

"Tell what?" Dutch Shea stared into the viewing room. The casket was closed. There was an American flag draped on top of it, and on top of the flag a fireman's hat. Standing at attention at either end of the coffin were two firemen in blue uniforms and white caps. Dutch Shea tried not to think of carbon granules in the bronchial passages and fat globules in the lung tissue.

"You're always making some kind of smart crack," Tommy Sweeney said.

"I wasn't." He edged toward the viewing room. One of the firemen standing attendance at the casket sneezed, spraying mucus on the flag. Tommy Sweeney glared at him, and then, as if noticing for the first time the scarcity of mourners, said defensively, "There's going to be a big turnout, you can bet on that."

"I'm sure," Dutch Shea, Jr., said.

"It's a bad time to come is all. Everyone's out getting a bite to eat."

Tommy Sweeney's embarrassment touched him. I guess there's a first time for everything, he thought. "The big crowd's usually after dinner."

"That's right," Tommy Sweeney said. "Remember when we used to have wakes in the house?"

Dutch Shea, Jr., nodded.

"Sandwiches and coffee and maybe a nice piece of brisket. Kept the women busy. The men talked. Those were the days all right."

"They were," Dutch Shea, Jr., said. He remembered his father laid out under the oil portrait of Pius XII at D.F.'s house and the voice whispering loudly as the priest saying the rosary intoned the Third Sorrowful Mystery, "Stop stuffing your face with the shrimp, Edso."

"I wanted Kev laid out at our house," Tommy Sweeney said, "but the judge put her foot down. At least at our house there would have been just him. They got two others here. One of them is colored. It doesn't seem right."

Dutch Shea, Jr., nodded again. Race was a subject he was not prepared to discuss with Tommy Sweeney under the best of circumstances.

"We got the big room, though. I think some of their colored are just resting up in here."

"That could be."

"They'll have to go when our crowd comes in."

Another nod. Nodding was always the easiest way to avoid engaging Tommy Sweeney in conversation.

"The judge is freshening up."

"Ah." Always "Ah" or "Mmmm" when Tommy mentioned Martha. Never appear too interested.

"For the governor. She wants to look nice when the governor comes."

Look nice. Wash your hands. Put on your first communion dress. Dutch Shea wondered if Tommy would ever accept the fact that Martha had navigated puberty. No, probably not. Tommy Sweeney still thought puberty a dirty word. He nodded toward the casket. "I think I'll go in."

"Beat the rush," Tommy Sweeney said. "A Hail Mary would be nice."

Dutch Shea, Jr., knelt at the prie-dieu in front of the flag-draped coffin and marveled at the effort it must have been for Tommy Sweeney not to mention BEAUBOIS, Robert NMI. For the judge's sake, he was sure. It was difficult not to think of the fire while praying before the last remains of Kevin Cloonan. Praying. So that was what he was doing. Cold bastard. He would have Marty Cagney check out if there were any fire code violations at the Cuthbertson in the morning. It was not much, but it was a start. Marty Cagney was good at that sort of thing. The impersonal clues in the bureaucratic record seemed to interest him even more than the soiled sheets of infidelity.

Enough of that.

Pray.

Hail Mary, full of grace . . .

He wondered how long he would have to stay at the wake. Probably until the governor came. The poor boy in the casket did not know he had become a campaign stop.

But what the hell am I doing?

. . . the Lord is with thee, blessed art thou . . .

He rose and did not know where to go. Not to the lounge with the firemen, that was for sure. And certainly not here staring at the coffin. It might give me ideas. Goddamnit, Martha, where are you? Maybe Ben Goldman was in his office in the back. For its minuscule retainer, the Association of County Funeral Directors was more trouble than it was worth, but at least its problems were non-felonious. Go back, see the Boomer, pretend he was on the job. Waste not, want not and let's hear it for the ACFD.

He walked down the corridor past the two smaller viewing rooms. As he passed the second, he saw an incredibly aged woman laid out, her tiny wizened face almost lost in the folds of white satin. That face . . .

Oh, God.

Not Annie O'Meara.

He thought his heart would stop. Why hadn't anyone told him?

Make sure.

Take a close look.

He tiptoed into the viewing room as if afraid he would wake the woman in the casket, leaned over the edge and examined the face. White wispy hair barely covered a pink scalp. Just like Annie. The same thin lips. It had been so long since he had seen her at the Arthur K. Degnan Senior Citizen Center. Why do all dead people look alike? Where was the guest book? There. The cover page said, In Memoriam—Elsie McGoorty. His relief was palpable. Sorry, Elsie. I hope God knew what He was doing, but better you than Annie. A fine kettle of fish that would be.

He sat for a moment staring at the body of Elsie McGoorty. What a place for a guilty conscience.

Down the hall he could hear voices on a television set.

"Jaworski's back . . . he looks into the end zone . . . throws . . . touchdown, Carmichael . . . Eagles lead . . ."

The Boomer was in.

He knocked on the door and entered the office. Ben Goldman quickly moved to switch off the television set.

"Caught you," Dutch Shea, Jr., said.

"Son of a bitch," Ben Goldman said. A guilty smile. "I got the points." He pointed to Dutch Shea's cast. "What happened?"

Dutch Shea started to tell the story, but saw that Ben Goldman quickly became bored with it. The Boomer's only real interest in crime was if it produced a victim upon whom he could practice his art. A near-miss was a client lost. "The governor's coming," he interrupted.

"So I hear."

"And the TV boys. I'm going to turn on the sign

161

outside. You get a wide shot, the sign will show up good on the eleven o'clock news."

"You've got to think of things like that," Dutch Shea, Jr., said.

"Right. He gets out of the car, I'm going to be right there."

"'Welcome to Goldman and Flowers, Governor. See what we can do. You won't get such a good look the next time you come through.'"

"It's good business."

"Of course." The walls of the office were decorated with photographs of the Goldman & Flowers handiwork. A United States senator lying in state in the Capitol rotunda. A welterweight contender killed in an automobile crash with a pair of boxing gloves on top of his coffin. A bishop. A mother superior. Why do all dead people look alike, Dutch Shea, Jr., wondered once again. It must be something to do with dust thou art. Here was a new specimen with a particularly grotesque smile on its face. He tapped the photograph. "Who's this one?"

Ben Goldman named a local philanthropist. "A real pain in the ass. The widow wanted his hair dyed when I was all done. Okay, I aim to please, I dyed the hair. Blond. He's seventy-seven years of age, but if she wants blond hair, then blond she gets. Then she wants a smile on his face. I tell her his false teeth don't fit. She insists." He shrugged. "He had beautiful eyes, she says. She wants them open. When's the last time you see one with its eyes open?" Ben Goldman looked furtively at the television set. "I'm telling you, Dutch, what you got to put up with in this business."

Dutch Shea turned the football game back on. The sun was shining in San Diego. ". . . a fifty-five yard field goal . . . Eagles up by ten with fourteen seconds left . . . and now a word from STP . . ."

"Turn it off," Ben Goldman said. "Bastards." He

picked an advertising layout from the clutter. "My Christmas special."

This must be a first, Dutch Shea, Jr., thought. He spread the layout on the desk. There was a spray of roses drawn at the top and then the copy:

AN OFFER TO AREA RESIDENTS

To ease death at this hour

A GIFT FUNERAL

Goldman & Flowers Mortuary & Memorial Park announces through this advertisement an offer to families bereaved during this Christmas season.

A FUNERAL AT NO COST

If death occurs in your family between the hours of noon December 21st and midnight December 31st, call Goldman & Flowers immediately. We will take the entire burden of the funeral off your shoulders—AT NO COST TO YOU.

This city has been good to us, has accepted us, has helped us establish an outstanding place in the business community with a service dedicated to helping families through their hours of grief when life—as it does for all of us—stops inevitably. This is our way of saying thanks.

Sincere. From the Heart. NO STRINGS AT-TACHED. If death strikes, you have but to call for your

GIFT FUNERAL

Remember—a funeral is a way of saying thank you and good-bye.

"What do you think?" Ben Goldman said.

"It's unique, Ben," Dutch Shea, Jr., said carefully. "Even beautiful in its way."

"Merchandising. That's what's missing. People are too goddamned afraid of death, you ask me."

I am. Yes. "You can do an Easter special, too."

"If this one works out, sure."

"Like white sales," Dutch Shea, Jr., said. "Dollar days." Free dishes, Blue Chip stamps, two-for-one discounts. Suicide rates rise, life support systems are unplugged. "But in good taste."

Ben Goldman looked at him closely. "It's okay, then?"

"I'm interested in the phrase 'no strings attached.' You mean the sky's the limit? Teak casket, brass handles, the college choir?"

"You're crazy."

"Then you've got to list the strings."

"Who says?"

"The attorney general. Truth in advertising."

Irritation mottled Ben Goldman's face. "Can't you even say thanks without the goddamn attorney general looking over your shoulder?"

Dutch Shea, Jr., picked up the layout. "What's the maximum you have in mind?"

"A thousand," Ben Goldman said sullenly.

"Tax included?"

"No."

"Honorariums?"

"No."

"Plot?"

"Hell, no."

"Transportation?"

"No."

"Give a twenty-mile limit," Dutch Shea, Jr., suggested.

"Why?"

164

"Because a funeral is a way of saying thank you and good-bye."

Ben Goldman nodded.

"Anybody?"

"They got to live within the goddamn city limits."

"Good idea."

"You mean I got to put all this in the ad?"

"Small print," Dutch Shea, Jr., said. "A footnote. It might be nice to have an asterisk after 'at no cost to you.' An asterisk is always discreet."

"What happens if I don't put it in?"

"Put it in, Ben," Dutch Shea said. "It's the thought that counts."

Ben Goldman sat down heavily. "You notice the attorney general never goes after Teddy Arbatis?" Teddy Arbatis was a cut-rate undertaker and a constant source of annoyance to the ACFD. He was now offering six-dollar cardboard coffins. Three dollars for the container, which he bought from his brother, a box maker, and for another three dollars his wife lined the container with cheap satin and fitted it with a kapok-filled pillow. "You know what he's up to now?"

Dutch Shea, Jr., shook his head.

"A lot of people don't like to go out in a paper coffin, right? Even if it is only six bucks. Makes them look like cheapskates."

"I guess."

"So he rents them a catafalque. Reusable. All nice polished wood, the works. And he sticks the cardboard job inside. Like it's a million-dollar goddamn funeral. Next day he's got the catafalque working again. For some other cheapskate. We got to get an injunction, Dutch."

"It doesn't sound illegal, Ben."

"Why not? He's got the goddamn thing working six days a week. Anything that goes to the cemetery should stay there, you want my opinion."

"It's just a service."

"What about truth in advertising?"

"What about it?"

"You think it makes sense for a guy to fool all his friends into thinking he spent a wad on his mother? When he's only put her in a paper job."

Dutch Shea, Jr., took a deep breath. "Think of it as a kind of year-round special."

"I give a quality funeral," Ben Goldman said. "You got any idea how long cardboard lasts after it gets into the ground? Until they hit the cemetery gate. They're home pushing down the chicken a la king and mom is already saying hello to the worms."

"Maybe it's an idea whose time has come, Ben."

"And that's all you got to say? Goddamnit, Dutch, what are you doing for us anyway?"

Dutch Shea, Jr., edged toward the door. "I'll look into it. Don't forget the asterisk."

The crowd had grown. It spilled out of the viewing room into the corridor, a milling mass speaking in subdued tones. Every chair was filled. The lounge was stacked with overcoats. Each time the front door opened, there was a blast of cold air and the crowd peered to see who had come in. Nuns. Priests. Firemen. Politicians. Dutch Shea wondered how many actually knew Kevin Cloonan. Two weeks before the election the wake was the place to be. Even Elsie McGoorty and the black man in the third viewing room benefited as the overflow took over their chairs. He looked for Martha and heard someone say, "Your Italian types are barbers, the Irish tend to favor the water commission."

Martha nodded discreetly. A warning nod. Stay away. She was standing next to the coffin with Judge Cooney, the presiding justice of the superior court. B. Eustace Cooney. Formerly Brendan E. Cooney until a late marriage with a rich and ambitious wife. The fat fraud would change his name to Cooney Eustace if he could get away with it. Or Eustace Cooley. He had once challenged Eustace Cooney as the trial judge of a murder case in which he was court-appointed defense counsel. With cause. On the grounds that since Judge Cooney had indicated he would run for district attorney at the next election, he had only assigned himself the case because the publicity of a highly visible murder trial would aid his campaign. The accused was a black man who had slain his wife and triplet daughters with a hatchet. Harlow T. Jefferson. The challenge was upheld and Judge Cooney reassigned off the case. And a fat lot of good it did for Harlow T. Jefferson. He still got life. And I made another enemy. This place is crawling with them. Look at Martha now. Monsignor Hawkes had joined her and Judge Cooney. The chancellor of the archdiocese. Dermot Hawkes and Eustace Cooney. That's a two-horse parlay. Monsignor Hawkes had fired him as counsel for the archdiocese the year before.

"Holy Mother the Church must think of its reputation, Mr. Shea," Monsignor Hawkes had said.

"Of course," Dutch Shea, Jr., had replied.

"We have no complaint otherwise about our representation, Mr. Shea."

"I'm glad to hear that, Monsignor."

"The representation you have given us the last—how many years is it?"

"Seven."

"Hmmmm. That long." Monsignor Hawkes had stared into the middle distance. "I hadn't thought that long." He smiled. "Of course that was before my time."

"Of course."

"The fact is, Mr. Shea, your defense of Mr. Mendel . . ."

"Mandel."

". . . is a source of some embarrassment to the archdiocese." That same bleak smile. "So . . ."

"I'm fired."

"That's a rather abrupt way of putting it."

"Then how should I put it?"

Monsignor Hawkes sucked on his lower lip. "We are looking for counsel less associated with the more raffish elements of the community."

"Myron would like that."

"Myron?"

"Mr. Mandel. He's usually called a pimp. Not raffish."

A frozen stare. Monsignor Hawkes had not offered his hand. "I think that takes care of everything, Mr. Shea."

Someone bumped into him and he lost sight of Martha. He found himself in the middle of a conversation. Two men with beads of sweat on their foreheads continued talking as if Dutch Shea, Jr., had been present all along.

"I like the open casket myself, don't you, Leo?"

"The last look, so to speak," Leo said. He mopped his forehead and looked at the door as another mourner entered the funeral home.

"When Moon Walsh passes away, Moon Walsh wants everyone to have a peek. To make sure I didn't go to Philadelphia."

"Moon's a card, isn't he?" Leo said.

"Absolutely," Dutch Shea, Jr., said.

"Georgie Sullivan had a closed casket," Moon Walsh said. "You ever know Georgie? He had the piles."

"Never had the pleasure," Dutch Shea, Jr., said. He was wedged against the wall and could not extricate himself.

"His brother Charlie was the assistant sanitation

commissioner," Leo said. "Charlie had a closed casket, too, Moon."

"It must be some kind of family trait," Moon Walsh said.

"Of course, it's hard to keep it open after a fire, I hear," Leo said. "The testicles is all that's left is what they tell me."

"Is that right?" Moon Walsh said. "I wonder where they put the rosary beads." He looked at Dutch Shea, Jr. "I never seen one laid out didn't have the rosary beads, did you?"

"Come to think of it, no," Dutch Shea said.

"It's not a wake without the beads in the fingers," Leo said. "Of course, if he don't have fingers, that's another story."

"It's a nice point if the testicles is all that's left," Moon Walsh said.

"I don't think they'd put them there, Moon," Leo said. "It would be disrespectful, I think."

Moon Walsh and Leo waited for Dutch Shea's opinion. "I never thought of that," he said. The answer seemed to satisfy them.

"I'd like to ask Monsignor Hawkes about that," Moon Walsh said. "He married my wife's niece. Regina that lost a foot of her small bowel. Diverticulitis." The front door opened again. "Who's that just come in, Leo?"

Leo craned his neck. "Pepper Hurley from the Firemen's Benevolent."

"You knew he'd be here, Pepper," Moon Walsh said, and suddenly he and Leo disappeared toward the door, leaving Dutch Shea, Jr., as if he had never intruded on their conversation. Once again he caught a glimpse of Martha but she was across the room talking to a lawyer in the attorney general's office and there were too many people between them to get to her.

Somewhere he heard Tommy Sweeney say, "I hope God knew what He was doing."

More people pushed into the corridor and he escaped for a moment into the small viewing room where the black man was on display in his casket and he heard someone say, "You hear what Abraham Lincoln said when he woke up after a four-day drunk?"

"What?" someone else said.

"'I freed the who?'"

"Oh, that's rich, Danno. You got to tell that one to Billy Dwyer."

"What do you mean? It was Dwyer told it to me."

"He's heard all the stories, Billy."

"He tells me the firebug took a lie detector test. They got that bastard by the balls."

Thank you, Danno. And you, too, Billy Dwyer. The DA's office had not mentioned a lie detector test.

Not that I ever did when I was in the DA's office.

He moved along the wall, a half-smile on his face, avoiding eye contact. He was at the lounge now, hemmed in by firemen, some in uniform, the rest looking uncomfortable in civilian clothes. A young uniformed fireman was talking expansively.

"So we walked into this little alcove, Hackett and me, and the glass from the window was all black and scattered over the floor, and he says, Hackett, not here. Too much smoke, look at the glass, no way. Okay, so then we walk past the alcove and down the hall and he says, getting closer. Like he's playing pin the tail on the donkey. And then we come into this service area and he says, school's out, this is it, Hackett, you're a genius. The son of a bitch is good and he knows it. There's this sink, what's left of it, I mean, is all clear, not black at all, just melted and crazed, you know what I mean?"

Dutch Shea, Jr., nodded vigorously. Too vigorously. The other firemen smoked and stared, bored, hearing an old story, not willing to acknowledge the genius of Hackett.

The young fireman continued, talking directly to Dutch Shea, Jr., an audience of one, a captive listener.

"That only happens when a fire gets a little goose. From a flammable liquid, so to speak. It gets hot so fast, it means it's had a little help. From a firebug, so to speak . . ."

"Dr. Torch," an older fireman said. The others snickered.

The young fireman faltered, sensing disapproval, as if he had admitted a stranger to the lodge.

"Go on," the older fireman said. It was a rite of passage, a lesson to be learned: finish, but hereafter hold your tongue around civilians.

"He says get a shovel, Hackett," the young fireman said. "Like the reason I'm there is to do his shoveling." He was lowering his opinion of Hackett, trying to win back the approval of his elders. "Shovel here, he says. Shovel there. Big with the orders. And then he brings in a hose and hoses the whole goddamn floor clean and there's this spot, it's all charred and spongy underneath. Here's where it started, he says, it's a dead giveaway. Hell, a rookie would know that." So much for Hackett, Dutch Shea, Jr., thought.

The older fireman tapped a cigarette ash into his palm and then deposited the ash into the cuff of his trousers. "The liquid, whatever it was, gas, kerosene, is what made the floor spongy." He was like a traffic policeman giving a ticket, dutifully explaining a section of the motor vehicle code and how it had been violated. "And charred. A fire spreads up, not out. An accidental fire, only the upper half, the upper two thirds of the room would have burned bad. Badly," he corrected. "If there's kerosene or gas . . ." He shrugged.

"It burns down and out," the young fireman said. "You know this Hackett?"

Dutch Shea, Jr., detected the hint of truculence. "I'd like to meet him," he said. An attendant carrying a large and ugly floral display pressed past him, and he used the display as cover to ease out of the lounge. He had not really noticed the flowers before. Banks of them. Sprays and wreaths. Wrapped in purple satin lettered in gold. Pax. Hook & Ladder Company 41. The legion of Mary at St. Dominick's R.C. Church. From Your Friends in the Police Department. American Legion Post No. 1 (William C. Westmoreland Post). The Blessed Martin Society St. Martin of Tours R.C. Church. Pax again. The Firemen's Benevolent Association. B.P.O.E. Lodge No. 9. Dutch Shea, Jr., studied each purple sash. Reading the lettering was a way not to talk.

"You know Frankie Trantino?" A short fat woman dressed in black. She spoke out of the side of her mouth as if she were passing a secret.

"No," Dutch Shea said.

"Kev's best friend in the department." The woman picked a blossom from a spray. "He's going to sing at the funeral."

"That's nice."

" 'Because.' "

"Because what?"

"That's what he wants to sing, Frankie. 'Because.' Father McIntyre over to St. Justin's wants him to sing 'Lovely Lady, Dressed in Blue.' 'Because' was Kev's favorite, though. Not 'Lovely Lady.' "

Dutch Shea searched for an escape route.

"He sings out at the Red Coach weekends. Frankie Trent."

Dutch Shea wondered if he had missed a connection. "Frankie who?"

"Trent. That's Frankie's singing name. Frankie Trantino. When he's out at the Red Coach. On Ninety-one. The Bloomfield exit. Frankie Trantino is Frankie Trent

172

weekends. He ends up every show with 'Because.' Don't tell the Fire Department, though."

"That he ends every show with 'Because'?"

"No. That he's Frankie Trent."

"I won't," Dutch Shea, Jr., said.

"They've had a lot of trouble at the Red Coach." The woman still had not looked him in the eye. "Fire code violations."

Dutch Shea, Jr., wondered how the woman had such a fund of information about the Red Coach and Frankie (Trent) Trantino, but not enough to ask.

"When it was burned down that time, they say Arnie Doyle did it for the insurance."

"I never heard that."

"That's why Frankie's Frankie Trent at the Red Coach."

"I can see why."

"Kev really loved the way he did 'Because,' Frankie." The fat woman began to sing softly, looking at the flowers, not moving her lips. "'Because God made you mine, I cherish thee.'" She hummed a few more bars. "It's a wedding song. That's the reason Father McIntyre wants 'Lovely Lady.' He thinks it's more appropriate for a funeral. Even though it was Kev's favorite, 'Because.' What do you think?"

"I'd go for 'Because,'" Dutch Shea said desperately. Frankie Trent. Arnie Doyle. He wondered if he were the only person in the funeral home not to have heard of these mythic figures. Georgie Sullivan who had the piles. His brother Charlie in the Sanitation Department. Billy Dwyer and Pepper Hurley and Moon Walsh. Martha was shouldering her way through the crowd. Thank God. "Look, there's Judge Sweeney. Would you excuse me?"

Martha shook his hand coolly. "How are you, Jack? I'm glad you could come." Impersonal and automatic, as if he were another body to shuffle through the receiving line. Under her breath she said, "You look blitzed."

"Thank you, Judge. I hope God knew what He was doing." She looked at him sharply and then her face softened almost imperceptibly. Quietly he added, "I'd also like to fuck your socks off."

"That's so nice of you to say, Mr. Shea. I really do appreciate it."

She still held his hand. He took her by the arm. The mourner's stance. People gave them room. "I'm glad you do, Your Honor. Perhaps later."

"I'd have to see about that, Mr. Shea." She was wearing black. High neck and long sleeves. Her hair was pulled back tight behind her head. He remembered she had told him once that she had an obscene caller. Her courtroom was one of the few with a telephone on the bench and she was regularly interrupted, no matter how often she had the number changed. The calls were always at the most inopportune time. In the middle of a hearing. While giving instructions to a jury. The caller whispered what he would like to do between her legs. What he would put in her mouth. How he would lubricate her for buggery. She never reacted lest it affect the proceedings. "I think it can be arranged."

"You once told me about a caller, Your Honor. While you were on the bench."

"It's an apt analogy, Mr. Shea." Martha nodded so brusquely at a man trying to get her attention that he peeled out of her sight line.

"One should never lose one's control."

"One shouldn't," Martha said. She was looking over his shoulder. "Ever."

He caught the note of caution and turned around. Dermot Hawkes and Eustace Cooney seemed to hesitate when they saw it was he Martha was talking to.

"I didn't expect to see you here," Eustace Cooney said. Plump and florid, a white silk handkerchief flow-ing out of the breast pocket of his blue double-breasted blazer.

"Why is that, Eustace?" Dutch Shea, Jr., said pleasantly.

"Under the circumstances," Eustace Cooney said.

"You sound like you're running for office again, Eustace. You could have been a winner last time." He held up his hand and pretended to read from an imaginary campaign poster. "Vote for Eustace Cooney —The Judge Who Gave Harlow T. Jefferson a Fair Trial."

Eustace Cooney flushed.

"Not much appeal for the law and order crowd," Dutch Shea, Jr., said. "But a winner with that innocent until proven guilty bunch. Your support's always been a little soft there."

Eustace Cooney turned away abruptly. Dutch Shea, Jr., ignored Martha's signals and smiled broadly at Dermot Hawkes. "It's been a long time, Monsignor."

Dermot Hawkes made no effort to shake hands. "Yes." He was well-fed and distant. "How are you, Shea?"

Oh, Shea was it? If that's the way he wants to play it, it's okay by me. Can't make Martha any madder than she is already. "Fine, thank you." Another smile. "You've gained weight." And a third. "Dermot."

Monsignor Hawkes ignored him and shifted his body so that he stood between Dutch Shea and Martha. "I think I'd like to begin the rosary in a few moments. I am told the governor won't be here until after the rosary."

"Of course," Martha said.

The noise level in the corridor was rising. "I saw you on television the other night," Dutch Shea, Jr., said.

"You did," Monsignor Hawkes said. He was trying to move away. The smile on his face excluded Dutch Shea, Jr.

175

"You mentioned the bishop is thinking of using seminarians to break the gravediggers' strike."

"I mentioned the possibility. I don't think I mentioned strikebreaking. That would be your interpretation."

Dutch Shea, Jr., noticed Dermot Hawkes's smooth dark jowl and caught the fragrance of sandalwood. "Perhaps I was being raffish."

"Perhaps you don't think this poor boy deserves the dignity of a final resting place."

"Perhaps I was thinking of the gravediggers," Dutch Shea said. He smiled at Martha. She was tense, watchful, ready to intercede if civility was further strained. "They're a tough bunch."

"You represent them, then?"

"No."

"Then I don't think there's much to talk about, is there?" A dismissive glance. And then a nod at someone behind Dutch Shea, Jr. It was like the snapping shut of the confessional window. For your penance, say . . .

Dutch Shea stood his ground. "You bring in the seminarians, you'll get ninety seconds on the evening news and half a grave dug. Then the cameras will disappear and the gravediggers will stay out all winter. All the bishop will have to show for it is a couple of calluses when someone hands him a shovel on camera. Unless of course he hands the shovel over to you."

A warning look from Martha.

Dermot Hawkes stared. His fleshy jowl shook slightly. "I appreciate your astute analysis."

"It's on the house."

"Yes." Monsignor Hawkes turned his back and leaned close to Martha. "I'm going to say the rosary now, Judge Sweeney." He took her by the elbow and steered her away. "If we could move people into the other room."

Dutch Shea, Jr., remained in place alone, as the mourners slowly pushed past him into the main viewing room. There was the low buzz of a crowd trying to keep quiet and then he could hear Monsignor Hawkes's carefully modulated voice. "In the name of the Father and of the Son . . ." He knew Martha was furious with him. He was like a loose cannon. Dermot Hawkes and Eustace Cooney. Both targets of opportunity. Oh, Christ. Now he would have to be repentant with Martha. Suddenly he wanted her terribly and he could feel himself starting a hard-on.

". . . and blessed is the fruit of thy womb, Jesus."

Sweet Jesus. What a place to get a hard-on. He put his hands in his pockets. Did it show? Mash it down. He looked furtively around and saw Barry Stukin winking at him. Good God. Why was he here? Ah. The governor, of course. That did it. He was limp again. Sorry about that, Martha. Where was Barry Stukin now? There he was, trying to follow the rosary responses. Now he glided along the rear wall of the viewing room, smiling, excusing himself, squeezing an occasional elbow. Then he was at Dutch Shea's side.

"I think they call this the cigarette break," Barry Stukin whispered into Dutch Shea's ear.

The air on the veranda of the funeral home was crisp and cold. By the front walk, Ben Goldman's neon sign glowed in purple: GOLDMAN & FLOWERS MORTUARY. And in smaller letters, Peace of Mind Guaranteed. Dutch Shea, Jr., wondered if the Boomer was going to add, "Holiday Specials."

Barry Stukin lit a joint. "The one legacy of my radical past."

"I think you could probably get yourself off," Dutch Shea, Jr., said. "You had enough practice. When you were poor and happy."

"Happy but poor," Barry Stukin corrected.

177

"I hear your shoes cost two fifty."

Barry Stukin regarded a well-shod foot. "Long lasting." He took a hit and offered the joint to Dutch Shea, who shook his head. "Why you here? Martha?"

It did not surprise Dutch Shea, Jr., that Barry Stukin knew about him and Martha. Barry made it his business to know what was going on. Information was a card to play. A way to cause a second thought, a moment's hesitation, a suspicion that there might be other aces up his sleeve. A window was open down the veranda and he could pick up Monsignor Hawkes's solemn tone. "The Second Sorrowful Mystery. The Scourging. Our Father, who art in heaven . . ."

Dutch Shea, Jr., said, "What about you? Don't tell me. You want to see the governor. About decriminalizing grass."

Barry Stukin smiled, took a last toke and field-stripped the joint. "Eustace Cooney wants to move up to the appellate bench. I said I'd help out."

"Swell."

"I saw you two talking. Eustace looked as if he'd swallowed a tainted oyster."

"I told him his campaign slogan last time should have been 'Vote for Eustace Cooney—The Judge Who Gave Harlow T. Jefferson a Fair Trial.' "

Barry Stukin shook his head slowly. "Give it a rest, Jack. So you got him reassigned. You got a new judge and Harlow T. still got life. So there you are."

"So there I am. The story of my life." Dutch Shea, Jr., shrugged. "What do you get out of helping Eustace onto the appellate bench?"

"It never hurts to do someone a favor, Jack."

"I think that's called quid pro quo, Barry."

"So there you are. It's nice to have friends, Jack."

"I'll try to remember that."

Inside the rosary droned on.

". . . pray for us sinners now and at the hour of our death."

"Amen."

"Glory be to the Father and to the Son and to . . ."

Barry Stukin stood by the window and listened. "World without end, amen. Hey, I like that. I really do. That's a concept I can get behind." His breath was frosted. "You keep up with this mumbo-jumbo, Jack?"

"It passes the time."

"In other words, you're hedging your bet."

Dutch Shea, Jr., smiled. "You remember Larry Shugrue?" Larry Shugrue was formerly chief county marshal. "I was having coffee with him the morning he died. He always had clam chowder during coffee breaks. Clam chowder and oyster crackers."

"I remember."

"He was telling me that morning about the world's laziest colored man. He always said 'colored,' Larry. You couldn't get him to say 'black.' 'Colored is what they are and colored is what I'm going to call them,' he'd say. Anyway, the world's laziest colored man was fucking a horse. Except he was so lazy he wouldn't get on with it. He just backed the horse up against him and said 'Giddap. Whoa, back.' And he slurps up a spoonful of soup and says, 'May God strike me dead for telling that one, Dutch.' And with that he keels over into the clam chowder. I thought he drowned. Myocardial infarction, the medical examiner says."

Barry Stukin contemplated Dutch Shea, Jr. "I never heard that one before. True story?"

Dutch Shea, Jr., shook his head. "No. But it heads off a lot of conversation about God. People hear it and they say, 'Wow.' Or 'Gee.' Or 'I'll be damned.' And then they tell a few jokes."

"So you are covering your bet. In case there's something to it."

"Wow. Gee. I'll be damned."

"No trespassing," Barry Stukin said. "Keep off the grass."

Dutch Shea, Jr., shrugged.

Barry Stukin wiped his tinted glasses with a silk handkerchief and tried another subject. "I'm handling Carmine Cantalupo now."

"I know."

"He likes you, Carmine."

So much he doesn't take my five-dollar bill in the collection plate. "I don't think I've ever said two words to him."

"He said you did him a favor once."

Dutch Shea, Jr., wondered when the subject had come up. And why. He could not think of any two people he less wanted to investigate his life. "Not really. I talked a little sense to someone once."

"He appreciates it."

And was in a position to show his appreciation. He suspected that was the message Barry Stukin was trying to convey. What does he know that he shouldn't know? He felt like a secret agent who was beginning to lose his nerve, tired of examining every word for its coded undertone. The front door opened and he could hear Monsignor Hawkes. "The Fifth Sorrowful Mystery. The Crucifixion and Death. Our Father . . ." The door closed and the voice faded.

"You worked out a deal yet?" Barry Stukin said.

Dutch Shea shook his head.

"Cop him, Jack. Plead him guilty. Even with the full pop, he'll be out in twelve years. Thirty-two years old and his asshole stretched."

"Whatever happened to innocent until proven guilty?" Dutch Shea, Jr., said. He felt sententious.

"Shit, you lost that illusion before you took the bar exam," Barry Stukin said. "The system is lubricated by

180

a presumption of guilt. They got a confession on your kid. And a polygraph test."

"You know an awful lot."

"I know you should plead him. What have you got against plea bargaining all of a sudden? It's the Drano that keeps the system unclogged."

"Remind me to write that down, Barry. I don't want to forget it."

Barry Stukin could not be deflected. "Tell it to your night school class," he said. "Hell, it's the most important thing they'll learn. Delay. Stall. Continue. Hope to Christ a witness has an automobile accident. A stroke. Moves to Tucson. Then it's time to deal, my friend, close the file, you scratch my back, I'll scratch yours."

Dutch Shea, Jr., knew that Barry Stukin was right. The accused were like markers on a board; the game was to measure the worth of felony against felony. Yet it was something he did not care to admit out loud. "You don't play the game, you play the players," he said sarcastically.

"It's something to consider," Barry Stukin said quietly. He ran a thumb and forefinger down each side of his trim beard. "When the DA's holding a confession and a polygraph test."

They stared at each other in the darkness. Dutch Shea, Jr., had an absolute sense that somewhere beneath the layers of cynicism Barry Stukin was trying to warn him. It was as close as Barry could ever come to acknowledging friendship.

"In case I need a friend."

"You can't have too many." Down the street two cars skidded around the corner and headed toward the funeral home. "Cop him, Jack. The only cases that go to trial are the unimportant crimes of important people."

181

The cars pulled to a stop and people piled out. Sound men, cameramen and reporters from two different television channels. The governor must be on his way. A blond woman reporter and a glowering male reporter in a yellow blazer with the channel number stitched to the breast pocket. A can of Alberto VO5 hair spray was produced and the two reporters passed it between them. Friendly competitors, Dutch Shea, Jr., thought. He heard the growl of more engines and then three motorcycle policemen turned into the street and behind them came a limousine. The woman reporter tossed the can of hair spray into the front seat of her radio car. Minicam lights flooded the sidewalk.

"What about the important crimes of unimportant people?" Dutch Shea, Jr., said.

"They can't pay you," Barry Stukin said.

III

Now: his hair was mussed in the gusty night wind and thinner than it looked mornings in the shaving mirror. Mistake No. 1: he should have asked Laurel if he could use her hair spray. He had seen the can through the car window. Alberto VO5. Funny what you remembered. Question: why were all women television newscasters named Laurel? Or Heather? Heidi was another favorite. The male reporter in the yellow blazer was Sid. Oh, oh. A career mistake there. Paul would have been more soothing. He was Mr. Shea. The governor was Governor. How did my tie get way over there? The knot looked as if it were trying to hide under the collar. Look at the camera. The governor looked at the camera. Laurel and Sid looked at the camera. Christ, where was I looking? Furtive was the word that came to mind. Cornered wasn't bad either. Sid said, "Now let me get this straight, Mr. Shea . . ." Fuck you, Sid. He switched channels. Laurel was staring directly at him. Laurel didn't blink. The wind did not muss a single blond hair. Laurel said, ". . . confrontation between prominent local attorney John Dutch Shea . . ." She made it sound hyphenated, like David Ormsby-Gore.

Oh, shit.

Martha would not look at the television set. She lay on the bed staring at the ceiling. She was naked. He tried not to look at her bush. Prettier than Laurel's, he was sure. He wondered if Laurel put Alberto VO5 on hers. He remembered the song that Hugh Campion used to sing. With a crucial ad lib in the lyrics. "Your eyes, your lips, your pubic hair / Are in a class beyond compare . . . They wouldn't believe me / They wouldn't believe me . . ."

Before he became Father Hugh, of course.

Hugh, you'd get a laugh out of this.

"Oh, shit." This from Martha. Very uncharacteristic of Judge Sweeney. Judge Sweeney did not indulge in profanity or scatology. Except in the throes of rapture. In the throes of rapture Judge Sweeney used the basic Anglo-Saxonisms. Nowhere else.

"Oh, shit," Martha repeated. A comment in itself.

This was how it had started.

The governor stepped from his limousine into the minicam floodlights.

Tommy Sweeney elbowed next to him and said, "I hope God knew what He was doing."

Eustace Cooney shook the governor's hand. As did Barry Stukin.

Ben Goldman maneuvered the governor and the camera crews in front of his neon sign: GOLDMAN & FLOWERS MORTUARY. Peace of Mind Guaranteed.

The governor said it was a sad occasion.

Sid put a microphone in the governor's face and asked if his campaign needed this kind of stop.

The governor said, "Sid, tragedy knows no politics."

Laurel put a microphone in the governor's face and asked if he planned to attend the wake or funeral of any other fire victims.

The governor said, "Laurel, I mourn for all the

victims of this tragic act. I mourn as the governor of this state. I mourn as a private citizen."

Monsignor Hawkes shook the governor's hand.

The governor said, "Stand here, Dermot, next to me."

A tight shot of the governor. The cold had reddened his cheeks.

Eustace Cooney leaned into the picture.

Laurel and Sid both said, "Governor . . ."

The governor said, "As a private citizen I hope justice will be done. As governor of this state, I will do everything in my power to insure that justice is done. Tomorrow morning I will instruct . . ." He switched to Channel 3.

"All steps necessary . . ." Back to Channel 18.

". . . to bring this man . . ." Channel 3 again.

". . . a man guilty . . ."

". . . of eighteen ghastly murders . . ."

". . . deed must be . . ."

". . . punished . . ."

". . . and justice done . . ."

Sid said, "Governor . . ."

The governor said, "I think you misunderstood, Sid . . ."

Laurel said:

The governor said, ". . . 'alleged' is implicit, Miss Henderson . . ."

". . . of course . . ."

". . . he should be . . ."

". . . presumed . . ."

". . . I really would like . . ."

". . . please, boys . . ."

". . . to say a prayer . . ."

". . . at the casket . . ."

". . . a little room . . ."

". . . please, boys, please . . ."

". . . Sid . . ."

". . . Laurel . . ."

". . . too much concern . . ."

". . . for the . . ."

". . . criminal . . ."

". . . glamour . . ."

". . . ous fig . . ."

". . . ure . . ."

". . . give the governor room . . ."

". . . and not enough . . ."

". . . for his vic . . ."

". . . tims . . ."

". . . please . . ."

". . . boys . . ."

A disembodied voice on the sound track. "I hope God knows what He's doing."

A mass of people pushing toward the veranda steps. The neon in Peace of Mind Guaranteed began to fizzle. In the glare of the camera lights the Victorian funeral home with its turrets and cupolas looked like a gingerbread haunted house. The governor bobbed and weaved amidst the crowd and seemed trying to resist the impulse to raise his hands over his head in a victory salute.

"Who?" That was Sid into an open mike.

". . . Mr. . . ."

". . . Beaubois's attor . . ."

". . . lawy . . ."

". . . John . . ."

". . . Dutch . . ."

". . . Shea . . ."

Look at the goddamn camera. For the record, describe yourself, what animal do you remind yourself of? Not a lion. Nor a tiger. An eagle, nay. Ferret. Weasel. I look like something out of *Bleak House*. Not entirely trustworthy.

The camera never lies.

Never!

A grim goddamn thought.

Sid pressed close.

Laurel stepped on Sid's mike cord and elbowed closer. So much for friendly competition, the sharing of a can of Alberto VO5.

"Why are you . . . Considering . . . here . . . Isn't it odd . . . After all . . . Beaubois . . . your client . . . Cloonan . . . wake of . . . accused of . . . alleged . . ."

He did not call Laurel Laurel or Sid Sid. The governor looked, whispered, discovered who had usurped his air time, his Laurel, his Sid.

Dutch Shea, Jr., said.

Heard himself saying.

Watched himself saying.

"I'm glad you used the word 'alleged.' Unlike the governor who . . ."

". . . do you mean . . ."

". . . are you accusing . . ." Hard little number, Laurel. Tight lips. Unsuccessful orthodontry. Keep the lips tight and the bad bite doesn't show. Good reporters have bad bites. Hence tight-lipped.

"I am only saying . . ."

". . . you are only . . ."

". . . only saying what . . ."

". . . that the governor is a lawyer. Which presumes he went to law school . . ."

". . . are you implying . . ."

". . . degree . . ."

". . . inferring . . ." Sid did not know the difference between infer and imply.

". . . . ."

". . . we have a concept in our legal system of innocent until proven guilty. The system is lubricated by that . . ."

Barry Stukin was cut into the picture. Barry Stukin seemed to be mouthing, "Oh, no."

". . . presumption of innocence . . ."

". . . Mr. . . ."

". . . Dutch . . ."

"Perhaps the governor slept through that class. He might have had a date that day. He might . . ."

A litany of mights.

"Who the . . ."

Fuck was bleeped out. One of the governor's aides.

". . . is this guy . . ."

"Mr. Dutch John Shea are you Yale implying Law slept through magna cum School Review laude inferring." Sid again. Dear Sid stop Infer does not mean imply stop Fools give you reasons wise men never try stop Cordially stop. ". . . I mean who the . . ."

Bleep.

A montage:

Hackett's friend being restrained.

Tommy Sweeney interrupted in mid-"I hope God knew what . . ."

Ben Goldman working on his neon sign which now read, "P ace o M nd ranteed."

Tommy Sweeney shouting, ". . . defending that guilty . . ."

Son of a bitch was bleeped out.

Sid: "Fire Captain Thom . . ."

Laurel: "Much decorated veteran Th . . ."

Here it comes:

". . . there are no guilty people . . ."

". . . people like you should be . . ." Hackett's friend.

". . . until the courts find them guilty . . ."

". . . you never defend . . ."

". . . never they are innocent until . . ."

". . . are you implying . . ."

". . . you inferring . . ." SIDSIDSID.

". . . that there are no guilty people . . ."

". . . yes, that is exactly what I am inferring . . . implying . . ." Okay, Sid, you win. The weasel was still not looking at the camera. Nor the ferret. Two microphones stuck in his face like licorice ice-cream cones. You're going to say it, aren't you?

"I am not prepared to discuss the intricacies of the law with you assholes."

So there.

Laurel's channel edited "assholes," held on "you" and then cut to a full face of "This is Laurel Henderson reporting direct from . . ."

Sid's channel bleeped out the whole phrase "with you assholes" and cut to Barry Stukin who put his hand in front of his face.

Said Sid: "Now let me get this straight, Mr. Shea . . ."

Said Laurel: ". . . confrontation between prominent local attorney John Dutch Shea . . ."

Said Martha: "Oh, shit."

He knelt on the threadbare rug and fitted her legs over his shoulders.

"No."

"Yes."

He foraged. Wondered how many lawyers had ever gone down on a judge. Thinking the thought was a kind of abasement in itself. Getting even for being a cuckold. What is a cuckold? A cuckold is a man who knows the difference between infer and imply.

Grazed.

Imagine: imagine being cuckolded by Byron Igoe. Byron Igoe with a piece of green vegetable stuck in his braces. Byron who said, "I'm sorry for your trouble." That year's version of "I hope God knew what He was doing."

Said he: "Why?"

Said Lee: "It rained for a week. I had a flat tire on the Merritt Parkway. An old man stopped and changed it for me in the rain."

"Why?" This was later. A day, maybe a week. The debriefing melded together into one conversation. She was a willing witness, volunteering nothing but never failing to answer. Bored. Tired.

"The sink backed up. I went on a diet and lost five pounds. I felt sad. I ordered you ten pairs of white cotton boxer shorts from Brooks Brothers."

He did not say he didn't want ten pairs of white cotton boxer shorts. He said, "Why?"

"I had a mole burned off my back. It was benign, remember? I found a tube of Ortho-Gynol in Cat's medicine cabinet. We went to that dinner at the Club. The man at the next table choked on a piece of steak and he coughed it up when you used the Heimlich Method on him and then he finished his dinner and ordered a second piece of pecan pie and sent us each over a brandy. Christian Brothers."

Ortho-Gynol. The Heimlich Method. Christian Brothers. Lee always had the gift of specificity. "Why?"

"We had an argument on the way home and then we watched Dick Cavett in bed. Aretha Franklin sang 'ABC' with the Jackson Five and then we balled and the other guest was that man who talks to dolphins."

Whose name she had not caught. Because they were balling. Specificity was a victim of balling. He had never heard her say "balled" before. He wondered if it were the Byron influence. "Why?"

"Why does anyone?" An answer more than a question, a verbal shrug.

"Why?"

"Because they want to stop time. Because they want to find time. Because someday they're going to realize they haven't stopped time and they haven't found time, all they've done is waste time."

An answer over several sessions.

"Oh, God," Martha said.

Which was better than "Oh, shit."

Further thoughts during cunnilingus. Does one "do" cunnilingus? Or does one "commit" it?

One "commits" a sin.

Scratch "commits."

" 'A bad agreement is better than a good lawyer.' Italian Proverb." Cat had embroidered that on a sampler for him one Christmas. Nervy little miss. Lee thought it was hostile. But Lee had gone to the ladies' room. That was hostile. There was another sampler, more embroidery, every Christmas, every birthday. She must have ransacked *Bartlett's* and *Mencken's*. " 'A lawyer and a wagon wheel must be well-greased.' German Proverb." " 'No lawyer will ever go to Heaven as long as there is room for more in Hell.' French Proverb." " ' "Virtue in the middle," said the Devil as he sat between two lawyers.' Danish Proverb." " 'I am a lawyer so I can never get away from evil.' Kafka."

Right on, Franz.

That was the last sampler. Hard to embroider when your head is in a cut-glass bowl of sorbet in a restaurant on Charlotte Street.

"Oh, God."

Fact: Martha is here. Indubitably.

Nonfact: not home. Not with Tommy. Here. With him.

Me.

Why? Because of this indubitable act? Hardly. Because a choice had been made. A commitment. In an hour of need. To him.

Me.

191

One commits a sin.

"Oh, God."

"Oh, shit."

He remembered.

"I could have you up before the board of ethics on this," Judge Sweeney had said. This was the second Monday of the Gentle Davidson trial.

"I realize that, Your Honor. That's why I'm here. Why I requested to see you in chambers."

"You met this juror . . ."

"Juror number twelve, Your Honor. Mrs. Foxx."

"With two x's."

"Yes, Your Honor."

"And of course you told her . . ."

". . . that I would have to leave this engagement and report our meeting to Your Honor when court convened this morning."

"So far, so good, Mr. Shea."

"Thank you, Your Honor."

"Except for the nature of the social engagement."

"A rather loose interpretation of that phrase, Your Honor."

"I'm surprised at you, Mr. Shea."

"Yes, Your Honor."

"Do you do this sort of thing often?"

"That was the first time, Your Honor."

"You're not under oath, Mr. Shea."

"It was the first time, Your Honor."

"Of course . . ."

"It was the first time, Your Honor." Insistently. He had heard about Structured Setting Martha. The Fireman's Daughter. Don't let her push you around.

An icy smile. Not even a smile, really. A movement of the lips. "This juror . . ."

"Number twelve . . ."

"Miss Foxx . . ."

"Mrs. Foxx, I think, Your Honor . . ."

"She was one of the guests . . ."

"Not exactly a guest, Your Honor. One paid a fee to attend this social engagement . . ."

"How much was the fee, Mr. Shea?"

"Twenty-five dollars a couple . . ."

"A couple . . ."

"Yes, Your Honor."

"And were you part of a couple?"

"No, Your Honor."

"Why was that, Mr. Shea?"

"I knew the host, Your Honor."

"You have charming friends, Mr. Shea."

"He was a client of mine, Your Honor."

"You are in no position to raise your voice, Mr. Shea."

"I'm sorry, Your Honor."

"I hope this service was not part of his fee."

"No, Your Honor."

"Then how did you happen to attend this social engagement?"

"Well, since my divorce, my client . . ."

"Has been looking out for your welfare . . ."

"Goddamnit . . ."

"Don't take that tone of voice with me, Mr. Shea."

"I'm sorry, Your Honor."

"Proceed, Mr. Shea."

"Look, Your Honor. I had never attended one of these evenings. I was bored, I shouldn't have gone, I was wrong. I'm divorced, I'm going through male menopause, you name it, I can give you every excuse, what it still boils down to is that I behaved like a horse's ass, like a kid jerking off, and I'm sorry if my language offends you, but you don't have to tell me what a fool I made of myself."

"I suppose your being here, Mr. Shea, is a mitigating circumstance."

"If it's not, Your Honor, I could be disbarred."

"The courts have said this is not a criminal activity, Mr. Shea."

"I don't think I could run for United States senator with it on my record, though."

"Are you planning to run for the Senate, Mr. Shea?"

"No, Your Honor."

"This woman. Mrs. Foxx. You did not know she was attending this social engagement."

"That is correct, Your Honor."

"Until she began fellating you?"

"Yes, Your Honor."

"I would have thought you might have noticed, Mr. Shea."

"One tends to be very busy at this kind of social engagement, Your Honor."

"With other couples?"

"Yes, Your Honor."

"And when you looked down, when you were not quite so busy, you saw juror number twelve?"

"Yes, Your Honor."

"And what did juror number twelve say when she was aware who you were?"

"'Oh, oh.'"

"'Oh, oh?'"

"Yes, Your Honor. I said perhaps we should talk."

"And there was high hilarity from the rest of the couples, Mr. Shea?"

"Your Honor, this is very difficult . . ."

"One unfortunately hears a great deal about fellatio in a courtroom, Mr. Shea. I once prosecuted a case when the verdict turned on whether the defendant of aggravated assault against a prostitute was or was not circumcised."

"I see, Your Honor."

"So you had this talk with Mrs. Foxx . . ."

"Yes, Your Honor."

"And she knows you are here."

"She knew I was going to see you in chambers, Your Honor."

"I suppose I should see Mrs. Foxx."

"Yes, Your Honor."

"Mr. Shea, I will dismiss Mrs. Foxx as a juror. I will use the loosest possible interpretation of social engagement. I would not like to see her reputation tarnished. And I will accept her word and your word that the meeting was unplanned and accidental except insofar as it conformed to the geometry of the social engagement."

"Thank you, Your Honor."

"As for you, Mr. Shea, I will not bring you before the board of ethics."

"Thank you, Your Honor."

"I do not wish your thanks, Mr. Shea."

"Oh, God."

The television set glowed. No sound. Only a satellite station program guide on the cable network. Channel B. *Romper Room. Straight Talk. Let's Make a Deal.* It occurred to him suddenly that the TV set he always kept on was like a child's night-light. He was afraid of the dark. Sleep brought dreams.

Bad dreams.

Cat's night-light was shaped like the man in the moon. My moon lamp, she called it. When she was older, she got a Goosey Gander. A large electrified goose.

Goosey Gander.

He could not call Lee. House rule. Lee was never called the same night Martha was on the premises. Even after Martha had vacated said premises.

D. F. Campion's .38 was still in the drawer in the bedside table. In its Milwaukee Legster. Have to get rid of that. He remembered shooting a handgun on the Police Department range when he was in the district attorney's office. The objective, the instructor said, is not to shoot the target in the head. That, the instructor said, assumes that all parts of the head are equal. All parts of the head, the instructor said, are not equal. The objective, the instructor said, is to cut the medulla oblongata. The medulla oblongata, the instructor said, is the widening of the spinal cord at the base of the spine. In order of preference, the instructor said, the targets are one, into the open mouth toward the center of the skull; two, straight into the rear of the head where the skull meets the spine; three, one-half inch to the rear and one inch down from the ear opening; and four, below the ridge between the eyes at a downward angle.

The instructor said.

Cut the motor nerves in the pelvic girdle and he'll go down.

The instructor said.

The objective is a no-reflex kill.

The instructor said.

He picked through the pieces of paper on the floor of the living room. Names, court dates, memoranda, telephone numbers. Bail bondsmen, fire marshals, health inspectors, social workers, probation officers. Measure the worth of felon against felony. Not bad. Bureaucrat against bureaucracy. Building & Safety Department. Animal Regulation Department. Sewer & Storm Drain Maintenance Bureau. Whose child fell into a storm drain and drowned?

He could not remember.

Méndez. López. Gómez. Vásquez. Jiménez. Benítez. One of those.

He picked up a letter almost hidden under a stack of recent appellate decisions. It read: Unified School

District Et Cetera & So Forth; Mrs. Andrew Wolferman Et Cetera & So Forth.

Dear Mrs. Wolferman,

We are sorry to hear of the early death of your husband, Andrew Wolferman, August 27th. Please accept our sincerest sympathy. Mr. Wolferman was a model teacher in this school district for 29 years.

We regret to inform you, however, that an audit of his salary payment record reveals that he was overpaid a net amount of $57.69.

This overpayment occurred when he was paid 8 hours service for teaching at the West Middle School on August 28, the day after his death.

The result is a gross overpayment of $102.70. Adjustment for withholding tax and retirement deductions in the amount of $45.01 leaves a net overpayment of $57.69.

Please send me your remittance in the amount of $57.69 immediately so that we may clear this overpayment from your husband's record.

Retention of salary overpayment to which you are not entitled constitutes an illegal act.

Yours truly,

Fred Becker
Deputy Director of Payroll Administration

cc: Overpayment Control #033040
STRA Unit
PERS Unit
Acctg. Sect.— Accts. Rec. 1-0731-1-1020-5342

Ooops. Meant to do something about this.

Not right now.

He put the letter underneath the pile of appellate decisions.

Later.

Crabs are notorious for feeding on dead human remains. A fact he had picked up along the way. In the practice of criminal law.

Next to bone, skin is the most resistant tissue in the body. Another fact he had picked up along the way. In the practice of criminal law.

Carbon granules.

Fat globules.

You use your practice to keep a shield between you and the world, Martha had said before she left. Like a condom.

Like a condom. Judge Sweeney had a gift for turning a phrase.

The law is your prophylactic.

Nicely put, Martha.

You're a conscientious objector to your own life. Another eloquent opinion from Judge Sweeney.

A conchie.

A CO.

Not bad. Postcoital tristesse a la Judge Sweeney.

He lay on the bed. There were two of Martha's hairs on the pillow. A daub of lipstick. A hint of perfume. He looked at the program guide on the silent television screen.

Let's Make a Deal.

All things considered, not a bad idea.

I am my father's son, Dutch Shea, Jr., thought.

I am an embezzler.

BOOK THREE

Inadmissible Evidence,
Sustained Objections,
Structured Settings,
Random Thoughts et cetera
Remembered the Instant Before Death

1. BEAUBOIS, Robert NMI. Why does he remind me of IGOE, Byron III? Little By. Son of Big By. Who humped my wife. Jumped my wife. Bumped and pumped my wife. Little By. Who needs a father. Son of Elaine. Who needs a husband. To hump and jump and bump and pump. Elaine of the three-million-dollar portfolio. Three. Million. Dollars. Clams. Potatoes. Smackeroos. Three million reasons to become the father of Little By. Who reminds me of BEAUBOIS, Robert NMI. Why By? The neck, that's why. The acne. A mountain range of eruptions and oozing carbuncles. Wonderful word, carbuncle. One of the best. Next to smegma, the ugliest in the language. Smegma has carbuncle beat by a car length.

BEAUBOIS, Robert NMI, fingered a boil on his neck, testing its readiness for squeezing. "I don't like it here."

"Why not?" Dutch Shea, Jr., said. He breathed through his mouth. Force of habit. The smell in the county jail always made him retch. "It's safe, the locks are terrific, the security's good, nobody breaks in." Ho, ho, old joke. Only the defendants are new. The criminal lawyer as terminal cynic.

Ho.

Ho.

"They shit in the stew at dinner."

"Who?"

"The PRs."

"Why?"

"Because the niggers pissed in the soup at lunch."

"That explains it, then."

The boil exploded and a missile of pus splattered against the plastic cubicle divider. Beaubois patted the bleeding cavity with a clean white monogrammed linen handkerchief.

"Expensive handkerchief."

"I sucked someone's cock for it."

So much for small talk. "I guess you don't want a single cell, then?"

Beaubois laughed. "I can take care of myself."

"You've had enough practice," Dutch Shea, Jr., said. "I've looked at your record."

"This is a bum rap."

"You confessed." Dutch Shea stared at the ceiling of the interrogation room. Dried excrement was caked to the plaster. Someone had drawn a penis entering the shit. He wondered how the artist had got up there. A new dimension to climbing the walls. "In writing. Signed."

"What was I supposed to do after ten hours? They didn't even let me take a piss."

"You also flunked the lie detector test."

Beaubois's fingers searched his neck for another ripe zit. "Wow."

Dutch Shea waited for a moment. Then: "That's it? Wow?"

"Yeah."

"Okay."

"I mean, all the time I was taking it, the guy giving it to me, the operator guy, I mean, he had me looking at this picture of that hotel. When it was burning, I mean. He let me feel it, the picture, run my fingers over it . . ."

A role model for Little By. "And it turned you on."

"Yeah. Shit, yeah."

A deep breath. This was one to make you shiver. "I suppose I can get behind that."

"But I did not set this one."

"Honest Injun?"

"I didn't."

"So let's hear your story."

2. "So he spends the night, my grandson," Marty Cagney said. "When he grows up, he's going to be a jockey, I think. Short like his father, dumb like his mother. Nice enough kid, though. Orderly. Always making lists. He goes to bed, I go through his pockets."

Dutch Shea, Jr., turned away from the Mister Coffee machine and stared at Marty Cagney. "Force of habit, I suppose."

"Hell, yes," Marty Cagney said. "So he's only thirteen, the kid, but what the hell, it's a good age to learn there's people who'll go through your pockets, you give them half a chance. It's a good day, you learn something like that. And anyway, he's such a hotshot, he shouldn't leave the coat on the floor, and the pants. I pick them up, then I got the right to go through them. And what do I find in the pocket but a list. Very neat. One, two, three, four. The nuns teach him that at St. Gerald's. They know all the disco steps, the nuns these days, but they still teach neatness. One, get a haircut. That's the first thing on the list. Two, get bike fixed. So far, so good. Three, Granddad's birthday present. I figure the kid's not so bad, he's got it down on his list to get me a present. Four, jerk off. In his own handwriting. Let me ask you, Dutch, you think he thought he was going to forget? I was a kid, it wasn't the sort of thing slipped my mind. I didn't have to put it on a list either. The nuns those days, they saw your list, four, jerk off, they'd send you down to Father Kavanagh in the principal's office, and he'd look at number four on your list and he'd break your spleen. It's a new world, Dutch. You know what I did? I wrote five, go to confession, and stuck it back in his pocket, the list."

Dutch Shea, Jr., nodded and smiled. Peekaboo Cagney. He could not imagine anyone ever calling Marty Cagney "Peekaboo." It looked nice enough in the Yellow Pages, it caught your eye, but in the flesh Marty Cagney was not a Peekaboo type, not a man you easily called "Peek." It occurred to him now that Marty Cagney did not look well. His color was gray and pasty and he seemed to have trouble breathing. Dutch Shea, Jr., handed him a cup of coffee and wondered suddenly if Marty Cagney were going to die. The thought made him shiver involuntarily. Another link with Lee broken. Oh, God.

"What's the matter?" Marty Cagney said.

"Nothing," Dutch Shea, Jr., said. "Sorry."

A shrug. "A real sweetheart, your guy." Marty Cagney shifted his weight. The chair could not seem to accommodate his bulk. "So what do you want me to do, help you get him back on the bricks, he's such a sweetheart."

Back to business. "I didn't say you had to fuck him, Marty."

"No offense, Dutch."

Dutch Shea sat down behind his desk. It had started to rain again.

"He rolls into town at four thirty the afternoon before the fire. One-way bus ticket from New Haven. Hangs around the Greyhound station until maybe seven o'clock. Probably trying to get picked up. Hits the Cuthbertson about eight thirty, tries to roll a queer and gets tossed out on his ear. That brings us to nine o'clock. The fire is reported at twelve thirty, he gets busted approximately six A.M. ten miles from the fire. It's the time between nine at night and six in the morning I'm interested in."

Marty Cagney looked doubtful. "You're not forgetting the lie test, are you, Dutch?"

"No, Marty, I'm not forgetting the lie test and I'm not forgetting he's queer as Dick's hatband and I'm not forgetting his confession and all the other arson beefs and I'm not trying to tell you chicken shit is chicken salad. This is a kid who gets a hard-on when he looks at a match. So all the time he's taking the test the operator lets him feel up photographs of the fire. I think I might be able to piss all over that test. And I don't need you to tell me I could be pissing in the wind and might get wet."

Marty Cagney smiled equably. "You pay the bills, Dutch, and you always pay on time."

Always.

A BMW 528i.

LEE S.

Paid in full.

Dutch Shea, Jr., cleared his throat. "Here's his story."

"Corroborated?"

"Of course not. That's where you come in." DIS-CREETLY DETERMINING WHAT WAS DONE—WHERE & WITH WHOM. "He takes a bus out Farmington to the combat zone. Goes into a drugstore, doesn't know which one, the black guy at the cash register asks him to leave."

"Why?"

"'He was hassling me.' Quote unquote. He hangs around awhile, finds a diner, gets a plate of baked beans, the beans cost fifty-five cents. He's still hungry, so he mixes up some hot water and ketchup and asks the waitress for some crackers to dip in it. She tells him to get lost."

"They're like that, waitresses," Marty Cagney said. He was writing in a small spiral notebook. "What time is it now?"

"Ten thirty, getting on to eleven."

"The buses have stopped rolling, it's going to be a little tight getting back downtown by midnight," Marty Cagney said. "Unless he hitches a ride."

Dutch Shea, Jr., put his feet on his desk. "That's exactly what he does do. Going in the other direction. Toward Elizabeth Park."

"Elizabeth Park," Marty Cagney said. "At that time of night. Fancy that."

"A guy in a Jag. XJ6L. 1979. Silver. Fuel-injected. A burled-wood dashboard. Stereo tape deck. Eight track. Hitachi."

"He remembers that, does he?"

"He says he stole one once, a Jag. And so he did. He also says the Hitachi isn't standard. Audiovox is."

"They played some music, then?"

"I guess," Dutch Shea, Jr., said. "The driver is a guy in his fifties. Blue blazer with gold buttons. Little anchors on the buttons. And a gold Rolex watch."

Marty Cagney put down his pencil and notebook and slowly massaged the bridge of his nose. "Why do I get the feeling, Dutch, that someone blew someone in that Jag?"

"Because you've got a dirty mind, Marty."

"This guy in the Jag, I don't think he's going to be too anxious to help you out."

"That was my feeling."

"If your guy is telling the truth, that is."

Dutch Shea, Jr., paused and listened to Alice March type in the outer office. "If you can't argue the truth, Marty, argue the facts. If you can't argue the facts, argue the law."

Marty Cagney picked up his pencil. "It must be midnight now."

"Close. My guy gets out to take a leak and the Jag takes off. Leaving him in Elizabeth Park."

"He's been so observant so far, he doesn't happen to catch the license plate, does he?"

"The last two numbers. Seventy-eight or seventy-nine. Or maybe eighty-seven or ninety-eight. Or ninety-seven or eighty-nine."

Marty Cagney wrote the numbers down.

"The Jag also has a bumper sticker that says, EGAN—AGAIN."

"Another vote for the governor," Marty Cagney said. "What's he do now, your guy?"

"He sacks out in someone's garage. Breaks a window in the side door and lets himself inside."

"Where?"

"I don't know. The cops retraced his route with him and he couldn't find it."

"Anything special in the garage?"

"Two hamsters in a cage."

"Swell."

"A dog starts barking before dawn and he splits. He falls asleep at the bus stop where he gets busted."

Marty Cagney closed his notebook. "Argue the law, Dutch."

Dutch Shea, Jr., shrugged. "Just see what you come up with." As an afterthought, he added: "Check out the Cutherbertson, too, Marty. Fire code violations, safety violations, you know what I mean."

"Anything funny that might have gone down."

"That sort of thing, yes."

"I'll check it all the way back to day one," Marty Cagney said.

Afterthoughts.

That sort of thing.

Day one.

Four, jerk off.
Five, go to confession.

3. Remember.

> "It came upon a midnight clear
> That glorious song of old.
> From angels bending near the earth
> To touch their harps of gold."

How he remembered.
Thayer Pomfret's adolescent voice cracking. A warning glance from his father. Thayer Pomfret's piano teacher striking a chord. Wilson Pomfret blowing into his pitch pipe.

> "Away in a manger, no crib for his bed . . ."

Oh, how he remembered.
Wilson Pomfret's annual Christmas sing at the state prison. Featuring his sons, Thayer and Nelson, and their piano teacher, Alice J. Buckley, pounding the keys, mangling the notes. The inmates, shadowy figures in the cell doors, arms extending through the bars. A tone on the pitch pipe.

> "Joy to the world, the angels sing . . ."

Yes, remembered.
Wilson Pomfret in a red Santa suit and a white cotton beard passing out presents after the carol sing to the children of inmates gathered for Christmas visiting day. Scaled-down tables and chairs in the visitors' center,

mended toys to play with, a ragged tree with broken ornaments.

Remembered.

Thayer Pomfret chewing on an oatmeal cookie: "My father says he knows your father."

John Shea, Jr., chewing on an oatmeal cookie: "My father says your father is performing a corporal work of mercy."

"What's a corporal work of mercy?"

"I don't know."

Later. John Shea, No. 89415, Cell C-27, third tier, East Block: "I don't think you should have told him that, Jack."

"I'm sorry."

"It was just a little joke. A private joke."

"Well, what is a corporal work of mercy anyway?"

"In this case, it's a way of letting God know you're around."

"Does God know Mr. Pomfret?"

D. F. Campion said, "I think He does."

Remembered East Block.

The Christmas tree atop the cell block. The reindeer, bells, holly, the golden tassels and the strings of Christmas lights festooning the cells.

Merry Christmas.

¡Feliz Navidad!

The Salvation Army packages. One apple, one orange, one package of gumdrops, one printed message from the Psalms: "I said, Lord be merciful unto me; heal my soul for I have sinned against Thee."

Remembered.

"There's no decorations on West Block." Said John Shea, Jr.

"That's right." Said John Shea, Sr. No. 89415, Cell C-27, third tier, East Block.

"Why's that?"

"The harder types are in West Block."
Remembered the disappointment.
"Aren't you a hard type?"
Remembered the prison newspaper with the brief holiday messages from inmates to those on the outside.

> Big Ed: Keep it cool, li'l brother.
> Wish you were here instead of me.
> The Eagle.

> Hogjaw: Merry Christmas, sucker. Keep
> punching and stay out of here. See you
> in March. Your daddy, Papa Dave.

Remembered.
Wilson Pomfret said, "How are you, John?"
"As well as could be expected, Wilson."
"You could use a cigarette lighter."
"No lighter fluid. They're afraid we might make bombs."
Remembered the tingle at the idea that No. 89415 would bomb his way out of the penitentiary.
"And no homemade cookies, candy or fruitcake."
Remembered the suggestion of a smile on the face of No. 89415, remembered the slight mocking tone in his voice.
"Any food has to be in a sealed unopened container."
"I guess they have their rules."
"I guess they do."
"Well . . ."
"Thanks for the thought, Wilson."
Remembered. His father talking to Wilson Pomfret who was wearing a red Santa suit with a white cotton beard. Remembered it was the last time he saw him. In East Block. West Block was for the hard types. There

210

was an inmate in West Block who had stolen the leather straps off the electric chair and in the prison shop cut them into wristbands and sold them to other inmates.

Remembered that his father did not have a leather wristband.

4. From the Personals column of the *Singles Free Press:*

FOOTLOOSE & FANCY FREE, 35-ish, intelligent, slender, good-looking. Dreamy yet intense. Grass widow (twice!). Freaks out on good talk. Wants to meet similarly inclined (45 tops) for fun & frolic. SFP Box 3600.

Dear Footloose,

I am a lawyer, 42, divorced. Intelligent. I like excellent conversation and criminals. Perhaps I fit your bill.

Actually he was forty-six.

5. Annie O'Meara's room was on the third floor of the Arthur K. Degnan Senior Citizen Center.

"You didn't bring no Snickers, Mr. Shea," Annie O'Meara said with disappointment.

"Only the ice cream, Annie."

"Snickers is my favorite, unless it's Butterfingers. You like Butterfingers, Mr. Shea, or Snickers?"

"Either one." There was a pink bald spot on the top of her scalp and what was left of her white hair fell straight down at the sides like a fright wig. She was wearing a white flannel nightgown printed with likenesses of Ringo Starr. He wondered if he should ask where she got the nightgown.

Annie O'Meara helped herself to another spoonful

of ice cream. "Is this Howard Johnson's? They got the twenty-eight flavors, Howard Johnson's."

"Baskin-Robbins."

"Them with the thirty-one flavors," Annie O'Meara said. A dribble of ice cream obliterated one of the Ringo Starrs on her nightgown. "That's three more than Howard's. That's a swell trick, having three more flavors than Howard's. You can buy Snickers at Howard's, though, Mr. Shea. I bet you didn't know that."

Dutch Shea shook his head.

"Thirty-one flavors," Annie O'Meara said. "Think of that. Vanilla, chocolate, strawberry. Them's the basics, Mr. Shea. Coffee, chocolate chip, peppermint stick. That's a grand flavor, the peppermint stick. Rocky road." She spooned another helping of rocky road into her mouth. "I could never understand how they get those little marshmallows so even in the rocky road. Just one to a spoonful. You'd think they'd all be at the bottom. There must be a trick to it, getting the marshmallows even like that. Pralines and cream. That's another one of them trick flavors. They've got a lot of trick flavors, Baskin's. Maybe that's why they got three more than Howard's. Pistachio. Remember Charlie Moran that was famous for the pistachio ice cream? Always the pistachio for Charlie . . ."

How many conservators would listen to Annie O'Meara list the thirty-one Baskin-Robbins flavors? Dutch Shea, Jr., thought. He wondered if she would follow with Howard Johnson's twenty-eight.

"How's my Dome Petroleum, Mr. Shea?"

It took him a moment to realize that Annie O'Meara was talking to him. Her flashes of lucidity were like oases in a desert of senility.

"Up two points," Dutch Shea, Jr., said.

"Two and an eighth," Annie O'Meara said. Money seemed to be the only subject that could draw her back to reality. "The boys at Dome really know their buttons. I like someone really knows his buttons, Mr. Shea. That's why I'm glad you're watching out for me."

A bleak smile.

"Stay out of CDs. Mr. Shea. You got to watch out for the interest rates. Fluctuates, don't you know? So stay out of the CDs. It's the principal we're interested in. And the tax exempts. I don't like the tax exempts. You show me someone in municipal tax exempts and I'll show you someone doesn't know his onions. My late husband, Mr. O'Meara used to say that. 'Doesn't know his onions.' That was a big difference between him and me. He'd say doesn't know his onions and I'd say doesn't know his buttons. There's a lot of difference between buttons and onions, Mr. Shea. Onions you eat. In a salad. Buttons are good on a shirt."

Dutch Shea nodded.

Annie O'Meara licked her spoon. For the first time she seemed to notice that there was something physically different about Dutch Shea, Jr.

"You got a white thing on your arm, Mr. Shea."

"A cast."

Annie O'Meara nodded approvingly. "There's nothing like a cast for making a man look grand. Like he's been in a war. You must be some kind of war hero, Mr. Shea. How many Japs did you kill? I never did like the Japs. They're yellow, you know. It's got something to do with all that rice they eat, them being yellow. It's not one of my favorite colors, yellow. Green's my favorite. Green's the color of pistachio ice cream. You remember Charlie Moran? That was famous for the pistachio ice cream. Always the pistachio for Charlie. You think it would've turned him green. The Chinese is yellow, too. Stay out of Liberty Bonds, Mr. Shea . . ."

He knew it was useless to seek a connection.

"A twenty-five-dollar bond for eighteen seventy-five.

That's no return. And you got to lick all them little stamps, put them in a booklet. Liberty stamps they're called. You get the stamp taste all over your tongue, you don't know your onions. He was a grand man, my late husband, Mr. O'Meara. He put me in Dome . . ."

Dutch Shea, Jr., stayed with Annie O'Meara until suddenly she went to sleep. He promised to stay clear of Liberty Bonds and tax exempts and certificates of deposit. Then she just closed her eyes in midsentence. She breathed evenly when she slept. The tiny pictures of Ringo Starr on her flannel nightgown seemed to dance over her slight withered form.

6. Was it that day? Or another day? The day that Roger Mullady tapped on his shoulder.

"I wonder if I might have a word with you, Mr. Shea? Just a word. A chat, if you like."

"Certainly, Mr. Mullady." Roger Mullady was the administrator of the Arthur K. Degnan Senior Citizen Center, a round man in a dark suit with rimless glasses and a permanent mirthless smile on his face. His office was on the first floor. On the wall behind his imitation walnut desk there was a large framed photograph of an austere-looking man.

"And how do you think Mrs. O'Meara is getting on?" Roger Mullady said.

"I was wondering about her nightgown. The Ringo Starr nightgown."

"Ah, yes." Roger Mullady meshed and unmeshed his fingers. "She won it in a contest. We encourage our guests to enter all the contests. It keeps the mind active. Twenty-five words or less, it's a real challenge, Mr. Shea. First prize on this one, as I recall, was a romantic cruise on the Princess Line to romantic Acapulco. South of the border, down Mexico way, Mr. Shea."

"And what if she had won?"

"Oh, but she did win. That beautiful nightgown. Twenty-five words on why she admired the Princess Cruises. Because their stock has a good earnings record, Mr. Shea. Doesn't miss a dividend. Our Mrs. O'Meara keeps up with those things." Roger Mullady clasped his hands and smiled at Dutch Shea, Jr. "I'm only sorry she didn't win first prize. The romantic cruise. I think she would have reflected great credit on the Arthur K. Degnan Senior Citizen Center."

"South of the border, down Mexico way."

"You have a gift for words, Mr. Shea. I must see you in court sometime. I suspect there is no jury that could not be swayed by your words." Roger Mullady removed his glasses and pinched his nose, slowly, his eyes closed, as if examining his conscience. "You know, Mr. Shea, there is a matter of some delicacy we should discuss."

His face was composed. "And what is that, Mr. Mullady?"

The mechanical smile. "Well, Mr. Shea, there are certain—and I hope the word is not too harsh— delinquencies in our Mrs. O'Meara's accounts here at Arthur K. Degnan's."

Dutch Shea stared at the photograph on the wall behind Mullady's desk. Never answer too quickly. Outwait him.

"Who is that?"

Roger Mullady swiveled in his chair and stared at the photograph. "That is Arthur K. Degnan himself. A man I knew personally."

An opening. A man who knew Arthur K. Degnan personally would be aching to tell about it.

"I thought he was dead."

"Before his time, Mr. Shea."

"A man of excellent reputation, I am told."

215

"A giant, Mr. Shea. A giant in the senior citizen field. Until Arthur K. Degnan entered the field, no one had thought of franchising senior citizens' centers." Roger Mullady bowed toward the photograph. "There is nothing stronger, Mr. Shea, than an idea whose time has come."

"I agree totally," Dutch Shea, Jr., said. In the back of his mind he seemed to remember that Arthur K. Degnan's franchising of senior citizens' centers had landed him in prison in another state. No. Indicted but not convicted. A timely and fatal stroke before jury selection. Best not to mention prison. Not while Mullady was feeling so reverential toward Arthur K. Degnan. Take the bull by the horns. Always the best tactic when a defensive posture was expected. "I think, Mr. Mullady, you are talking about Annie's bill here being nine months in arrears. Or is it ten?"

His brusque irritability startled Roger Mullady. The mechanical smile wavered. "I am sure there is no real problem, Mr. Shea."

"Well, is it nine or ten, Mullady?" A further show of impatience for effect.

Roger Mullady went to a file cabinet. Dutch Shea drummed his fingers on the arm of his chair.

"Nine, Mr. Shea. There's another bill due the fifteenth of this month."

Dutch Shea, Jr., shook his head and smiled. "It's not worth the trouble being a conservator, Mr. Mullady. Too much trouble. Too much bookkeeping. And if the truth be told, the fee's not worth a damn. I could murder Solly."

"Solly?"

"Judge Baum. Solly Baum. The probate judge. An old friend. We were law partners once. Before he went to the bench. He appointed me conservator. I took it as a favor. That's a good lesson, Mr. Mullady. Never do business favors for your friends. You're bending over, trying to make a putt, and there's Solly saying, 'How'd you like to take over the Annie O'Meara estate?'" A self-deprecating chuckle. "I missed the putt and got the estate."

Roger Mullady nodded quickly. Too quickly. Dutch Shea was sure he did not play golf. The golf course was a boardroom from which he was barred. Dutch Shea leaned over an imaginary putter and addressed an imaginary ball. "As you know, I must make a complete accounting to the court of probate, and as I am sure you also know, Mrs. O'Meara's—Annie's—holdings are many and varied."

Roger Mullady's eyes blinked. And blinked again.

"Difficult to locate," Dutch Shea, Jr., said. He sat down. His voice sounded bored. "In a number of different accounts, a number of different banks, a number of different safe-deposit boxes." He took a deep breath. "Whatever."

"I understand perfectly."

"And because of the intricacies of probate law, expenses against her estate must be kept to a minimum until there is a complete accounting." He smiled ruefully. "This must be tedious for you. I'm a criminal attorney, Mr. Mullady, and to be quite frank, probate law bores me stiff." He leaned forward. "I'm not even sure I understand it sometimes."

Roger Mullady laughed heartily.

Dutch Shea lowered his voice conspiratorially. "To be perfectly honest, I prefer criminals. Especially guilty ones. The colored boy you know stuck up that gas station. He doesn't give you any trouble, he puts himself completely in your hands, no back talk, he just wants you to cut him the best deal you can. It's the innocent ones that are all the trouble, believe me."

"I can see that, yes."

Another smile. "This is not to imply, of course, that Annie is any trouble. She's giving me all the help she can, but in the privacy of this room I think I can say her mind is not what it was."

He waited for Mullady to nod in agreement.

"And again in the privacy of this room, I expect you are aware of the size of her holdings."

For a moment Dutch Shea, Jr., thought that Mullady was going to turn to the photograph of Arthur K. Degnan for advice.

"I would not like you to break any legal confidence, Mr. Shea. Any court order. Although, in some ways, I think of myself as Annie's conservator also . . ."

"Of her health and welfare."

"Exactly, Mr. Shea."

"And doing a damn fine job, Mr. Mullady."

"Why, thank you, Mr. Shea."

Dutch Shea stared at the photograph of Arthur K. Degnan. "Well, Annie's not a rich woman, by any means, but her holdings are extensive. A few securities, some bonds, real estate, a little jewelry . . ."

He reached under the cast and began to scratch his wrist. Mullady waited expectantly.

"In the vicinity of a quarter of a million dollars." He stifled a yawn. "That may be conservative. Perhaps three hundred thousand."

"I see." Mullady took a deep breath and then exhaled. "She has a will . . ."

Dutch Shea, Jr., reacted sharply. "Mr. Mullady, the court of probate would move to take disciplinary action if I divulged . . ."

"Believe me, I had no intention, Mr. Shea . . ."

Dutch Shea, Jr., held up his hand. "And I'm sorry if I seemed to imply . . ."

They smiled at each other across the desk.

"Do you own this franchise? This Degnan?"

"I am only the manager." Roger Mullady wore the

look of the capable man unappreciated in senior citizen circles, forced to suffer fools gladly.

"It's a sad business. But rewarding for those who have a gift for it. Rewarding in many ways." He paused to let Mullady reflect on what he had said. "Those contests. Were they your idea?"

"It's a principle I would like to see further adopted in the senior citizen field, Mr. Shea."

Dutch Shea, Jr., rose. "You should have a franchise of your own, Mr. Mullady. Annie is very happy here, you know."

"I'm glad to hear it."

"She has no next of kin. This is home."

"Ah."

"I'm sure she's told you how much she enjoys Bugs Bunny."

Mullady looked at him blankly.

"The Saturday cartoons."

"Ah, yes."

Dutch Shea, Jr., pursed his lips and stared out the window, as if contemplating a thought too ill-formed to be mentioned. "Perhaps provisions might be made . . ." He shook his hand as if to wave away the idea.

Roger Mullady meshed and unmeshed his fingers.

"I am glad we have had this chat, Mr. Shea."

"So am I, Mr. Mullady."

"There is a load off my mind."

"And mine."

7. From *The Sunday Messenger* at St. Robert Bellarmine's Roman Catholic Church:

SINGLE IRISHMAN

We are looking for an unmarried Irish gentleman, age 50 or older. Work evenings answering tele-

phones and general maintenance. Live in, with
comfortable room, all utilities included. Require
good moral character and temperate habits. Funeral home in Canaryville. Good salary. PHONE
12:00 Noon to 5:00 P.M., 268-0703.

He hung up when someone answered.

8.   CROSS-EXAMINATION

BY MR. SHEA:

Q. Sergeant Dwyer, did you instruct your officers
to solicit acts of prostitution over the telephone?

A. No, sir, I did not.

Q. What did you tell them?

A. I advised them to call the outcall service and
request that a girl be sent to their locations.

Q. For what purpose?

A. For the purpose of conducting a prostitution
investigation.

Q. And you instructed your officers to say that
over the telephone to the outcall service?

A. No, sir.

Q. I have nothing further.

CROSS-EXAMINATION

BY MR. SHEA:

Q. Now Sergeant Hughes, I want to be very
precise. Did you avail yourself of this offer for a
blowjob or a half-and-half?

A. Well, sir, I said I agreed and then I walked out
of the room and gave a signal to Sergeant Dwyer

and he entered the room and proceeded to arrest the . . .

Q. You actually agreed to engage in an illegal act?

A. Yes, sir, so I wouldn't look funny.

Q. Half-and-half or a blowjob?

MR. TORIZZO: Objection, irrelevant.

EXAMINER LEFEBVRE: Overruled. The witness is directed to answer.

A. Half-and-half.

EXAMINER LEFEBVRE: What's that? The witness is directed to speak up.

A. Half-and-half.

Q. You prefer half-and-half to . . .

MR. TORIZZO: Objection.

EXAMINER LEFEBVRE: Sustained. Strike the question. Mr. Shea . . .

MR. SHEA: I'm sorry, Your Honor . . .

EXAMINER LEFEBVRE: You may continue. Don't let it happen again.

Q. Was Mr. Mandel there at any time when you agreed to let the masseuse perform an illegal act of half-and-half on you?

MR. TORIZZO: Objection, argumentative.

EXAMINER LEFEBVRE: Sustained as to the form of the question. You may restate the question, Mr. Shea.

Q. Was Mr. Mandel there at any time you had these half-and-half conversations with this girl?

A. No, he was not.

Q. Did you talk to Mr. Mandel on the telephone?

A. No, I did not.

Q. Do you know if Mr. Mandel sent the girl out?

A. No.

Q. Do you know who sent the girl out?

A. I do not know.

Q. I have nothing further.

"Well," Thayer Pomfret said in the corridor during the recess, wiping his half-glasses with the triangular tip of his Cottage Club tie, "it's a lot more educational in there than working on a decedent trust."

"Just another day at the factory," Dutch Shea, Jr., said. He wondered how many Cottage Club ties Thayer had in his closet. Day after day the same bloated gold and blood-red stripes.

"Where do these girls come from, Jack?" Thayer concentrated on the cleanliness of his spectacles. "These masseuses?"

The ironic and almost imperceptible pause between "these" and "masseuses" made him flash with annoyance. "What masseuses, Thayer? I didn't see any masseuses in there. We've been examining vice cops all morning."

"The masseuses the vice officers arrested."

That cool reasonable decedent-trust voice reminded him of Judge Liggett. Less patronizing, but the same tone. Inform us about the lower orders, Jack. About the economics of anal sodomy. As if buggery were a possibility for an investment portfolio. Take It Up The Ass, Inc. "They're just girls. Girls who don't have a hell of a lot going for them." It struck him suddenly how much Thayer resembled Peter Jennings. Who had not been in the restaurant on Charlotte Street the night Cat was killed. Decapitated. Triangulated. Cat. Thayer's god-daughter. Thayer. Who looked like Peter Jennings and who had handled the legal work on Cat's adoption. The paper work. What information was in that paperwork? "Girls who might even have worked in the file room at Howard, Carey & Pomfret."

"I would tend to doubt that."

"Why? You don't have any girls who fuck your paralegals and dream of marrying a junior partner?"

"Perhaps. But it's a big jump from there to masseuse."

Why did Thayer's smile always irritate him so? "Not that big. It doesn't work out with the junior partner so she decides to peddle it, and when she gets busted, she gets a big thrill, there's a senior partner from the old law firm sitting there with the D.A., wearing his club tie from Old Nassau and getting his rocks off while she explains your basic nurse call and the best way to do Greek so it doesn't hurt, it hurts like a bastard you don't do it right. Never mind there's no need for you to give Johnny Torizzo any help, you're the general counsel for United Tel, you got a perfect right to be there, it's better than jerking off listening to her."

Thayer Pomfret smiled. "A morning in court does wonders for your disposition."

"Yeah, well." So I can't get a rise out of you, so what? Thayer was like Lee that way. He had often wondered why they had never gotten together when they were younger. It seemed the perfect mating of Episcopalian genes, a merger that could easily have been codified by Judge Liggett and Wilson Pomfret, a merger of minimum whereases. He thought of Thayer's bony index finger slipping between pliant belly and elastic panty band, through the hedgerow into the damp dark available cunt, finger followed by prick, a consummation the issue of which should have been two point seven children with last name first names, living in a house whose medicine cabinets were unsullied by Kaopectate or Preparation H. Did you ever go out with Thayer? he had asked Lee once. His lips were dry when he kissed, she had replied, anticipating where the line of questioning was leading. The whereas that Judge Liggett and Wilson Pomfret could not have anticipated.

Dry lips. Wonderful the pigeonholes of memory. The irritation subsided. "Sorry."

"Think nothing of it." Again the smile that was like a moat between them. "It just proves a point. I'm not hostile enough for the criminal bar."

"And I am." He thought of dry lips and did not get angry.

"All I'm saying is that it takes a remarkable degree of hostility to be a good criminal lawyer. That's why they're usually lone hands. A large firm can't accommodate them. They're like gunfighters."

Gunfighters die alone, he thought. "Is that meant to be a compliment?"

"If you wish." Words escaping through dry lips.

"Aren't you ever hostile?"

"How hostile can you be about a decedent trust?"

Decedent. Dead. Cat. If asked, would Thayer tell him the names of Cat's real parents? Correction: natural parents. He and Lee were her real parents. Would he? No. Of course not. Hostile bastard.

CROSS-EXAMINATION

BY MR. SHEA:

Q. Who did she commit this act of prostitution with, Detective Ito?

A. She solicited me.

Q. She didn't have intercourse with you, did she?

A. No.

Q. You called her for a massage?

A. Yes.

Q. Did she have two hands?

A. Yes.

Q. Appear to have five fingers on each hand?

A. Yes.

Q. Are you familiar with the manner in which massages are given by one human being on another?

A. Yes.

Q. Are they given with hands and fingers?

A. Yes.

Q. And she was massaging you?

A. Yes.

Q. And did she apply her hands and fingers to you through your clothing?

A. No.

Q. Were you nude?

A. Yes.

Q. Was your entire body nude?

A. Yes.

Q. And this was to entice her into making some sexual advance to you?

A. No.

Q. Ah. What was the purpose, then?

A. She told me to remove all my clothing.

Q. And you always follow orders.

MR. TORIZZO: Objection.

EXAMINER LEFEBVRE: Sustained. Rephrase the question.

Q. Was your state of nakedness in line with any policy of the vice squad of this city's Police Department?

A. No.

EXAMINER LEFEBVRE: Speak up.

A. No.

Q. I see. But in order to facilitate your investigation, you thought this was the proper procedure?

MR. TORIZZO: Objection, calls for a conclusion. Mr. Shea is badgering the witness, Your Honor.

MR. SHEA: Your Honor, I just have this witness naked on a bed with an equally naked masseuse performing five finger exercises on him. I wouldn't call that badgering, Your Honor, I'd call that . . .

EXAMINER LEFEBVRE: I don't care what you'd call that, Mr. Shea, and I don't want it on the record.

MR. SHEA: Certainly, Your Honor. Is Mr. Torizzo's objection to the witness's nakedness overruled . . .

MR. TORIZZO: Your Honor, the objection was to Mr. Shea's badgering of this witness . . .

MR. SHEA: Who has twelve years of exemplary nakedness, excuse me, service in the vice squad.

MR. TORIZZO: Your Honor . . .

EXAMINER LEFEBVRE: You're out of order, Mr. Shea.

MR. SHEA: I am truly sorry, Your Honor. I beg the court's pardon.

EXAMINER LEFEBVRE: Just watch out, Mr. Shea. You may continue with this witness.

Q. Now where were we? Oh, yes. On the bed. Now Detective Ito, were you being observed by any other officer at the time all your clothes were removed?

A. No.

Q. And did this girl touch your penis or your testicles during the course of this massage?

A. Yes.

Q. And you allowed that to happen freely and voluntarily, is that correct?

A. No.

Q. Did you try and stop her from doing that?

A. Yes.

Q. How did you try to stop her?

A. I told her to massage my ankles.

Q. Did you become sexually aroused?

A. No.

Q. When she was massaging your ankles, was Mr. Mandel present?

A. No.

Q. Did you ever talk to Mr. Mandel about this girl?

A. No.

Q. As far as you know, Mr. Mandel never had any connection with this girl?

MR. TORIZZO: Objection, calls for a conclusion.

EXAMINER LEFEBVRE: Sustained.

Q. I have nothing further.

9. Innocent? No. I don't think you've broken the law, Myron, but you're not innocent. You're a pimp. You send girls out and the girls usually end up with a cock in their face, and that's a pimp, you hold it up to the light. What you've done, and I've got to congratulate you for it, is you've found a way to make an end run around the law. It's a nice touch, and I'm going to juke you through that loophole in the law, but you're not in. the massage business, Myron, you wouldn't know a deltoid if it hit you in the face. You were in the massage business, you'd hire some 212-pound Swede with fingers like grappling hooks that could crack your toes and make your neck stop hurting, but the trouble with a 212-pound Swedish masseuse is that she'd also cause terminal soft-on, and I never met a girl you hired was in the soft-on business. The only exercise they get, your girls, is getting down on their knees to cop some guy's joint or maybe to say a prayer their next trick isn't undercover vice. What I'm trying to tell you, Myron, is don't be so fucking greedy. You send these girls out on a thirty-dollar massage, they kick back twenty-five to you, they make five bucks. It's common sense, they've got to hook. So why not charge forty, split it fifty-fifty? There's enough doubt there, I can half convince a jury you're a legitimate businessman, they're not Carmelite nuns.

A combination of things he told Myron Mandel.

Thought he told Myron Mandel
Wished he told Myron Mandel.
Didn't care whether he told Myron Mandel.
One or all of the above.

10. From the effects of John Shea, No. 89415, Cell C-27, third tier, East Block.

Dutch—

How's this for a poem?

> "If I could have my last wish,"
> Said the prisoner one day,
> As they led him from the death cell
> To the chair not far away.
> "Please grant me one request, sir,
> Ere you tighten up the strap.
> Just tell the warden,
> I would love to hold him on my lap.

Not bad, huh? Har, har. I ordered peaches. In January. It's as good as a reprieve. Har, har. She was a twat. So long.

Your pal, Billy McGurkin.

The twat was the woman for whose murder Billy McGurkin was executed.

11. Elaine Igoe bent close and crooned softly into his ear.

> "Again,
> This couldn't happen again.
> This is that once in a lifetime,
> This is that moment divine . . ."

228

Leonard McNamara & His Fabulous Five slammed into another chorus. A crush of couples shuffled on the dance floor. The bright overhead lights glinted cruelly off the polished parquet floor and off the necklaces and pendants and chokers and bracelets of the dancers, casting into relief every imperfection of skin and make-up.

"You sing wonderfully, Elaine." They were alone at the table. The Touhys and the Rooneys were dancing. "Let's leave these two lovebirds alone," Roger Touhy had said to Greg Rooney. Marian Touhy and Regina Rooney had giggled. Roger Touhy was almost drunk and had knocked over the chrysanthemum centerpiece. Roger Touhy thought busing was a goddamn shame.

Marian Touhy waved from the dance floor.

"Let's dance again," Elaine Igoe said. Her hair was sculpted and bouffanted. She wore a royal blue velvet dress with puff sleeves, a high ruff collar and a gold cord that wrapped twice around her waist.

"No, let's sit this one out, Elaine." She's dressed for a coronation, he thought suddenly. It's an outfit she could wear when Prince Charles takes over. Elaine Igoe, representing St. Robert Bellarmine parish. Not missing a word. I, Charles Philip Arthur George Mountbatten-Windsor, Prince of Wales and Earl of Chester, Duke of Cornwall and Rothesay, Earl of Carrick, Baron Renfrew, Lord of the Isles and Great Steward of Scotland . . . What a story to tell at the communion breakfast. The thought cheered him. "I've been stepping on your toes all night."

"Oh, Jack, you dance beautifully."

He smiled and toyed with a matchbook. The matchbook cover said, Mother Cabrini Hospital Women's Auxiliary Dance.

Leonard McNamara's music covered the silence.

"You think the bishop will come?"

"I don't think he goes to dances, Elaine."

Elaine Igoe fluttered her false eyelashes. One of them was coming loose. "He's such a swinger, Jack, you never know."

Another awkward smile. He pretended to watch the dance floor. There was an enormous tinted photograph of Mother Cabrini above the bandstand. Elaine Igoe hummed another chorus of "Again," moving her head to and fro in time with the music.

". . . da da that once in a lifetime,
da da that moment divine."

This moment divine, this divine moment.

"What are you reading, Jack?" A bright, interested voice.

"Oh, just the menu, Elaine." There was a calligraphic menu at every place setting. The words "In Memory of Mother Cabrini" were scrolled at the top. Elaine seemed to be waiting for him to say something. He read the menu aloud: "Chicken in Aspic with Ham Cornucopias Filled with Vegetables or Braised Tongue Served with Pureed Spinach."

"A good choice, don't you think?"

He nodded.

"I had the chicken."

"I had the braised tongue."

"Oh, Jack. Always doing something different."

He studied the menu and read aloud again. "Mixed Green Salad of Lettuce, Romaine and Chicory. Hot rolls and Butter. Baba Ring with Compote of Fresh Fruits. Madeleines."

Elaine Igoe said, "That must be the dessert."

"I think it is, yes." There was one more listing on the menu. "Coffee."

Leonard McNamara & His Fabulous Five segued

into "Guilty" and Elaine Igoe sang softly along with them:

> "Is it a sin, is it a crime,
> Loving you, dear, like I do?
> If it's a crime, then I'm guilty,
> Guilty of loving you . . ."

He smiled at her. A beaming smile. A lustrous smile. A smile that seemed glued to his face. A rictus of a smile. He hummed, "Dada da dada da dee da . . ."

"Oh, Jack, that's wonderful."

"Dee dee da dada da da."

"Oh, Jack."

A riff on the drums. Leonard McNamara unhooked his saxophone and said, We're going to take five, folks, and then back to the big drawing, an all-expenses trip for two to San Juan, Puerto Rico, five glorious days, five fun-filled nights, in just five minutes, *cinco*. Another riff. The crowd moved off the dance floor, pushing past the tables. Glazed eyes, slack smiles, a blended buzz of voices. Eustace Cooney, in velvet dinner jacket and plaid cummerbund, averted his eyes. Vote for Eustace Cooney—The Judge Who Gave Harlow T. Jefferson a Fair Trial. The only benign thought of this benighted evening.

Roger Touhy said, "Goddamnit, I need a drink." His face was beet red and there were beads of sweat on his brow.

Greg Rooney said, "That's work, cutting a rug." He wore wire-rimmed glasses and was a urologist. J. Gregory Rooney, M.D.

"I should say," Dutch Shea, Jr., said.

Regina Rooney said, "Next dance with me, Jack."

Roger Touhy said, "His dance card is all taken up, right, Elaine?"

"Oh, Rog," Elaine Igoe said.

231

Greg Rooney read from the back of the menu: "Chairman of the Entertainment Committee—Mrs. Byron Igoe."

Marian Touhy said, "Hurray for Elaine."

Mrs. Byron Igoe. Widow of Mr. Byron Igoe. Who was the fornicator of Mrs. John Shea. And cuckolder of Mr. John Shea. A silence fell over the table.

Regina Rooney righted the centerpiece.

Roger Touhy said, "At least you didn't use that chairperson crap, Elaine."

All at once everyone was speaking.

Greg Rooney said, "I like the way you gave it to the governor, Jack."

Roger Touhy said, "You really showed it to that son of a bitch, Jack."

"Do you think the Republicans have a chance, Jack?"

"That Egan's a four-flusher, don't you think, Jack?"

"Well, he's not going to get my vote."

"Thanks to Jack."

"He's some guy, Elaine."

Roger Touhy said, "Hey, did you know Leonard McNamara's Father Bill McNamara's brother. At Precious Blood."

"Is that right?"

"That's some tough parish, Precious Blood."

"Precious Blood on the floor is what they call it."

Roger Touhy said, "You know Tommy, the bartender downstairs?"

"The colored one?"

"That's him."

"I didn't know you're getting so friendly with the colored boys now, Rog," Greg Rooney said.

"You got an awful big mouth for a urologist," Roger Touhy said. "A pecker checker."

"Oh, Rog," Marian Touhy said.

"Better hide the J&B, Marian," Greg Rooney said.

"Anyway," Roger Touhy said, "he goes to Ireland last summer, Tommy."

"Ireland. You got to be kidding."

"Ireland. And he passes himself off as the dinge bishop of Jamaica."

"Oh, Rog, you're impossible."

"That's a scream, Rog."

"I'm not kidding. He rents himself a bishop's outfit and says he's the bishop of Jamaica. A real darky. Says Mass, preaches a sermon, lets the micks kiss his ring. He would have got away with it, but May Quinn spots him."

"May Quinn from St. Robert Bellarmine's?"

"Jerry Quinn's widow."

"Well, May Quinn says, 'I know him. That's Tommy, the bartender at the Club that makes the best fizzes in the archdiocese.' "

Regina Rooney said, "Well, that's one thing May Quinn's an expert on."

Marian Touhy said, "Fizzes."

Greg Rooney told about a woman in New Mexico who cooked a burrito for her husband and reported that there was a picture of Jesus burned on the tortilla.

"Oh, Greg."

"No, it's true. It was in *U.S. News and World Report* last week. You see it, Jack?"

"I missed it, Greg."

"You ever know a pecker checker didn't get *U.S. News?*" Roger Touhy said.

"Rog is at the J&B again," Greg Rooney said.

"What's a burrito?" Elaine Igoe said.

"One of those Mexican dishes," Regina Rooney said.

" 'Jesus on a tortilla,' she called it," Greg Rooney said. " 'I don't know why this has happened,' she says, 'but God has come to me through this tortilla.' "

"In *U.S. News.*"

"I swear to God. The bishop out there doesn't know to shit or go blind."

"Greg."

"Excuse my French."

"Tommy the bartender ought to go out there as bishop."

"Wouldn't that be a riot?"

"How do they explain it, Greg?"

"Skillet burns."

"Those Mexicans."

Roger Touhy said, "I cooked a tortilla once and there was a picture of Mickey Mantle on it."

"Oh, Rog."

Ruffles and flourishes from Leonard McNamara & His Fabulous Five. The crowd hushed. Leonard McNamara stepped to the microphone. And now . . . the moment . . . you've all . . . been waiting for . . . the grand prize . . . San Juan . . . five glorious . . . fun-filled . . . habla espanol . . . who'll be the lucky couple . . .

Elaine Igoe reached under the table and squeezed Dutch Shea's hand.

Leonard McNamara fished into the bowl, held up a chance and read, "Larry and Sue Dillon, you here, Larry and Sue?"

Roger Touhy said, "Ah, shit."

Marian Touhy said, "I really wanted it for you two. If two people ever deserved it, it's you and Elaine, Jack."

Regina Rooney said, "Why don't you go anyway?"

Greg Rooney said, "That's a hell of an idea, Jack. We'll chaperone, Regina."

Elaine Igoe said, "Brandy, Jack?"

"Thanks, no, Elaine." He prowled Byron Igoe's study, picking up Byron Igoe's golf trophies, keeping the room between Elaine and himself.

"You didn't drink hardly a thing all night."

"I have to be in court in the morning."

"Wasn't it a wonderful dance?"

"I'm really glad you asked me, Elaine." All the way home in the car she had told him the plots of all the television shows she had seen that week, complete with commercial interruptions. And then Mary Tyler Moore said to Ted, What do you want to be, Ted? And Ted said, ambassador to Honolulu, and then there was a commercial, and then Lou Grant said . . .

"Can you imagine the Rooneys?" Elaine Igoe said. "That suggestion."

Dutch Shea, Jr., studied a silver cup:

BYRON IGOE
1ST PLACE—MEMBER-GUEST TOURNAMENT, 1975
74-77/151

He put the cup down.

"Do you like Tom Brokaw?" Elaine said. "On the *Today Show?*"

"I'm not generally up that early."

"I think he's wonderful."

He nodded, and kept nodding, not knowing what to say.

"His wife's name is Meredith."

"I didn't know that."

"Meredith Brokaw."

Additional nodding.

"Her birthday's Christmas Day. You think she only gets one present?"

"That's an interesting question, Elaine."

Elaine Igoe said, "Make love to me, Jack."

He remembered the cellulite deposits. He remembered the photograph of Byron in the round silver Tiffany frame on the hall table upstairs. He remembered won-

235

dering if she put it there before she went out that night,
taking it from the bedside table. He remembered that she
used Aim toothpaste and he remembered that she had
prescriptions in her medicine cabinet for Compazine
suppositories and Septra DS for cystitis and Hydro-
Diuril for premenstrual symptoms and Naturetin-K for
bloat. He remembered that Lee used Naturetin-K and he
tried not to remember Elaine's financial statement. He
remembered she did not come and he remembered she
said it had never been like this and he remembered
rememberedremem

12. Her gynecologist had recommended the salpingogram when she could not get pregnant. A simple
procedure. The cervix was dilated and the uterus
injected with dye to see if the fallopian tubes were
blocked. If the tubes were blocked, that was the reason
conception did not take place.

QED.

Lee was against the idea.

"Why is it always the woman? Why can't it be your
fault?"

"Lee, we're not talking about fault. It's no one's
fault."

"Why can't you get checked? Go do what men have
to do?"

"All right. I'll call Greg Rooney. He's a urologist.
Then will you get the goddamn salpingogram?"

Lee agreed.

Reluctantly.

And he had made an appointment with J. Gregory
Rooney, M.D.

"The hell do you mean, self-gratification?" Dutch
Shea, Jr., said.

J. Gregory Rooney, M.D., wiped his aviator goggles
on his white medical coat. "Call it self-abuse, then."

"Remember Sister Geraldine. The one with the gold tooth at St. Rita's, taught us the Sixth Commandment. 'Thou shalt not beat thy meat,' I think it said."

"It's a hell of a thought, Jack," J. Gregory Rooney said. "The fact is, you want a sperm count, I got to have something to count. Preferably yours. It just so happens I got a rubber right here. In the desk. Sheiks. Remember them? We used to steal them from Arthur's Drugstore, we were kids. You go into the can and belt away. When you're finished, put the rubber in this little box here and give it to Miss Hannecy on the way out. I send it down to the lab and in three days I know if you're shooting blanks or not. Which is the point of the exercise."

"A urologist." Dutch Shea, Jr., shook his head.

"It puts me in Sea Island twice a year, Jack. Lee Trevino gives me golf lessons. He helps me with my grip, I tell him how to keep his prostate in tip-top shape. A lot of money in peckers, you get right down to it."

"What do you tell the nuns, you go back to St. Rita's for reunions? That you keep a bunch of rubbers in your desk drawer?"

"Free samples, Jack," J. Gregory Rooney said. "Just go whack off. How many doctors you know will tell you that? It's not like you're learning something new. You want, I got some pictures will help you along."

J. Gregory Rooney called in a week.

"I wouldn't vouch for the caliber of the gun, Jack," he said. "a bazooka it's not. But you're not shooting blanks either."

Lee put the salpingogram off for two months. Finally she made the appointment and he drove her to the clinic. Her tubes were blocked. The gynecologist put the X rays on the light board and said the most common cause of blocked tubes was pelvic inflammatory disease. Lee did not speak on the way home. He wondered how she was going to handle the pelvic imflammatory disease. It was not the easiest subject to work your way into. He did not expect her to say, Gee, a pelvic infection, I wonder how I got that? That was the style of some women he knew, but not Lee's.

She did not beat around the bush when they reached the house on Asylum Avenue.

"I had the clap when I was at Smith."

"I had it once, too." In fact he was not sure whether he had ever had it. The smear of the persistent drip had turned up negative on the slide. He just wanted to make her feel better.

"It doesn't matter from whom. No one you know."

"I didn't ask."

"I gave it to someone else. That's how I knew I had it."

"I didn't ask that either."

"Christ, you're noble," she said. "I know why you want a child."

"Lee, I'm not even sure I do."

"Because of your father."

That was when he kicked the bathtub and broke his toe. The funny thing was, she was probably right. All a baby really meant to him was something to prove the blood was not all bad. A new generation that had nothing to live down.

The twists and turns of memory. Cat. Always memory returned to Cat. Oh, Cat. Thank God your mother had the clap. Imagine a child half hers and half mine. A mutant seed.

Cat, Cat. I honor the genes that produced you.

13. *A day in the life.*

Harriet Dawson was arraigned at ten A.M. and the charges against her were dismissed by eleven.

"How we going to handle this one?" Judge Blatt said in chambers. He leaned back in an overstuffed leather chair and filed his nails with an emery board. On the wall above his desk there was a gallery of photographs of the judge shaking hands with a number of politicians.

"The DA wants to kick it down to manslaughter with a bullet," Dutch Shea, Jr., said.

"Just a touch," Johnny Torizzo said. "She's out in eight months, I'll throw in time off for time served."

"No deal," Dutch Shea, Jr., said. "You charged her with felony murder, I'm comfortable going to trial with that."

"She ran over that kid with a lawn mower," Johnny Torizzo said. "A baby. Nine months old."

"No deal," Dutch Shea, Jr., said.

"She was drunk," Johnny Torizzo said.

"Says who?" Dutch Shea, Jr., said.

"The arresting officer."

"He got the tests to back it up?"

"He said her voice was garbled and incoherent."

"She'd just run over her grandchild. Baby Harriet, I think her name was. How else is she supposed to sound?"

"She admitted she was drinking."

"A couple of beers."

"She could hardly stand up."

"Johnny," Dutch Shea, Jr., said. "You want to go to trial, I'll put your cop on the stand." He counted off on his fingers. "He got her name, he got her address, he got the kid's name, she told him what happened and how it happened. Her voice was so fucking incoherent, how'd he manage to get that all down?"

"Gentlemen, gentlemen," Judge Blatt said. He ran his tongue over his teeth, cleaning them of any small food fragments. "I'm inclined to dismiss."

239

"Your Honor . . ." Johnny Torizzo said.

"Christ Almighty, Johnny," Judge Blatt said, "you want this in the papers every day?"

"Is that the bottom line?"

Dutch Shea remained silent. Judge Blatt put on his jacket and then his black robe. "The bottom line, Mr. Torizzo, is that she has already lost the child. Incarceration will not bring the child back. Understood?"

Johnny Torizzo shrugged. "Just trying, your honor."

"Fine. Give my best to Theresa."

Johnny Torizzo nodded and left Judge Blatt's chambers. The judge picked up the calendar and said, "Don't you have something else here today?"

"Number ten, Your Honor," Dutch Shea, Jr., said. "A345144. Considine. Packy Considine. He's down for sentencing."

"The wheelman on the armored car robbery?"

"The same."

"He stole the car with the bumper sticker, right?"

"I'VE GOT MY SHIT TOGETHER BUT NOW I CAN'T PICK IT UP."

Judge Blatt laughed. "You talk to him about a deal?"

"He said stand-up guys don't fink."

"Stand-up guys do nine-to-fifteen."

"That's what I told him, Your Honor."

"I don't know how you did it," Harriet Dawson said. She threw her arms around Dutch Shea's neck and kissed him on the lips, her tongue searching for an opening in his mouth. "I'm going to bake you some apricot muffins, you hear?"

"I hear."

"They'd've been that little girl's favorites, she'd've lived."

"I'm sure."

"I can't get that little girl out of my mind." Hector

and Leo stood behind Harriet Dawson. It appeared to Dutch Shea, Jr., that both were trying to goose her.

"It's all over, Mrs. Dawson. Try not to think about it anymore."

"Baby Harriet." Harriet Dawson slapped Hector's hand away from her bottom and then Leo's. "Guess I got to get on with living."

"You do that." Dutch Shea, Jr., watched Harriet Dawson depart through the swinging doors of Department 124, whooping with laughter as Hector and Leo grabbed for her bottom. One down, one to go. He searched the courtroom for Charlie Considine. Packy's brother. Better to break the bad news to Charlie before he heard it firsthand from the bench. Nine-to-fifteen. A serious pop. A carrot for Harriet Dawson, a stick for Packy Considine. The way of the world. There was no sign of Charlie. He was probably on the pay phone. Charlie Considine was always on the telephone.

"Who you looking for?" Barry Stukin said. He was sitting in the jury box next to a black lawyer in a three-piece beige suit with gold buttons.

"Charlie Considine," Dutch Shea, Jr. said. There was a low din in the courtroom. Lawyers sat sidesaddle in the public seats, their lips glued to the ears of their clients, hands covering their mouths so that no one could eavesdrop.

"He still fencing?" Barry Stukin said.

"You mean can he turn over a hundred thousand rolls of film in twenty-four hours, yes, that's what you mean by fencing."

The black lawyer immediately perked up. His name was Clarence Banks and he was always on the lookout for a new client. "He got anything outstanding?"

"No, Clarence," Dutch Shea, Jr., said. "Unless you want a truckload of Feminique. I think he's got a buyer, though. A chain of all-night drugstores in Cleveland is what I hear. He's got about as many brains as a Rolaid, Charlie, but he's a genius when it comes to unloading hot stuff. Power tools, calculators, your video recorders. Especially the Jap stuff. Hitachi, Sanyo, Mitsubishi. He loves the Japs. Sony, Seiko, JVC, Panasonic. You can't beat the Japs for good work, Charlie says. It's because they got small hands, he says. Phillips wrenches, Charlie pays you cash on the barrelhead. Paper Uncle didn't print, twenty-five cents on the dollar. Horowitz on RCA, twenty-five thousand six-track tapes, the best of Vladimir, Charlie Considine knows where to unload it."

"You can't say he's not eclectic, Charlie," Barry Stukin said. He had a blue silk handkerchief tucked up the sleeve of his gray suit jacket.

"He better be eclectic, the amount it's cost him in Packy's legal fees over the years," Dutch Shea, Jr., said. "The first time he goes in, the shrink at the farm writes he's the type of personality will spend half his life in prison. That was one shrink was on the money. With about nine dollars change. He's thirty-seven, Packy, he's spent seventeen years in the slam, and he's looking at nine-to-fifteen in about forty-five more minutes. Which is what I got to break to Charlie, he ever shows up." He scanned the calendar. "What've you got?"

"Number 5," Barry Stukin said. "Trial setting."

Dutch Shea ran his finger down the list. Number 5 was Stark, Katherine, 192.1, 1 Ct. "Manslaughter. What is this shit? You don't try manslaughter, you cop to manslaughter."

"Thanks, Jack," Barry Stukin said. "Every time I'm around you, I feel like I'm back in law school, getting the benefit of your knowledge."

"Don't tell me, Johnny Torizzo's the prosecutor," Dutch Shea, Jr., said. He had no interest in Katherine Stark's one count of 192.1. "Martha tells me a great story about him. She's in chambers with him and Bernadette Hanrahan. Bernadette's client is that dyke radical, wanted to blow up Channel 3, the one that looked like Sylvester Stallone, Emma something. Hanratty. So they're shooting the breeze about this and that, discovery, and Johnny says to Bernadette, 'You're spending a lot of time alone with her.' And Bernadette says, 'She's in solitary,' and Johnny says, 'Makes me wonder what you two do when you're alone in there,' the little prick. 'Come on, Johnny,' Martha says, and Bernadette says, 'That's all right, Your Honor, we don't do anything in there, nothing. Which is what Theresa tells me she and Mr. Torizzo do at night in their bedroom.' 'Now wait a minute,' Johnny says, and Martha says, 'You started it, John.'"

"So don't ask why he wants to take it to trial," Barry Stukin said. "He's a shitheel is why. We'll bring in a jury panel and then he'll stand up and say, 'At this time, Your Honor, we want to formally drop our complaint against the accused, we're not satisfied with the quality of our case,' and then Stanley Blatt will feed out some crap about Abraham Lincoln and the nature of justice, he can't come up with anything King Solomon might have said on the subject, and they'll both be on the six o'clock news that night on Channel 3 that Emma Hanratty should've blown up."

"Oh, oh," Dutch Shea, Jr., said. "Here comes Charlie now."

"So how's the fencing business," Dutch Shea, Jr., said after breaking the news as gently as possible to Charlie Considine. They sat in the far corner of the jury box. On the bench, Stanley Blatt was dispensing with the cases on his calendar as quickly as they were called.

"I don't do that anymore, Dutch."

"You don't do it any less either, Charlie."

243

"Always the jokes with you, Dutch." Beads of perspiration crowned Charlie Considine's brow. Even in the middle of winter Charlie perspired. He always carried a handkerchief in his right hand to mop the sweat away. "We could appeal."

"Appeals cost money," Dutch Shea said. He watched as Judge Blatt agreed to a motion for the appointment of doctors.

"I gave you the house in Wallingford," Charlie Considine said. The house in Wallingford was a collateral payment for Packy Considine's latest defense.

"The house in Wallingford is in what we charitably call a changing neighborhood. You had two mortgages on it and an equity of exactly . . ."

Dutch Shea put on his glasses and checked the Considine folder. He knew to the penny what the equity was, but he believed in the purposeful pause.

". . . of exactly $6794.91. By the time I got the place appraised and paid off the back taxes you forgot to tell me about and checked out the title and the variances and paid the real estate agent six percent for unloading it, I came out with a little less than thirty-one hundred dollars." He paused again. "Plus it was the first house I ever saw that had seventy-nine power lawn mowers." Dutch Shea peered over his glasses. "In the living room."

"That was a mistake, Dutch, I told you that," Charlie Considine said. He patted the moisture from his forehead. Dutch Shea wondered if the handkerchief were surgically implanted in Charlie's hand. "The jigaboos must've been using the house to dump hot stuff."

"Oh. That explains it." On the bench, Stanley Blatt set a trial date of the first Monday in November for Barry Stukin's 192.1.

"Packy don't like the joint, Dutch."

244

Dutch Shea, Jr., waved to Barry Stukin as he left the courtroom. "Why not? You don't see the jigaboos dumping their hot lawn mowers there."

Charlie Considine's face sagged. "What's it going to cost, the appeal?"

"Quality advocacy, Charlie. Ten K."

"I don't have that kind of dough, Dutch." Charlie Considine was almost whimpering. "You know what I got? Tupperware. Sheets. Twelve thousand dildos. A load of macadamia nuts. It takes a lot of macadamia nuts to add up to ten K."

"Then he should've taken the deal. All he'd be staring at is grand theft, auto, he testified against his pals, got him into this scrape."

"Stand-up guys don't fink, Dutch."

"Then the world has taken a turn for the better since sunrise, Charlie."

The bailiff called A345144, Considine, Arthur aka Packy, for sentencing. Dutch Shea, Jr., led Charlie Considine from the jury box to the defense table.

"You got the illegal search as grounds for the appeal," Charlie Considine whispered. "They had no reason to stop that car."

"Charlie," Dutch Shea, Jr., said. "That bumper sticker might just as well have said, PACKY CONSIDINE—BANK ROBBER."

A marshal led Packy Considine into the courtroom from the holding tank on the floor below. He was wearing blue denims stenciled with the words, COUNTY JAIL. He winked at his brother and at Dutch Shea, Jr.

"Unload him, Charlie," Dutch Shea, Jr., said. The marshal patted Packy Considine down and then unlocked his shackles. "Dump him like you're going to dump that load of dildos."

"I promised I'd take care of him, Dutch. I promised the old lady."

"Charlie, that was thirty years ago. He wasn't even jerking off then, Packy."

"Yeah, he was, Dutch. Into a picture of James Garner."

The marshal led Packy Considine to the defense table. The two brothers punched and pummeled each other on the shoulders.

"Charlie," Packy Considine said. "Char-LEE."

"Pack," Charlie Considine said. "Pack-EE."

They fell into each other's arms.

"There's a statute of limitations on promises, Charlie," Dutch Shea, Jr., said.

The bailiff motioned Charlie Considine to the spectator seats.

"I promised, Dutch."

"I'm sorry, Charlie."

"Char-LEE."

A day in the life.

Anodyne for the nights in the life.

14.

Dear Lawyer,

Well, it's funny the kind of answers you get from an ad like that. Pervs, mainly. (That's short for perverts.) It makes you wonder if you should take a chance. Like all I have is one thing on my mind. I feel like a g.d. fool. (You know what "g.d." means.) Anyway, I will take a chance. With you. My name is Dot. (Short for Dorothea.) I'm 38, if you have to know the honest truth. I like a good joke, too. Oh, yeah, I nearly forgot. 521-1336. I mean, how were we going to get acquainted? It's not my real phone (remember those pervs!!!!), but I'll be there Wednesday, 5:30 to 6:30. And feeling foolish if

you don't call. Comme ci, comme ca, as the
French say. (My only French expression.)

"Is this Dot?"

"Yes."

"This is the lawyer."

"Hi."

"Hi."

"I mean, you got a name?"

"Oh. John. Jack, actually."

"Jack. I think I like John better. Hi, John."

"Hi."

"You're a lawyer."

"That's right."

"What kind of cases do you handle, John?"

"Well, right now I have one in front of the Public
Utilities Commission."

"Hey, I'm impressed. The Public Utilities Commission. You for it or against it?"

"That's funny."

"I like a good joke."

"That's what you said."

"I did?"

"In your letter."

"Oh, yeah. You gay?"

"I hope not."

"I hope not, too, ha, ha. I mean, the reason I asked
is I heard a real cute one, and I thought if you were gay
you might be offended, but if you were gay, why did
you make this telephone call, right?"

"Right."

"So anyway, here's the cute one. Why does it take
five fags to change a light bulb?"

"I don't know."

"One to change the bulb and four to say, 'Fabulous.'
Isn't that cute?"

"Yes."

247

"As I said, I love a good joke. Breaks the ice, don't you think?"

"Sure does."

"Well, Mr. Public Utilities Commission lawyer, we going to meet?"

"I'd like that."

"You know the Chateau Blanche?"

"I know the Chateau Blanche."

"The Neptune Room?"

"Yes."

"They have a Happy Hour in the Neptune Room. I bet I've seen you there. I love the Happy Hour, don't you?"

"Absolutely."

"Fifty cents a drink, you can't beat that. And all the rumaki you can eat."

"Rumaki?"

"Those bacon things. Wrapped around the pineapple. The toothpick holds them together. Can't forget the old toothpick."

"Oh, those."

"Bet you didn't know they were called rumaki."

"I call them bacon things."

"That's cute. Well. You game for Happy Hour?"

"Sure."

"Friday. How's that?"

"Fine."

"I'll be the one drinking the Pisco Sour."

15. "You know that show on television, *The Dating Game?*" Marty Cagney said.

Dutch Shea, Jr., nodded. He wondered if the rain would ever stop. And wondered if Marty Cagney rambled on to all his clients this way. Or only to those whose wives' adultery he had investigated.

"Well, they got a version out of San Francisco now.

248

The Gay Dating Game. I kid you not. The cable picks it up. Three o'clock in the morning." Marty Cagney shrugged. "I have a little trouble sleeping."

"It happens."

"You, too?"

A noncommittal smile. He was not prepared to discuss his sleepless nights with Marty Cagney.

"Yeah, well." Another shrug. "So I was watching this *Gay Dating Game* last night. Just like the real one. Three contestants. Seven gold chains and eleven shirt buttons unbuttoned between the three of them. I counted."

"Professional interest." Three contestants. Two less than necessary to change a light bulb. Why do I get told all the gay stories all of a sudden? Is it something I give off? Christ, that would have solved a lot of problems.

"That's it. And then there's the guy who's it. The one who picks the contestant he gets to date. Guys, Dutch. On TV."

"It's three in the morning, Marty." He must remember to watch *The Gay Dating Game.* The shows he watched during the sleepless nights all seemed to be sponsored by a local Volvo dealer crooning about the Volvo's life expectancy of seventeen point nine years. He did not like to comtemplate that seventeen point nine. He was not sure he could handle another seventeen point nine years. That would bring him up to sixty-four. Will you still need me, will you still feed me, when I'm sixty-four?

No, not that song. The one Beatles song he knew. He used to sing it to Cat.

Will you still need me . . .

Yes.

Will you still feed me . . .

Yes.

When I'm sixty-four? . . .

Daddy, you'll never be sixty-four.

Cat, Cat. Who would have thought she had the life expectancy of a Volvo?

"Anyway." Marty Cagney was still talking. "This guy says, 'Contestant number one.' And then they cut to contestant number one. Two chains, four buttons unbuttoned. 'If I was a potato, would you fry me, bake me or mash me?' I'm telling you, Dutch, I wish he asked me that question. He reminded me of my son-in-law."

Marty's son-in-law. Formerly married to Marty's daughter. Mary. Mary who wanted to open a gay bar. Mary whose son had to remind himself to masturbate.

Families.

Will you still need me, will you still feed me, when I'm sixty-four?

Not when you have a Volvo's life expectancy.

A quick smile. An ostentatious check of his watch. Tap the face. Put it up against his ear. All to indicate it was time to get down to business.

"What have you got?"

"That building's got a history of wiring defects," Marty Cagney said. "All duly noted here." He handed a folder across the desk with an apologetic smile. "I got to charge you for the typing, Dutch."

"Of course, Marty." He wondered if Marty Cagney would ever stop being embarrassed in front of him. Stop. No good can come from thinking that. He buried himself in the folder. There was something soothing about the Cuthbertson's history of wiring overloads and electrical failures, in the names of the building inspectors and fire examiners and city marshals who had censured the hotel. No LEE S here. No daughters with the life expectancy of a Volvo.

"I talked to the tenants," Marty Cagney said. "The day of the fire, an old guy named Corcoran on the third

250

floor blew a fuse. He had a radio, a refrigerator, a hot plate, two fans, a lamp and a TV set plugged into the same extension cord. Plus there was no hot water that day."

"So." Dutch Shea looked up from the folder.

"The heater blew out. Gas fueled. It's right under the utility room where the fire started. Second time in three weeks it happened. They called the gas company. I got a record of the call."

"You do your homework, Marty."

"Circumstantial, Dutch, but what the hell? There's a lot of ways that fire could have started. . . ."

He picked up the note of disbelief in Marty Cagney's voice. Smoke. That's all it was. Smoke. He half-listened and tried to penetrate the Cuthbertson's maze of ownership. The holding companies, the subsidiaries, the partnerships. The genealogy of a welfare hotel. Originally called The Embassy. He liked that, the spurious sound of it. He sorted through the title transfers and the mortgage defaults and the refinancings and the zoning applications. The history of the Cuthbertson was a history of indebtedness. Perfect for a welfare hotel. Marty Cagney's thoroughness was like a narcotic. The Simla Corporation built the hotel. He tracked the Simla Corporation through bankruptcy, default and foreclosure. Then FHI took over. FHI had trouble making its payments. FHI unloaded it onto the Charter Oak Corporation. Charter Oak renamed the hotel. The Embassy became The Allen House. Classy.

Classy. And a warning light.

Marty Cagney said, ". . . and a fire alarm ten days ago. Two fags were making it guess where?"

"Where?" Distractedly. The Allen House.

"The utility room. In a moment of careless rapture, one of the fags dropped the joint he was smoking into the rag pile."

251

"Oh." That warning light. The Allen House. He remembered The Allen House from his father's funeral. D.F. owned it.

Oh, God.

"Which started a fire," Marty Cagney said. "You all right, Dutch?"

"Fine, Marty." FHI. Another warning light. Frog Hollow, Incorporated. The partnership between his father and D. F. Campion. FHI. The acronym had slipped by him at first.

"A lot of fags end up in that utility room since the cops started cracking down on the men's room in the bus station. Three busts in two months."

"That's terrific, Marty." The Charter Oak Corporation. One of D.F.'s companies. Now he remembered.

Remembered.

Even with BEAUBOIS, Robert NMI, he could not seem to escape memory.

". . . a complaint the day of the fire."

"A complaint?" A pro forma question. He didn't care about the complaint. It was memory that kept on intruding. History. The past.

Why would FHI sell the hotel to the Charter Oak Corporation?

Why would the left hand not know what the right hand was doing?

Why do I want to know?

"Kids sniffing glue, Dutch. A complaint the day of the fire."

"Oh."

Will you still need me, will you still feed me, when I'm sixty-four?

LEE S.

Cat. Who had the life expectancy of a Volvo.

The Allen House. FHI. The Charter Oak Corporation.

Why do I want to know? Why would I want to know? When I have spent a lifetime trying not to know.

"I'll check your sweetheart's movements out myself," Marty Cagney said.

My sweetheart. BEAUBOIS, Robert NMI. My sweetheart was supposed to protect me from memory.

All my sweethearts were supposed to protect me from memory.

When you can't trust your sweetheart, who can you trust?

16. "What I don't want, and I want to tell you this frankly," Francis Noonan said, "what I don't want is the Crime Commission on my ass. I'm in the construction business, for Christ's sake. You're in the construction business, you deal with guys with names like Dino and Luigi, got the alpaca sweaters in every color. Every one of them's a close personal friend of Frank's, hear them tell it. The only reason he didn't sing at their granddaughter's first communion, Frank, was he had this benefit, build a hospital in Vegas. Dino Z. and them. You know Dino Z.? Wears the yellow alpaca all the time with the mother-of-pearl buttons and the little golf hat says Pequod CC on it. The reason he wears the Pequod CC hat is he clipped a couple of guys and buried them under the ninth fairway when he built it, Pequod, the story is. You deal with people like that, like Dino Z. there, you run a fleet of diesels can carry a million cubic feet of dirt. He puts a body under my dirt, Dino Z., all I did was supply the dirt, not the stiff, if he was a stiff when the first load fell on him even.

"I was a nun, I wouldn't know people like him, Dino. I'd know people like Monsignor Quinlan at Regina Coeli. I was a nun, as a matter of fact, I wouldn't question Monsignor Quinlan too close about his brother Teddy, was in Sammy Cohen's buying a vicuña jacket the day Hooky Rothman gets his. He brung Hooky in with him, some people say, not that I always believe what some people say, and this guy comes in with a piece looks like a BAR and plays Tic Tac Dough all over Hooky, and you'd've thought Teddy Quinlan never heard of him, Hooky. 'I see a body lying there,' he tells the cops, Teddy, 'and I says to myself, Why, it's Mr. Rothman.' Forgetting it was Hooky was putting him into the vicuña in the first place.

"So the thing of it is, dirt's big business, you want to get right down to it, and the people in the dirt business, well, I deal with a lot of people pick their teeth after they eat, and they eat a fuck of a lot of pasta, you want the honest to God truth. But me, me I go to Mass on Sunday, I'm not playing golf, and I make my Easter duty, and the archbishop wants to build a new parochial school, all he's got to do is lift up the horn and Francis Xavier Noonan is writing out a check. I buy a table for ten at all Matty Dineen's dinners, even though I was governor of this state and I had Matty as water commissioner, I'd count the dams and the reservoirs every morning just to make sure they was still there. Johnny Falanga, he's running for reelection, he wants to change the lettering on the city trash cans from CITY ON THE MOVE to HERE'S JOHNNY, I step up to the table.

"I don't want to antagonize anyone, is the reason, and that's the way of the world, I shit you not. You antagonize a guy and what this guy does to you is this. You underbid somebody six dollars a ton to haul a load of asphalt, you got all the right mileage specifications, you're within the zone requirements, and all of a sudden the Transportation Department says you can't use the city tunnels because they just did a new study, came out yesterday, and what they found is there's more traffic delays in tunnels and the asphalt you're bringing into town might fall below the required three hundred degrees, there's ever a traffic jam in the Charter Oak Tunnel, so they're going to get different transportation, and that's what happens, you dumb fuck, you don't buy one of Matty Dineen's tables for ten. Get it?"

"Got it," Dutch Shea, Jr., said. "What I don't get is why you're coming to me."

"Who'm I supposed to go to?" Francis Xavier Noonan said. He weighed close to three hundred pounds and he wheezed when he talked. "Thayer Pomfret? He helped set up the Crime Commission, for Christ's sake. Forget that. He's a good citizen, though what the world does not need is another good fucking citizen, you want my opinion. The good citizens, they don't just want to get rid of the ginneys, they want to get rid of the spaghetti, too, you want my opinion. But forget that. He was running for Congress there, I even get on his bandwagon, it didn't matter I knew he was going to get his ass handed to him, with a pair of Jockey shorts thrown in. I was with him, up the North End there, covering my bet, you never know, miracles might happen, the Atlantic Ocean might dry up, too, and he walks into Vito Scalisi's joint and orders drinks all around, and a Perrier for himself, no shit, hand on the Bible.

"So it's the week after the election, and I figure he ever wants to run again, he might need to know a couple of ginneys, and I send him Quino Cianfrani, he's got something up before the Planning Commission, and he don't need a lawyer the only two Latin words he knows is habeas corpus. 'How do you spell that?' he says to Quino. 'Capital C-I-A-N-F-R-A-N-I,' Quino says. 'Cianfrani.' 'I see,' Thayer says. I never call him Thayer in my life, we didn't have many first name Thayers over on Sisson Avenue there, although I call him shithead a couple of times. 'Cianfrano.'

'Cianfrani,' Quino says. 'I see,' he says again, writing it down like somebody just shit on his pad. 'Cianfrani.' Looking through his tortoise shell glasses. Quino's got the tinted specs and the blow-dried razor cut and the modified Mister B collar and at this point he's probably thinking he'd like to put me under the ninth fairway at Pequod there, I think he's getting a hard-on thinking about that, as a matter of fact. 'And your first name is Quino,' shithead says. 'Uh-uh,' Quino says. 'Pasquale. Quino's my nickname.' 'And a nice nickname it is,' he says, Pomfret. I think he's already working the Crime Commission over in his mind. 'Short for Pasqualino,' Quino says. 'I see,' Pomfret says. He hasn't taken a crap in three weeks and his eyes are too close together, and he's wondering who the moron is sent him Quino Cianfrani, which is why I don't go to Thayer Pomfret, one reason anyway."

"I thought there probably was a reason," Dutch Shea, Jr., said.

"Exactly," Francis Xavier Noonan said. "Which is why I want your help. How well you know Waterbury? It doesn't matter you do or you don't, one place is just like another. I got this new company, I call it United Sanitation for now, I got thirty trucks, I got the drivers, real rocks, guys who wear their Camels rolled up in the sleeve of their T-shirt there, and I got this site in Waterbury, four hundred acres, and I want to turn it into the biggest landfill in the state. You follow me so far?"

"So far," Dutch Shea, Jr., said.

"I'm going to put in a three-story baler, that son of a bitch will be able to compact fifty cubic cards of garbage into a package the size of a case of Bud. A Sara Lee German chocolate cake, maybe even. You like it?"

"So far."

"You like the name?" Francis Xavier Noonan said.

"You deal with garbage, it's hard to come up with a name, you know what I mean?"

"I know what you mean."

"I'm not married to United Sanitation, is what I'm trying to say. General Compaction, I been playing around with that. Reduction Associations, that's another one. You got any ideas, I'd like to hear them."

"What about General Compaction, a division of United Sanitation?" Dutch Shea, Jr., said.

"A division of United Sanitation," Francis Xavier Noonan said. "I like that." He repeated the name and whistled. "It's a thing of beauty is what this operation is. It will solve the garbage needs of this state into the twenty-first century."

"I lie awake nights, Francis, wondering what we're going to do with the garbage in the twenty-first century," Dutch Shea, Jr., said, "and I shouldn't've bothered, you thought it all out yourself."

"I'm glad you feel that way," Francis Xavier Noonan said. "Carmine thought you might."

"Carmine."

"Cantalupo. He did me a favor once. Barry Stukin says you did him a favor once, Carmine, I cut you in on this, you help me set it up, I'm square with him, Carmine, he's square with you. It's not so complicated, you stop to figure it out."

"No, I guess it's not."

"You ever know his daughter, Carmine? Sara. I hear it's tougher getting into the number forty-three bus than it is getting into her."

"I really don't know her."

"Give me a son every time," Francis Xavier Noonan said. "Tougher'n hell to knock up a son."

"I suppose."

"Anyway," Francis Xavier Noonan said. "I was thinking about five percent." He waited for a response and got none. "I mean, plus your fee, of course. I don't want to imply you do this on a contingency basis. You get your fee plus the five, it could be worth a fortune. Barry tells me you won't look the other way, someone waves a fortune your way. Which is what I'm doing, you got nothing against garbage."

"Barry Stukin," Dutch Shea, Jr., said slowly.

"You got a real pal there," Francis Xavier Noonan said.

"I figured he was behind this."

17. He watched the woman at the bar order another Pisco Sour. Her hand went up, her finger pointed to her empty glass and she said, "Again, Mickey." Lee did not drink Pisco Sours. Nor did she know the first name of many bartenders. And if she did, she never said, "Again, Mickey." Not her style. He wondered if that was why he married her. He could not think of any other reason. They had slept together that whole summer. Her coolness in bed impressed him. She stripped the foil from the condom and then slipped it on him. Efficient. No wasted motion. The woman's job, she said. Of course he did not know then of the pelvic inflammation. One pelvic infection would tend to encourage precaution. He was surprised when he asked her to marry him. It was spur of the moment. It had simply never occurred to him to ask any other woman to marry him. Certainly none of the intense young advocates who had shared his bed in law school. Certainly not Clarice. Oh, God, Clarice. Over whom he had once masturbated. No. That was a furtive nocturnal groping he preferred not to remember. Lee. She was taking a shower. He pulled back the curtain and asked her. Her hair was lathered with Prell Concentrate and the white suds poured down between her breasts. She did not seem to think it odd that he asked her in the shower. She did not even turn the water off.

She said she would have to ask Father. Father. Fairfax Liggett was not a Dad type. Nor a Daddy. Never Pop. Not in a million years. Father. Father objected. Father demanded clarification. Obiter dicta from the bench. A statement of intentions. A definition of assets. Voir dire.

It's like he's setting a trial date, Lee.

That's the way he is, Jack.

What if he says no?

He won't.

But what if he does?

I'll marry you.

Why?

Because I love you.

Love. A concept he always had difficulty with. Notice "concept." He sounded like Judge Liggett. He suspected the judge would have called love a "concept."

Because I love you.

Yes, she said it. Said it a lot. Said it before Byron Igoe. Said it after Byron Igoe. Said it even when they were splitting up.

You know, Jack, I really did love you. You just never believed me. That was part of the problem. It might even have been the problem.

True thing. One of Cat's sayings. True thing.

Did I love Lee? Lee who did not drink Pisco Sours. What does it matter now?

The woman at the bar was looking at him over her Pisco Sour. Not a bad face. Just a face with a lot of miles on it. A face that had seen too many Pisco Sours.

"Hey, you."

For a moment he thought she was calling for Mickey, the bartender. "Me?"

"Your name wouldn't happen to be John, would it?"

"No," he said. "Dutch."

* * *

18. "The word 'alibi,'" Dutch Shea, Jr., said, "should never, repeat never, be used by a defense attorney." He glanced around the drab classroom. One fluorescent cylinder flickered, another was burnt out. The Spanish graffiti on the walls had repulsed repeated Ajax rubdowns. Dimly he could make out, *"Viva la huelga,* mother . . . ." Black paint had been splashed over ". . . fucker." What *huelga,* what mother-fucker? Some of his students stared back blankly at him. The Art of Cross-Examination was an elective. He knew that most of the students took it because he had a reputation as an easy grader. The hour provided them an opportunity to bone up on Principles of Realty Law. No matter. Most would fail the bar exam anyway. And the course effectively subtracted one evening from his week.

"Why is that, Mr. Shea?" That would be Mr. Flatow. Bernard Flatow was never without a question. Bernard Flatow had seen every episode of *The Defenders* and *Judd for the Defense.* Bernard Flatow often contradicted him with a point of law raised by E. G. Marshall on *The Defenders.*

"Because it connotes something contrived, Mr. Flatow."

"Then what should I use, Mr. Shea?"

"You might try 'explanation.'"

"When E. G. Marshall uses 'explanation,' Mr. Shea, he always puts 'straightforward' in front of it. 'Straightforward explanation' is what he always says."

"That's a very good point, Mr. Flatow."

E. G. Marshall had a lawyer son on *The Defenders,* he seemed to recall. And he had a lawyer father. Will wonders never cease? He turned and wrote on the blackboard. "The Myth of the Expert Witness." He liked to work with his back to the class. It added dramatic effect when he turned and confronted them

with a punch line. He called for examples of expert witnesses and with each answer wrote on the blackboard. "Pathologist." "Handwriting expert." "Fingerprint expert." That was the one he wanted. With his back still to the class, he said, "An expert witness is so called because he can expertly espouse anything to support . . ."

He turned to face the class. ". . . whichever side of the case calls him."

An expected chuckle from the class. Even from those studying Principles of Realty Law.

"Now. How does a defense attorney destroy the credibility of an expert witness?"

It was meant as a rhetorical question, but of course he should have counted on Bernard Flatow. "E. G. Marshall always refers to the expert as 'sheriff' or 'officer' so that the jury gets the idea he's not totally objective."

"Very interesting." A girl in the back of the classroom was staring at him. She must have come in when he was writing on the blackboard. He wondered why she was so familiar. "First you must learn the vocabulary of the expert witness. Let us take for example the fingerprint expert."

"Fingerprint experts almost always appear for the prosecution," Bernard Flatow said.

"Can we thank you for that revelation, Mr. Flatow, or E. G. Marshall?"

The class laughed. Bernard Flatow flushed. A cheap shot. He wished he had not said it. The girl in the back did not smile. Pale skin. Pale red hair. A cheap overcoat she did not take off.

"You'll never know as much as the expert witness, of course, but with a little reading in the literature of fingerprinting, you will learn what a ridge is, a whorl, a loop, an arch, a delta, a core. You will learn dots, or islands, as they are sometimes called. You will learn about ridge beginnings and short ridges and split ridges or enclosures. And above all you will learn about bifurcations."

The girl was not taking notes. She just stared at him. She reminded him of a nun out to break her vows.

"Mr. Shea, that's an awful lot to learn, man." That was Mr. Miranda. Mr. Miranda was always looking for a way to cut corners.

"Defense is an exercise in learning and forgetting, Mr. Miranda." And so is life, my friend, so is life. It was forgetting he had so much trouble with.

The girl. He was sure she was someone he should have forgotten.

"Man, why should we learn all that shit?"

That was Mr. Jackson. The only black in the class. At least Mr. Jackson did not call him "Dude," as he did all his other instructors.

"Because you wish to get your client off, Mr. Jackson."

"Shit, man, that dude is guilty."

A laugh from the class. At least they seemed to have absorbed the basic principle of criminal law.

"All right, then, because you wish to impute the testimony of an expert witness. To call into question his expertise."

"Make that honky look like an asshole."

"Concisely put."

The girl frowned. He bet she had never heard scatology in her parochial school classrooms. A sure thing, that bet. She looked as if she expected him to give Mr. Jackson a dose of the rubber hose.

Like a nun out of uniform.

Uniform.

Now he had it.

"Now we are told by our expert witness that no two fingerprints are identical . . ."

Maid's uniform.

"Your questions must be precise . . ."

Maeve.

"With the proper foundation . . ."

Maeve Kelleher.

"No shortcuts . . ."

D. F. Campion's maid.

"For example, our fingerprint expert. First you ac-knowledge his degrees, his courses of study, his exper-tise, as it were. Then you begin to chip away. 'Do you agree . . .'"

Distant cousin of Kathleen Donnelly.

"'. . . that there are at least two hundred and twenty million people in the United States?'"

Kathleen. Into whose armpit Clarice had stuck a wad of Juicy Fruit.

"'And if we are to assume that each has ten fingers, would that not total two billion two hundred million fingers?'"

Kathleen. With the pale red pubic hair.

"'In fact, is it not true that no one has ever compared the hundred and twenty fingers on the hands of the members of this jury to determine whether any of them has similar points of identification, let alone the more than two billion . . .'"

What was Maeve Kelleher doing here?

Never ask a question without knowing the answer. The very basis of the art of cross-examination.

This was one answer he did not want to know.

"It was my night off, you see," Maeve Kelleher said. She chewed on the slice of orange from her Tom Collins. "Uncle Dominick . . . Mr. Campion, that is . . . he always lets me have one night a week off. And all day Sunday, after lunch."

He remembered.

263

The one night a week with Kathleen.

"I usually go to the pictures."

"But not tonight."

"I'd seen them all. Except the one with Al Pacino. I don't like Al Pacino. I don't favor Italian men, to tell the truth."

"I see." The ice in his drink had melted, but he did not ask for any more. The waitress had looked closely at Maeve when she ordered the Tom Collins, obviously knowing she was underage. No sense going through that again. A grown man pouring Tom Collinses into a minor was a problem he did not care to add to his old kit bag.

"You know, I never thought of that."

"Of what?"

"That there are more than two billion fingers in America. But if you know your multiplication tables, there'd have to be."

"Yes."

"It makes you realize how big America really is."

That was one way to think of it, yes. Or you could think the Chinese had eight billion fingers, so take that, America. Good Lord, I'm beginning to think like a Galway farm girl. A reversion back to the bogs. Maybe I'd be better off back in the bogs. With a background tenor chorus singing, "Too-ra-loo-ra-loo-ra."

For Christ's sake, grab hold. "Maeve, why did you come to my class tonight?"

She started nibbling on the orange rind. "Well, I heard you were such a grand lawyer."

"That never brought you to my class before."

Maeve Kelleher drank her Tom Collins through a straw, as if it were a milk shake. "I got a letter, you see."

He wished Bernard Flatow were conducting this questioning. E. G. Marshall was sure to have a theory about letters received by Irish domestic servants. Or better yet, call on Mr. Jackson. Mr. Jackson would know how to handle it. What is this letter shit, bitch?

"From Kathleen. Kathleen Donnelly."

Of course. Why should he expect his luck to change? He hoped his face expressed disinterest. "Really."

"Yes."

"Interesting." Not convincing. He did not do a good languid. Another tack. Introduce an element of doubt. Of someone only dimly remembered. "The one who used to work for Mr. Campion." Better. And the "Mr. Campion" was a good touch. No familiarity. Not with the household help.

"You were asking about her, remember?" Just a hint of truculence. A brazen number, this Maeve.

"Really." Back to languid. "A cousin, wasn't she?"

"Third cousin."

"Once removed. That's the one, isn't it? From . . ." As if his memory faltered.

"Sligo."

"That's it." A smile just condescending enough to suggest that the genealogy of Irish servant girls was not all that engaging. But he knew suddenly that he was only delaying the inevitable. He wondered what Maeve Kelleher was up to, wondered what small extortion was about to be exacted.

"She said to say hello."

Was that it? Was that all there was? Hi, hello, how's it going, remember me? He remembered the birthmark in the small of her back. Pale brown birthmark. Pale red pubic hair. "How'd she happen to write?"

"Well, I wrote my da . . ."

For the first time Maeve Kelleher did not look at him. Becoming evasive, was she? Well, you started this, Maeve. And you're not going to get any help from me.

". . . I said we'd been talking about her."

"Who?"

"You and me. That night at Mr. Campion's. When you were asking all the questions." There was a look of sullen defiance on Maeve Kelleher's face. "And my da must've said something to her da."

"In Sligo." He wondered if Maeve had a birthmark in the small of her back.

"And I guess her da wrote her." A pale brown birthmark. And pale red pubic hair. "In the state of Nevada."

Ah. That state of Nevada. That state of apprehension. That state of expectation. "And she wrote you."

"That's right."

"And said to say hello."

Maeve nodded. He looked at her and did not say anything. Your serve, Maeve.

"We used to talk about her a lot in school," Maeve said finally.

He did not reply.

"The parents talked about her, too. When they thought we weren't around."

She's circling the subject as if it's prey, he thought. The subject of Kathleen Donnelly.

"She was fast, they said."

Fast. The anachronistic quaintness of the word seemed not to apply to Kathleen Donnelly. "And that was disapproved of."

"Only by the priests. And the nuns."

So they were in on it, too. Fast Kathleen. Object of clerical novenas. "But not by the girls in school."

"The girls used to whisper she had a baby."

Fast Kathleen. "Women do."

"She wasn't married, you see."

266

Fast Kathleen. Kathleen with the pale brown birthmark in the small of her back. His? No, not possible. It was nearly a year after they stopped seeing each other that she left D.F.'s. And once a week during that year, she passed him the peas and the succotash, this woman in the white maid's uniform, fast Kathleen with the pale red pubic hair.

"She never named the da."

He wondered if Maeve expected him to deny paternity.

Kathleen.

Why do I only feel relief that I am not the father of your child?

Fast Kathleen.

One night a week and every Sunday after lunch.

And one weekend.

After the salpingogram.

No. That was too easy. That made it seem like cause and effect. That gave him motive. And motive was a very poor explanation of character. The one viable *pensée* of John Shea, Jr.

He looked at Maeve.

Fast Maeve. Who did not favor Italian men.

Available Maeve. Of that he would make book.

What did she suspect? What did she expect? Perhaps only to find in his bed a ticket to the city of Las Vegas in the county of Clark in the state of Nevada. A Galway dream, a Sligo finale.

Kathleen said to say hello. Not bloody likely. Not her style at all. Keep your bloody Kelleher nose out of my business was more the style of Kathleen Donnelly of Sligo. Kathleen with the pale brown birthmark, Kathleen with the pale red pubic hair.

Would it ever end?

This banquet of memory.

He contemplated Maeve Kelleher. Suspecting

Maeve, expectant Maeve, fast and available Maeve. Keep your bloody nose out of my business. A command that would pique the Galway nostrils. Oh, God, child, fast and available child, go back to Ireland. You are a memory I cannot afford.

"If you write, tell her I said hello."

BOOK FOUR

I

"I'm the sort of priest," Hugh Campion said, "strangers tell dirty jokes to." He corrected himself. "To whom strangers tell dirty jokes. On the way up here, on the plane, the man sitting next to me, he said, 'Father Hugh, did you hear the one about the Polish bank robber?' A nice man. He watched the show. He told me he added Tabasco to my recipe for omelette fines herbes and it was a triumph. I don't think he was the sort of man who would tell a dirty joke to his parish priest."

"What about him?" Dutch Shea, Jr., said. Through the plate-glass window that enclosed the veranda of the Club, he could see a small tractor rolling a distant fairway in the pelting rain.

"What is there to know?" Hugh Campion said. A red silk handkerchief stuck out of the breast pocket of his black clerical suit. "He had one of those plastic briefcases with his company's name printed on it. United Technologies, I think."

"I mean the Polish bank robber."

"He tied up the safe and blew the guard," Hugh Campion said.

Dutch Shea, Jr., laughed. In the distance, the greens-keeper jumped off his tractor, replaced a divot, then rolled over it and continued down the fairway.

"Most priests," Hugh Campion said, "If they meet a stranger on a plane, they get asked about the difference between sanctifying and actual grace or mortal and venial sin." He chuckled. "When I was in the seminary, old Father Devlin, Dirty Devlin, we called him, I never knew why, Father Devlin said that the difference between mortal and venial sin varied from parish to parish. It was my first exposure to situation ethics." Hugh held the white wine under his nose before taking a sip. "Dirty Devlin was the one who called the vow of chastity putting on the tin pants."

"Maybe that's why they called him Dirty Devlin," Dutch Shea, Jr., said.

"The point is, Jack," Hugh Campion said, "that I never get asked how St. Blaise got to be such an expert on throats. Or in the temporal line, how to counsel Mrs. Sullivan, the president of the Altar Society, when her daughter, Sister Alice, the Mercy nun, falls in love with her mother superior. Not me. I'm the sort of priest people sidle up to. 'Sidle.' It's the operative verb for the people I come into contact with. 'Father Hugh,' they say, 'did you hear the one about.' If I ever write my autobiography, I'm going to call it, 'Did You Hear the One About—Memories of the Green Room by Hugh Campion, C.P.'" Hugh took another sip of wine. "'C.P.' That stands for celebrity priest. A small and select ministry. Somehow I don't think God had *TV Guide* in mind when he urged the spreading of the Word."

"You really thinking of writing your autobiography?"

"It's a gold mine, I'm told," Hugh Campion said. "Big bucks. Recipes, Tin Pan Alley and the confessional. All I need is a goddamn dog. Publishers take me to lunch at The Four Seasons. The chef invites me into the kitchen, Mick Jagger gives me the finger and then says I'm a beautiful guy, Stevie Wonder gives me the latest spade handshake." Hugh peered over his wineglass. "You know, I've always been two handshakes behind those spade musicians."

"Go easy on the Catholic stuff, one publisher says. Go easy. Christ, it's been twenty years since I met a monsignor. The people I see call nuns 'darling.' I'm not even sure I can name the Popes since Pius the Twelfth. And I only remember him because I go into Poppa's house and there he is staring at me in the front hall. Poppa tells me he's going to leave me that painting in his will. I think he's trying to tell me if Pius were still pope, I'd be lucky to be a curate at St. Finbar's in Collinsville."

"You've seen D.F., then?"

"Oh, hell, yes," Hugh Campion said. He raised an eyebrow and smiled. "A guerrilla skirmish. We snipe at each other from the underbrush. He asked me about Septuagesima. Out of the blue. What I thought of it. There's not a hell of a lot you can say about Septuagesima, is there? I don't think he thought I knew what it was. And then he asked if I knew Perry Como. I think there was a connection there, but I didn't get it." Hugh shook his head. "Actually Clarice asked me to talk to him. She wants his financial support. You can imagine how far I got."

"I was there the night she mentioned sex clinics for emerging nuns."

"Yes." Hugh Campion drew the word out. "Another Campion contribution to eccentric Catholicism." He paused. "Did you know she's thinking of running for Congress? I didn't pass that on to Poppa. There's a time and place for everything."

"She's not serious?"

"I think she said she was kicking it around. Getting

273

some input. Running it up the flagpole to see if anyone will genuflect. I thought of a swell campaign slogan. 'Vote for Clarice Campion—Recently a Nun.'"

"It's an enthusiasm, Hugh. It will pass."

"It's really not that bad an idea, Jack. Look at the boobs we have in Congress now. Clarice would be a refreshing change. From convent to Congress. It's a plausible step. Congress needs a virgin. It's an un-tapped constituency. Think of Clarice as the head of a major new pressure group."

"Poor Clarice," Dutch Shea, Jr., said. He wondered how many conversations about her he and Hugh had encoded over the years. It was always impossible for either of them to speak directly about her. One was always perplexed, the other protective; one ironic, the other resigned.

"Yes, Poor Clarice," Hugh Campion said. "I some-times think 'Poor' is her first name. Right there on her birth certificate. 'Poor Clarice Campion.' It's a double name, like Mary Anne or Betty Lou." Hugh speared a wedge of lemon with his fork. "Poor Clarice. That's the problem, right there." He squeezed the lemon over his sole. "You know, she always wanted to marry you, Jack."

Dutch Shea, Jr., did not respond. What was there to say? That he knew and was indifferent? Or that he didn't know and was obtuse? Across the dining room he could see Greg Rooney trying to get his attention. Greg Rooney who had laboratory proof that he shot live ammunition. Although never into Clarice Campi-on, the former Sister Domenica. And at another table Harry Pyle sat with Thayer Pomfret. Two more vectors from my past, he thought. The Club seemed criss-crossed with them today. Thayer who had arranged Cat's adoption. A subject he did not wish to contem-plate. It had always seemed so inextricably entangled with his own blemished parentage. Your dad is your dad. Something Cat could never say. Leave it alone, sealed in red tape. Another uninvestigated mystery. My life is a Chinese box full of uninvestigated mysteries. Shake that thought off. Look at Harry Pyle. Pretending he doesn't recognize me. Harry Pyle whose marriage to Serafina Cantalupo he had brokered. After a fashion. In this very dining room. He wondered if Carmine Cantalupo had cut his son-in-law in on the garbage caper. Or if it were an offer only reserved for slightly tainted members of the bar.

"Another demented idea," Hugh Campion said. "Like wanting to run for Congress. When you weren't available, she upped her sights and became a bride of Christ. I suppose it wasn't bad as marriages go. Seventeen years is a pretty good run these days."

Hugh paused while the waitress topped his wineglass. She had a worn Irish face and wore a small gold cross around her neck. She leaned close to Hugh and whispered, "Would you like another piece of sole, Father? Chef is saving one just for you." She nodded at Dutch Shea, Jr. "No extra charge, Mr. Shea. And there's a lemon surprise that's not on the menu. With real whipped cream, not Cool Whip." She leaned close again. "The Protestants get the Cool Whip. They don't know the difference."

Hugh Campion shook his head and said no, he could not eat another bite and please, would she thank the chef?

"Nora," the waitress said. "Nora Marinan. From St. Jude's."

"Thank you, Nora," Hugh Campion said. He waited until Nora Marinan was out of earshot. "Imagine that. The Protestants get the Cool Whip. There's a lesson there."

"How they fuss over Father," Dutch Shea, Jr., said.

A quick smile. "Just like I'm a real priest," Hugh Campion said. He raised his hand in greeting to someone across the room. "Who's that waving at us? The one that looks like a fighter pilot."

J. Gregory Rooney was wearing his yellow-tinted aviator glasses.

"Greg Rooney."

"I thought so. Transy."

"A class ahead of you, two ahead of me."

Hugh Campion cocked a finger at J. Gregory Rooney. "He taught me how to masturbate. I sometimes think it's a pity it didn't take."

Dutch Shea, Jr., laughed. Hugh, sweet Hugh. "He's a urologist now."

"That's the same racket."

Oh, yes. The same racket. *You go into the can and belt away.* The semen was counted. *A bazooka it's not.* Then Part II of the deal: the salpingogram. *The most common cause of blocked tubes is pelvic inflammatory disease.* And so on to Kathleen Donnelly. Who was there. Like Mount Everest. To be climbed. Mounted. Mounting her mound. Lee wasn't even first to play around. At least I don't think. That was certainly food for thought. Play around. A slippery combination of words. Fool around. Even more shifty. Fuck around. Pithy. To the point. Fucking around with Kathleen Donnelly. *They learn to cook and clean and shave under their arms.* If they don't want a wad of Juicy Fruit up there.

Memory.

And here comes another shard of memory. Eustace Cooney. Taking a table and casing the room. Pretending not to see me. As usual. Still claiming I cost him the DA's office. Well, at least I helped. And got a fringe benefit. No cases heard by Judge Cooney since that challenge. Vote for Eustace Cooney—The Judge Who Gave Harlow T. Jefferson a Fair Trial.

Memory.

Your dad is your dad.

"You look terrific, Hugh."

"It's dealings with women that age people, Jack," Hugh Campion said. "That's why priests and queers always look terrific." He flicked a bread crumb away with his napkin. "How's Lee?"

Speaking of dealings that age people. "All right."

"Do you see her?"

"We talk." Q. *Why did you go into the ladies' room alone that night?* A. *Why did you pick that restaurant?* She answered questions with questions now. He supposed it passed for talk.

"Would she ever have married Byron Igoe?"

He surveyed Hugh. His face was lightly tanned. Lee once said that Hugh was never out of season. "That's an unpriestly thing to ask."

"True. But you can't say I've been a raving success as a priest."

He remembered the empty sperm sacs noted on Byron Igoe's autopsy report. "An automobile accident tends to make such questions moot." And he thought of Elaine. Who had cellulite deposits on her thighs and whose calls he had not answered since that night. *What night?* That night. *Describe that night.* The night I came over her Caesarean scar. *It's what they call a bikini incision, Jack.*

"The thing I remember about Byron," Hugh Campion said, "is that little piece of asparagus in his teeth, in his braces, when he came to your dad's wake. When your dad died."

Your dad is your dad.

"Do you ever think of your dad, Jack?"

"Sometimes." *The harder types are in West Block.* A good thing to remember. All things considered. I mean, who would want to be a second-generation candy ass in East Block?

"I mean about what happened to him?"

You mean, why did FHI sell The Allen House to the

277

Charter Oak Corporation? You mean, why did the left hand not know what the right hand was doing? "Not really." *My life is a Chinese box full of uninvestigated mysteries.* "It happened."

"You've got no interest?"

"Hugh, I was a child. It was thirty years ago. He's dead."

Headlines: INSURANCE SCANDAL. SHEA CHARGED. ACTED ALONE, SHEA SAYS.

"Maybe you're smarter than all of us, Jack," Hugh Campion said.

ACTED ALONE, SHEA SAYS. A peculiar assertion, that one. Rich with innuendo. "How's that?"

"The way you prefer not to examine your life."

NO FURTHER INDICTMENTS WILL BE SOUGHT, DISTRICT ATTORNEY SAYS. So saith the DA.

"Oh, for Christ's sake."

ACTED ALONE, SHEA SAYS. So saith Shea.

SHEA. A good, crisp headline name. But not with O'MEARA. A bad headline pairing. Too many vowels.

You're damn right I prefer not to examine my life. Where the hell does it get you?

But.

An exception.

Exceptions make the rule.

"Hugh . . ."

"I'm sorry, Jack. It's none of my business."

"Don't be silly." Be casual. Clear the throat. Dab at the lips with the napkin. Get the tone right. The funny - thing- happened -on - the -highway -of -life tone. The finger- snapping- something- just-occurred-to- me tone. "Something just occurred to me. Do you remember a girl who used to work for D. F.?" There. It was too late to go back. "A hell of a long time ago." He waved good-bye to J. Gregory Rooney. *A bazooka it's not.* "One of those Irish bogtrotters." With pale red pubic

278

hair. "Kathleen." Slowly. As if not quite sure. "Kathleen Donnelly."

Hugh looked startled. "Clarice put Juicy Fruit in her armpit."

"Yes, that's the one."

"Whatever made you mention her?"

"The new girl . . ."

"Maeve . . ."

". . . she told me the other night she was in Las Vegas. Among other things."

"Sweet Jesus." Hugh Campion stared out the veranda window into the rain. "Poppa fired her." He seemed far away. "She's the only one he ever fired."

"Yes." A pause. "I think because he thought I was sleeping with her."

Hugh stared at him.

And kept staring.

"Were you?"

"Yes." *A bazooka it's not.* "My first venture into infidelity." He felt as if he were in confession. Offer an extenuating circumstance. "Actually my only one."

The truth.

Not that the truth is ever a defense.

Lee didn't know. Or did know. It didn't matter. She didn't care. Or wouldn't have cared.

If she knew.

Byron was later. Years later. It wasn't a score she was settling.

Didn't care. Or wouldn't have cared. That says it all.

No, not all. *You know, Jack, I really did love you. You just never believed me.*

Hugh was still withdrawn, distant. "I never knew that."

"I think you were the chaplain on that cruise ship around that time."

279

The distance evaporated. "One of my early priestly triumphs," Hugh Campion said. A sudden sad smile. He touched Dutch Shea's arm and held his thumb and forefinger together and made the sign of the cross over the table. The sad smile seemed riveted to his face. *"Te absolvo,* Jack."

II

What he did not tell Hugh Campion:

That he had taken Kathleen Donnelly to a convention of trial attorneys in New York. That he had not delivered his paper, "Conflicts in Representing Multiple Defendants." That he had not participated, as scheduled, in seminars on "The Right to Refuse Urine Tests in Narcotics Cases," "The Discriminatory Use of Peremptory Challenges" and "Toward a New Theory of Prostitution Defense." That he and Kathleen Donnelly had spent much of their time in the bar of the Park East Lounge on Madison Avenue. That he and Kathleen Donnelly had made love standing up in the ladies' room at the Park East Lounge. That it was the only time he had ever made love standing up. That he had seen Veronica Lake drinking at the bar of the Park East Lounge after making love with Kathleen Donnelly standing up in the ladies' room. That the three drunk men with Veronica Lake had called her Ronny.

What he had never told Cat:

That there was a reason why he remembered seeing Veronica Lake in the Park East Lounge.

Oh, yes.

Fact: Cat did not know who Veronica Lake was.

Olden times, Daddy.

Olden times to Cat was the moment before she was born.

Fact: Cat was not even born when he and Kathleen Donnelly saw Veronica Lake in the Park East Lounge.

The night they had made love standing up in the ladies' room.

The night he should have been a panelist on the seminar on "The Right to Refuse Urine Tests in Narcotics Cases."

They're from Sligo, the Donnellys.

She had told him about Sligo the afternoon he cut the seminar on "The Discriminatory Use of Peremptory Challenges." In bed. At the Americana Hotel. There was a poem about Sligo. She knew only one line:

> "But the haunted air of twilight is
> very strange and still . . ."

They had spent a lot of time in bed at the Americana Hotel during that convention of trial attorneys. He supposed they were in bed when he did not deliver his paper, "Conflicts in Representing Multiple Defendants." He was sorry about that. It was a good paper. He had worked hard lining up precedents: *Reynolds* v. *Cochran*, 365 U.S., 525, 530-531, [1961] on the constitutional right to chosen counsel; *Tillotson* v. *Boughner*, 350 F2d 663, 666 [7th cir., 1965] on resisting disclosure of an individual client's identity where it would be incriminatory to the client.

He was a real lawyer in those days.

When he was committing adultery with Kathleen Donnelly of Sligo.

In the haunted air of twilight.

He tried to imagine Elaine Igoe reciting a poem in bed.

Elaine who did not come and who said it had never been like this.

Or Lee.

No poetry from Lee.

Or cellulite either.

Lee came.

She could not be faulted on that score.

He dialed Lee's number again. Still busy. He wondered if the phone were off the hook. Why? To whom was she not reciting poetry? With whom was she coming? .

Still busy.

And still raining outside. He wondered if the rain would ever stop.

Tillotson v. Boughner.

A precedent.

Precedents are the cornerstones of the law. So saith Martha Sweeney. Delivered when the Right Honorable Martha Sweeney, judge of the superior court, was the featured speaker at the annual dinner of the County Bar Association.

Polite applause.

The cornerstones are made of cheap cement, he had told her in bed later that same evening.

Told the Right Honorable Martha Sweeney, judge of the superior court.

Prior to or subsequent to the performing of consensual sodomy.

With the Right Honorable Martha Sweeney, judge of the superior court.

Who came.

Like Lee.

Like Kathleen Donnelly. Who served him seconds on succotash.

It's dealings with women that age people, Jack. That's why priests and queers always look terrific.

Poor Hugh. Mustn't forget Hugh. Hugh who had

absolved him. Absolution from the chaplain of *Hollywood Squares,* Hugh had said.

"As a priest, I'm a joke," Hugh Campion had said over brandy at lunch.

"I want to get involved," Hugh Campion had said over a second brandy.

No, you don't, Hugh. Involvement is the last thing you want. Hugh the worker priest, Hugh the leper colony missionary was like Clarice the congresswoman.

"I'm due in court, Hugh." Always a good out. "A PUC case."

A PUC case indeed. Was he trying to persuade Hugh he had a classier clientele these days?

Court was restful. A refuge. A moat against my life. *Like a condom. The law is your prophylactic.*

"Sergeant Casey, let's take this one step at a time. You called one of Mr. Mandel's outcall services."

"Yes. The Farmer's Daughter."

"On a telephone?"

"Yes."

"On a telephone in the Chateau Blanche Motor Hotel." *Subject A wearing white halter dress checks into Chateau Blanche Motor Hotel, 1 Constitution Plaza, driving silver BMW 528i, license plate LEE S.*

"Correct."

"The outcall service did not call you, right?"

"Yes."

"You called it?"

"Objection, asked and answered. Mr. Shea is badgering the witness."

"Overruled."

"Did Mr. Mandel answer the telephone when you placed your call to The Farmer's Daughters outcall service?"

"I don't know."

"Did a man answer the phone?"

"No."

284

"Then a woman answered the phone?"

"Yes."

"Then if you made an inductive leap you could assume that if a woman answered the telephone, that woman was not Mr. Mandel?"

"I suppose."

"And what did you ask this woman?"

"I said I wanted a massage."

"She did not ask you if you wanted a massage. You asked her?"

"Right."

"Just a massage?"

"I said I wanted a massage and extras."

"And what did the dispatcher do then?"

"She hung up."

"Did you call again?"

"Later."

"On that same telephone in the Chateau Blanche?" *Subject A exits Chateau Blanche Motor Hotel, 1 Constitution Plaza. Subject A is barefoot and is carrying what appears to be one pr black satin sandals in hand.*

"Yes."

"Did Mr. Mandel answer?"

"I don't know."

"Did a woman answer?"

"Yes."

"So making that same inductive leap you made earlier, we can assume the woman was not Mr. Mandel."

"I suppose."

"And what did you tell this woman this time?"

"That I wanted a massage."

"And extras?"

"Just a massage."

"Did this woman, this dispatcher, ask your name?"

"Yes."

"And you gave it to her?"

"Yes."

"Your real name?"

"No."

"Just a name?"

"Yes."

"Did she ask your telephone number?"

"Yes."

"And you gave it to her?"

"Yes."

"And your address?" *Subject A tips doorman Michael Haughey 45¢ and departs Chateau Blanche Motor Hotel in silver BMW 528i, license plate LEE S.*

"Yes."

"Did she ask how you intended to pay for the massage?"

"Yes."

"And what did you say?"

"Cash."

"And what did she say then?"

"She said she would contact a masseuse and the masseuse would call me within twenty minutes."

"Then what did she do?"

"I don't understand the question."

"Did she hang up?"

"Yes."

"Did she solicit you?"

"I don't understand the question."

"How long have you been in vice, Sergeant Casey?"

"Eleven years."

"And you have never learned the meaning of the word 'solicit' as it applies to Section Six Forty-seven of the state penal code?"

"She did not solicit."

"And did Mr. Mandel solicit?"

"No."

"You in fact called the outcall service?"

286

"Yes."

"And you in fact did the only soliciting?"

"Objection . . ."

Point made. It was a game of points. That's all it was. Run. Goal. Basket. Touchdown. A game in suit and tie instead of helmet and padding or short pants and funny shoes. Each case with its own game plan. Xs and Os. Hit the open man. Pick and roll. Move the runner over. Run to daylight. Weak-side dog. Memorize the play-book. Is Mr. Mandel under arrest? Under indictment? Charged with any violation of the criminal statutes? Questions from the playbook. No. No. No. Three points. Like a field goal. Have you conducted many outcall investigations? And is Mr. Mandel's the only investigation you have conducted whose purpose was the termination of telephone service? Yes. Yes. Basket. Two points.

His telephone rang.

Let it ring.

The light on the answering machine glowed red, then went off.

"Jack, it's Elaine . . ."

Wrong game plan. Wrong game. Definitely the wrong game.

Back to the full-court press:

"Your Honor, the Police Department Mr. Torizzo is representing has an obligation and a duty in the presence of sufficient proof to arrest people they believe are guilty of crimes. The Police Department has not in this case. In other words, the Police Department cannot prove that Mr. Mandel has done anything illegal and so in the absence of that proof the intervenors have chosen to move against Mr. Mandel's telephones. The intervenors ask us to believe that Mr. Mandel's poor telephones have been ordered removed because they transmitted some evil or immoral or illegal communication. The intervenors ask us to believe that these are bad telephones and that bad telephones like bad dogs and bad children must be punished . . ."

Not bad.

He played good defense.

He was a prospect.

A first-round draft choice.

Drafted by Myron Mandel.

That was the catch.

"Jack, it's Elaine . . ."

Better Myron.

He tried Lee's number again. Your Honor, would you direct the witness to answer: Why were you in the ladies' room alone that night?

Busy.

A newscaster was talking on television. Sid. My old buddy Sid Infer-Imply. Sid seems to have graduated to the anchor chair. He turned up the volume. Sid was using his sincere voice. His another-tragedy-on-the-highway-of-life voice. Sid's sincere voice clashed with Sid's yellow blazer. Dateline Bergen County, New Jersey. There are eight million stories in Bergen County; this is one of them. A child in the backseat of a police car. Then a spokesman for the district attorney. The spokesman talked about charges. Child abandonment. Endangering the welfare of a child. Then a shot of a car lot. Then a close-up of a Corvette. Sid was talking sincerely off camera. A 1977 black-and-silver Corvette. Mint condition. Lowered. Duals. Hard and soft tops. Get on with it, Sid. Value $8800, according to the Kelly Blue Book. The Blackstone of the used car business, that Kelly Blue Book. Sid, the story is slow in developing. And now the car dealer. Looking uncomfortable. A pencil holder clipped to his shirt pocket. Get on with it, Sid. Why all this sincerity?

Oh, God.

A couple had tried to trade the boy in the back of the police car for the Corvette. Their son. Four years old.

Oh, Cat.

Sid said maximum penalties would be sought. Said Sid. Child abuse. Conspiracy to sell a child. Three-to-five on each charge.

Oh, Cat.

Cat. Do I really remember you? Or do I only have an idealized memory of you? A pastel memory. With all the darker hues erased. Did the Cat of memory correspond to the real Cat? Or in grief have I beatified you beyond recognition?

I can't think that.

Cut to the car dealer. The hand holding the microphone belonged to a reporter named Bob.

"My first reaction, Bob, was to make the swap. Put them into the 'Vette . . ."

Cut to the Corvette.

Voice-over: "But I knew that was wrong. A gut instinct. I mean, what would that kid do when he wasn't a kid anymore? How would he cope with life knowing he was traded for a 'Vette, know what I mean?"

Back to Sid. Nodding sincerely. "Indeed."

Said Sid.

Sid said.

God, I hate the nights. The nights were a prison of memories. Strike prison. Mustn't think about prison.

Lee's line was still busy.

He opened the drawer in the bedside table. There it was. The Milwaukee Legster. And the .38. *Popular with detectives, undercover agents and the CIA. You can't beat that for references. Those guys are champs.* What a messy way to do it? Do what? It. Everything splattered all over the walls. Not that it would harm the decor. Not of this apartment. A bag over the head. A bag would do the trick. A bag would catch it all.

Details, details. Now for the last words. Last words were important. He wondered what his father's last words were. Before he stepped off his bunk in East Block. Before the wet sheet broke his neck.

I only regret that I have but one life to lose for my country. No. A bit much.

It is a far, far better thing I do. Uh-uh. Too literary. *Ils ne passeront pas.* Come on. No jokes.

I believe in God.

Hmmm. Not bad. A touch ostentatious. But what the hell? A small quibble. And a way to hedge the bet. In case there was a big lollipop in the Great Beyond.

I believe in God.

I like it. It's got size. I like the parameters. A lot of dimension there.

He put the .38 back in the Milwaukee Legster and the Milwaukee Legster back into the drawer. He felt immensely better.

Back to the tube. He switched channels. Enough of you for one evening, Sid. Over to Cavett. Cavett was smiling. Who are those people with him? One with a beard. One who laughed politely. Ho, ho. Ha, ha. Now the fat one. The fat one wore a sweater. The fat one looked like Queen Victoria. Cut to the tepid one. The tepid one also had a beard.

Who were they?

Book critics. Thank you, Dick. You never leave your audience in the dark. Kazin and friends. Dick was impressed.

If you're impressed, Dick, that's good enough for me.

Now he had the dynamic. *Upstairs, Downstairs* on the book beat. The older bearded one was Richard Bellamy. The tepid bearded one was Hudson. Damply deferential to the older beard. Hudson treated the polite laugher and the fat one as if they were footmen.

Lord Bellamy seemed to be having a good time.

Not so Queen Victoria. Queen Victoria was sadly, badly, desperately in need of a diuretic. Naturetin K for bloat. Naturetin K would suck the bloat out of him.

He remembered that she had prescriptions for Compazine suppositories and Septra DS for cystitis and Hydro-Diuril for premenstrual symptoms and Naturetin K for bloat.

Queen Victoria was talking. The perspiring prole, swaddled in his sweater. Eyes shifty, evasive, never making contact with the camera. Aware of the pecking order on the panel and sullen about it. Resentment dripped from every chin.

He nodded. But did not sleep. Could not sleep. Did not wish to sleep.

He snapped awake. Queen Victoria was still talking. All butch and bluster. Upstaged on *Upstairs, Downstairs*.

Dozed again.

Sleep = dreams. DREAMS = BAD DREAMS. Cat. A part of whom was on a Jewish Bentley. On the bonnet, the detective from Scotland Yard had said. The bonnet and the boot. A different language on the other side of the pond.

The telephone rang.

And rang.

Elaine, I'm not quite ready to deal with you yet. On the plus side, there's the scratch. The dinero. The long green. On the minus side, there's the cellulite.

He switched on the answering machine.

"Jack, it's Lee." The former Lee NMI Liggett. The former Mrs. John Shea, Jr. Now in proper Emily Post fashion Mrs. Liggett Shea. Fancy that. Mrs. Liggett Shea calling at this time of night. "Did you see the news? Turn it on. Channel Three." Click.

Channel 3 was Sid. Did Mrs. Liggett Shea lust for Sid?

Sid was still sincere. ". . . cameras on the scene and

will cover this continuing story as long as time permits . . ."

What continuing story is that, Sid? Someone trading their kid in on a Trans-Am?

What's the Kelly Blue Book on a kid?

What was the Kelly Blue Book on Cat?

Cat.

Said Sid: ". . . the rain that has plagued this city for the last three . . ."

MEMO TO SID: Can rain "plague"? Just checking, Sid.

Sid said: ". . . finally caused a tragedy tonight . . ."

What did Lee see in Sid? It must be Sid's yellow blazer. Try this on for size: Mrs. Lee Liggett Shea Sid.

Said Sid: "To repeat our report from earlier in the newscast, the deluge has caused a section of the hillside at the Goldman and Flowers Memorial Park cemetery to collapse. Torrents of water, mud and boulders have sent corpses and coffins tumbling into a residential neighborhood adjoining the memorial park . . ."

Uh, oh. Boomer, you've got a big problem on your hands. You better begin your Christmas special today.

Sid said: "The area that collapsed was a recent addition to the Goldman and Flowers holdings . . ."

Holdings. That's what he said. Holdings. Said Sid.

Sid said: "A number of bodies were recently reburied in this new fill area of the memorial park after an older section of the cemetery was sold for a medical plaza . . ."

Boomer, I think you are going to need a lawyer.

A clip of the Boomer at the opening of the Goldman & Flowers Medical Plaza & Annex.

A shot of the collapsed hillside.

Suddenly he began to feel uneasy.

Said Sid: "Three corpses have been found in one resident's yard . . ."

A shot of the yard. Three mounds on the front lawn were covered with Fire Department tarpaulins.

It wasn't an itch for Sid that made Lee call.

Please, God, don't let it be what I think it is.

Sid said: "Residents . . ."

A close-up of a resident. An older woman in rimless glasses smiled at the cameras. Under the camera lights her face glistened in the rain. Off camera a reporter shouted: "What was the status of the bodies on your lawn?"

"Mostly torsos." The woman wiped the rain from her face. "A few limbs." A smile for another reporter. "Arms and legs, you know . . ."

Please, God. Lee can sit on Sid's face if this isn't what I think it is.

Said Sid: "The grim job of cleaning up . . ."

Please.

Sid said: ". . . and identifying the bodies thrown from their final resting places . . ."

No.

The final resting place was under the Goldman & Flowers Medical Plaza & Annex.

A Goldman & Flowers Enterprises, Ltd., company.

Said Sid: "Only one body . . ."

Just one.

Sid said: ". . . has definitely been identified . . ."

Definitely.

Said Sid.

Oh, God.

". . . that of the late John Shea . . ." Of course "late," you dumb bastard. He was under the goddamn medical plaza.

Lee. No wonder she called. To warn him. He was sure of that. An act of kindness.

Sid said: ". . . the leading figure in a famous local real-estate scandal . . ."

There was a shot of his father on the steps of the old superior court building. Black-and-white film, cracked and jumpy. There was a vague smile on his face. He

293

stared directly at the reporters, listened politely to every question. I have no comment. I'm sorry. Please, no comment.

It had been over thirty years since he had heard that voice.

In this case, it's a way of letting God know you're around.

The harder types are in West Block.

I'm sorry. I have no comment. There was the same touch of irony, the same sense of distance.

His telephone rang.

Said Sid: ". . . tried and found guilty . . ."

Another call.

A lot of people must be watching Sid tonight.

Sid said: ". . . sentenced to . . ."

A still of his father after sentence was passed. Again staring directly at the camera.

The harder types are in West Block.

No, they weren't.

A still of his father entering prison.

I am older now than he was then.

Said Sid: ". . . committed suicide in prison after serving only . . ."

Older than he was then.

Sid said: ". . . no one else was ever indicted . . ."

The camera panned over the three tarpaulin-covered bodies.

One of those? Which one? How did they identify him?

A third call.

He erased the answering machine. I don't want to know who called.

No sympathy, please.

Said Sid: ". . . the father of prominent local attorney, John Shea, Jr., who recently, in a story covered by this reporter, cast aspersions on the legal qualifications of Governor . . ."

294

There he was.

No irony. No distance. No staring directly at the camera. As furtive as Queen Victoria over on the Cavett show.

I am not prepared to discuss the intricacies of the law with you assholes.

Sid said: ". . . and is now defending accused murderer, Robert Beaubois, the man alleged by the district attorney's office to have set . . ."

Sid was sincere.

So sincere.

Fuck you, Sid.

III

Morning.

Mornings were always better. Or so they say.

"I wake and feel the fell of dark, not day."

That was more like it. The curse of the Irish, remembering poetry. "But the haunted air of twilight is very strange and still." A curse visited even on Kath- leen. Kathleen of the pale red pubic hair. Enough of that. "I wake and feel the fell of dark, not day." No wonder. Gerard Manley Hopkins, S.J. Society of Jesus. Oh, to be a Jebbie this morning. This fell of dark.

Shave, shower. A splash of Brut, a touch of sandal- wood, a dab of Lilac Vegetal. A melding of scents.

On this fell of dark.

A serious suit. Black knit tie. White button-down shirt. No, change the shirt. Button-down shirts were preppie.

Button-down shirts were for Cat.

He changed the shirt, inserted the collar stays. Serious business. The reburial of one's father was always serious business.

On this fell of dark.

A check in the mirror. Jut-jawed. Steely-eyed. Ramrod straight. And morally gelatinous.

On this fell of dark.

Mr. Goldman would see him at eleven. Mr. Goldman was booked until eleven. Mr. Goldman would be attending the recently bereaved.

Myron Mandel on the line. "Listen, I didn't know your old man died in the slammer. Is this going to fuck up my case?"

Count on Myron. Always to the point.

D.F. Campion on the line. "He should've been buried at Mount St. Benedict's."

"He was a suicide, Dominick. They don't bury suicides in consecrated ground."

Matter of fact. No quaver in the voice. The tone picked up from the old black-and-white newsreel footage on the television screen the night before.

Visine for the eyes.

To *The Times,* Channel 3, the *Record,* WBIG, Channel 18: I have no comment.

On this fell of dark.

Martha Sweeney on the line. "There've been bad geologicals on that property since 1927."

Oh.

"I had my clerk search the titles this morning."

Ah.

"You can sue his ass, Jack."

No way.

Mr. Goldman was still busy. Mr. Goldman said please wait.

So Martha had already checked the geologicals. Of course she would have. It went with her lust for precedents. He wondered if she had ever done a geological on him.

Some slippage here.

A fault line there.

Ancient slumping.

He was a walking slide area.

He got up, stretched his legs, walked down the corridor. The guest book for the viewing room nearest Ben Goldman's office said, IN MEMORIAM—HAROLD PUGH. There were no names in the guest book and only one mourner sitting in front of the casket. Dutch Shea wondered if he should take a look. Death seemed to fascinate him today. And why not? About my age, Harold. Doesn't seem to have missed many meals. Call Harold anything, but don't call him late for chow. There was a button missing on the sleeve of Harold Pugh's suit jacket. And what appeared to be a soup stain on his tie. Why am I doing this? He felt a tap on his shoulder. The other mourner was standing next to him.

"John McNulty." The voice was resonant. A tall man with a long nose and a funeral manner. "You must be a friend of Harold's."

"Not exactly."

"Harold had so many friends."

"I'm sure."

"I bet you have a lot of anecdotes."

"Anecdotes," Dutch Shea, Jr., said hesitantly.

"About Harold's sense of humor."

"Not really, no."

"What about his zest for life?"

Dutch Shea, Jr., shook his head. He wondered if he should make up something. Harold was Harold, that was good enough. Something along that line. Old Harold, he was something else. Nothing too definite. Nothing you could get booked and fingerprinted for. Accessory after the fact. How else to explain why he was checking out a complete stranger. Try this one out. Actually I don't know Harold. I'm from the State Board of Funeral Directors and Embalmers. Just checking out Goldman's work. He did a hell of a job, don't you think? Considering what he had to work with. It comes to skin tones, there's nobody better than Goldman.

"I'm going to speak at Harold's service," John McNulty said. An unctuous tone crept into his voice and he clasped his hands in front of his chest.

"Then you knew him?"

"Oh, no, I never met him." John McNulty took a business card from his vest pocket and handed it to Dutch Shea, Jr. The card said:

LAST WORDS & KIND THOUGHTS

A Service for the Bereaved
John Francis McNulty, Principal Speaker

In the lower-left-hand corner, there was a telephone number and printed discreetly in the lower-right corner the words, RATES ON REQUEST.

"Yes," Dutch Shea, Jr., said. He wondered if that were the most appropriate response. "I see." He tried a third time. "Interesting."

"I like to talk to the friends of the deceased," John McNulty said. "To see what he was really like. A funeral, after all, Mr. . . ."

"Shea."

"A funeral, after all, Mr. Shea, is only a way of saying thank you and good-bye."

"I guess I've never thought of it that way." Dutch Shea nodded toward the casket. "I wish I had known him better."

John McNulty suddenly became guarded. "You're not a creditor by any chance."

"No."

"I am glad. Harold had a number of creditors, I'm afraid. He went bankrupt."

"That is too bad."

"Four times."

No wonder the guest book was unsigned. But then you would have thought Harold's creditors might have come to make sure. "That must make your job more difficult."

"There's always a little good in everyone, Mr. Shea."

"Of course."

"I think, Mr. Shea, that what I want to say about Harold is that he was a big guy . . ." John McNulty paused and for an instant Dutch Shea wondered if that were all there was to say about Harold Pugh. "A big guy," John McNulty repeated, and then he found the rhythm, ". . . a big guy whose endless buoyance was wholly infectious, climbing hill after hill . . ."

He looked at Dutch Shea, Jr., for a response.

"That says it," Dutch Shea said.

"I think so," John McNulty said. Once more he clasped his hands in front of his chest. He stared at Harold Pugh and lowered his voice. "But hills, as we all know, have a downslope as well." He was emoting now. "And if Harold unknowingly hurt any one of us, well . . ." A dramatic pause. ". . . well, he always hurt himself more."

"That captures him, all right." I'm getting caught up in this, he thought. He tried to imagine John McNulty speaking at his father's funeral. Finding anecdotes to illustrate the bright patches on the downslope of life. Better yet, book him for my own funeral. Yes, Jack Shea took the money, but think how hard it was to get away with it.

"I appreciate that," John McNulty said. He seemed quite pleased. "Then I'd like to say that Harold was the kind of man who could stand in the middle of a burning house and tell you what a beautiful view of the azure sky you had through the burned-out roof."

Dutch Shea nodded. If such were the case, he

suspected Harold might have set the fire for the insurance. He glanced at the body. Now that we're on a first-name basis, Harold, I'm Jack. Some people call me Dutch. You can call me Jack, I'm so familiar with your bankruptcies and all. At least you're all in one piece, Harold. Limbs and torso all glued together, it looks like. It was hard to imagine the lump under the yellow tarp as his father. He wondered at the condition of his father's clothes. No soup stain on the tie, he was sure of that. And all the buttons on the jacket. Even on the downslope of life, John Shea, Sr., had all the buttons on his jacket . . .

"The thread is not broken by death." John McNulty was performing again. "By that rainbow whose end we cannot see." He looked at Dutch Shea, Jr. "I like that theme, don't you?"

"Very much."

"Do you know if he was Rotary?"

"No."

"I like to throw in the clubs. Rotary always sends a delegation."

Another nod.

"And then I want to end with the love that forgives, triumphs, endures," John McNulty said. "What do you think?"

"I think you might end with forgives."

"Good idea, Mr. Shea."

Behind them a woman entered the viewing room and discreetly cleared her throat. Ben Goldman's secretary. "Mr. Goldman will see you now, Mr. Shea."

2

"He fired you?"

"He fired me."

"Why?"

"He said the Association of County Funeral Directors couldn't stand the notoriety of a lawyer whose father had died in prison. He said it was bad for the ACFD's image."

"What about cemeteries that collapse, what does that do for the old image?"

"Martha, don't get upset."

"That's what I don't understand, your not being upset." Martha's voice rose. "There's a medical plaza over where your father used to be. That's the first thing to be upset about. And where they put him was about as stable as a bowl of ice cream. So parts of your father end up on someone's lawn and what happens? You don't get upset. And you get fired."

"Calm down. Take the long view."

"Jack, I don't understand you."

"Hell, I'm not sure I understand myself."

"Where they going to put him?"

"That's all taken care of. A new plot. We just have to work out the cost."

"The cost."

"Martha, don't shout."

"Are you trying to tell me you're going to have to pay to rebury your father?"

"Well, to be perfectly frank, I did think he had perpetual care and that that would cover it."

"It doesn't?"

"Well, he says perpetual care as it applies to the cemetery business actually means gardening. Mowing the grass, a little weeding, a bouquet on Memorial Day, that sort of thing. There are no provisions for reburial. A new casket is a fairly large item."

"Jack, I have difficulty believing what I'm hearing."

"Look, it will work out. I think what he doesn't want is a mental anguish suit. If I don't file, all it will cost is a new perpetual care contract. It's only pennies."

"Jack, this is your father you're talking about . . ."

"Martha, I want it over with. That is the bottom line. I want him back in the ground. I want it off television and out of the newspapers. If it is going to cost me a little money, then it is a price I am more than willing to pay."

"All right, Jack."

"And look at the bright side."

"Are you trying to tell me there's a bright side?"

"I pinched a piece of literature off his desk. For a new kind of hearse."

Martha Sweeney took a deep breath and stared.

"An RV."

"RV?"

"Recreational vehicle. Listen to this. 'The RV as funeral coach was conceived by Adam Hruska, a Des Moines, Iowa, funeral director who has contacted an Indiana firm to manufacture the vehicles for sale to funeral homes. Hruska asserts the deal will add life to the RV industry.' Great stuff, right?"

Martha kept staring.

"Ninety thousand bucks. And what do you get for your ninety grand? Listen. 'The RV combines the traditional roles of hearse, flower car and limousines on the trip to the cemetery.' This part I really like. 'The vehicle can carry thirty-eight passengers and thirty floral arrangements as well as the deceased.' Mustn't forget the reason for the party. 'This draws the family together, along with the clergyman.' That's Hruska, said that. 'You don't have to hurt someone's feelings by telling them they have to ride in the second car instead of the lead car.' And get this. There is even room for a wet bar.''

"Jack . . ."

"Wait a minute. One last great touch. 'You push a button and the table holding the casket slides out automatically. You can have it slide out the left side or the right side. This precludes worry about finding the ideal parking spot.' A lot of thought went into this, Martha. You don't want to hold up traffic, you can snap Mom or Dad out of there in jig time. Thirty-eight relatives pile out of one car, things won't get all backed up.''

"Jack, I think you're crazy."

"Could be."

"I think you're losing your grip. I think you're seriously dissociated . . ."

"You think I belong in the bin?"

"I think you need help."

"Possible."

"Jack, Jack . . ."

"Let's fuck."

"Now?"

"In this haunted hour of twilight."

"Here?"

"Why not?"

"Jack, these are my chambers, for Christ's sake."

IV

Hugh Campion, in black cassock, white surplice and funeral stole, blessed the grave. "O God, by whose mercy the soul of the faithful departed, John, finds rest, bless this grave and appoint it and release the soul of thy servant, John, from every bond of sin . . ."

Elaine Igoe wept loudly. Keening, I'd call it, Dutch Shea, Jr., thought. Hardly appropriate for a man dead more than thirty years. Elaine, I am not impressed. He glanced at D. F. Campion. D.F.'s face was even more choleric than usual. The old man could hardly contain his anger with Clarice. Rosary beads threaded through her fingers, Clarice Campion patted Elaine on the arm. It was Clarice who had invited Elaine Igoe to the reburial. Clarice had enlisted Elaine in her fight for nuns' rights. Elaine believes nuns should be liberated, too, Jack. Hell, yes, Clarice. What else could he say? That nuns' rights were a way for Elaine to get close to him? Maybe I should just tell Clarice that Elaine has cellulite . . .

Hugh Campion sprinkled the grave with holy water. "Grant to thy departed servant, John, O Lord, we beseech thee, this favor: that he who desired to do thy will may not receive punishment for his deeds . . ."

No punishment. I like that. Fellowship in the choir of angels rather than the fellowship of the structured setting.

Structured Setting Martha.

"Do you want me to come?"

"Good God, no. It's going to be tough enough to get through without you there."

"I wonder if any judge has ever been fucked in chambers before."

"Precedents, Martha. Always looking for precedents. The cornerstones of the law."

The mechanical gravedigger was parked just beyond the casket. A plastic casket. The best that Boomer Goldman would come up with. The Boomer also refused to give him a new perpetual care contract. The Boomer was acting as if the corpses were at fault for the cave-in.

"From the gate of hell," Hugh Campion said, incensing the plastic casket.

"Deliver his soul, O Lord." Clarice and Elaine responded with fervor. D. F. Campion mumbled. Silence from the closest living relative of the deceased. The formerly buried. John Shea's body lies a-moldering in the grave. Thirty years a-moldering. A mote in the eye of God, but thirty years is thirty years. He wondered if the Boomer's embalmers had spooned the remains into the plastic casket. Swept up the dust with broom and pan. He looked around. Five mourners on this rainswept day. Not like the last time. The first time. No Twomeys and Clarkins, no McNultys and Maras, no Galvins and Riordans and Bolands and Bogans. No Liggetts and Pomfrets, no Cahills and Keleghans. Definitely no Byron Igoe. Just the widow Igoe, who was even now belting out a response. "May perpetual light shine upon him."

Elaine Igoe turned the perpetual light of her smile upon him.

She wasn't even there the first time. The first time with the lobster Newburg and the creamed chicken in patty shells and more goddamn shrimp than you can shake a stick at, it must have set D.F. back a mint, and isn't it swell him taking in little Dutch, Jr., a champ like his dad, little Dutch, big Dutch and D.F., they were like this, it's the least D.F. could do, a spread like this, considering . . .

Considering what?

"God the Holy Ghost," Hugh Campion intoned.

"Have mercy on the soul of the faithful departed, John," Clarice and Elaine responded in unison.

He had difficulty thinking of his father as the faithful departed. Just departed. Long departed. So long departed that he had spent the morning in court. A drunk driving case. No reason not to treat it as a normal day just because his father was being reburied. The long departed. A jail-house lawyer, my old man, the genuine article. He'd understand, right? Right. Keeps your mind off things, right? Right.

What things?

Off considering what, for one thing.

A good thing to keep your mind off, considering what.

Consider nothing but the arresting officer on the stand. The arresting officer said the defendant was drunk. The arresting officer said the defendant had failed the pupillary reaction test. The defendant. The 502, driving under the influence. The 502 was guilty as hell. The 502 also paid in cash. Up front. A 502 who pays in cash is a good client to help keep your mind off things.

Concentrate on that pupillary reaction test.

The old pupillary reaction time defense.

Questions, questions, questions. Questions to keep your mind off things.

How exactly did you measure this slow reaction time, Officer? Mechanically? Scientifically?

Oh, only with a flashlight. And based on your long professional experience as a police officer.

Ah.

Yes.

Mmmmm.

Questions, questions, questions.

Questions about the arresting officer's familiarity with the effects of ocular motor nerve weakness.

Oh, not familiar.

Ah.

Yes.

Mmmmm.

Questions about the arresting officer's familiarity with the effects of atrophy of the optic nerve.

Oh, not familiar.

Mmmmm.

Well, then, what about the Argyle Robertson syndrome of locomotion ataxia? Familiar with that, are you?

He especially liked that question. Like the way the arresting officer began to fidget. *Defense is an exercise in learning and forgetting.* Who said that? I did? Oh. Well. The things I've learned and forgot. Fatteh's *Handbook of Forensic Pathology.* How about Harrison's *Forgery Detection?* And Moenssen's *Scientific Evidence in Criminal Cases?* That was a read. A real page-turner. And don't forget the Argyle Robertson syndrome of locomotion ataxia.

A way to pass the morning. The morning before the afternoon your old man is reburied. The old faithful departed himself. Who died in the slammer. With a wet sheet around his neck. That was one way to depart faithfully. Nothing like dipping into the Argyle Robert-

308

son syndrome of locomotion ataxia to keep your mind
off things like that.

"All ye angels and archangels, all ye orders of
blessed spirits . . ." Hugh was deep into the litany.

"Pray for the soul of the faithful departed, John."
Teamwork from Elaine and Clarice. Give each a tam-
bourine and they could work up an act. The Faithful
Departed. A good name for a rock group. He and Cat
used to make up names for rock groups. The Interna-
tional Jewish Conspiracy, the Israeli disco favorite. The
Golden Oldies, from Sun City to you. Moby & The
Dicks. Don't tell your mother that one, Cat. Oh,
Daddy. Cat would like The Faithful Departed. Being
faithful departed herself.

"St. Catherine, St. Barbara, all ye holy virgins and
widows . . ." Virgins & Widows. Not bad either.

"Pray for the soul of the faithful departed, John."
Considering . . .

Considering what?

Consider the soul of the faithful departed, John.
Before he was faithful departed. When he was faithful
and present.

He had gone from the courtroom to the library, from
the Argyle Robertson syndrome of locomotion ataxia
to the yellowed newspaper files.

Not the best way to keep your mind off things.

Considering.

Considering the headlines.

INSURANCE SCANDAL.

SHEA CHARGED.

ACTED ALONE, SHEA SAYS.

NO FURTHER INDICTMENTS WILL BE SOUGHT, DISTRICT
ATTORNEY SAYS.

So. There it was. The insurance was on a housing
development called Albany Heights. Not real heights.
A landfill. But Albany Landfill was not a name for a
housing development. Albany Landfill did not sing.

Not like Albany Heights. Postwar housing for our returning vets. WE OWE THEM SOMETHING. Not a bad slogan, that. LO DOWN. FHA AVAILABLE. Ranch luxury and 1½ ba.

"From all evil."

"O Lord, deliver him, thy servant, John."

Thy servant, John. Was that a step up or a step down from faithful departed John? Questions, questions. Thy servant John had taken out completion bonds and liability insurance on Albany Heights. As required by state law. Just a formality. To ensure the completion of all that ranch luxury. Or so Thy servant, John, said. Thy servant, John, collected prorated shares of the insurance and completion bond premiums from his investors. Then Thy servant, John, neglected to buy the insurance. Thy servant, John, kept the premiums.

Why?

ACTED ALONE, SHEA SAYS.

NO FURTHER INDICTMENTS WILL BE SOUGHT, DISTRICT ATTORNEY SAYS.

Considering . . .

Considering what?

"From the rigor of thy justice."

"Oh, Lord, deliver him, thy servant, John." D. F. Campion's voice joined with Clarice and Elaine.

Tough luck for Thy servant, John. A small earthquake. The first in seventy-one years. The landfill moved. A gas line ruptured.

FIRE DESTROYS HOUSING DEVELOPMENT.

A housing development with no liability insurance. And no completion bond. Because Thy servant, John, had pocketed the premiums.

Why?

ACTED ALONE, SHEA SAYS.

Thy servant, John. Shortly thereafter the faithful departed John.

310

Albany Heights.

Annie O'Meara.

The sins of the fathers.

Etc.

Christ Almighty!

"From the gnawing worm of conscience . . ."

"O Lord, deliver him, thy servant, John."

Not to mention Thy servant, John, Jr.

It just keeps gnawing away, that legless old bilateral invertebrate. Ugly as hell, that old worm. Almost as ugly as the capybara. Oh, Christ. It's bad enough making connections. Why make connections comparing uglies? He remembered the sign on the cage: A COUSIN OF THE MOUSE AND THE GUINEA PIG, THE CAPYBARA IS THE WORLD'S LARGEST RODENT. Its cage was next to the pony cart ride in the Central Park Zoo. Kathleen Donnelly was with him. It was the afternoon he cut the seminar on "The Discriminatory Use of Peremptory Challenges." He had never seen anything so unattractive. It had a snout and webbed feet and no tail and brown hair and pale pink legs. And was just about big enough to pull the goddamn pony cart. Kathleen clung to his arm. Did she shiver or did he just imagine it? Did he really think the rodent a sign, penance for an adulterous weekend, or did he just now imagine it? Did we ever fuck again? Or did she just pass him seconds on succotash? Memory failed in the presence of the plastic casket, in the presence of the faithful departed, Thy servant, John.

From the gnawing worm of conscience, O Lord, deliver me, Thy servant, John, Jr.

"King of awful majesty . . ."

"We beseech thee, hear us."

"Lamb of God, who takest away the sins of the world . . ."

"Grant unto him life everlasting."

311

"Eternal rest grant unto him, O Lord."
"And may perpetual light shine upon him."
"May he rest in peace."
"Amen."

2

Hugh Campion leaned and kissed his father on the cheek. "I've got to go, Poppa."

He had never seen Hugh kiss D.F. before. Never. Not even when he was a child. Did I kiss my father good-bye the last time I saw him? That Christmas in East Block. No. No kisses allowed in the penitentiary.

He walked Hugh to his car. "Thanks, Hugh."

"It was the least I could do, Jack." Hugh searched the sky for rain. "I hope you didn't mind the rather gloomy litany."

"Not at all."

"All that talk about evil and God's wrath and eternal flames and intolerable cold."

"I rather liked that gnawing worm of conscience myself," Dutch Shea, Jr., said.

"Ah, yes," Hugh Campion said. "I do, too. Keeps me from forgetting *Name That Tune.*" He opened the car door and placed his surplice and funeral stole on the front seat. "By the way, I said Mass this morning at juvenile hall. A wonderful turnout for a weekday. Standing room only, as we say in show business."

"Wonderful, Hugh." No need to tell him that inmates who went to Mass used the thin onionskin paper in the chapel missals to roll joints.

He walked back to where D. F. Campion was standing uncomfortably with Clarice and Elaine Igoe. In the distance behind them, the mechanical gravedigger was scooping dirt over the plastic casket in the open grave.

"Oh, Jack." Elaine Igoe held a wadded Kleenex in her hand. Her eyes were swollen with tears.

"Thank you for coming, Elaine." She pressed her hand into his, mashing the wet Kleenex into his palm.

"Can we get together?"

"Soon, Elaine."

"Clarice is doing the most wonderful things for the nuns." He wondered if Clarice ever got used to people talking about her as if she were not there. "I really would like to help her out."

"That's a wonderful idea, Elaine." Maybe I should tell her I jerked off fantasizing about Clarice once. That would test her commitment to nuns' rights. Beat my meat. Pulled my pud. Thinking of Clarice. Poor Clarice. Who had also wanted to marry him. Who smiled at him now over Elaine's shoulder.

"There are a few legal problems I'd like to talk to you about."

While I'm counting your cellulite ridges. And tracing your bikini incision.

"I think you'd need a tax lawyer for that, Elaine." Like the faithful departed, Thy servant, John. Who pocketed the premiums.

Like father, like son.

"That's what I was wondering, Jack. Is nuns' lib tax deductible?"

D. F. Campion coughed loudly. Dutch Shea, Jr., moved between D.F. and Elaine. The old man could not even hear nun's liberation mentioned without choking.

"Taxes aren't really my field, Elaine."

Elaine persisted. "But surely you'll agree that Sisters should join the sisterhood."

More coughing. D. F. Campion's face was mottled with fury. Clarice clapped her father on the back.

"We'll talk, Elaine." He turned and kissed Clarice on the cheek. "I'll take you home, Dominick."

Home. The house on Prospect Avenue. Site of the wake for the faithful departed, thy servant, John.

Was it ever my home? Or Kathleen's? Or were we both just boarders?

Questions, questions. I am assaulted by questions.

Clarice squeezed his hand and led Elaine Igoe down the slope to her Saab. For the first time he was aware of Clarice's license plate.

PAX.

A little more high-minded than LEE S.

3

"Tax deductible," D. F. Campion said. The purple was fading from his face. "Sisters. Sisterhood. *Sisterhood*. Good Catholic girls joining that bunch of deviates."

"Mmmmm." Dutch Shea, Jr., concentrated on the traffic. He was not about to engage in a colloquy with D.F. about Clarice and Elaine. "Mmmmm." He turned left into Park Street. D.F.'s idea. The old man had insisted on driving through Frog Hollow on the way home from the cemetery. Through the heart of the heart of Frog Hollow. The old Irish ghetto. Where D.F. was born. As was the faithful departed. Thy servant. John. Sr.

"Sisterhood," D. F. Campion repeated. His voice trailed off. Park Street secured his attention. He stared out the car window. The store signs were all in Spanish. Bodega. Botanica. Supramarketa. "The PRs have taken over the neighborhood."

"Mmmmm." The Puerto Ricans were as unspeakable to D.F. as the sisterhood.

"Park up here in front of St. Lawrence O'Toole's."

He maneuvered the car into a parking space. Two small boys began polishing the fender with a chamois cloth. He gave them a quarter.

314

"You'll spoil them," D. F. Campion said.

"They'll scratch it with glass if I don't," Dutch Shea, Jr., said. His own apartment was two blocks away on Washington Street. Where the faithful departed started out, I end up. Now that is irony. He remembered an old Irish saying: the first generation makes it, the second generation enjoys it, the third generation loses it. Frog Hollow wisdom, his father called it.

My father.

Did he really enjoy it?

Will I lose it?

Am I losing it?

Have I lost it?

Questions, questions.

"I was baptized here," D. F. Campion said. St. Lawrence O'Toole's was a grimy, nondescript red-brick pile. "Made my first communion here. Was confirmed here." The Mass board in front of the old church indicated that its name had been changed to La Purisima Concepción. "Why'd they want to do something like that?"

"I don't think St. Lawrence O'Toole has an awful lot of meaning down here today," Dutch Shea, Jr., said noncommittally.

"Why the hell not?" D.F. was standing in front of a store window. The faded gold leaf sign in the window said ROPA—DAMAS Y CABALLEROS Y NIÑOS.

"Good question, Dominick."

D. F. Campion suddenly smiled. "I remember my pa one time. There was a big K of C shindig in the parish hall. Old Maurice Burke was the bishop then. A numbskull if ever there was one. He believed in the elves. Probably because he looked like one himself. Couldn't have been more than four feet high. They said he wore high heels under his cassock to make him look taller. A terrible tiny man. Anyway. My pa kneels to kiss his ring and this midget says to him, 'I hear you got

315

a grand new set of false teeth, Dominick.' Like it's something my pa wants known to all the ginneys and Polacks in the K of C. 'Simply grand, Your Excellency,' says my pa, and he proceeds to bite the dwarf in the finger when he kisses the ring. Oh, he was a grand man, my pa. He took no back talk from elves."

The memory seemed to cheer D. F. Campion up enormously. He stopped in front of a bodega. In the window a butcher was plucking a scrawny chicken. On the steps of the store a small dark-skinned boy regarded D.F. balefully. The old man patted him on the head. "Where are you at school, lad?"

"Yo no se."

"Well, go to a parochial school, you want my advice. You tell your mother you want to go to St. Lawrence O'Toole's. You go to a parochial school, people know you're smarter and you get a better job. Something where you can wear a sweater and a tie. Never underestimate a tie, lad. You wear a tie and you can get into accounting, and that's a fact. Work with numbers. One, two, three, four, five and the rest . . ."

"Uno, dos, tres . . ."

"Whatever you say." D.F. barged ahead. "And when you retire, they give you a dinner and a nice watch. Make sure it works, and if it doesn't, get something better than a trip to Providence like that nitwit Artie Nangle."

The child shrank away from D.F.

"So mind me, you go to a parochial school. Mark my words, you can always tell a lad from St. Lawrence O'Toole's. They're all in accounting."

The boy ran into the *bodega*.

"They've got no head for numbers, the Spanish," D. F. Campion said. "It comes from eating beans."

From inside the shop a sharp-faced woman smiled at Dutch Shea, Jr. He smiled back and tried to place the face. Too much makeup. A professional smile. Now he had it. Ynez Cano. His next-door neighbor. The prostitute in 3-G who recorded *Days of Our Lives* on her Betamax X2 while turning a trick. Ynez Cano had a head for numbers. The money was in her purse before she undid a button.

Puta. Why am I more at home with *putas* than with elves and accountants?

D. F. Campion beckoned from the corner of Hungerford Street. "Oh, this was a wonderful neighborhood, Jack." He pointed across the street to an old three-story, two-family frame house. "That's where I was born. My pa was an alderman." Sheets hung from the windows of the house and shutters were missing. At least two windows appeared to be broken. From one a girl leaned out and yelled, "Marta." Her voice carried across the gathering afternoon shadows. "Your dad lived in the other half. His pa was a policeman."

A policeman. He remembered an old photograph. A man with a bushy mustache, a high starched collar and a short-billed policeman's hat. He wondered what his policeman grandfather would have thought of his son and grandson.

"The three Ps," D. F. Campion said. The light changed and for a moment the old man was surrounded by people crossing the street. He never stopped talking. "The police, politics and the priesthood. That was the only way a mick got out of the Hollow in those days. The Yanks wanted to keep us here and don't you forget it."

More than sixty years ago and still the bitter edge. What is D.F. trying to tell me? Why does he insist on this enervating voyage of memory? Who was even President sixty years ago? Wilson? Harding? These were memories he could neither share nor contem-plate. An ancient voyage from steerage to suburbia, from poverty to wealth, from law abiding to law breaking. Why today? On this day of days. Stupid question. Because it was this day of days.

"Over there." D.F. was pointing at another house farther down Hungerford Street. "That's where Ignatius Delaney lived. The elevator operator at United Fire. Looked like a prune. Didn't move his bowels twice in forty years. But when he died, he was the largest individual stockholder in the company. Every day, up and down in that elevator. 'Good morning, sir.' 'Good morning, Ignatius.' But what a head for numbers. He bought a few shares and he always took up his options. Even when he was saying, 'We'll take you right up to six, sir, the express this morning, sir.' He was always listening in that elevator, picking up the tips and he knew enough what to do when the stock split. Fifty years he went up and down, down and up, it froze his bowels solid, and when he retired they had a lunch and you know what they gave him? A pen and pencil set. Him with a hundred ninety-five thousand shares. And you know what he said, him with his hundred ninety-five thousand shares? 'Thank you, sir.'"

D.F. turned suddenly and walked back toward the car. The little boy in front of the bodega saw him coming and once again disappeared into the store. Dutch Shea, Jr., trailed behind. He could guess the moral behind the Ignatius Delaney saga.

"It wasn't my way, Jack, all that bowing and scraping. Nor your dad's. It was the harp loonies that named him Dutch. You know why? Because he had such a hard head. No 'Yes, sir,' and 'Thank you, sir,' out of your dad, Jack. A real hard head."

He remembered the ironic smile, not the hard head.

The sadness in the eyes. The polite detachment. He knew his father detested his nickname.

Like father, like son.

He wondered if anyone had ever described him as hard-headed.

Muddleheaded, perhaps.

Softheaded.

You play life on the dark keys, Jack. Lee had said that.

And I'm beginning to hear the melody.

He drove through the late afternoon traffic. Beside him, D. F. Campion seemed caught in his own thoughts. He did not speak until the car turned on Washington Street and passed Dutch Shea's own apartment.

"Why don't you move out of this crummy neighborhood?"

"Because it suits me," Dutch Shea, Jr., said. "And besides, you were just telling me what a great neighborhood it was."

"Before you were born," D.F. said. "Before the PRs and the boogies moved in. When I was just starting out and your dad was my lawyer, that was when it was a swell neighborhood. I owned the whole shebang one time. Every building. Frog Hollow, Inc. Your dad and me. The Brennans and the Dennehys lived over here then. And the Doyles and the McCaheys and the Sullivans."

"Stout men all." Frog Hollow, Inc. FHI. Which sold The Allen House to the Charter Oak Corporation. Which was D. F. Campion.

Why?

Why would the left hand not know what the right hand was doing?

Why did his father pocket the premiums?

Considering . . .

319

Considering what?

"Go ahead and laugh," D. F. Campion said. "But the Brennans and the Dennehys paid their rent on time. It's Méndez and López over here now and me no comprende rent, hey, you take food stamps. They wouldn't have pulled that on me and your dad, Jack. We were a pair, him and me. All the micks were dying to get out of Frog Hollow and here's me and your dad, two harps calling ourselves Frog Hollow, Inc. The Yanks didn't like that, buster, I'm telling you. A mick wasn't supposed to get rich. Not a penny did they lend us. Four-flushers, the bunch of them. Your late father-in-law. His Honor. That made Nelly Treacy tell the dirty joke at the Club. Billy McCahey, every St. Patrick's Day, he'd put a sack of shit on the judge's doorstep. He never made the connection, your father-in-law, between the shit and St. Patrick's Day."

"I'm sure he didn't." Dutch Shea, Jr., doubted that St. Patrick was even included in Judge Liggett's communion of saints.

"Those were the days, I'm telling you, buster."

Those were the days. The days that sent his father to prison. The good old days. Poor pure Irish, rich bad Yankees. The good old days that were somehow entwined with his own decline. He looked at D.F. slumped against the car door and with a sharp, painful awareness he knew that Dominick had died a little today. Suddenly he did not want to know what D.F. was trying to sort out, did not want to know how many memories the old man was trying to erase. He would not ask, could not ask. The habit of not asking was too ingrained.

Leave it be.

There was enough death for one day.

From all evil, from Thy wrath, from the rigor of Thy

320

justice, from the power of the devil, from the gnawing worm of conscience, from long-enduring sorrow, from eternal flames, from intolerable cold, from horrible darkness, from dreadful weeping and wailing, O Lord, deliver me, thy servant, John, Jr.

And from memory.

BOOK FIVE

I

Raining. Pelting. A cloudburst and he had no raincoat. He eased the Toyota through the courthouse parking lot. Nothing like a little rain to show the deficiencies of a Corolla. The brakes were watersoaked. Jam them in this mess and it'd skid right into a Cad or a BMW. Fuck BMWs. Especially the 528i's. LEE S. Calm down. It's only a little rain. It'll stop. No spaces in the lot. Not one fucking parking space. I'd like to own a parking lot. With my own permanent space. Name stenciled on the asphalt. A parking lot. Not a bad investment. All it needed was a little venture capital. Annie O'Meara's Dome is what you mean. Those boys at Dome really know their onions. Or is it buttons. Venture capital. Drop that idea fast, buster.

He turned at the end of one row and slipstreamed up another. No spaces here either. Just four more BMWs. What is it with BMWs and lawyers? What's the appeal? Maybe a car to fuck in. The bucket front seats in Lee's 528i folded almost clear down. All she had to do was rest her feet on the dash and Byron could have hammered away like she was on a down mattress. Rain thoughts. Parking lot thoughts.

There. Was that a space? The next row.

But no. A Porsche 911 Targa was parked diagonally across two spots. With the license plate that told it all. STUKIN. Barry Stukin's new boat. Forty thousand dollars worth of Kraut steel. Engineered with the same efficiency that produced the Auschwitz ovens. What masochism made rich Jews prefer German cars? STUKIN. You miserable bastard. Parking across two spaces so no one can scratch your baby. STUKIN. Christ, I hate vanity plates. LEE S. So I've got to get soaked because you need two spaces. Fuck you, jack. And that gumbah you sent me, while you're at it. Fat Francis. *What I don't want, and I want to tell you this frankly, what I don't want is the Crime Commission on my ass.* Favors I don't need. Fuck STUKIN. And LEE S, too. In the ass. A nice thought. He had never done that.

There was a clap of thunder. And still not a space. Suddenly he slammed the Corolla into reverse and skidded to a stop behind STUKIN, showering spray. *Barry tells me you won't look the other way, someone waves a fortune your way.* So you want two spaces, do you? *You got a real pal there.* Fuck you, real pal. He was out of the Corolla and into the rain. On his knees beside STUKIN. Fingers fumbled for the air nozzle on the right rear of the 911 Targa. The Auschwitz gas guzzler. Try a flat, STUKIN. The rain poured down his nose, soaked his suit. Did Byron really fuck Lee in LEE S? A car rolled by. Another BMW. A 733i. The driver stopped, rubbed the condensation from his window, tooted his horn, shook his fist. But didn't get out. Getting out meant getting wet. With rain down the collar, rain in the shoes. He gave the BMW horn tooter the finger and moved around to a second tire. In case STUKIN thought he could drive away on the spare. Fuck LEE S. In her 528i. The air whooshed out of the Michelin radial like life itself.

Ahhh.

He felt better.

Wet, but better.

2

"Mr. Shea."

Mr. Shea, in dry clothes now, a Burberry umbrella courtesy of Alice March dripping at his feet, reshowered, resplendent in clean suit, shirt, tie, socks, shined shoes, dry and still feeling better, cleansed, said, "Your Honor."

"I don't see your name on my calendar this morning." Martha Sweeney, sensible black glasses perched on the tip of her nose, hair tightly knotted and held in place with a tortoise-shell barrette, a snub-nosed Smith & Wesson .38 hidden on her hip in a snapaway holster, peered at him from the bench. Stern Martha Sweeney. No-nonsense Martha Sweeney. Structured Setting Martha Sweeney. Who already this morning had sentenced a first offender, armed robbery, 211, P.C., to five years in a structured setting. Which was the reason for the Smith & Wesson. Sentencing made some defendants volatile. And there was another sentencing on the calendar. Martha always wore the .38 when she sentenced. "Are you appearing?"

"No, Your Honor." The only reason I am in this courtroom is to take you to lunch. As you well know. In the Sonesta Room at the Chateau Blanche Motor Hotel for the quarterly luncheon of the County Bar Association. No-host bar, peanuts and cheese dip gratis. An opportunity to meet your peers in law enforcement and get stiff.

"Number six on my calendar, A610559, Raines, Roscoe C., for arraignment, you see it?"

"Yes, Your Honor." Burglary, 459, P.C., one count, receipt of stolen property, 496, P.C., one count, possession of a controlled substance, 11350, P.C., one count.

"Mr. Lee of the public defender's office was going to handle this matter, but there's been a death in the family and he is unable to appear and the PD doesn't have another attorney immediately available. I wonder if you can handle the arraignment."

"I'd be glad to, Your Honor." As a favor. He smiled at the bench. I bet I am the only person in this courtroom who knows you have a healing Bartholin cyst. Which makes lubricity difficult. And has thus inhibited your sexual activity for two weeks. Inhibited but not stopped. There is more than one way to skin a cat.

"Is something amusing you, Mr. Shea?" Brusque and forbidding Martha Sweeney. Who knew what he was smiling at. Who did not think a lanced Bartholin cyst was a laughing matter. Who did not like him smiling at her in front of her clerk and tipstaff and bailiff and the off-duty policemen waiting for their collars to be called. A lawyer whose organ she had contemplated. An attorney familiar with her Bartholin cyst. "If this strikes you funny, I can keep the accused in custody until the public defender can assign an attorney who will find the charges a good deal more serious than you appear to."

The off-duty policemen snickered. The only other person in the well of the courtroom was a very pregnant Latin woman with a front tooth missing.

"I'm sorry, Your Honor." He tried to look properly chastised. "Excuse me." He took the defendant's file from the tipstaff and sat down in the jury box. Egg-

328

crate lighting illuminated the dirty walls. The clock was stopped. On the wall next to the clock a sign said, POL CE OF ICERS MU T DISPLAY APPROPRAITE ID. He had never noticed that "appropriate" was misspelled before. So much for my powers of observation.

RAINES, Roscoe C. Dutch Shea, Jr., looked at the photograph stapled to the accused's police jacket. Negro, 32 years old, hair conked. Don't often see a black with conked hair these days. The man looked vaguely familiar. He leafed through the jacket. No wonder. A record that went back seventeen years. Reform school, county detention, state penitentiary. Must have seen him when he was run through here before. There certainly were enough opportunities.

Okay.

RAINES, Roscoe C. Apprehended with a nineteen-inch JVC color television set and a glassine envelope containing a controlled substance, to wit, cocaine. RAINES, Roscoe C., claimed to have found the nineteen-inch JVC in an alley.

Lucky man, Roscoe. I've lived in this city all my life and I've never found a TV set in an alley.

Who's the prosecutor? He checked the calendar. Alonzo Perez, deputy district attorney. A new boy. Fresh out of law school. An equal opportunity DA. No need to deal yet. Let's see how good he is first.

He stared at the photograph of RAINES, Roscoe C. Familiar face. No, he hadn't prosecuted him. Or defended him. He considered going downstairs and taking a look. RAINES, Roscoe C., was in the basement lockup waiting for his case to be called.

No.

He had already been in one lockup this morning. Seeing BEAUBOIS, Robert NMI. BEAUBOIS, Robert NMI had used up his tolerance for the criminal element today.

"So far your story checks out pretty well."

The scraggly hair, the pustuled neck. "You think I was fucking lying or something?"

"The truth has never exactly been your long suit, Bobby." Marty Cagney had winced at that point. Marty Cagney had never addressed any prisoner by his Christian name.

"Listen, man, I'm looking at eighteen counts of murder one."

"That's a better reason than most to lie," Marty Cagney said quietly.

"Fuck you, Pop."

Marty Cagney shrugged.

"Marty retraced your steps," Dutch Shea, Jr., said. "You left out a couple of things."

"Like what?"

"Like the black guy at the drugstore."

"He was hassling me."

"Maybe because you were trying to steal some Dilaudid from the drug drawer."

"You going to believe that coon, man?"

"Your choice, Bobby. The Dilaudid or eighteen counts of murder one."

"Fucking nigger."

"That brings us to Tiny Naylor's."

"Who the fuck is Tiny Naylor?"

"Tiny Naylor's is where you bought the baked beans."

"For fifty-five cents." Beaubois primed a pustule.

"The only place out there that sells baked beans for fifty-five cents," Dutch Shea, Jr., said. "The waitress wouldn't give you extra crackers."

"Cunt."

"So you mixed up the hot water and ketchup and threw it at her. I got to hand it to you, Bobby. You left your signature wherever you went."

Beaubois squeezed. A drop of blood replaced a whitehead. "You find the guy in the Jag?"

"You fuck him?"

"Hey, listen, man . . ."

"Bobby, you went to the joint the first time when you were fifteen years old. They could fly the Goodyear blimp up your ass right now and it wouldn't touch the sides. I asked you. Did you fuck him?"

"I went down on him."

"What about him?"

"He couldn't keep it up."

"Anything else?"

"He had a birthmark on his cock. A big purple birthmark."

Marty Cagney's eyebrow moved a fraction.

"Okay. Let's go to the house with the hamsters."

"It was a garage."

"How'd you get in?"

"I broke a window."

"What time?"

"Midnight. Twelve thirty."

"You left when?"

"Sunup. A little before."

"Why?"

"I fucking told you. A dog began barking."

Dutch Shea, Jr., stared up into the mirror. A guard was watching, hand on his revolver. "Tell him, Marty."

Marty Cagney opened a spiral notebook. "A woman on North Steele Road, a Mrs. Finley, heard a window break that night and called the police. The call was logged in at twelve thirty-seven A.M. and never investigated. At five nineteen A.M., Mrs. Finley called the police again. Her dog was barking, she suspected intruders. Again the call wasn't answered. That call's also on the division log. Later that morning she reported her garage had been broken into. Someone had broken the window in the outside door and let himself in."

Beaubois smiled. His teeth were stained and gummy. "See."

"Tell me about the hamsters," Dutch Shea, Jr., said.

"What hamsters?"

"The hamsters in Mrs. Finley's garage. There were two of them in a cage, remember?"

"So what?"

"So what did you do to them?"

Beaubois looked from one to the other. "They were hassling me."

"They were hamsters, for Christ's sake. You strangled them."

Beaubois shouted back. "They were hassling me."

Oh.

Of course.

So.

On the upside, BEAUBOIS, Robert NMI, was a sociopath and a psychopath. But on the downside, it was likely that BEAUBOIS, Robert NMI, did not set the fire in the Cuthbertson. Not if he was in a garage on North Steele Road at 12:37 A.M., he didn't.

Someone else torched the Cuthbertson.

Formerly The Allen House.

Formerly owned by the Charter Oak Corporation.

A spin-off of FHI.

Frog Hollow, Incorporated.

Your dad and me. Two harps calling ourselves Frog Hollow, Inc. The Yanks didn't like that, buster, I'm telling you.

"You did a hell of a job, Marty," Dutch Shea, Jr., had said when they left the county jail.

Marty Cagney always did a hell of a job.

"To tell the truth, Dutch, I can't say I'm crazy about putting that nutcase back on the bricks," Marty Cagney said. "You ever been hassled by a hamster?"

Objection. Irrelevant.

"And what about our pal in the Jag?"

"The one with the blue blazer and the purple birth-mark. Another swell job by Marty Cagney. Who had checked out all the 1979 fuel-injected Jaguar XJ6Ls currently registered at the Department of Motor Vehicles. Thirty-one of which were silver. Seven of which had license plates whose last two digits contained a combination of the numbers 7, 8 or 9. Two of which had bumper stickers that said, EGAN—AGAIN. One of which was owned by a man with a purple birthmark on his genitalia.

Who had left BEAUBOIS, Robert NMI, in Elizabeth Park at midnight the night of the fire.

"I think we'll keep him in the bullpen for a while, Marty. In case we need him. No sense in causing trouble if we don't have to."

No sense indeed.

I already have more trouble than I need.

Except that Marty Cagney always did such a hell of a job.

LEE S.

For example.

The Allen House.

For example.

"Marty, there's something else I'd like you to do for me."

"Sure, Dutch."

"There's someone I'd like you to track down. A woman. I think she lives in Las Vegas."

A woman with pale red pubic hair.

Just in case I need more trouble.

Trouble. RAINES, Roscoe C. He stared at the conked hair. Why do I know that face?

Martha was sentencing again. BUTTANDA, Federico Fernando, stood before her in his jailhouse denims.

Dutch Shea, Jr., checked the calendar. A habitual offender. 487, P.C., grand theft, auto. Five counts. Clarence Banks was defending. Lucky you, Federico. Clarence advertised.

CLARENCE BANKS
Certified Specialist in Criminal Law
Minimum Fee: $5000

And then a list:

Closed Cases (Partial List):
Acquitted.
Acquitted.
Acquitted.
Dismissed.
Dismissed.
Hung Jury.
Convicted of lesser manslaughter.

Clarence never seemed to lose one.

Jesus. What kind of dummy gets caught five times stealing a car? Lowered, probably. With duals. And a squirrel tail on the antenna.

A dummy who deserves Clarence Banks as his attorney.

Five years for BUTTANDA, Federico Fernando. Light for a habitual. Martha must be feeling charitable today. Or Clarence had dealt someone away. Another listing probably. Convicted of lesser.

"Hey, lady."

Martha looked up. She moved almost imperceptibly in her chair. Getting the .38 onto her hip, Dutch Shea, Jr., bet.

"You forgetting something, lady?"

334

Martha stared at the defendant for a moment. "Ah, yes. Mr. . . . ." She adjusted her glasses and examined the defendant's jacket to ascertain his name.

"Buttanda," Clarence Banks offered.

"Thank you, Counselor. I am aware of the defendant's name."

Bad move, Clarence. For five K, you don't show up Her Honor on the bench.

"Mr. Buttanda wishes to get married to"—Martha picked up another piece of paper—"a Miss Rosario Augustina Mota . . ."

The pregnant Latin woman with the missing front tooth beamed in the front row of spectator seats.

"Before he is"—Martha faltered momentarily as she searched for the appropriate words—"remanded to the state penitentiary . . ."

That's how to sugarcoat it, Martha. You're all heart.

". . . to the state correctional facility . . ."

Keep trying, Martha.

Rosario Augustina Mota stepped across the bar and stood beside her intended. She kept her hands clasped under the bulge in her stomach as if she were trying to keep the baby in until the ceremony was performed and its legitimacy was guaranteed.

"Mr. Shea."

"Your Honor."

"I wonder if you'd be a witness to this matter with Mr. Banks?"

"Certainly, Your Honor." Leave it to Martha to refer to a wedding as "this matter." He walked to the defense table.

"How are you, Dutch?"

"Fine, Clarence. How you going to list this one?"

Clarence Banks gave a booming laugh.

"No losers in your ad, Clarence. I didn't know you were batting a thousand."

335

"Shit, Dutch, when Ford runs an ad, does it say it just had two hundred thousand Mustangs recalled?"

Federico Buttanda and Rosario Mota were talking quietly in Spanish, holding each other's hands.

"Name familiarity, Dutch, that's what I get out of those ads."

Name familiarity. I've got entirely too much of that, Dutch Shea, Jr., thought.

"Gentlemen."

"Your Honor."

Dutch Shea, Jr., took his place beside Rosario Mota. She began weeping.

"By the laws invested in me . . ."

The door to the holding tank opened and a marshal brought in the next defendant. RAINES, Roscoe C. He was in jail denims and handcuffs. The marshal unlocked the cuffs and motioned for Raines to keep standing until the marriage ceremony was completed.

"Rosario Augustina Mota, do you take this man . . ."

Dutch Shea, Jr., glanced across the courtroom at Raines. Suddenly he realized why the face was familiar.

That son of a bitch.

"*Sí.*" Tears rolled down Rosario Mota's cheeks.

Roscoe Raines stood at ease, thumbs hooked into his belt loops.

You got any nicknames? Like Ramblin' Man? Chocolate Lightning? Sable?

Ain't you got no suede?

"Federico Fernando Buttandez . . ."

"Buttanda, lady."

"Excuse me." A flash of annoyance passed over Martha's face. "Federico Fernando Buttanda, do you take this woman . . ."

I bet you wear a rubber when you fuck.

You some kind of pimp lawyer.

Man, that's a heavy job, a pimp lawyer. I get some ladies, I don't want no lawyer lives like this.

He wondered if Raines had recognized him.

You motherfucker, what you looking at?

". . . I pronounce you man and wife."

Pimp laywer.

Well, you are being defended by a pimp lawyer now, baby.

Federico Buttanda and his wife embraced. Rosario buried her head into her husband's shoulder and sobbed.

Martha coughed. "Mr. Buttanda."

"Lady."

"I don't want you petitioning me for an annulment in six months because you haven't consummated your marriage."

Buttanda looked bewildered.

Rosario wailed.

Roscoe Raines laughed.

At least someone thought it was a funny joke, Martha.

Martha Sweeney looked embarrassed.

No one seemed to know how to end the scene. Finally Martha nodded at the marshal, who came over and gently pried the newlyweds apart. Clarence Banks shook hands with his client and then led Rosario back to the spectator seats.

Roscoe Raines slapped his knee and bent over giggling.

Martha banged her gavel.

Federico Fernando Buttanda disappeared through the door to the holding tank with the marshal. He did not look back at his bride.

The bailiff called docket number A610559.

"Mr. Shea, are you ready?"

337

"I'd like a few minutes to talk to my client, Your Honor."

"We'll take a recess."

Roscoe Raines sat sullenly in the jury box. "Man, I found that TV set."

"Don't jive me, Roscoe." No, he has no idea who I am. I'm just some honky he stuck up. We all look alike.

"Man, why would I jive you? You my lawyer. You going to get me off this beef?"

"I'm a pimp lawyer, Roscoe. You sure you want a pimp lawyer?"

"Shit, man, pimp lawyers know all the tricks. I don't want no lawyer handles niggers who steal TV sets. Big-time pimp lawyer, that's what I want." He leaned close. "You really a pimp lawyer?"

If it's an act, it's a good one. "You said it."

"You got any leftover pussy, you let me know."

"You just keep your trap shut, Roscoe. I'll see what I can do."

"Your Honor, I ask that all charges against my client be dropped on the grounds that there was no probable cause for arrest."

"Denied, Mr. Shea. Are you ready, Mr. Perez?"

Alonzo Perez wore a three-piece suit and a mustache and wire-rimmed glasses. He was twenty-nine years old and looked younger. "Your Honor, I would like to call the arresting officer, Officer O'Dea, to the stand."

Martha looked at him in surprise.

This is an arraignment, kid, not a hearing. She wants to go to lunch.

Martha started to speak, then stopped.

You better not fuck up, kid. She's going to teach you a lesson if you do.

Roscoe Raines whistled softly between his teeth. "If you such a big-time pimp lawyer," he whispered, "what you doing here?"

"I fuck the judge."

A delighted, toothy smile. Life as understood by Roscoe Raines. "All riiiight."

Martha gaveled them into silence. How she would have loved to have heard that exchange.

Was there a life sentence for a contempt citation?

He winked at Roscoe Raines. You miserable shit, you stuck a .22 down my throat.

One of life's little ironies.

He remembered the old joke. New Jersey looks like the back of an old radio.

My life is like the back of an old radio. Everything connects.

My life is like New Jersey.

QED.

It must be watching Alonzo Perez that makes my mind wander. He doesn't know what he's doing. This turd sitting next to me is going to walk because Lonnie Perez thinks he's smart.

Alonzo Perez tugged his mustache and tried to look older. "Now, Officer O'Dea . . ."

Denis O'Dea was a large and none-too-bright young man in a plaid lumber jacket. His shield was clipped to his jacket and he talked police talk. He said he had seen the suspect emerging from an alley on Putnam Street carrying the alleged television set. When he tried to apprehend the suspect, said suspect dropped the set and attempted flight.

"I made an immediate surveillance of the area to ascertain whether the suspect was operating alone or with accomplices and when I determined he was alone, I gave chase and was able to apprehend him on the corner of Putnam and Grand. There I placed him under arrest and read him his rights."

Alonzo Perez nodded in satisfaction. "Thank you, Officer O'Dea."

The policeman looked at the prosecutor and then at the bench.

Martha's face was impassive. "You have nothing further, Mr. Perez?"

"No, Your Honor."

You nitwit, you didn't ask about the cocaine.

"Then shall I turn the witness over to Mr. Shea?"

Come on, Martha. You gave him one chance.

"As you wish, Your Honor."

Oh, Roscoe, you are a lucky man.

"Mr. Shea."

"No questions, Your Honor."

Looking disgusted, Denis O'Dea left the stand. When he passed Alonzo Perez, he closed one nostril and stuck a knuckle up the other and sniffed.

"Yes, Mr. Shea."

"At this point, Your Honor, I'd like to request dismissal of all charges against my client."

"On what grounds?"

"On the grounds that the People have not proved that the television set was stolen nor did Mr. Perez secure any testimony from the arresting officer about the alleged possession of a controlled substance, charge three, specification number . . ."

"I can read the charge sheet, Mr. Shea."

You got to give it to me, Martha. I don't want this sucker to walk any more than you do, but Structured Setting Martha has a history of landing on fuckups, whether prosecutor or defense counsel. Don't change your MO now.

"Request granted. Case dismissed."

Alonzo Perez looked as if he had been hit in the face with a shovel.

"Mr. Perez, I'd like to see you in my chambers."

"You're in for a tough half hour, Lonnie. He remembered his own session with Martha after his entanglement with the juror in the Gentle Davidson trial.

As for you, Mr. Shea, I will not bring you before the board of ethics.

Thank you, Your Honor.

I do not wish your thanks, Mr. Shea.

"Hey, man, thanks."

"Think nothing of it, Roscoe." He noticed Martha leaving the bench.

"I'm going to get my threads back, man, then I'm going up to the Property Office. I want my TV set."

He studied Roscoe Raines. *"Your* TV set."

"I stole that sucker, man, it's mine." Roscoe Raines laughed and punched him lightly on the arm. "You think they give me the coke?"

"I don't think so, Roscoe." The courtroom was clearing for lunch. "You don't remember me, do you?"

Immediately Roscoe Raines became guarded. "I never met no hotshot pimp lawyer."

"You stuck me up."

"You have a hard time proving that, man."

"The DA couldn't prove you stole the TV set either, Roscoe."

They stared at each other.

"Hey, man, what's your name again?"

"Mr. Hotshot Pimp Lawyer."

Roscoe Raines peered closely at him. "Hey, man, I remember you." He slapped his knee and snapped his fingers. "Irish, right?"

Dutch Shea, Jr., nodded.

Roscoe Raines grabbed his hand. "How you doing, Irish?" Then he felt the cast and his voice became apprehensive. "I didn't break your arm, right?"

Dutch Shea, Jr., shook his head.

"How you break it then?"

"I hit a TV set."

Roscoe Raines laughed delightedly. "No shit." He

punched Dutch Shea on the arm again. "That pimp. He fire you?"

"No."

"He need some muscle?"

"I don't think so, Roscoe."

"Shit." His voice brightened. "Good to see you, Irish."

"Thank you, Roscoe."

"No hard feelings, right?"

"Sure."

"You is hot stuff, Irish." He snapped his fingers again. "Listen. I was thinking. I got a case coming up in Department One Twenty-five."

"Oh."

"They say I raped some chick."

"And?"

"It was a misunderstanding."

"I see."

"Why don't you handle it for me? I got one of those PD dudes. He's dumber than this DA here."

"I think I'm booked up, Roscoe."

"Big pimp case?"

"Big pimp case."

He stood up. Roscoe Raines pumped his hand.

"See you, Irish."

"I hope not, Roscoe."

II

More bad dreams.

A priest, a rabbi and David Susskind.

The subject was suicide.

"The thing is, David . . ." Rabbi Steven ("With a *v*, David") Lesher talking. Rabbi Steven Lesher held his cigarette by its sides, between his thumb and index finger as if it were a joint. ". . . the thing is, your suicide makes a commitment to taking his own life. Your suicide . . ." Rabbi Steven Lesher took two quick hits off his filter tip. ". . . your *average* suicide, mind you, has a vocation . . ." Another hit. ". . . in the same way I had a vocation for the rabbinate and Lionel here . . ."

CUT TO: Father Lionel Gill, C.S.P.

". . . had a vocation for the priesthood, isn't that right, Lionel?"

Father Lionel Gill, C.S.P. vigorously shook his head. "I think that is absolute nonsense, Jewboy."

What!

He woke. Father Lionel Gill smiled benignly. The graphic said, Author ("Idle Minds, Satan's Workshops"), Lecturer, White House Priest. Rabbi Steven Lesher fiddled with the zipper of his warm-up jacket. David Susskind nodded.

". . . absolute nonsense, Steven."

Ah.

"The vocation, Lionel, is for life-ending. End it. Out. Finito."

Dozing again.

"Finito Mussolini, as it were."

And awake again.

Finito Mussolini.

Off with the audio. But not the video. My night-light. Why does a grown man need a night-light?

Silly goddamn question.

Martha Sweeney groaned, rolled over, rested her knee on his genitals, snored.

He considered masturbating. Sometimes he had masturbated when Lee was sleeping. Whacking away in tempo with her snoring. Racing to the bathroom to flush his seed. No telltale stains to indicate auto-adultery. Which was more unforgivable than the real thing.

Or so he had told himself.

Proximity makes the heart grow colder.

Martha snored.

Who to conjure up?

He remembered pale red pubic hair.

She had no telephone listing in Las Vegas. No sweat, Marty Cagney had said. He knew a private investigator in Vegas. First you check the printout of power meter readings. If her name is on it, then you have an address. If you have an address, you can get a telephone number. Easy as pie.

Hair pie. Pale red hair pie.

An idle mind is Satan's workshop. Or someone's workshop. The workshop of that gnawing worm of conscience.

344

Which is why he kept his days full. And why he detested the nights. And kept a night-light on.

The mind was on idle at night. The worm gnawed.

Think of the days. The days were beginning to worry him now. Signs and portents. The days were getting out of sync. That was it. A sync problem. The gears not meshing properly. Matching felon with felony no longer seemed to fill the bill. His practice was supposed to keep his mind off the nights. And now the days were becoming as dangerous as the nights.

Consider this day. The day just past. The luncheon for the County Bar Association. Bonhomie at the no-host bar.

"So I said to him, 'Lew, you're going to have to do a touch. They insist, the Strike Force. As an example. A year. Minimum security. White-collar slammer. It's the best I could work out.' He takes it like a champ. 'So I go to prison,' he says. 'You seen Haldeman? He looks terrific. Got his hair styled now. Ehrlichman? Never looked better. I'm too old and too ugly to get buggered, so why worry? It's only a year. You get out every weekend and at my level of sexual activity, that's more than enough. It'll do me a world of good.' Seventy-two years of age, Dutch, you got to admire a guy like that."

Dutch Shea, Jr., nodded. White-collar crime was a subject he did not care to discuss. He moved down the bar. The conversations washed over him.

"Here's a guy, he offers Larry DeNiro six lecture dates, big conventions, twenty-five hundred a pop, and he swears on a stack of Bibles he's not trying to bribe a judge. 'He's a hell of a talker, Judge DeNiro,' he says. You been up before Larry, you know how he talks. Angelo Santangelo got him appointed when the governor wanted the Teamsters' endorsement. He's got trouble understanding traffic cases, Larry. I think he thinks we got a wire on him, which is why he reports the lectures . . ."

"I tell him he needs a tax shelter and what does he do? He buys a middleweight. Cowboy Chocolate. 'You got to be colored to be called Chocolate,' he says to this middleweight. 'Why?' the middleweight says . . ."

"Anyway, it's hot, so they all decide to go swimming over to the pool at Transubstantiation High. Everybody jumps in except Fat Eddie Keenan, he says he can't swim. Well, you know Guido and that bunch, always joking around. They undress him, Eddie, take off all his clothes, and throw him into the pool over to Transy there. Jesus, they nearly shit, is the story I get. He's got this hairy chest, Eddie, like a gorilla, except now there's these raw hairless blotches on it. A head of lettuce has got more brains than Guido, but he knows what those blotches mean. It means Fat Eddie's been wired and the blotches are from putting on and taking off the Fargo unit. They tape it on is what they do. You see those blotches, it's like a sign saying, I'm a snitch. What they do is, they try to drown him in the pool. Imagine that. At Transy. Guido went to Transy is what's so funny about it . . ."

"Kenny Ito's working undercover, you know Kenny, right? The Jap. So he's sitting in a hot tub with this chick and he testifies she tries to go down on him. She never gets her hair wet, he says, Kenny. I cross and I say how deep is the water in the tub. Four feet, he says. 'Your Honor,' I say to Judge Sweeney, 'I would like the court to appoint a surveyor.' 'Why is that?' Judge Sweeney says. 'Your Honor,' I say, 'if the water is four feet deep, as Mr. Ito has testified, and if my client never got her hair wet, as he also has testified, then Mr. Ito is some kind of man and I would like the exact specifications of his manhood.' 'Case dismissed,' Judge Sweeney says. . . ."

He had heard the story from Martha. Even Martha was sometimes not exempt from the rancid view of human behavior that prevailed in a courtroom. Are we all tainted?

Or am I just trying to rationalize?

He had not told Martha about Roscoe Raines. She would have wondered why he had not had him arrested. Fat chance of making that stick after all this time.

Anyway his cast was coming off this week.

And he did not want an argument with Martha.

He looked around the crowded convention room. Who did he want to see? Not Barry Stukin. He suspected Barry Stukin knew it was he who had let the air out of his tires. Too bad. Fuck him.

Not Solly Baum. Certainly not Solly Baum.

Nor Eustace Cooney.

He was not up to talking to Eustace Cooney just yet about his silver fuel-injected Jaguar XJ6L. With the Hitachi stereo and tape deck. And the bumper sticker that said, EGAN—AGAIN.

So Judge Cooney was queer.

He certainly had a purple birthmark on his cock. One notices those things in the shower room at the Club.

This was going to take a certain amount of delicacy. One did not call a nominee for the appellate bench as a hostile defense witness casually.

Not with my background with Eustace.

Not with my background, period.

Not to mention my foreground.

Eustace Cooney was someone he wanted to trot out only as a last resort.

And yet.

Eustace Cooney's purple birthmark. An unimpeachable alibi for BEAUBOIS, Robert NMI.

Talk about a million laughs. A moment to savor. Another monologue engulfed him.

"Burial instructions. Be explicit, I tell my clients.

Have it down on paper. You get a daughter-in-law doesn't know your wishes, with every good intention she'll pop you into the ground someplace you don't want to be. You take Buddy Lupin. He's in Miami Beach, he meets Georgie Jessel at a wedding, he says it changed his life. I got it down in black and white. He wants his remains shipped to Israel and buried in the George Jessel Forest . . ."

He could think of worse places to be planted. Popped into the ground. Where his father was, for example. Where Cat was. The three parts of Cat. Arm off the Bentley, head out of the Waterford crystal bowl. Who knew how many parts his father was in? Mostly torsos, a few limbs, the lady on television had said. Never a Shea in one piece. Collect the appendages and pop them into the ground alongside the toastmaster general. In the George Jessel Forest.

The Jessel.

I'm going to be buried in the Jessel.

He liked the sound of it.

Together again in the Jessel. The Shea Family. Cat, Jack and the faithful departed.

Thy servant, John. What did I call him? Daddy? Father? Sir?

I can't remember. I cannot remember. Will I forget what I called Cat? Catherine Liggett Shea. Wonder if I called her Catherine or Cathy. Who will be the custodian of Cat's memory after . . .

After what?

After I'm in the Jessel.

Thinking about it, are you?

Semper paratus.

He spotted Thayer Pomfret across the room. Thayer had handled Cat's adoption. Thayer was her godfather. Thayer would know who the custodians should be. A man wearing a Cottage Club tie and drinking a perfect martini, straight up, no olive, no twist, Thayer Wilson Pomfret II, TWP II, button-down shirt, cuffs on his pants, shoes that tied, Mr. Center Vent himself.

And my friend.

Putative friend.

Alleged friend.

"I just heard Clarence Banks say he was a sacrificial lamb in the game of political chess," Thayer Pomfret said.

Dryly. Thayer was nothing if not dry. *He hasn't taken a crap in three weeks and his eyes are too close together.* Wisdom from Francis Xavier Noonan. *Your pal with the fifty-seven teeth in his head.* Wisdom from D. F. Campion. *Dry lips.* Wisdom from Lee Liggett Shea. "Haven't you ever mixed a metaphor, Thayer?"

"No."

"I suppose you haven't."

Thayer Pomfret smiled over his martini. Even in the jammed Sonesta Room, there seemed a distance separating him from everyone else. "I'm sorry about your father, Jack."

"Nothing to be sorry about, Thayer. He's been dead over thirty years."

"I mean the way this happened."

"It happened."

"Yes. I suppose that's the best way to look at it."

Together again in the Jessel. The Shea family. "It tends to make you think of blood and family."

"Yes. I can understand that."

"And kinship." He remembered Thayer and Wilson Pomfret that last visiting day at the state penitentiary. Wilson Pomfret in his red Santa Claus suit and his white cotton beard. *My father says your father is performing a corporal work of mercy.*

"Yes."

"How things connect."

349

"Yes."

Now or never. I've laid down enough foundation. "Thayer, you handled Cat's adoption."

"Yes."

"I'd like to know who her parents are."

"You know I can't give you that information, Jack." Without hesitation. No eyebrow flickered, no muscle flinched. No hiding behind faulty memory or sealed documents. I can't. Equals I won't. Equals I know.

"Think of it as a corporal work of mercy."

"What the hell is a corporal work of mercy?"

"You asked me that once."

"I don't know what you're talking about."

"She's dead, Thayer."

"The law still applies, Jack."

"I want to tell them what she was like. I want her remembered."

"You remember her. Lee remembers her." An imperceptible break in his composure. "I remember her." He was arguing. Presenting a case. In summary. "D.F. remembers her. Hugh. Clarice. Her friends. Your friends."

My friends.

Alleged friends.

Putative friends.

"I want her parents to know."

"That is privileged information, Jack."

"Fuck privileged information."

His voice reverberated. People turned. People stared. I am making a scene. I am not drunk, people. I am only working on my second drink, people. Plus two handfuls of pistachio nuts. Which is why my fingers are all red. From shucking those goddamn shells.

Pistachio nut shells. Pistachio ice cream is made from pistachio nuts. *Remember Charlie Moran that was famous for the pistachio ice cream?*

350

He saw Martha trying to ascertain what the commotion was all about.

And Eustace Cooney clucking disapprovingly. That rock of the law. The Gibraltar of the courtroom. Solomon with a purple birthmark.

Don't cluck at me, faggot.

Elizabeth Park blowjob.

An aisle seemed to clear and he headed back to the bar. Solly Baum tried to intercept him. Friend of the faithful departed, Thy servant, John. About that little matter of probate, I bet. He wondered if he should ask Solly if he had ever known Annie O'Meara's friend, Charlie Moran, that was famous for the pistachio ice cream.

No, that tack wouldn't work. Try this: I know I'm a little late with Mrs. O'Meara's accounting, Solly, but this thing with my father, my dad, my daddy, has got me all turned around. Give me a couple of weeks and I'll get it all straightened out, I'll go see Mrs. O'Meara, et cetera and so forth and let me waltz you around again, Kathleen.

Kathleen.

The lobby seemed safer. Offered cover. Beat a hasty retreat.

Barry Stukin cut him off at the cigarette counter. "Jack, is there anything wrong?"

Pink shirt, cream collar, cream cuffs. The picture of a Porsche driver. "Fuck you, mister, and the Porsche you rode in on."

Barry Stukin shot cream cuffs and gold cuff links. "So it was you who let the air out of my tires. Someone saw you. I didn't believe it."

"Now you can."

"I got soaked."

"I figure you probably did. I figured you probably ruined that three-piece suit with the nice little ticket pocket."

"Why?"

"You sent me the garbage man."

"I don't know what you're talking about."

"Francis Xavier Noonan. Who is going to solve our garbage needs into the twenty-first century."

Barry Stukin scratched under his watch band. "If I made a mistake, I'm sorry. I was just tossing some business your way."

"I don't need your charity."

"Jack . . ." Barry Stukin took a deep breath. "I just heard . . ."

"Heard what?"

Another deep breath. "The word is that you might be a little short."

Short. A word rich with innuendo. "Not so short I need your fucking gumbah clients."

There.

Casualty report: two (2) friends, real or putative; one (1) angry judge of the superior court (albeit not so angry that Her Honor's knee was not currently resting on counsel's genitalia).

"Jack, I think you ought to see a psychiatrist."

"No way, Martha." Perhaps a priest. Bless me, Father, for I have sinned. Oh, have I sinned.

"You're obviously under a great deal of stress."

"No shrink."

Damage control: I just heard. The word is. Short. Five letters riddled with innuendo. Broke. Busted. Tapped out. So tapped out that you've been dipping into someone's estate. So tapped out that the judge of probate is making funny faces.

The word is. I just heard. How? Did it really matter? From Solly Baum, perhaps. Friend of the faithful departed, Thy servant, John. Is Jack Shea all right? He can't seem to get it together. I can't get him to give me an accounting. The verbal doodling of a concerned friend.

The word is.

I just heard.

He wondered if the word came with a name attached. Mrs. O'Meara. Annie. What did they know about Annie? Would they ever know why she disliked chocolate burnt almond ice cream? The nuts stick in my dentures, Mr. Shea. Even the Polident can't get them out. And that Polident is the best there is, Mr. Shea. What do you use, Mr. Shea? The Colgate? I hear the Aim is very good.

The word is.

I just heard.

Damage control advisory: abandon ship.

Martha snored.

III

Reconstruct.

I'm going to bake you some apricot muffins, you hear?

I hear.

They'd've been that little girl's favorites, she'd've lived.

He remembered. Harriet Dawson giggling the day the charges against her were dismissed. Leo giggling. Hector giggling. Leo and Hector goosing Harriet.

I'm out a batch of apricot muffins.

He folded over the top page of the autopsy report.

This is the well-developed, obese unembalmed body of a 64-inch, 155 pound, 39-year-old Negro female. The hair is black and shows a normal female distribution. The eyes are brown, the scelerae are white, the pupils are round and equal. There is bleeding from both nostrils and pink froth in the mouth. The neck is symmetrical. The breasts are large and pendulous. The abdomen is convex. The extremities are unremarkable except for a surgical incision indicating a colostomy was performed to create a permanent artificial opening in the colon to effect an artificial anus.

So Harriet Dawson had a colostomy. A fact he had not known. No reason that he should have. Still. One liked to know the little things. Like Annie O'Meara's taste for rocky road ice cream. Maybe Purvis was responsible for the colostomy. *Harv was hard to birth. I had to have stitches to tie up the tear in my thing. Purvis said it didn't matter. We could do it in the other place.* He had said, *Your rectum.* She had said, *That's the place.* Hector had killed Purvis. And now Leo had killed Hector and Harriet.

No other surgical scars or tattoos are noted except for the effects of five (5) gunshot wounds.

Five (5) gunshot wounds. And four (4) in Hector. It all came under the heading of Domestic Argument in the police report. A rather flexible definition. Leo must have been wrought up. Not that anyone would ever know why. The SWAT team had taken Leo out. End of domestic argument. Harv was in jail, Mavis was whoring. Leaving counsel for the defense to make the identifications.

There are no deformities. There is no jaundice or edema present. Examination of the limbs and antecubital fossae reveals evidence of old needle tracks.

He glanced down the corridor at Martha. She sat on a bench, trying not to look at the autopsy photographs on the walls. A suicide who had held a hand grenade against his stomach. A three-year-old girl whose nipples had been pulled off with a pair of pliers. Martha lit a cigarette. Martha who rarely smoked. It was best to smoke in the morgue. Smoking cut the smell. She had insisted on coming with him. Better coming to the morgue at three in the morning than staying alone in his apartment. Not even a question about why it could not wait. Sparing him unnecessary lies about not being able to sleep. She seemed to understand that he wanted to come.

He pulled on the cigar Jerry Costello had given him. A foul fat cheap cigar. Like Jerry Costello. It was Jerry Costello who had called him. Just a bunch of niggers, Dutch. You know why so many colored got killed in Vietnam, Dutch? The lieutenant would shout "Get down" and they'd all get up and start dancing.

At two A.M.

In bed with a judge.

Jerry Costello knew the man to call.

Knew he would come.

Knew his man.

A man who would listen to his jokes.

He read: GUNSHOT WOUNDS. Gunshot wounds one through four were "not immediately life threatening." Which left Gunshot Wound #5. The one that did the trick.

Gunshot wound #5 is a penetrating wound of the chest.
ENTRANCE WOUND: This is situated in the left anterior chest 12 inches below the vertex, 5½ inches to the left of the midline. It is circular, ³/₁₆ inch in diameter with a laceration abrasion to the right ½ inch in diameter. There is no sooting or stippling of the surrounding skin and no gross powder residue in the wound track.
EXIT WOUND: None.
PROJECTILE: A relatively well-preserved lead bullet is recovered from the right posterior chest wall.

DIRECTION: The gunshot wound track passes from left to right, to the back 45 degrees and slightly downwards.

COURSE: The gunshot wound passes through the skin, fat and muscle of the left anterior chest wall, enters the left thoracic cavity through the 2d intercostal space, perforates the left upper lobe of the lung, enters the mediaastinum and perforates the body of T5, exits the right pleural cavity through the 6th intercostal space adjacent to the spinal column and ends in the muscle of the right posterior chest wall.

EFFECT: As a result of the gunshot wound, there is left hemopneumothorax fracture of the thoracic spine at the level of T5 and contusion and softening of the thoracic spinal cord also at the level of T5.

OPINION: This gunshot wound is immediately life threatening.

A simple declarative sentence. Unequivocal and absolute. Easily diagrammed. Subject, predicate, unambiguous modifers. This gunshot wound is immediately life threatening.

Not unlike my days.

Not to mention my nights.

No wonder he found a certain comfort here.

Leo was in the cold room. Tier after tier of bodies, five stretchers to a tier. One tier held only infants·in paper bags.

Jerry Costello checked the toe tags. "Wyzansky. Must be a Polack. Listen, Dutch, what do 1776, 1812 and 1914 have in common?"

"I don't know, Jerry."

"They're adjoining rooms in the Warsaw Hilton."

"You're a scream, Jerry."

Leo was wrapped in butcher paper. Jerry Costello

ripped the paper away. The tearing noise seemed to reverberate off the walls.

Most of Leo's head had disappeared. Leo who had goosed Harriet. Harriet who was going to bake him a batch of apricot muffins.

"There ain't no dignity in death, Dutch."

"I guess, Jerry."

"You hear about the nigger track team?"

"I missed that one, Jerry."

"They set them off with a burglar alarm."

"You're a scream, Jerry."

Hector was on a table in the autopsy room. Hector who had goosed Harriet. Harriet who was going to bake him a batch of apricot muffins. A sign on the wall said, EAT A TOAD FOR BREAKFAST AND THAT WILL BE AS BAD AS YOU FEEL ALL DAY. There was dried blood on the floor and dried blood on the telephone and there were jars full of organs and chemical beakers filled with body fluids. Hector was being reassembled.

"Listen, Dutch," Jerry Costello said. He sneaked a look at Martha through the open door of the autopsy room. "You think she puts out, the judge?"

"Why don't you ask her, Jerry? You got your courtroom tie on? The one that lights up and says, FUCK YOU. Show it to her. I'll bet she'll think it's a bundle of laughs."

"I got to figure you're getting in, Dutch."

"Why's that, Jerry?"

"It's two o'clock in the morning when I call you and when you show up here, she's with you. Maybe you picked her up on the way down, but it's not the sort of place you bring a date, you want my opinion. So that means she was with you and the only reason anyone's at that shithole you call home is you're getting in."

"No wonder they made you a detective, Jerry."

They walked down the corridor to the bench where Martha was sitting.

"Jerry was just showing me what a great detective he is, Martha."

Martha Sweeney nodded. Inhaled deeply, exhaled a cloud of smoke.

"What great powers of induction he has." Jerry Costello flushed. "Isn't that right, Jerry?"

"Dutch is always joking, Your Honor," Jerry Costello said. The network of veins in his bulbous nose was slowly reddening. "I know your dad pretty good. Tommy."

2

The telephone rang.

A hang-up.

"Why?" Martha Sweeney said.

Why?

The eternal question.

Why did I do it or why am I telling you?

Last things first. Why am I telling you? I'm dotting the i's and crossing the t's. The morgue does that to you. A naked black woman with a colostomy, 155 pounds of dead fucking weight, that is a large last straw, but there you are, a last straw with a convex belly and large and pendulous breasts and no jaundice and no edema and no new needle tracks on the antecubital fossae, a last straw that shat through her pussy and ran over her granddaughter with a power mower and now she was dead and Leo was in the cold room and Hector was on the autopsy table, and that is it, I am folding my hand, throwing in my cards, waiting for the next deal whatever it might be, I don't give a fuck, I waive my Miranda rights, anything I might say can be held against me, fuck it, I've had it, that is why I am telling you.

Why did I do it?

Another question altogether.

The telephone rang again.

Deep breathing and then another hang-up.

"Why?"

He had asked Lee why.

It rained for a week I had a flat tire on the Merritt Parkway an old man stopped and changed it for me in the rain the sink backed up I went on a diet and lost five pounds I felt sad I ordered you ten pairs of white cotton boxer shorts from Brooks Brothers I had a mole burned off my back it was benign remember I found a tube of Ortho-Gynol in Cat's medicine cabinet.

So much for why.

Why is a question calling for a nonresponsive answer.

The telephone rang a third time.

"You made a whore out of my daughter." Pronounced whoore. Then a click.

Jerry Costello certainly hadn't wasted any time getting hold of Tommy Sweeney. He could imagine the conversation. First a couple of dirty jokes. What's a colored track team in Vietnam doing dancing in rooms 1776, 1812 and 1914 of the Warsaw Hilton? That's the capital of Poland, Tommy. By the way, I saw the judge . . .

"Who was that?" Martha Sweeney said. Whore, whoore, whoooore.

"Wrong number."

"Why?"

We had an argument on the way home and then we watched Dick Cavett in bed Aretha Franklin sang "ABC" with the Jackson Five and then we balled and the other guest was that man who talks to dolphins.

"Why?" The whore, whoore, whoooore sat on the couch, one leg tucked underneath her, warming her hands with a mug of instant coffee, the afghan he had taken from the house on Asylum Avenue wrapped around her shoulders.

The house on Asylum Avenue.

The house Judge Liggett had bought him and Lee as a wedding present.

After a fashion.

"Pride." He was surprised to hear the sound of his own voice. Pride. A better beginning than *it rained for a week,* but he suspected it was less responsive. "Judge Liggett died." Sitting on the toilet. Wearing a nightshirt. A stroke. He never even fell off the toilet seat. A fact he had not told Lee. A fact he would not tell Martha. Although applicable. As applicable as *I had a mole burned off my back it was benign remember I found a tube of Ortho-Gynol in Cat's medicine cabinet.* "He was broke."

"Judge Liggett?" Surprise. Men like Fairfax Liggett did not die broke. Nor die on a toilet seat with a nightshirt pulled up over aged spindly legs. They died in bed rich in honors and worldly goods.

"Dead broke. He speculated. In the commodities market, of all places. Pig futures. Among other things. He didn't miss a roll of the dice, the judge."

"Did Lee know?"

"Only that he died broke. Not about the house on Asylum Avenue. He gave it to us as a wedding present. Except he kept the deed. And kept on refinancing it."

"Why didn't you just sell it?"

"Lee wouldn't have had a place. I had moved out. It was during the time she and Byron . . ."

Marty Cagney time. DISCREETLY DETERMINING WHAT WAS DONE—WHERE & WITH WHOM. *Subject A wearing white halter dress checks into Chateau Blanche Motor Hotel, 1 Constitution Plaza, driving silver BMW 528i, license plate LEE S.*

"And you paid it off."

He nodded.

"The grand gesture. The nobility of Jack Shea." Martha shook her head. "You goddamn fool."

No objection.

"What was the indebtedness?"

"Approximately a hundred and fifty thousand."

"Jesus, Jack."

There was no need to comment.

"What did you do?"

"I paid it out of the various estates I was entrusted with. I always thought it would work out. It was a one-man office, I had my own accounting system, Solly Baum was always appointing me conservator or referee or guardian of some new estate or other. I'd draw something out of one account and pay it into another. No one ever knew. Most of the people were senile or mentally incompetent, so it was unlikely that *cestui que trust* or *cestui que use* would ever apply to the court for audit . . ."

"So you kept on robbing Peter to pay Paul?"

"And Matthew, Mark, Luke and John, too."

"It's not funny, Jack."

"Christ, Martha, I know it's not funny. I felt like a juggler on a high wire. I never slipped. And then . . ."

Martha cupped the coffee mug in both hands and let the steam rise over her face. "And then what?"

"Cat died."

Two words. No translation necessary. I lost my grip. Stopped caring. Let things slide. Like father, like son. Son of the faithful departed, Thy servant, John.

"I was into Mrs. O'Meara's account this time." *I like someone really knows his buttons, Mr. Shea. That's why I'm glad you're watching out for me.* "I got behind on her bill at the convalescent home where she's staying." *Oh, that Bugs Bunny, Mr. Shea. I wet my pants when I see Bugs.* "The supervisor complained to the probate court. I think I plugged the hole too late." *You should have a franchise of your own, Mr. Mullady.* "It's only a matter of time before Solly orders a hearing."

Neither one spoke. The silence was interrupted by the ringing of the telephone.

"Whoremaster." Click.

The least of my sins. And the quaintest.

Martha Sweeney said, "Who was that?"

"Nobody."

"Who was it?" The judicial warning.

"Tommy."

"Goddamn him." It was a moment before Martha spoke again. "How much are you short?"

"Almost two hundred now."

She did not say anything.

"I kept hoping for a windfall."

"I loved you, Jack."

Loved. Past tense. Arrivederci, sayonara, au revoir, auf Wiedersehen.

"I'm an officer of the court. You've made me aware of a felony. I could be charged with misprision."

He attempted to smile. "I'll never tell, Martha."

"Goddamn you, Jack."

"I'm sorry, Martha."

IV

Thoughts while traveling west, economy class.

Economy-class thoughts.

DEMOCRATS ATTACKING WINDFALL PROFITS. Newspaper headline.

I kept hoping for a windfall.

Windfalls I have known.

Elaine Igoe is a windfall.

It is also a prison between her cellulited thighs. A West Block. For harder types than I. For hardier types than I.

Carmine Cantalupo is a windfall.

You shouldn't've said that to Barry Stukin, Mr. Shea.

Said what, Mr. Cantalupo?

He's a good boy, Barry Stukin, Mr. Shea.

Indubitably, Mr. Cantalupo.

You did me a favor, Mr. Shea.

Not really, Mr. Cantalupo.

Take a look at my grandsons, Mr. Shea. This one's Rocco, this one's Guido, this one's Lou. Nice boys.

I'm sure they are, Mr. Cantalupo.

Take a look at my granddaughters, Mr. Shea. This

one's Ames, this one's Lindsay, this one's Daisy. Funny names for girls, don't you think, Mr. Shea?

If you say so, Mr. Cantalupo.

That's the great thing about America, Mr. Shea. A man like me, a gumbah, like you say, he can have granddaughters with names like that. Ames and Lindsay and Daisy.

I see your point, Mr. Cantalupo.

My daughter, Serafina, she's very happy, Mr. Shea.

I'm glad, Mr. Cantalupo.

Harry Pyle's a nice boy, Mr. Shea. He don't understand the fruit business, but he's a nice boy.

I'm glad, Mr. Cantalupo.

You can call on me, Mr. Shea. Anytime.

Thank you, Mr. Cantalupo.

I'm good for it.

Thank you, Mr. Cantalupo.

No strings.

Thank you, Mr. Cantalupo.

"Sir, would you please pull down the window shade?"

"Why?"

"So the other passengers can watch the movie."

"I don't want to watch the movie."

"Sir, it's very difficult for them to see the movie if your shade is up."

"That's their problem."

"Sir, be a good sport."

"Miss, I'm a lawyer. A pimp lawyer. And nowhere on this ticket does it say that a pimp lawyer has to be a good sport."

"Sir, you're making a scene."

"No, miss, I just want to look out the window. I don't want to watch Barbra Streisand taking a bath with Kris Kristofferson."

"Sir, I'll have to call the captain."

"I'd be glad to meet him."

"Sir . . ."

"It's a great country, miss, when you can be a gumbah and have granddaughters with names like Ames and Lindsay and Daisy."

She's a photographer, Dutch. At the Flamingo.

What kind of photographer, Marty?

A cocktail photographer, Dutch. In the lounge. One of those broads that takes pictures of guys with hair in their ears that are there with dames they're not married to.

Thanks, Marty.

You know a comedian named Jackie Gross? The one that started out in a strip joint in the North End. His name was Jackie Grossbart then.

I defended him once. Violation of the liquor laws.

Really. It's a small world, Dutch.

What about him?

Well, he has a game show now. *Beat the Rap,* I think it's called.

So.

She's tied up with him, my man in Vegas says.

The only thing wrong with oral sex is the view.

What's that, Dutch?

One of Jackie Grossbart's jokes, Marty.

You're not short, Mr. Shea. You're not tall, but you're no shrimp. I often wonder why they call shrimp short. They're curved and they've got a shell, but they're not short. Jockeys are short, and midgets. You ever know any midgets, Mr. Shea? They used to have a midget here at Arthur K. Degnan's. Artie Kinsella. He died. Maybe because he was so short. A lot of fish don't have shells, Mr. Shea. Fillet of sole. I never had a piece

366

of fillet of sole that had a shell. Alaska cod. Mr. O'Meara used to love his Alaska cod. It didn't have any shell on it is the reason why. Every Sunday morning, Mr. O' Meara wanted his Alaska cod. A special treat. Better than a physic, Mr. O'Meara always said. You don't eat Alaska cod, Mr. Shea, you should take a regular physic. Mr. O'Meara loved his physics. He didn't have his regular physic, he'd get all bent over and curled up. Looked like a shrimp. Maybe that's why they call shrimps short. They don't take physics. I expect it would be hard to give a shrimp an enema, don't you, Mr. Shea? That's a funny job for a man, giving a shrimp an enema. I bet he owns a Studebaker. A man who gives a physic to a fish is a man who owns a Studebaker, Mr. O'Meara always used to say. It's a funny thing about Studebakers. They seemed to attract that sort. Maybe that's why they went out of business. How's business, Mr. Shea? My Dome still okay? That bunch at Dome, they don't drive Studebakers. Not a shrimp in the crowd. They're generally tall in the oil business, Mr. Shea. Comes from the Alaska cod and regular enemas . . .

Did you tell her?

Yes.

And?

I think, Martha, she wanted me to take an enema.

I loved you, Jack. You just never believed it.

No, I never believed it.

You always did play life on the dark keys.

And the melody lingers on.

I'm glad you came by. I never thought I'd say that, but I am.

So am I.

Is this what you'd call a mortal sin?

No. In the eyes of the Church, we're still married.
So we can fuck to our heart's content.

That's how he remembered it. Which is not to say that is how it really happened. Read the lines a different way. Eliminate the filters. Use harsh natural lighting. Was it a grudge fuck?

A mutual grudge fuck.

Who else have you told?
Judge Sweeney.
Why did you tell him?
Him.
Because we went to the morgue together. To identify a client of mine. She had a colostomy. It seemed the thing to do.

You can go to D.F.
No.
Why not?
Because I can't. Because in my bones I know he was tied into that thing with my father. He was in it up to his eyeballs. I've known it all my life. I don't know how and I don't know why and I've never wanted to know.

Then he owes you, Jack.
I still can't go to him, Lee.

Did I say that?
Or wish I had said that?
In any event, she knows.
Did she always know?
Know as long as I did?
Probably.

* * *

Why were you in the ladies' room that night?
Because she had just told me she was pregnant.

Cat.
That absurd, obsessive question. Why were you in the ladies' room that night? That question I never expected to have an answer.
Because she was pregnant.
Cat.
Who dug a wraparound burgundy-colored Danskin skirt from her backpack and a pair of lace-up lavender espadrilles and that blue button-down Brooks Brothers shirt with the frayed collar. Even a disposable Bic razor to remove the stubble from her legs.

No, Daddy, I just want to see her.
You want to buy some Lowestoft?
Daddy, don't be a pain in the ass.
Cat.
Oh, my God, Cat.
So that was the answer.

That's why she wanted to see me that night, Jack. Alone. It's the sort of thing a daughter tells her mother. You never gave me much credit for being Cat's mother, but I did raise her. I took care of her the day she got her period the first time and I remember when she was a little girl she called my bedroom her sweet second room and she called spaghetti buzzghetti and she called people who came to the house hellos. She said where you was and where did the morning went and you told Thayer, you son of a bitch, you wanted someone to remember her. So she told me she was pregnant, it was an accident, and she wanted to know what to do and I went into the ladies' room because I knew I was going to cry and I didn't want to cry in front of her and I

369

wanted to get the tears out of the way so I could act sensibly and then I heard the bomb and when I finally got out part of her was in the sherbet and part of her was in the street and you, you son of a bitch, you want someone to remember her.

> I'm going to marry
> A boy named Harry.
> He rides horses
> And handles divorces.

"Ladies and gentlemen, will you please fasten your seatbelts and extinguish all smoking materials as we are about to land at McCarran Field in Las Vegas, Nevada . . ."

V

He stayed at the Flamingo. In the lobby the girl at the Avis counter asked if he had heard about the Polish bank robber: he tied up the safe and blew the guard. The bellman said if he wanted company the girl at the Avis counter gave the best French on the Strip. When he got to his room, he called the telephone number Marty Cagney had given him for Kathleen Donnelly. The operator cut in and said the number had been temporarily disconnected and that there was no new number. She was not listed in the telephone book nor with Directory Assistance. He dialed Jackie Gross. His answering machine said, "Hi, this is Jackie Gross. You know what bowling is? Polish tennis. But speaking seriously, my wife is a real Jewish cook. I ask her, 'What are you going to make for dinner?' and she says, 'A reservation.' For more of the same, catch me at ten and midnight at the Riviera. At the sound of the beep, kiss my ass."

Uh-uh.

He unpacked and took a shower. In the bathroom there was a plastic kit of courtesy toiletries—razor, blades, toothpaste, two toothbrushes, comb, shaving lotion, breath mints, an aerosol can of orange-scented vaginal spray and a tube of K-Y jelly. The Muzak in the bathroom was playing the selected hits of Buddy Trillin & The KayCees, now exclusively in the Stardust Lounge. He dialed Jackie Gross again and when the machine answered hung up once more.

How to announce himself on that machine.

Mr. Gross, this is John Shea. I'm an attorney.

No. That was a style that would not work with, "At the sound of the beep, kiss my ass."

Something breezier was called for. Jackie. This is Dutch Shea. Your old lawyer. When your name was Grossbart. May you have carbuncles on your private parts. Remember that one? Your Yiddish curses. May you be going downhill in a car with no brakes. May your Mercedes break down in Israel. May your nose be covered with warts. You always could break me up, Jackie.

Has it really come to this?

Something cooler, more distant. In the Thayer Pomfret manner. Would you have Mr. Gross please call John Shea, Jr., at the Hotel Flamingo?

As if the voice on the answering machine was not that of Jackie Gross but of his butler.

Perfect.

He stared into the mirror. This was the first bathroom he had ever seen with two telephones. One next to the toilet. Was any business that important? What did it say about the business at hand? Is this the perfect office for a second-generation embezzler?

Thoughts while sitting on the crapper. In the Flamingo Hotel. In Las Vegas, Clark County, Nevada.

Why am I here?

Because when the earth yielded the faithful departed, Thy servant, John, I lost the right not to investigate the uninvestigated mysteries of my life. A rather fragile right in the first place. Not even a right. A choice. A wrong choice? A practical choice. At least until the earth moved and surrendered the remains of John Shea, Sr. Now the Chinese boxes must be opened. One by one. Each to yield the surprise that was not quite a surprise. Like the Christmas present one always knew one was going to get.

Why am I here?

To find Kathleen Donnelly. Formerly a waitress in the state of Nevada. Now a photographer at the Flamingo. Who takes pictures of men with hair in their ears. Who is kept by Jackie Gross.

That Kathleen Donnelly.

Who had a daughter.

Maeve Kelleher said.

A little girl, sir.

Maeve Kelleher said.

She'd be about my age now, sir.

Maeve Kelleher said.

Oh, she gave her up, sir.

Maeve Kelleher said.

A long time ago.

Maeve Kelleher said.

When she was just a little baby, sir.

Maeve Kelleher said.

He called the Flamingo employment office. Teri referred him to Kelly. Kelly referred him to Brandy. Brandy referred him to Sandy. Sandy said that Kathleen Donnelly was no longer employed at the Flamingo. Sandy said that Kathleen Donnelly had given no notice and had left no forwarding address.

Sandy asked if he were in law enforcement.

Sandy asked if there were any criminal charges outstanding against Kathleen Donnelly.

* * *

"At the sound of the beep, kiss my ass."
"Would you have Mr. Gross please call John Shea, Jr., at the Hotel Flamingo?"

It's the sort of thing a daughter tells her mother.
And not her father.
No, Daddy, I just want to see her.
You want to buy some Lowestoft?
Daddy, don't be a pain in the ass.
She'll ask if you've shaved your legs.
Then I'll do it.
I better go along with you.
No.
Somebody needs to referee.
I can handle it, Daddy.
It's the sort of thing a daughter tells her mother.

Tell me about Kathleen Donnelly, Dominick.
Eamon Donnelly's widow. That hit the fellow from Planned Parenthood in the face with her handbag.
No, not Eamon Donnelly's widow.
I don't know who you mean, then, Jack.
You fired her. You told me she was in Las Vegas. You said she was a bad apple. You said you had her checked out. You said you had to watch out for that type.
I don't remember saying that, Jack.
You did, Dominick. You also said Thayer Pomfret did a little legal work for you once.
It was nothing important, Jack
He also handled Cat's adoption.
I remember that.
I was just wondering if the legal work he did for you had anything to do with Cat.
Don't be silly, Jack.
Or with Kathleen Donnelly?
I don't know what you're getting at.

374

Is Kathleen Donnelly Cat's mother, Dominick?
Don't be silly.
Is she, Dominick?
How am I supposed to know?
Is she, Dominick?
That's the silliest thing I ever heard.
Is she, Dominick?

Objection. Argumentative. Badgering the witness.
Sustained. Strike from "I don't know what you're getting at." You may continue, Mr. Shea.
No further questions.

Famous last words.
I only regret that I have but one life to lose for my country.
It is a far, far better thing I do.
I believe in God.

There was no call from Jackie Gross. At nine thirty, he left the Flamingo for the Riviera. In the lobby of the Riviera, there was a photo blowup of Jackie Gross wearing a golf cap and carrying a putter over his shoulder along with the words, TWICE NIGHTLY—10 AND MIDNIGHT.

"Dutch." The speaker was very fat and was wearing a sea-green short-sleeved leisure suit. The girl at his side towered over him. "Small world, Dutch. Francis Noonan."

"Hello, Francis."

"Say hi to Sherry, Dutch."

"Shelley." The girl leaned on Francis Xavier Noonan's shoulder and tried to fix the strap on one of her pumps. When she bent over, her breasts were revealed to the nipples.

"Say hi to Dutch Shea, Jr., Sherry."

"Shelley."

"I'm here on a convention, Dutch. The hod carriers. Sherry's helping me have a good time. Tell Dutch that swell story you told me, Sherry."

Shelley straightened up. "You hear the one about the Polish bank robber?"

"I heard that one."

"What did I tell you, Sherry? He hears all the jokes, Dutch. A laugh a minute. And a hell of a lawyer. You know that little matter we talked about, Dutch? Something has just come up, I want to talk to you about it when we get home."

"Fine, Francis."

"And Dutch, don't miss Jackie's show. You remember Jackie, don't you? When he was at ChiChi Carinici's joint up the North End there. I spotted him then. I shouldn't be in the fucking gravel business, I should be a talent spotter . . ."

"Nice to see you, Francis."

"We'll talk, Dutch. And you want some company, Sherry here's got some swell friends, right, Sherry?"

"Shelley."

Jackie Gross said, "I used to play with my diddy when I was a kid. I mean, I was a workaholic with my diddy. Two-fisted, you know what I mean. My old man says to me, 'Listen, you keep whacking that thing, you're going to go blind.' Wow. No kidding? 'No kidding,' he says. 'Blind.' So I say, 'How about I keep doing it until I need to wear glasses?'"

Jackie Gross said, "Appearances are important, right? Take a look at me. Pretend I'm a lifeguard. How far out would you go?"

Jackie Gross said, "Hey, where'd you go to school? Notre Dame? That's French for football."

Jackie Gross said, "Speaking of doctors, ladies and gentlemen, I go see my doctor, his name is J. Brooks

Schwartz. You got a Jew doctor and he's got an initial and a last name before you hit the Schwartz, already you're in shit up to your collarbone. So he says to me, J. Brooks Schwartz, I got good news for you and I got bad news for you. The bad news is terrible, the good news is terrific. So I say to him give me the bad news first. And he says to me your tests came back, you got six months at the outside, then the toilet, you're in it, over and out, start the end credits. So I pick myself off the floor and I say to him what's the good news? And he says to me I finally fucked my nurse . . ."

Jackie Gross said, "You been a beautiful audience, I love you all, now I got to go take a dump, get ready for my next show . . ."

2

Jackie Gross said, "You want some J&B, Dutch? Daniel's? Tanqueray with a twist? I got all the brands. Chivas. That Turkey stuff. Stolich—you know the one I mean, that Russian shit—Stolichnaya, that's the one. Olives, onions, chee wees. No salted peanuts. Bad for the bowels. Clogs the sewer. You like the joint?"

Dutch Shea, Jr., glanced around Jackie Gross's living room. Except for the mirrors, everything was white. White sofas, white chairs, white rugs, white picture frames. White end tables, white coffee table, white side tables. White breakfront. White ice bucket. White glasses. "I like the theme, Jackie."

"This is class, Dutch," Jackie Gross said. He was also all in white. Shoes, socks, slacks, belt, polo shirt and cardigan. "Not like those places on the Sahara golf course. Pit bosses live there. You want to live next door to a pit boss, you'll have a swell time there. This place is private. Listen, you know who's on the board of this club? Vaughn Monroe. Henry Ford's brother. People like that. Vic Mature."

"That's swell, Jackie."

"I never expected you to turn up, Dutch."

"I've got some business here, Jackie."

"Business, Dutch. You can make a mint in Vegas. A lawyer like yourself. Let me pass the word. I'll never forget what you did for me, Dutch. You get my Christmas card?"

"Every year."

"I got your name on my Rolodex."

"I'm honored, Jackie."

"I bet you never thought I'd have a Rolodex when I was at ChiChi's."

"I spotted you then, Jackie. I shouldn't be in the legal business. I should be a talent spotter."

"Dutch, you're the best. Let me make a few telephone calls. Somebody tells me Tommy Leonetti's looking for a new lawyer. What a set of pipes, Tommy. Lou Kalish was his attorney. He passed away last week, God rest his soul. You believe in God, Dutch?"

"I've never given it much thought."

"I do, Dutch. Nothing formal. I don't go to temple or any of that shit, but I know there's a big guy up there, and that big guy, Dutch, you don't want to get on the wrong side of Him. It makes you think."

"I can see that, Jackie." Dutch Shea, Jr., prowled the living room. He picked a book off an end table. It was the only book visible. The title was *The Giant Book of Insults*.

"That's a hell of a book, Dutch. That's what I mean about the big guy." Jackie Gross was pointing at the ceiling and beyond. "I was in a bookstore. Now I don't go into many bookstores. I mean, the only thing I learned how to read when I was a kid was 'Sold for the Prevention of Disease Only.'" Jackie Gross waited for the laugh. "But I found myself walking into this bookstore. Like someone was pushing me in. The big guy. And I head right to this counter and there it is. *The Giant Book of Insults.* It's a gold mine, Dutch. The big guy was watching out for me, I got to believe that."

Against his will, Dutch Shea, Jr., yielded to curiosity. "Why's that, Jackie?"

Jackie Gross held up *The Giant Book of Insults.* "With this book, I can squelch any heckler." He pressed it into Dutch Shea's hands. "Go on. Give me a drunk. 'He should get his jocular vein cut.' I'm telling you, Dutch, you can really shut people up. You let the hecklers take over your act, you're dead." Jackie Gross held an imaginary microphone, snapped an imaginary mike cord and addressed an imaginary heckler. "You say a thousand things, but you never say goodbye. I don't know what makes you tick, but I wish it was a time bomb. Your idea of fun is to throw an egg into an electric fan." Jackie Gross sat down. His forehead was covered with sweat. "See what I mean, Dutch?"

Dutch Shea, Jr., nodded noncommittally.

"That's why I got a special feeling about the big guy."

"I can see that, Jackie."

Jackie Gross stood up. "Listen, Dutch, it was good to see you. You want to see some shows, let me fix it for you. You want a piece of ass . . ."

Dutch Shea, Jr., remained seated. "Actually, Jackie, the reason I'm here has nothing to do with the big guy."

"Oh. You want to cut up a few touches about old times. At ChiChi's."

"No." Dutch Shea, Jr., felt his shirt dampen in the frigid air conditioning. "Actually I wanted to ask you about a woman named Kathleen Donnelly."

"Come again?"

"Kathleen Donnelly."

Jackie Gross's back was to Dutch Shea, Jr. "You're going to have to give me a little help, Dutch."

"You were banging her."

Jackie Gross turned around. "Listen, Dutch, keep it down. I got a family."

"And you know Vic Mature."

"Yeah, I know Vic. What's he got to do with this?"

Dutch Shea, Jr., lifted a framed wedding invitation off the coffee table.

Mr. and Mrs. Arnold Kepesh
cordially invite you
to the wedding of their daughter
Brenda Maxine
to that rising young comic
Jackie Gross
on Sunday March 19, 1970
Temple Beth Emanu-El

He read it twice to make sure he was not hallucinating and then carefully replaced it.

Was it even possible to continue a conversation about Kathleen?

Yes. You have traveled too far. How many miles to Babylon? Three score miles and ten. Can I get there by candlelight? Yes, and back again.

"Kathleen Donnelly."

Jackie Gross snapped his fingers. "The Irish girl."

"Yes."

"The one with the red hair."

"That's the one."

"I haven't seen her in a long time, Dutch. A couple of years."

"Where's your wife, Jackie? Brenda, isn't it?"

"We leave her out of this, Dutch, you understand?"

"I thought she might like to know you paid the rent

on Kathleen Donnelly's apartment right up to the first of the month."

"Jesus, Dutch, you do your homework. Tommy Leonetti, he'll be in good hands, you take him on."

"Where is she?"

Jackie Gross closed the sliding doors into the living room. "You got to believe me, Dutch. I don't know."

"I don't believe you, Jackie. I don't think Brenda Maxine will either."

"Jesus, give me a break, Dutch."

"You got the big guy in your corner, Jackie, you don't need a break from me."

Jackie Gross began turning off the outside lights one by one. "It's true. She left town a couple of weeks ago."

"For where?"

"I don't know. She was talking about going back home. To Ireland, for Christ's sake. I told her she wanted to step in cowshit, I knew a couple of places a lot closer than that."

"Why?"

"You want it straight?"

"Straight."

"No more horseshit about Brenda?"

"Not if you play it straight."

"Okay." Jackie Gross turned off the last light. Only the glow of the pool lights lit the living room. The reflection of the water shimmered on the ceiling. "I meet her five years ago. I'm over at the Flamingo, she takes my picture, we get talking. It turns out she's from the old hometown and one thing leads to another, you know what I mean?"

Dutch Shea, Jr., stared out the glass doors at the swimming pool. "She had a child."

"Dutch, I had nothing to do with that, I swear. She was just a kid when that baby was born. I got no illegitimate kids, I always wear a rubber, I'm very careful about that. I play twenty-two weeks a year in the lounge, I'm not careful, someone can take me for a lot of money."

"Where is the child?"

"She gave it up for adoption when it was born. Back in the old hometown. She never talked about it much. Except . . ." Jackie Gross's voice trailed off.

"Except what."

"It died."

"How?"

"Some kind of bomb. I never got it straight. I got kids of my own, you know what I mean? Every one of them a pain in the ass, you know what I mean? I had a bomb, I'd set it off myself under my kids. I got a daughter, she's seventeen . . ."

"How did she know?"

"Know what?"

"That the girl died."

Jackie Gross flicked the pool lights off and then on again. "Every month she got a check . . ."

"From whom?"

"Someone in the old hometown. A lawyer, I think. The one that handled the adoption."

"He told her?"

"I don't know who told her, Dutch. Somebody did. It shook her up a lot. She got to be a pain in the ass about it, you want to know the honest truth. That's when I began to phase her out."

"You didn't need the aggravation."

"I got enough aggravation, Dutch, for the both of us."

"But you didn't phase her out completely?"

"Just out of the starting rotation, Dutch. I put her in the bullpen."

"You're a prince, Jackie."

382

"I appreciate that, Dutch."

"One last thing. Why did she take off?"

"Someone began sniffing around."

"Who?"

"A private detective. And I think the lawyer who was sending the checks had something to do with it. She got spooked. I go see her one night two weeks ago after my ten o'clock show and she's packing. I tell her to stick around, we'll go out after my midnight show, eat a little Chinese, and you know what she tells me? Get stuffed. That's English for go fuck yourself. I was going to slip her a couple of hundred, but no fucking way after that, you know what I mean, Dutch?"

Dutch Shea, Jr., sank back into the overstuffed down pillow of the white couch. The reflection from the pool undulated on Jackie Gross's face.

"One thing I'd like to ask you, Dutch, you don't mind."

In the darkness, Dutch Shea, Jr., nodded.

"What's your angle in this?"

"It's a legal matter, Jackie."

"You're the lawyer for that kid?"

"In a way."

"I thought it had something to do with that. I got that message on my machine and I said to myself . . ."

"I wanted to tell her what the child was like."

"You knew it, then?"

"Yes."

"Well, if it's so important, Dutch, why don't you tell its old man?"

For a moment, Dutch Shea, Jr., could not breathe. Not here. Not in Las Vegas, Nevada. Not in an all-white house in the desert. Not from a lounge comic. Not from Jackie Grossbart who said the only thing wrong with oral sex is the view. Who said bowling was Polish tennis.

Who said.

Who said, "She used to work as a maid in the old hometown. When she come over from Ireland. Someone was shtupping her. The son. Now here's the great thing, Dutch. He's a priest. Can you beat that? A priest."

BOOK SIX

John Shea, Jr.

I

"I will go unto the altar of God." Ralphie Keogh was off and running.

"To God, who giveth joy to my youth," Ralphie Keogh's acolyte replied, struggling to keep up.

It took Ralphie Keogh just seven minutes to zip through the Confiteor, the Introit, the Kyrie, the Gloria, the Collect and the Epistle. Not bad for a Sunday, John Shea, Jr., thought. Not up to the weekday record when he had a golf date, but not bad. Ralphie Keogh wore a golf glove on his left hand. John Shea, Jr., wondered how many priests in the archdiocese said Mass wearing a golf glove. Perhaps the bishop had given Ralphie a special dispensation. There were a lot of golfers at St. Robert Bellarmine's. Golfers gave a lot of money to archdiocesan charities. Certainly more than the Puerto Ricans in the South End. Ah, yes. Ralphie Keogh had talked to him about the Puerto Ricans in the South End this very week. Specifically about Hugh Campion and the pastor of La Purisma Concepción, Father Silvio Garcia. To the consternation of Father Ralphie Keogh, Hugh had proposed Father Silvio Garcia for membership in the Club.

"You got to talk him out of this, Jack," Ralphie Keogh had said.

"I can't, Ralphie," John Shea, Jr., had said. "The covenants of the Club are quite clear. Membership is automatically offered to the governor, both United States senators and to the pastor of every church to which a member belongs."

"Well, who the hell belongs there, then, Jack?"

"Hugh. He's attached there temporarily and has assumed full parish duties. So he's well within his rights to put up Father Garcia."

"I got nothing against Silvio, Jack. He's a hell of a priest, they tell me."

"I'm glad to hear that, Ralphie."

"But golf's not his game. Jai alai, maybe."

"I don't think he plays jai alai."

"There's a lot of swell baseball players came out of Puerto Rico. Roberto Clemente."

"I don't think the Red Sox want him either, Ralphie."

"Would you tell me what Hugh is up to, Jack?"

"He wants to be involved, Ralphie. Good works. Breaking down social barriers. I think this comes under that heading."

"He's a goddamn troublemaker, you ask me," Ralphie Keogh said.

A point well taken.

Father Hugh.

Father.

Cat's father.

Father of Catherine Liggett Shea.

Father. Pater. Père. Poppa. Pop. Pa. Daddy. Dad.

Your dad is your dad.

And my dad was fucked over by your dad.

Something Hugh didn't know.

As he did not know that his coupling with Kathleen Donnelly had produced issue.

Te absolvo, Jack.

D.F. had assured him that Hugh did not know.

D.F. had gone to the bishop and the bishop had arranged a transfer. A posting to the National Broadcasting Company. Technical adviser to NBC's *Father Brown* series. Fame. Fortune. *Name That Tune.* The Golden Medley. The perfect soufflé.

And no knowledge of his issue.

Te absolvo, Jack.

SHEA, Catherine Liggett, female, Caucasian, 18. Time of death: 2057 GMT.

Your dad is your dad.

Time for the sermon. Ralphie Keogh walked to the pulpit. My God, he's swinging an imaginary putter. Ralphie Keogh did not waste much time on the announcements. He got to the point quickly.

"I don't want you to think of heaven as a par three hole, my brethren. Heaven is a par five with a dogleg. A lake in front of the green. Sand traps all around it. Tough cup placement. Over a gully and a bad break near the hole. In other words, heaven is very easy to bogey, my brethren. The saints are the only ones that birdie it. And I don't see any saints sitting in front of me this Sunday morning at St. Robert Bellarmine's . . ."

Roger Touhy nodded vigorously. Roger Touhy had a nine handicap.

Greg Rooney nodded vigorously. A seven handicap. With help on his grip from Lee Trevino. One of the perks of the pecker checker business. *A bazooka it's not.*

Hugh had the bazooka.

And no knowledge of his issue.

The fruit of his loins.

Te absolvo, Hugh.

Ralphie Keogh was gesturing with his left hand. The one with the golf glove. He made hell sound like a sandtrap. John Shea, Jr., stared at the wall behind the altar. Something new was hanging there. It looked like a knitted version of The Last Supper. He checked the printed announcements. Yes, there it was. Da Vinci's Last Supper. A filet crochet rendering. Presented to St. Robert Bellarmine's Parish by Mrs. Byron Igoe.

Elaine. Where did she pick that up? She must have abandoned nuns' rights.

There she was. In the second row. He wondered if he could slip out without running into her. She would want to question him once again about BEAUBOIS, Robert NMI. Elaine had not approved of the dismissal of all charges against BEAUBOIS, Robert NMI.

"He's a homosexual, Jack."

"That's not against the law, Elaine."

"What exactly did you do?"

"It was the district attorney who asked that the charges be dismissed, Elaine."

"I don't see why."

"He didn't have a case. That's as good a reason as any."

"Somebody set that fire."

"But my client didn't."

"I don't know why you take clients like that, Jack."

"So they don't get sent to jail for setting fires they didn't set."

"A person like that."

"He's not a person, Elaine. He's a scumbag. Probably the worst scumbag I ever defended. He'd bugger little By right up the ass for thirty-five cents. . . ."

So much for Elaine Igoe.

Kiss that three million good-bye.

He felt inside his jacket to make sure the letter was still there. Yes. Of course. He had not let it out of his sight since he received it the day he returned from Las Vegas. It was in his jacket during the day, on the bedside table at night. He wondered how many times he had read it.

"You are hereby ordered to appear at a hearing before the judge of probate at 9 A.M. Monday November 21 for an accounting of the assets of Mrs. Walter M. O'Meara . . ."

Et cetera and so forth.

Barry Stukin had volunteered to represent him.

"I think I know how we can make restitution, Jack."

"It's not a matter of 'we,' Barry. It's a matter of 'I.' And I cannot make restitution."

"Christ, Jack, there's a lot of ways to get money. It's only two hundred."

"Only two hundred." John Shea, Jr., had smiled. "I remember when you used to defend for a lid. Now it's 'only two hundred.'"

"I'm smarter now, Jack. Not better. Just smarter. You never did get any smarter. And now you're two hundred in the hole, you son of a bitch, and I've got a terrible feeling you're better."

Better than what was never defined.

Time for communion. Ralphie Keogh placed the wafer on his tongue. "The body of our Lord, Jesus Christ, preserve thy soul unto life everlasting. Amen."

Unto life everlasting.

It had a nice ring to it.

A reassuring finality.

A touch of sanctifying grace to make the trip a little less bumpy.

He slipped out before the last gospel. There was a smell of snow in the air. A newsboy stood beside a pile of Sunday newspapers. John Shea, Jr., flipped past the comics to the front page. The headline said:

CUTHBERTSON ARSON CASE
BEAUBOIS'S ORDEAL: HOW JUSTICE WON OUT

Justice.

How the newspapers loved to talk about justice.

"You don't have a case and you know you don't have a case. Unless you want to put him on trial for being such a sweetheart. He was in town for fourteen hours and you know we can account for every second of it. Including the hour he was in Elizabeth Park with a judge's joint in his face. Now I don't want to call that judge, you can bet your sweet ass I don't want to call that judge, but you go to trial and I am going to put a respected member of the judiciary on the stand and I am going to ask that the courtroom be cleared and I am going to have the bench direct this respected member of the judiciary to unzip his fly so that twelve good men and true can examine his purple private parts. Now it is my ass in the courtrooms of this county if I do this, I won't even be able to get a traffic ticket fixed, but when it comes out, and I assure you it will, when it comes out you knew I had this evidence and I gave you the chance to drop the charges against my client, then you will be in the shit with me and I suspect we will drown in it together."

Which was how justice won out.

There was a photograph of Beaubois on the front page and one of himself and one of the district attorney and one of the presiding judge.

The district attorney quoted Thomas Jefferson: "The sword of the law should never fall but on those whose guilt is so apparent as to be pronounced by their friends as well as foes."

The presiding judge quoted Daniel Webster: "Justice is the ligament which holds civilized beings and civilized nations together."

He quoted no one. "I am pleased the district attorney has examined the evidence and found it wanting," he said. "I have no further comment."

BEAUBOIS, Robert NMI, said, "I am gone, man. I am gone."

Expurgated from, "I am fucking gone, man. I am fucking gone."

2

He let himself into his office. It was immediately apparent that Alice March must have come in yesterday and cleaned up. The lawbooks were back in the bookcases, briefs were filed and indexed, transcripts neatly piled and annotated, ashtrays emptied. Even the rings from damp glasses and coffee cups on his desk had been polished away. A bad sign. Alice must not expect him back for a while. Which meant she expected the hearing to go badly.

He wondered if she had already found a new job.

Still, Alice had hedged her bet. On his desk she had left a typed calendar of the week's appointments. "Monday, 9 A.M., probate court." Nothing else. Everything else canceled. Tuesday was another thing altogether. "9:30 A.M., Mrs. Krogh." Mrs. Krogh was a blackmailer. "11 A.M., Mr. Francis X. Noonan." About that little matter Francis had mentioned in Vegas. Francis was interested in how to get away with murder. Literally.

"What I want to ask you, Dutch, is a hypothetical question."

"Fire away, Francis." An unfortunate choice of words in light of what Francis Xavier Noonan had to say.

"Let us say a man is shot," Francis Xavier Noonan said.

"We are speaking hypothetically, I hope, Francis."

"Absolutely, Dutch."

"And this man who is shot is not shot accidentally."

"I would say the chances are very good it is not an accident."

"May I ask, Francis, what is your personal interest in such a hypothetical question?"

"No personal interest at all, Dutch. I am just fascinated by the law."

"So fascinated that you are willing to pay for my time to get the full benefit of my knowledge."

"That's the only interest I have, Dutch. Believe me."

"Belief doesn't enter into the lawyer-client relationship, Francis."

"Well, there you are, Dutch."

"Yes, here I am, Francis."

"Let us say, Dutch, that this man is shot three times."

"To make sure."

"It would have that effect, yes."

"Hypothetically."

"Of course. And let us say he is shot with three different guns."

"And I suppose those three different guns would be held by three different hands."

"You're on the money, Dutch."

"That would present a very interesting legal point, Francis."

"I thought it would interest you, Dutch."

"Especially as it concerns culpability."

"Meaning who gets stuck with the rap."

"That is one way of putting it, Francis."

"You think about it, Dutch, I'll come back."

Tuesday at 11 A.M.

Presupposing I am still practicing after Monday at 9 A.M.

Not seeing Francis Xavier Noonan was a benefit he had not counted on.

In the event of an adverse ruling.

He opened Mrs. Krogh's folder. Blackmailers were not usually that pretty. Of course Mrs. Krogh had vigorously professed her innocence. She was young. Twenty-two or -three. Brown eyes, black hair and a nose that almost tapered to a point. If not beautiful then close to it. Good teeth. But capped. She was too young to have had her teeth capped. He had examined her face for other imperfections. A pair of parentheses around her lips when she smiled nervously. And high on her right cheekbone a touch too much makeup. The cheekbone may have been discolored under the makeup. Black and blue. Perhaps from the attention of Mr. Krogh. Who was also charged.

". . . and I was attracted to him," Mrs. Krogh had said. There was a hint of elocution lessons in her voice. ". . . and I said I would like to suck his. . . "

Her elocution teacher would have been proud of her diction. The object of Mrs. Krogh's affection was Mrs. Krogh's gynecologist. The rendezvous took place in Mrs. Krogh's apartment. Where Mr. Krogh took an interesting roll of pictures. Which when developed were sent to the gynecologist. Who had gone to the police. Who had arrested Mr. and Mrs. Krogh.

"You didn't know your husband took these pictures."

"I swear."

"Or that he had a peek through which he could take photographs."

"I swear."

Mrs. Krogh also swore that she did not know who had sent the photographs to the gynecologist's wife and who was now sending the photographs to the gynecologist's neighbors and to the nursing nuns at Mother Cabrini Hospital.

Mrs. Krogh said she was an innocent victim.

Mrs. Krogh said she had always been led astray by her romantic nature.

Mrs. Krogh said she would divorce Mr. Krogh as soon as this nightmare was over.

Mrs. Krogh said she thought the gynecologist would be a very nervous witness.

"Yes, I suppose I would have to ask him if he did this sort of thing with his patients often. And I suppose I would have to ask him if the state board of medical examiners approved of this sort of thing."

Mrs. Krogh made an appointment to return Tuesday at 9:30 A.M.

Presupposing I am still practicing after Monday at 9 A.M.

Not seeing Mrs. Krogh Tuesday at 9:30 A.M. was another benefit he had not counted on.

Were there any other benefits he had not counted on?

Ah, yes. Myron. Mustn't ever forget Myron. Our municipal wart. Not seeing Myron would be another benefit he had not counted on.

Still.

He had been very good with Myron.

Quality advocacy for the municipal wart.

"Your Honor, Mr. Torizzo has suggested that it is the telephone that is the culprit in this case, not the person using the telephone. Mr. Torizzo, acting for the intervenors, must take this line because of what the evidence of his own witnesses has so amply demonstrated, and that is that my client, Mr. Mandel, did not use any telephone in any situation or under any circumstance whatsoever for any illegal purpose.

"The evidence is clear that Mr. Mandel scrupulously followed the law. Mr. Mandel has not been arrested. Mr. Mandel has not been indicted. Mr. Mandel is not the subject of any civil complaint nor is Mr. Mandel the subject of any abatement proceeding.

"There has not been a scintilla of evidence that Mr.

Mandel ever accepted one red cent from any of the witnesses who are alleged to have committed acts of solicitation or prostitution. There is no evidence that he lives off the earnings of prostitutes. There is no evidence that Mr. Mandel counseled or that Mr. Mandel advised or that Mr. Mandel assisted or that Mr. Mandel encouraged any violation of the law on the part of the independent contractors who worked for his agency.

"Is it any wonder then that Mr. Torizzo, acting for the intervenors, must concentrate on an electronic instrument rather than on a living, breathing human being who cannot be charged with the violation of a single statute in the whole of the state penal code?

"It must thus be pointed out that the use of a telephone is a significant and fundamental right in modern society which involves not only the right to work and the right to produce economically but also and most importantly involves the right of freedom of speech. If the Public Utilities Commission disconnects Mr. Mandel's telephones, they will deprive him not only of that right but also of the monetary value of his economic venture."

Myron Mandel was impressed. "I liked that freedom of speech shit, Dutch. That's what it's all about."

"It doesn't mean a thing, Myron. You're going to lose your telephones. Every one of them."

"I got my rights . . ."

"You're a pimp, Myron. And they're going to take out your lines because you are a pimp. But they can't prove you're a pimp. And because they can't prove you're a pimp, they can't deprive you of a right to make a living. So they're going to take out your lines one day and you're going to get new lines the next. You won't even be out of business twenty-four hours, Myron. That is what is meant by the scales of justice."

A rather loose interpretation of Daniel Webster.

Not to mention Thomas Jefferson.

And all the other spokesmen for justice plucked from *Bartlett's Quotations*.

Justice has a nose of wax. Clarence Darrow said that. He didn't know what it meant, but he liked the sound of it.

He wondered if there was a single member of the bar who did not have a copy of *Bartlett's* on his bookshelves.

A nose of wax.

I'll have to look into that.

He stared out the window at the superior court building. It was getting cold. He wondered if he should turn on the heat.

No.

Or go home.

Jesus, no.

He picked up the telephone and dialed his answering machine. There was a message from Thayer Pomfret. Thayer said he would see him in court in the morning.

Thayer Pomfret had volunteered to assist Barry Stukin.

Putative friends.

Friends.

"Thayer, let's cut the horseshit. If I know what happened, the information is no longer privileged. Right?"

"It's at least moot."

"D.F. bought the kid and set up the trust, which you administered. A check went out every month. Kathleen agreed not to see the child or to contact her guardians. Is that how it worked?"

"In general."

"No pictures, no information, right?"

Thayer Pomfret nodded.

"Then who told her Cat died?"

"I did."

"You sure as hell exceeded your authority on that one."

"I did it at Lee's request."

The breath seemed to leave his body. "Lee."

"She always knew. D.F. told her. You remember Judge Liggett didn't want you to adopt. D.F. kept pushing it. Lee's not stupid, Jack. She added it all up and then put it to D.F. That's when he told her."

"But not me."

"You didn't have to be convinced, Jack."

"Oh, Jesus."

Jesus.

What a tomb of secrets D.F. was.

So old, so fast. His shirt collar hung away from his neck now. He seemed lost in the folds of his suits.

"I was overextended, they were calling in my paper. Your dad gave me the money."

"Did you know how he got it?"

"Yes."

"Was it your idea, Dominick?"

He did not answer directly. "My God, Jack, who would've figured on an earthquake?"

"You both would have gone to prison."

"There was no sense in that, Jack."

"No, I suppose not." It had a certain irrefutable logic. As a lawyer, he would have to admit that. As a lawyer.

"I said I'd take care of you. I said when he got out it would be just like the old days."

"Of course."

"You're the only real son I've ever had, Jack."

"And that's why you got me the baby."

"She was my granddaughter. My only grandchild. The only one I'd ever have. I knew you'd love her. I knew you'd take care of her. I loved that little girl more than you'll ever know."

They were standing on the crest of a knoll at Mount

St. Benedict's cemetery. D.F. went there almost every day now. His wife's gravestone said, LILLIAN BURKE CAMPION—1913—1947. What was it D.F. had said about the way Lil Campion had died? Bingo! Light's out, time's up.

Bingo, light's out, time's up.

Yes.

"Let me make it up to you, Jack. Please, let me make it up to you."

Te absolvo, Dominick.

3

Home.

A clean white shirt laid out. All buttons sewed on. Solly Baum liked neatness.

Shine the shoes. The black shoes. Monday at 9 A.M. was not an appearance where one wore brown shoes with a blue suit.

A solid tie.

Unto life everlasting.

Per omnia saecula saeculorum.

Amen.

Those reassuring lyrics.

Dozing.

Keep your trap shut, Barry Stukin had said.

Speak when spoken to, Barry Stukin had said.

Thayer will present Judge Baum the details for the plan of restitution he's worked out with D.F.

Judge Baum will refer the matter to an administrative hearing by the board of ethics of the state bar association.

A letter of reprimand, Barry Stukin had said.

Maybe a suspension, Barry Stukin had said. Two months at the outside.

Two months?

Two months.

Are you telling me the fix is in?

No fix. An appreciation of services rendered to the bar of this great state.

What services?

Keeping a purple pecker out of the public record. The reputation of the judiciary remains untarnished. That carries a lot of weight, that shit.

You know, I think I liked you better when you couldn't take a leak without aiming it at the judiciary of this great state.

Shit, Jack, I liked myself better. But life goes on. When the going gets tough, the tough get going. You got to go along to get along. I know all the phrases now. That Nixon bunch. They had great phrases. A bunch of crooks, but great phrasemakers.

Dozing.

Awake. On with the TV. The night-light of my life. Time for my old buddy Sid.

Oh, Christ. Sid was talking to Hugh Campion. Hugh was walking a picket line. With the gravediggers at the Catholic cemeteries.

Sid said, "Hugh . . ."

Not Father Campion. Not even Father Hugh. Just plain Hugh.

"Hugh, what do you think of Archbishop Broderick's attempt to break this gravediggers' strike with seminarians?"

"I hate to think of seminarians as scabs, Sid."

A shot of Hugh signing autographs.

How many picketers sign autographs?

How many priests wear jeans and turtleneck sweaters?

"And I hate to call my own bishop a scab, Sid, but when he picked up that shovel for your minicam, that's what he became."

Trust Hugh to know the kind of camera.

Father Hugh.
Father of Cat.
Cat.

I'm going to marry
A boy named Harry.
He rides horses
And handles divorces.

From the gnawing worm of conscience, deliver me,
O Lord, Thy servant, John.
Thine other servant, John.
John, Jr.
Guardian of Cat.
Also faithfully departed.
In a number of pieces.
Three to be exact.
He heard a noise. An intruder? Roscoe? Wonderful
Roscoe. My answered prayer. The solution. Roscoe
with his .22. The favored weapon for contract hits.
Muzzle velocity 1000 feet per second. More than
enough to dispatch Thy servant, John, Jr., into life
everlasting.
Bingo! Light's out, time's up.
It was the wind, not Roscoe.
Roscoe, how comforting you would be.
Ah, shiiiiiit, Irish.
Ain't you got no suede?
I bet you wear a rubber when you fuck.
Ain't you got no remote?
I really picked shit when I picked you.
Honky welfare.
That does it, Roscoe. That is too much. You have
gone too far. You have insulted the custodian of a
Milwaukee Legster. With its snub-nosed .38. Popular
with detectives, undercover agents and the CIA. You

can't beat that for references, Roscoe. Those guys are champs.

In the drawer.

The Milwaukee Legster was still there.

I bet Jackie Gross doesn't have a Milwaukee Legster. What Jackie Gross has is all the brands. Tanqueray. Chivas. That Russian shit. That Turkey stuff. Olives, onions, chee wees.

Come again, Dutch?

Give me a little help, Dutch.

The Irish girl.

The one with the red hair.

Just out of the starting rotation, Dutch. I put her in the bullpen.

He wondered if Jackie Gross had told Kathleen Donnelly that the only thing wrong with oral sex is the view.

Kathleen. Who had never heard Cat say, "Where you was." Who had never heard her say, "Where did the morning went."

Or "flybutters."

Lee would remember.

Thank God, Lee would remember.

Kathleen, Kathleen. Vanished into the haunted hour of twilight.

He was awake. Cavett was on the tube. Queen Victoria was a guest again. Chins aquiver. No sweater this time. Just a shirt. A cosmetic mistake. The royal highness had titties. And the royal titties jiggled when the royal highness spoke. The royal eyes were still shifty. Who was he on with this time? A celebrity cop from Los Angeles. He had read one of the celebrity cop's books. It was full of cop tristesse. The celebrity cop was talking about lice. Hollywood lice. My street garbage, the celebrity cop said, is better than that Hollywood lice. My street scum. My vermin. My germs. My bacteria. My garbage.

403

Second time around for garbage.

The celebrity cop was certainly proprietary about his garbage.

Why not? It had made him rich.

A talk-show toughie.

A *Playboy* interview.

A Cavett guest.

A jouster with Queen Victoria.

Whose royal titties heaved.

The royal highness was not amused.

Blather, blather, butch and bombast.

So saith Queen Victoria.

Queen Victoria still needed Naturetin-K for bloat. Queen Victoria looked as if an OD on Naturetin-K was in order.

Elaine Igoe took Naturetin-K for bloat.

And Lee took Naturetin-K for bloat.

Did Cat take Naturetin-K for bloat?

She didn't take the goddamn pill. And got herself pregnant. And had to see her mother. And I made the reservation. And Peter Jennings wasn't there. And Lee was in the ladies' room.

All roads leading to the probate court Monday at 9 A.M.

Where the fix was not in.

Only an appreciation for services rendered to the bar of this great state.

Monday at 9 A.M. Keep your mouth shut.

Tuesday. Mrs. Krogh at 9:30. Mr. Noonan at 11. First, Francis, the district attorney would have to find the three guns. Then he would have to find the three hands the three guns were in. Then he would have to put the right gun into the right hand. Then he would have to figure out what bullet from which gun in whose hand was the most immediately life-threatening.

Tuesday.

My garbage.

And no proprietary interest.

He opened the drawer of the bedside table. It was still there. Popular with detectives, undercover agents and the CIA.

Those guys are champs.

Famous last words.

It is a far, far better thing I do . . .

I only regret I have only one life et cetera and so forth . . .

I believe.

I believe in music.

I believe for every drop of rain that falls, a flower grows.

I believe in Cat.

I believe in God.